A lake is the landscape's most beautiful and expressive feature. It is Earth's eye; looking into which the beholder measures the depth of his own nature.

Henry David Thoreau, *Walden*, 1854

the Shadow Year

Hannah Richell

First published in Great Britain in 2013 by Orion Books,
an imprint of The Orion Publishing Group Ltd
Orion House, 5 Upper Saint Martin's Lane
London WC2H 9EA

An Hachette Livre UK Company

1 3 5 7 9 10 8 6 4 2

A CIP catalogue record for this book is
available from the British Library.

ISBN (Hardback) 978 1 4091 4298 0
ISBN (Export Trade Paperback) 978 1 4091 4299 7
ISBN (Ebook) 978 1 4091 4300 0

Printed in Great Britain by Clays Ltd, St Ives plc

The Orion Publishing Group's policy is to use papers that are natural,
renewable and recyclable products and made from wood grown in sustainable
forests. The logging and manufacturing processes are expected to
conform to the environmental regulations of the country of origin.

www.orionbooks.co.uk

For Matt

PROLOGUE

It is the smallest details that come to her: the damp grass underfoot threaded with buttercups, the air humming with insects, the snap of her nightdress catching in the breeze. As she wanders out of the cottage and down towards the mirrored surface of the lake, her senses are heightened. She hears the splash of a duck hiding in the reeds and the slow drum of her heart in her chest. Just a few moments to herself, she thinks – to wash – to swim – to clear her mind and ready herself for what lies ahead. Soon she will be gone from this place.

Halfway down the ridge she stumbles on the uneven ground then rights herself, carrying on until she is at the water's edge. The lake lies before her, a blue eye gazing up at the sky. Shadows of slow-drifting clouds shift upon its surface and, as she watches them, the image shimmers like a mirage conjured in the heat of a summer's day. She blinks and the haze lifts.

She dips a toe into the cool shallows then wades out, thick mud and silt squeezing between her toes and a dark water stain creeping up the hem of her nightdress. Water ripples and disperses all around her and it must be the glare of the sun because increasingly it's as though she's looking at the lake through the grease-smeared lens of a camera – as if she wades not through a lake, but through a dream. The pebbles feel real enough beneath her feet, as does the cool water rising up towards her chest and all around the fabric of her nightie spreads out across the surface of the lake, floating like the petals of a flower. Real and yet not real. She shakes herself. Is this a dream?

Pushing off from the bottom, she swims out to where the water is dark and deep then stops to watch the breeze play across the surface, lifting it in choppy peaks. Her blood is cooling and she feels the weight of herself – her arms, her legs, the heavy tangle of her nightie, her slow-beating heart. Treading water, she sees the cottage tilt in the distance and the light waver across the treetops. It's a dream, she tells herself and lays her head back upon the water, suspended there between earth and sky, floating for just a moment upon the skin of the lake.

1

LILA

July

Lila sits at one end of a deserted picnic bench with a takeaway coffee cup before her. Although it's warm out – the warmest it's been for a while – the park is half empty; it is that strange, quiet hour when workers have retreated back to their offices after lunch but the schools are yet to spill children out of their doors. From where she sits Lila can see through the picture window of the park café where a woman restocks the drinks fridge, and a little further away to where a council worker bends over a bed of ragged marigolds. An empty can clatters past him, caught in the breeze. Closer, in the shade of a tall plane tree, stands a pram.

There is a baby asleep inside. Lila can just make out the curve of her face above a pale pink blanket. Her cheeks are rosy and one dark tuft of hair escapes from beneath her cotton hat. Lila watches, fascinated, as the infant grimaces in her sleep, her eyelashes fluttering once, twice before falling still again. The baby's mother is over by the paddling pool. She has taken off her shoes and socks and is splashing through the shallows with a young boy of about two or three. Lila sits on the bench and watches them from behind dark sunglasses, twisting her coffee cup in her hands.

'Look, Mummy, a bee.' The boy points to something in the water and his mother approaches and bends down next to him. Lila takes a sip of her coffee and allows her gaze to drift back towards the pram. She knows the model. She knows that the brake is on. She

3

knows that to release it you have to flick that white handle up 180 degrees. She practised it only weeks ago in the shop. She swallows down the bitter coffee taste in her mouth. God, it would be so easy.

The mother and her son splash to the far side of the pool. They scramble out and head to a clump of bushes near the café and begin to search for something with which to scoop the bee from the water. The boy scampers across the concrete then cries out. He fusses over his foot and his mother moves closer, brushing the dirt off his sole, hugging him, then rerolling his already wet trousers.

A weak sun filters through the branches of the tree overhead, sending patterns of light dancing across Lila's bare arms. From far away comes the sound of a football connecting with a boot, the delighted shriek of a child being pushed on a swing, the sound of a jet plane high overhead. The mother and boy enter the café. She sees them ask for something – a paper cup. Lila eyes the pram and then stands.

She ignores the pain in her ribs and focuses instead on the thud of her heart as she moves closer. The baby's lips are pursed now, opening and closing, suckling in her sleep. A fly buzzes over the pram's canopy, then lands on the pink blanket and creeps towards the baby's face. Lila takes another step forwards, fighting the urge to swat it away. Somewhere inside she registers the cold hollow of her heart. It would be so easy.

She reaches out and allows her hand to brush against the handlebar of the pram. The plastic is warm to her touch. The baby stirs. Behind her she hears the splash of feet in the paddling pool, the little boy's giggle. 'Get it, Mummy.' Lila gazes down at the sleeping baby and shudders. She lets out a long breath then steps backwards away from the pram, away from the baby. She turns and makes her way along the path leading around the pool where the mother and son work together to fish the bee from the water.

'He's alive,' she hears the boy cry in delight.

'Don't touch,' warns his mother, 'he might sting.'

The woman glances up at Lila as she passes and throws her a smile. Lila gives the woman the slightest nod, the hot sting of her tears hidden behind her sunglasses as she follows the path out of the park gates and makes her way over the zebra crossing and up the hill, her heart hammering loudly all the way home. Get a grip, Lila, she tells herself. Just get a bloody grip.

* * *

The man is at her front door as she enters through the gate. He stands with his back to her, dressed in motorcycle leathers and helmet, with one finger pressed insistently on the doorbell. 'I'm here,' she says.

When he turns, all she can see of his face are two dark eyes peering through the helmet visor. A walkie-talkie crackles at his lapel. 'Are you Lila Bailey?'

'Yes.'

'Delivery. You'll need to sign.'

She nods and accepts the electronic pad from his hands, scrawls her signature across the screen then hands it back to him. In return he offers her a stiff cream envelope addressed in neat handwriting. Without another word, he moves up the path to where his motorbike waits in the street. It starts with a violent roar and speeds away down the hill. Lila tucks the envelope under her arm and fumbles with her keys in the lock.

Inside, she bends carefully to retrieve the takeaway menus and bills scattered across the mat, adding them and the courier's special delivery to the growing pile of unopened mail on the hall table. It proves to be one envelope too many and the whole lot cascades to the floor in a splash of paper. She's tempted to leave everything where it has fallen until she remembers the mess will be the first thing Tom sees when he arrives home later that evening. Holding her ribs gingerly, she crouches down to gather the envelopes and restacks them onto the table in two neat piles. The last one she adds is the cream envelope from the courier. As she places it on the pile she feels a strange weight sliding and shifting within. She hesitates then shakes it. There is definitely something in there, something small but heavy rattling inside. Intrigued, she moves away from the pile, the envelope still in her hand, and carries on up the stairs.

In the bathroom Lila runs a bath, as hot as she can stand, and watches as the steam billows into the air and mists on the mirror over the sink. She breathes deeply, then reaches for her pills, swallowing two before taking up the envelope again.

The handwriting is unfamiliar and the postmark smudged and illegible. She slides her finger beneath the seal and pulls out a typed letter and several folded documents. She gives the envelope one last shake and watches as a heavy silver key drops into the palm of her hand. She stares at it for a moment then turns it over, feeling the reassuring curve of it between her fingers, and when she is ready she reaches for the letter and begins to read.

* * *

Tom arrives home an hour later. She sees his distorted face come into view through the filmy surface of the bath water. She watches his eyes widen, his mouth open in alarm, before rising up through the surface with a gasp, pushing her hair out of her face.

'Bloody hell,' exclaims Tom, one hand to his chest, 'for a second . . . I thought . . .' He shakes his head then stares at her. 'What are you *doing*?'

'What does it look like? I'm taking a bath.'

Tom runs his hands through his hair. 'Sorry, you scared me, that's all.' He takes a deep breath, loosens the knot of his tie then tries again in a steadier voice. 'How was your day?'

'Fine.' She reaches for the flannel. 'Yours?'

'Fine.' He hesitates. 'Did you get out?'

'Yes, I went to the park. It was nice.' She can't quite meet his eyes and busies herself instead with scrubbing her face.

'Good.' He smiles. 'Did you talk to Suzie about work?'

Lila nods.

'And?'

'It's pretty quiet at the moment.' The water is cooling. Lila sits up and wraps her arms around her knees, rests her chin on top of them. 'Most of our clients are cutting their budgets . . . she says I should take as long as I need.'

6

'That's good.' Tom looks about the bathroom, his eyes landing on the key on the sink ledge. 'What's this?' he asks, reaching for it and testing its weight in his hand.

'It came today.'

'What's it for?' He takes up the envelope and papers beside it.

'I don't know.' Lila tries not to feel annoyed that he's reading her private letter without asking permission.

'Who are Messrs Gordon & Boyd?'

'A solicitors firm, I think.'

He looks up from the typed sheet of paper. 'Is it something to do with your father's will?'

'I don't know,' she says, trying to keep her voice even. 'I don't think so. It's a different firm.'

Tom stares at her, the exact way she's seen him stare at a stranger, trying to size them up, figure out if they're friendly or hostile. He shrugs and places the key back on the edge of the sink where he found it. 'OK. I'll see you downstairs?'

'Sure,' she says, and she watches him go, waits for the door to close behind him before she twists the hot tap on again and slides once more beneath the surface of the water.

* * *

They eat dinner together in the kitchen, Lila in her pyjamas, her hair damp from the bath, Tom hunched over his plate, still wearing his crumpled work shirt and trousers. 'Did you see anyone today?' he asks at last, breaking the silence.

'No.'

'Make any plans for tomorrow?'

She shakes her head.

'Mum says she's going to give you a call. She's wondering if you fancy meeting her in town later this week?'

She eyes him carefully. 'I don't need you making arrangements for me, Tom.'

'It's not like that. She wants to see you.'

Lila raises an eyebrow before returning to the food on her plate. She's not hungry but she pushes the chicken around, tries to make it disappear by cutting it into smaller pieces.

He sighs. 'Lila, I get it. First your dad's heart attack . . . then . . .' He can't say it and she can't meet his eye. Tom clears his throat and tries again. 'I just don't think it's healthy for you to shut yourself away all day. You're grieving, yes, but you might feel better if you got out and about, if you saw a few friends.'

She shakes her head. 'I'm fine. I told you, I went to the park.'

'Yes, but just drifting around on your own isn't—'

'Tom,' she warns, 'stop trying to organise my life. Stop trying to *fix* me.'

He throws up his hands and they both turn back to their plates, nothing but the occasional scrape of cutlery to break the silence.

'So what are you going to do about that letter?' he asks eventually. 'Seems very odd, if you ask me.'

Lila nods. 'I know. Why would someone leave me a piece of land?'

'It could be part of the settlement of your dad's estate?'

She shakes her head. 'I don't think so. That was all wrapped up a few weeks ago. I received some money but there was no mention of any land. Besides, the letter says this is an *anonymous* gift.'

Tom frowns. 'Did you look at the map? It's a sizeable plot. Do you know the area?'

'No. It looks very remote . . . up on the edge of the Peak District. I've never even been to the Peak District before and I certainly don't know anyone from around there.'

The furrows in Tom's brow deepen. 'You should call the solicitors' office tomorrow – try to find out a bit more. They must be able to tell you *something*.'

'Yes.' She scrapes the remains of her uneaten dinner to the side of her plate then lays her cutlery carefully in the centre. 'I suppose if that fails I could just head up there and take a look for myself.'

Tom's hands fall still, his knife and fork hovering over his plate.

'Why do you look so surprised? I've got the map and that key. What would be the harm?'

Tom purses his lips. 'It all just seems a bit odd.'

'We could go together,' she tries. 'This weekend . . . or the next. It would be good to get away, even for just a little while.'

Tom hesitates. She can see that he is surprised by her sudden desire to *do* something and knows it must seem strange when she has spent the last couple of weeks holed-up at home, doing very little of anything besides sleeping and crying and wandering aimlessly around the house. But somewhere new and remote . . . somewhere no one knows them . . . somewhere where no one knows what's happened is strangely appealing.

But he shakes his head. 'I can't go anywhere – not until I've had my latest design passed.'

'Well,' she says, dropping her gaze to the table, 'I can always go on my own.'

'No,' says Tom quickly. 'I'd like to come. Give me a week or two and I'll come with you.' He pushes his plate away and smiles at her. 'You're right, it might be fun. A complete change of scene . . . an adventure.'

'OK,' agrees Lila. 'I'll wait. A week or two.' She reaches across for his plate, stacks it on top of her own and then carries them over to the bin where she dumps the remains of their uneaten dinner into the rubbish. Neither of them, it seems, is terribly hungry.

* * *

Later, in bed, Tom reaches for her and tries to pull her close. His fingers connect with the bruises on her ribs and she inhales sharply. 'Sorry,' he says, 'does it still hurt?'

'Yes.' She rolls away from him and stares into the darkness. Of course it still hurts. She is afraid it will always hurt, that the pain lodged in her chest is never going to go away.

'Sorry,' he murmurs again.

She can feel him shift on the mattress and knows that he is lying on his back staring up at the ceiling. They are only inches apart, but somehow the distance between them feels immense. There is still so much they haven't talked about – so much they haven't faced. Words

9

and scenes arrive unwanted in her head. She pushes them away and tries to focus instead on the gradual slowing of Tom's breath.

She knows she won't sleep. Her body is wired, her limbs restless, her mind galloping, but there is fear too – fear of sleep; fear of that sensation of tipping over the edge into darkness; fear of falling into oblivion. She waits until Tom is snoring gently, then slides silently out from between the sheets and tiptoes into the bathroom.

The bottle of pills is half full. The doctor has been generous with her prescription; she'd suggested she might stop taking them after a week or so, when the anxiety had begun to ease, but Lila's growing accustomed to that slow softening sensation that creeps up and dulls the pain, that blurs the sharp edges of her mind, and so she twists the lid off the bottle and swallows another two pills with water gulped straight from the tap.

Downstairs, the letter from earlier still lies on the dining table, the key glinting beside it in the glow of a street lamp. As she waits for the drugs to do their work she pulls out a chair and reaches for the key, holding it carefully in the centre of her palm. Sounds of the city echo around her – a distant siren, high heels clicking quickly down pavement, the faraway bark of a dog – and as the darkest shadows inside her head begin to soften and fade, she finds herself wondering about the mysterious key – and about the lock it will fit into – and about what might lie behind the door it opens.

2

JULY

1980

They appear in the kitchen one by one, seduced by the sound of clinking bottles and the heady scent of marijuana, until all five of them are slumped around the lopsided wooden table, swigging beer and passing spliffs. Someone hits play on the squeaky tape deck and the opening chords to 'Going Underground' start up, blaring out into the hot, still night. A lighter flares in the darkness. An ashtray is passed. A bottle is opened. Hanging in the smoke haze above their heads is an air of waiting: waiting for a breeze, waiting to move out, waiting for *real* life to begin.

'So I guess summer's arrived,' says Kat, swirling the remaining beer round and round at the bottom of her bottle. Her bare feet are propped on the edge of the table and she reaches up and lifts her damp, chestnut-coloured hair off the back of her neck, twisting it up into a knot before letting it fall heavily to her shoulders once more. 'It's *so* hot tonight.'

'I saw some kids frying an egg on the bonnet of a car earlier,' says Ben, sprinkling tobacco from a pouch along the length of a cigarette paper. 'It looked pretty good. I'd have eaten it.'

'Why am I not surprised?' asks Carla, rolling her eyes.

A candle flickers on the table between them, refracting off the empty beer bottles strewn around and casting them all in a strange, weaving light. Kat plays with the loose threads on her denim cut-offs. 'I suppose we should be grateful. It'll probably be pouring rain again next week.' She shakes her head in frustration. 'We should be celebrating . . . doing something . . . not just sitting here watching eggs fry.'

Simon gives a low laugh from the head of the table and spins the lid of his beer bottle before him like a top. 'You mean a last hurrah before we all head home to join the queues at the local job centre?'

'Look at us,' says Ben, licking the length of the cigarette paper and folding it with well-practised precision. 'Illustrious graduates, class of 1980. Three years in this place and all of us qualified to do little more than roll a mean joint and hold our liquor.' He twists the end of the joint then tears a small piece of cardboard from the cigarette paper packet, coiling it into a roach.

'Speak for yourself,' says Kat. She's spent the last few weeks filling in job applications and received nothing but the curtest of rejections so far, but she's still hopeful.

'Besides, I'm still not sure Mac here can hold his drink.' Simon nods across to where Mac sits slumped in the corner, his dark hair falling like a curtain across his face.

Ben laughs and snaps open his Zippo, puts the flame to the end of the joint and burns off the paper twist. Satisfied with his handiwork, he lifts the spliff to his lips and draws deeply, twice, until the cherry glows red. He takes another drag and then passes it on to Simon. Kat watches Simon inhale, the movement hollowing his face and exaggerating the high angle of his cheekbones. He tips his chin to the ceiling and exhales smoke in one long, steady stream above his head. He takes another drag and then passes it on to Carla. Kat is still watching him when he turns back to the table and catches her eye. He grins at her through the darkness.

The tape ends with a click. Kat stands to flip it over and when she returns to her seat, she notices how the candlelight has cast the five of them inside a golden bubble, the half-light masking some of the more unsavoury details of their student digs. Hidden out on the edges of the room are the lopsided electric cooker with its crusty hob, the ugly green damp patches blooming on the walls and the grimy cupboards with their ill-fitting doors hanging loose from hinges. Ben's tatty poster of a leotard-clad Kate Bush has begun to peel away from the wall at one corner while somewhere near the open back door is the overflowing rubbish bin spilling empty crisp packets and beer bottles onto the sticky linoleum. Behind her teeters a stack of dirty pots and pans that they long ago lost the energy to fight about. Kat knows eventually that someone will cave in and that from experience it will probably be her or Carla. Beyond the candlelight all the detritus and decay of their scruffy student house lurks, but for now it's just her and her friends and the music and the smoke haze hanging above their heads. Kat looks about at her odd, makeshift student-family and smiles. A golden bubble: she supposes that's what they've been living inside these last few years at university.

'Is he asleep?' Carla asks, nodding her head in the direction of Mac.

'Dunno. Mac!' Simon leans across and pokes him in the ribs. 'Mac, wake up.'

'What?' says Mac, flicking his hair out of his face and rubbing his eyes. 'I'm awake.'

'Sure you are.'

'Don't sleep,' urges Carla. 'It's one of our last nights together. Let's not waste it.'

One of their last nights together. 'Yes,' agrees Kat quickly, 'let's not waste a minute. Let's *do* something.' She peels a long strip from the label of her beer bottle. 'I mean, you're all complete pains in the arse to live with and everything, but even I can admit I'm going to miss this.'

'OK,' says Simon. 'What did you have in mind?'

'Tomorrow's supposed to be hot again . . . how about a trip to the seaside?' Carla leans into the crook of Ben's arm. 'Swimming . . . fish and chips . . . ice cream. You'd drive us, wouldn't you, Mac?'

Mac yawns. 'Sure.'

Simon shakes his head. 'Everyone will have had the same idea. It'd be unbearable. Besides, it would take us most of the day to get to the coast.'

'There's always the canal out the back,' grins Ben, taking a deep drag on the dwindling spliff before passing it on. 'You know, if you *really* want to swim.'

Kat gives a horrified laugh. 'You really are an animal, Ben. Only you could think of jumping into that cesspool.' She turns to Carla. 'And you sleep with this guy?'

Ben gives a loud, beery belch and then nuzzles his ginger goatee into Carla's neck. 'Don't be fooled by her ladylike exterior, she loves a bit of rough.'

'Yeah, yeah,' says Carla, cuffing him around the head.

Kat waves the joint on as it moves around the circle; she's drunk too much already and the hideous, patterned lino they have lived with for the last two years is beginning to shift and swirl alarmingly before her eyes. They are all silent as they consider their dwindling options, until finally Mac speaks up from the end of the table, his voice so quiet they have to lean in to hear him. 'There's a place . . .' he hesitates, 'a lake. Out in the countryside. I went there once when I was a kid.' He clears his throat. 'It was all right . . . you know . . . nice.'

'A proper lake?' asks Kat, narrowing her eyes.

'Yeah.' Mac nods, shaking his hair from his eyes. 'I could probably find it again.'

'How far?' asks Simon, the lid of his beer bottle now lying still in the flat of his hand.

Mac shrugs. 'I reckon an hour or two north of here.'

'What do you think?' Simon asks, turning to look at the others, his dark eyes flashing in the candlelight.

Carla reaches for the neck of her T-shirt and flaps it away from her skin. 'I'm so hot I'm almost tempted by the canal. You can count me in.'

Ben nods. 'And me.'

'Me too,' says Kat, placing the cool glass of the beer bottle against her forehead.

They all turn to look at Simon. He stares back at them, his eyes black and unreadable. Watching him, Kat feels the familiar catch in the back of her throat. *Say yes*, she wills.

In one quick move he spins the bottle lid into the air, catches it and flips it onto the back of his hand, inspecting it as if it were a coin. 'Let's do it,' he says with a grin, tossing his dark hair out of his eyes. 'We deserve a little celebration, right, before we pack up this place and leave . . . ?'

'Tomorrow?' asks Kat.

'Tomorrow,' he confirms and Kat feels her face relax into a smile.

* * *

She half expects the others to have forgotten the plan by morning, so it's a surprise to find them all squashed into Mac's clapped-out Fiesta and heading out of the city just as the clock in the Market Square chimes ten. Simon calls 'shotgun' and sits in the passenger seat next to Mac while Carla, Ben and Kat are left to squeeze into the back seat. All of them, it seems, are buoyed by the idea of escape. Carla has even found time to make cheese sandwiches and pack a cool bag with beer and lemonade, the glass bottles clinking cheerily in the boot as they drive out of the city.

'No funny business,' Kat warns, seeing Ben's hand creeping up the inside of Carla's thigh. She angles herself away from them and stares instead at the curve of Simon's neck, just visible through the gap in the headrest. She sees the faint sheen of sweat on his olive skin and the heart-shaped mole just below the lobe of his left ear where his hair curls. She thinks about reaching out to touch it, but she doesn't dare.

The city is already beginning to display the effects of another unexpectedly hot summer's day like a tourist sporting sunburn. The roads shimmer in the heat, oozing sticky black tar, while the grass along the verge begins to crisp and brown like burnt sugar. After a while, even with the car windows rolled down, it is unbearable, like sitting in the blast of a hairdryer. Kat eyes a large advertising hoarding for instant mashed potato, then turns her gaze enviously toward a cluster of little kids shrieking and spraying each other with plastic water guns on a street corner. Two women, their hair tied up in scarves, sit on a brick wall pulling choc ices from white paper wrappers while they watch the antics of the children. Slowly, slowly, the car creeps through the traffic and spills out onto the open road.

Kat thought it would feel good to do something, to go somewhere different but the longer she sits in the back of the tiny car, the more cramped it begins to feel. The halter ties of her bikini top are cutting into her neck and Carla's dimpled thigh presses hotly against hers; a layer of sweat builds between them, the skin of their arms occasionally brushing and sticking. Kat shifts closer to the window, cranky with the arrival of her hangover, the taste of last night's beer lying like a dusty carpet on her tongue.

'You're very quiet,' Simon says, turning to study her through his black Ray-Bans. 'Are you OK?'

She nods.

'Hung-over?'

She nods again and Simon smiles. 'I'm not surprised. Just looking at Ben's shirt is giving *me* a headache.'

'Hey, what's wrong with it? It's holiday attire, isn't it?' huffs Ben, holding out the lairy fabric of his Hawaiian shirt, but it is too hot for any of them to bother replying and Simon just turns back to the road. The grey ribbon of asphalt stretches endlessly before them; a road to nowhere, thinks Kat, and she rests her head against the side of the car to doze a while.

'So where exactly *are* we going?' she hears Ben ask an hour or so later as they pass through yet another picturesque village of topsy-turvy stone cottages and twisting country lanes. 'We're near the Peak District, right?'

'Yep. Heading north.'

'Are you taking us into the national park?'

Mac shrugs. 'I'm not sure. The lake might belong to the park, or it could be farmland.'

'Oh fantastic,' says Kat, opening one eye a crack. 'I didn't realise getting shot by an irate farmer was on today's agenda.'

'You said you wanted an adventure,' says Simon, turning round to face her again. 'I'm sure Mac knows what he's doing. Right, Mac?'

But Mac doesn't say a word; he is focused on the road in front of them, driving them deeper and deeper into lush countryside, past fields of rapeseed glowing golden in the sunshine and green pastures spotted with black-and-white cows.

* * *

Another hour passes and they distract themselves with 'I Spy' and squabble like kids over what music to play. The girls want Blondie but they're outnumbered and Ben's album goes on. 'The Clash?' groans Carla. 'Not again.'

Kat closes her eyes again and tries to block out the thrashing guitars. Her headache is getting worse.

'We must be nearly there,' says Carla, pulling her frizzy auburn hair up into a pineapple. 'It's pretty hot back here. We could do with a stop if it's going to be much further.'

'What do you say, mate?' asks Ben, leaning forwards between the two front seats. 'How much further?'

'I'm not exactly sure,' says Mac, without even looking up from the wheel.

'*You're not exactly sure?*' Kat is incredulous. 'I thought you knew where this lake was?'

Mac just shrugs.

'So when *were* you last up here?'

Mac shrugs again, his eyes fixed on the road. 'Can't remember.'

Simon studies Mac for a moment then bursts out laughing. 'That's what I've always loved about you, Mac: it's just *so hard* to shut you up.'

Kat leans her head against the side of the car and regards each of her friends in turn, tries to imagine what it will be like next week after their graduation ceremonies, when they pack up their student house and say their goodbyes. They've spent two years together in their shambolic red-brick terrace and while there have been arguments about washing-up and toilet paper, household chores and bills, she knows she will miss Ben's easy humour and Carla's warm generosity and Mac's strange, quiet manner. And Simon . . . well, she knows there will never be anyone else quite like Simon. In the short time she's known them, her friends have come to mean everything.

*   *   *

Twenty minutes later, Mac slows the car on a twisting country lane then indicates and turns up an overgrown track littered with rocks and potholes. It's obvious from the height of the grass growing down the central ridge of the trail that no other vehicles have passed that way for a very long time. Kat leans forwards and gazes out the window, scanning gaps in the hedge for a telltale spot of blue water shining in the distance; but there is nothing. As they bump along the uneven ground, the heat of the midday sun now beating down on them, Kat wills the journey to an end.

The hedgerows are high and bursting with thistles and thick, snaking briars. Nesting sparrows dart from the undergrowth as the car passes by, while cabbage whites flutter against the blue sky. A huge bee, drunk on pollen, wafts through the open window; Carla shrieks and flaps wildly until Ben manages to steer it safely out of the car. Far above them the silhouette of a hawk hangs black against the dazzling blue sky; Simon points to it and they all watch in awe as it hovers like a shadow above them.

They continue jolting their way up the track for a few more minutes until the hedgerow begins to crowd in on them from both sides and brambles screech and scratch against the car. 'Are you sure this is right?' asks Ben, leaning over again from the back seat. 'There's no way we'll be able to turn the car around if it gets stuck.'

'You'll see,' says Mac.

Ben and Kat exchange worried glances across the back seat but just a few hundred yards on and the track unexpectedly widens again. Mac pulls the car up onto the grassy verge and switches the engine off.

'I don't see a lake,' says Kat.

'We go through there.' Mac points to a wooden gate slumped on its hinges, only just visible through the thick brambles and tangled hawthorn branches. They stare at the gate. There is nothing but the heavy drone of insects and the car engine ticking beneath the bonnet to break the silence that has descended over them.

'Where does it go if we carry on up the track?' asks Simon, nodding ahead to where the trail winds up over a distant hill.

'Dunno,' shrugs Mac, 'the moors, I guess. But the lake's this way. Come on, grab your stuff.'

'We're walking?' asks Kat, horrified.

* * *

They pull their belongings from the boot – hats, towels, an old tartan rug, the bag of drinks and sandwiches – then take it in turns to clamber over the creaking wooden gate. The grass in the meadow on the other side is almost waist-high and bursting with ox-eye daisies and scarlet poppies drooping in the hot sun. They swish their way through in single file, Mac leading them down towards a thick line of trees in the distance.

The air is alive with insects and sunshine. Crickets leap from their path as they move through the tall grass. A huge blue dragonfly crashes into Kat and then zigzags off across the field, the deep thrum of its wings trailing away on the air. Ben, dragging the bag with one hand, has already sparked up another joint, the aroma drifting like exotic perfume. Kat can feel a trickle of sweat run from the hollow at the base of her neck down between her breasts; she wipes it with the hem of her T-shirt, then tucks the fabric into the elastic of her bra, exposing her midriff and lower back to the sun. Her hangover is definitely getting worse.

Once they reach the wooded copse on the far side of the meadow, they follow Mac through the shade of the trees, a damp earthy scent drifting up from the floor. Emerald ferns nod as they pass by and huge banks of nettles push up towards the canopy. It is quiet, nothing but their footsteps and the crunch of dry leaves and sticks beneath their shoes. Kat feels a million miles away from the bustle of the city.

Finally, they emerge from between a bank of alders but there is still no sign of a lake. Kat stomps behind the others out onto a grassy ridge, the drumbeat of her hangover building in time with her footsteps, until halfway along Mac pauses and looks about, as though checking his bearings.

Carla groans. 'Don't tell me, we're lost?' Her pineapple wilts in the heat, spots of pink colouring her plump cheeks.

'No,' says Mac with a shake of his head, 'we're not. Come on,' and he leads them to the far end of the ridge and then down a long slope of tufty grass before disappearing behind a thick hedge of blackberry brambles.

One by one they follow him round, Kat trailing miserably in the rear. As she emerges on the other side of the bushes she almost walks slap bang into Carla who has come to a sudden halt.

'Sorry,' she mumbles, then raises her head and looks out, following the others' line of sight to gaze down at the vista spread before them. She lets out a long, slow breath. 'Oh,' she says.

'Yep,' says Simon.

'It's . . . it's . . .' She can't find the words.

'. . . perfect,' says Carla, finishing her sentence for her.

'It's amazing,' crows Ben. 'There's absolutely no one here.'

Mac doesn't say a word; he just stands there with a sheepish grin spreading across his flushed face.

They are standing at the top of a grassy slope, gazing down into a small green valley – a basin of land seemingly hidden from the rest of the world by the emerald hills and shady woodland rising up on all sides to enclose it. Best of all, nestled in the trough of the hills and gleaming like a sheet of glass in the sunshine, lies a perfect, shimmering lake. The landscape is like a mirage after the long car journey and the hot trek through the fields and woodland. Kat shields her eyes from the glare of the sun and drinks it in.

She's never been very good at judging distances but the lake is a good size – at least three hundred yards across and perhaps half a mile or so long – definitely more lake than pond. It sits like a glittering blue eye, surrounded on all sides by fringes of woodland and the steep grassy hills. It's as though they have fallen into a secret valley – one cloaked in an air of strange, blissful solitude.

Kat pulls her gaze from the water and studies an old stone cottage set back from the shores of the lake: a simple construction with a solid square base, triangular roof, two square windows upstairs and two more downstairs flanking a rectangular front door. A chimney stack juts from either side of the roof and completes the symmetry of the old place, and looking at it Kat is reminded of simple childhood pictures drawn in crayon. Beyond the cottage she spies an old, misshapen barn, slumped at an alarming angle into the shoulder of the hills, and closer to the lake, stretching out from the shore, a rickety wooden jetty with an old tin boat tied by a fraying rope to a post nearest the water.

While the cottage, the barn, the jetty and boat all hint at past ownership, it is clear from the stillness of the scene around them, from the air of neglect and decay that has stolen over the remnants of the buildings, that there is no one there – and that there hasn't been anyone there for quite some time. Ben is right, she realises: they have the lake all to themselves.

A fish flips on the glassy surface of the water, breaking the spell cast upon them. With an elated cry, Simon sets off at a run down the bank, Ben and Carla following close behind. Simon hits the jetty first. He sprints down the length of it and peels off his T-shirt. Kat watches the movement of his muscles beneath his smooth olive skin, the shift of his ribs as he raises his arms above his head and dives in a near-perfect arc into the lake. He disappears below the surface – a pattern of concentric circles spreading across the mirror the only sign of his descent – before emerging moments later five or so yards further out, shaking the water from his dark hair. He yells again in delight and then disappears once more below the surface.

Ben is next. He trips down the jetty, struggling to reach the water while simultaneously removing his shirt and shorts. Finally, when he is down to a grey pair of Y-fronts, his white barrel chest exposed to the sun, he bombs into the water with an almighty splash. Carla, a little more sedate, peels off her pinafore dress and boob tube at the water's edge then wades through the shallows in her underwear before splashing out to where the boys are swimming. 'It's cold,' she shrieks.

'Not when you get used to it,' calls Simon from further out, sculling through the water on his back. 'It's lovely.'

'Come on,' calls Ben, turning back to Kat and Mac still standing on the shore, 'what are you two waiting for?'

Kat throws Mac a small smile – an unspoken apology for not trusting him to find the lake – then makes her way down the grassy bank to the water's edge where clumps of green reeds burst up towards the sky and water boatmen skate lazily in and out of their shadows. She stands for a moment, holding the yellow cotton fabric of her skirt up around her thighs, watching the reflection of the water dancing on her bare legs.

'Come on,' yells Simon, and it's the sight of him moving further away from her into the centre of the lake that does it. She shrugs off her skirt and top, throws them back onto the shingle then wades deeper into the shallows in her bikini. At first the water is warm, almost bath-like, with thick green weed that obscures the silt and stones resting on the bottom; but the deeper she goes, the cooler and clearer it gets, until it is so cold she instinctively raises her arms to shoulder height and holds the air in her lungs in a tight gasp. The water is almost up to her chest when she turns around and calls to Mac. 'Aren't you coming in?'

He regards her from the bank, his eyes obscured by the too-long fringe of his straggly brown hair, then shakes his head. 'Later,' he says and crouches down on his heels in the grass.

She eyes him there in his faded black T-shirt and ripped jeans and shakes her head. Typical Mac: always wanting to watch, always holding himself back. 'You're crazy. You must be boiling.' But she isn't going to waste time arguing with him. Holding her breath, she launches herself under the water, kicking out with her legs and using her arms to propel her to where the other three swim beyond the jetty, watching as bubbles of air leave her mouth and rise to the surface in a string of iridescent pearls.

When she breaks the surface, Carla is laughing and shrieking, trying in vain to sink Ben beneath the water. Kat watches them play-fight for a moment then turns away and swims out a little further to where Simon floats serenely, his body angled like a starfish to the sun. In the bright light his olive skin appears paler against the blue-green lake. She stares at him, sees the rise and fall of his chest, his long legs, his face utterly relaxed, content. She imagines swimming to him, wrapping herself around him, pulling him close, pressing her mouth upon his cool, wet lips, their hot breath mingling, the taste of him on her tongue. She wonders how he would react if she summoned the courage to go to him then shivers at the thought.

Simon's dark eyes snap open. He turns and stares at her and Kat blushes and wonders if he can tell what she's been thinking. 'He won't come in,' she says, not quite meeting his eye but nodding her head in Mac's direction. 'God knows why.' Simon stays silent, floating. 'I mean, we drive all this way and he just wants to sit there?'

The silence deepens until Simon flips onto his front and takes a couple of smooth strokes through the water so that he is right there in front of her, his skin shining wet, his chin dipping just below the surface, his full lips curving into a smile. He is so close she can see the tiny beads of water hanging on his long lashes and flecks of green the same colour as the lake shining in his eyes. He looks at her in that way he has, as if he is looking right inside her, gazing at her innermost secrets and Kat, feeling the quickening of her heart, tries to breathe. The moment stretches until, at last, he asks, 'Are you happy, Kat?'

She swallows and fights to hold his gaze. 'Yes,' she says, 'I think so.' She wonders if it's the right answer then takes a breath. 'I mean, I am right now, at this very moment' – the heat rises on her cheeks – 'if that's what you mean?'

Silence hangs between them. Kat holds her breath. *Kiss me.* The thought is so loud in her head she wonders if he has heard.

But he doesn't kiss her. Instead, he smiles again, his teeth flashing white in the sunlight and then he closes his eyes and leans back into the water, leaving Kat to hover there, her feet paddling up and down and her hands making little swirling movements just to keep herself in one place. She's been doing this for three years now, she thinks, treading water, trying to stay in one place – trying to stay at his side.

* * *

The first time she ever saw Simon Everard he'd been standing in a rowing boat in the middle of the lake on the university campus shouting through a requisitioned traffic cone, demanding action about the increased prices at the student refectory. Kat, watching him through narrowed eyes, had noted his faded Che Guevara T-shirt and his shoulder-length dark hair and put him down as just another wannabe revolutionary. There were plenty of them around. But the scene had provided a distraction and so she'd sat on the bank with a growing group of students and watched in amazement as one by one a steady stream of willing bodies had thrown themselves like lemmings into the water to take up the protest alongside him, while the university's security staff looked helplessly on.

'He's a bit of all right, isn't he?' a girl with long, glossy hair and the shortest shorts Kat had ever seen had sighed from the grassy slope beside her and Kat, turning back to assess the student again, had noted his broad shoulders and the lean muscles just visible beneath the fabric of his T-shirt, his striking face with its high cheekbones and strong jaw, his flashing dark eyes. Yes, he was definitely a bit of all right.

From that day on she'd noticed him everywhere. He was one of those people who commanded attention by his very presence, not just his good looks but by the confidence he exuded. It was as if just by walking into a room, or strolling through the student bar, he shifted the air around him in such a way as to turn heads. She'd watched him from a distance, always the centre of attention, surrounded by friends and admirers, but had never drawn close; guys like Simon didn't talk to girls like her; that much she knew.

Then, late one night, he was there, slumped in the corridor of her halls of residence, wearing nothing but a pair of boxers and a lopsided grin. She'd shifted the bag of library books on her shoulder and thrown him a sideways glance as she put her key in the door. He was obviously drunk as all hell.

She could have shut the door and left him but a guilty pang stopped her and at the very last moment she'd poked her head back into the corridor and asked, 'Are you OK?'

'Oh sure,' he'd replied airily. 'Just steeling myself for the walk across campus.'

'Dressed like that?'

'Seems so.'

It was then that she'd heard the sound of weeping drifting from behind the closed door opposite. 'Amy?' she'd asked, eyeing him carefully.

'Amy,' he confirmed.

'Is *she* OK?'

He'd nodded. 'She's fine.' Then, seeming to feel the need to explain further, 'We appear to have wildly differing views on how *exclusive* our dating arrangement was.'

'Oh.' For some reason she'd found herself blushing. 'I see.'

'My clothes are in there,' he'd said, jerking his head at Amy's door, 'but as she doesn't seem to be in a forgiving mood tonight, I guess I'm walking home like this.' He'd grinned again.

Kat barely knew Amy, a tall, willowy girl with drawers of designer clothes and a gaggle of look-alike friends. Kat had introduced herself on their very first day in halls, but since then Amy had barely given Kat a second glance. She knew she wasn't Amy's type, but she could see how this guy would be.

'Well,' Kat had said, deciding to extricate herself from the situation as quickly as possible, 'good luck . . . and good night.' She'd stepped back into her room and closed the door behind her with a gentle click then leaned against it, listening for the sound of his departure. His knock, when it came, vibrated like a drumbeat at her back.

'Listen,' he'd called through the door, making her jump out of her skin, 'I don't suppose I could borrow a T-shirt or something?'

She stood breathless on the other side of the door, silent and still.

'Anything, really . . . I'm not fussy. You see, I feel like a bit of an idiot.'

Still, she hadn't moved a muscle.

'I can return it to you . . . tomorrow,' he'd gone on.

Slowly, she'd turned and placed a hand on the doorknob.

'Please?'

With a sigh she'd opened the door. 'I doubt I have anything that will fit you,' she'd said, eyeing his smooth, broad shoulders.

'Well, could I come in for a moment at least?' He ran his hands over his bare chest, shivering just a little. 'It's draughty out here.'

Reluctantly she took a step back, holding the door open for him. He was the first man she'd invited into her room in halls and she resented the way he made her feel uncomfortable in her own space, the way he took in her few belongings with an unabashed, sweeping gaze. 'James Dean . . . Jim Morrison . . . Jimi Hendrix,' he'd said, commenting on her posters, 'You like a tragic hero, huh? Live fast . . . die young?'

She hadn't replied, but begun instead to search through a pile of clothes for something suitable he could wear. 'I'm not sure what I've got that's clean . . .' she'd murmured.

'Nice teapot,' he'd added, moving across to her sink and fiddling with the lid of the flowery number standing beside her tiny sink. 'Very fancy.'

She'd thrown him an irritated glance. 'Do you want my help or not?'

'Sorry.' He took a step backwards.

Her pink cheesecloth shirt had been the only thing that looked like it might fit. She'd turned and held it out to him. 'It's all I've got.'

'Thanks. You're a lifesaver.' He'd pulled it on hastily, doing up the buttons slightly wrong, then checking his reflection in her mirror. 'It suits me. I'll bring it back tomorrow. You're room 32—'

'324.'

'324. Right. I won't forget.'

Judging by how drunk he seemed, she'd seriously doubted he'd remember.

'I'm Simon, by the way,' he'd added, making for the door. She'd watched him go, a strange churning sensation in the pit of her stomach. 'Thanks,' he called over his shoulder, swaying away down the corridor. 'I owe you.'

She hadn't expected to see him or the shirt again but the following afternoon he was back as promised, still green with hangover, but true to his word. 'Just a little thank you,' he'd said, handing Kat her shirt, wrapped now around a bottle of wine. Kat had stared at the gift – she'd never drunk red wine before, she was more of a cider girl – then thanked him for the gesture and taken it from his outstretched hands. 'As I'm here, I don't suppose you'd make me a cup of tea?' he'd asked with a cheeky grin. 'In that fancy pot of yours?'

She'd eyed him for a moment.

'Or we could open this? A little hair of the dog . . . while I wait for Amy . . .'

Cheeky bastard, she'd thought; she could see he was used to getting whatever he wanted. 'Come on then,' she'd said. 'You'd better come in.'

It was an unlikely friendship, but over the space of a year, they'd grown close, eating lunch together in the canteen, drinking in the student bar, and bickering about music and politics over endless cups of tea as they perched side-by-side on the bed in her poky room. Even she was unprepared, however, when he'd asked her over a pint of cider in the union bar if she'd move into a house with him and some of his friends at the end of the first year. She'd stared into his dark eyes and felt her heart flutter alarmingly, like a caged bird.

'Great,' he'd said, smiling across at her. 'It's a four-bedroom place. My old schoolfriend Ben – we boarded together – he's going to share the largest room with his girlfriend Carla. She's fun, you'll like her.' She'd nodded, trying to stop an inane grin from spreading across her face. 'I'll take the room next to theirs . . .' he'd continued, 'and you can have the attic room?' She'd nodded again. 'Which just leaves the box room. We'll give that one to Mac.'

'Mac?'

'Yeah.' Simon had shrugged. 'He's a bit of an oddball . . . a loner. But Ben says he can score us good weed so I reckon we can put up with him.' He had leaned back in his seat and regarded her for a moment. 'You know what I like about you, Kat?' He hadn't waited for an answer. 'You're one of the few girls I know who has no agenda.' He'd looked at her from beneath the long sweep of his lashes. 'We can be *proper* friends, you know?'

'Yes,' she'd smiled weakly, 'I know.'

He'd been right, of course. It had been a lot of fun. For two glorious years they'd lived in their dirty, damp, falling-down student hovel and Kat had never felt so happy. Her new friends wrapped her in their warmth and good humour. They made her feel like she was one of them, part of the gang. It was something she'd never experienced before. For the longest time she'd never really allowed anyone to get close; she'd kept people at arm's length, had always been an outsider, for she'd learned the hard way and from a very early age how people could let you down; and yet somehow with Simon, she struggled to keep her defences up.

She'd tried hard not to love him, but as the terms rolled by, she'd found herself growing increasingly skilled at reassembling the shattered pieces of her heart. It seemed so senseless, how a person could feel *so much* for someone – so intensely – and for it to come to nothing. What a waste of emotion. What a waste of energy. Her only consolation had been the fact that, while other girls came and went, she, at least, was the constant in Simon's life – maybe not his girlfriend, but there in his orbit. She couldn't help harbouring the hope that one day it would be her turn, that he would realise that the person he was meant to be with had been standing there beside him all along.

Kat treads water and tilts her face to the sky, closing her eyes against the sun. She's been holding on to that hope for three years now, but time is almost up. Their future hangs wide open – as wide as the blue sky above her head – and in just a few days they will leave university to go their separate ways. Kat is coming to the painful conclusion that no amount of waiting or wishing is going to make Simon fall in love with her.

She dives below the surface, reaching out for the bottom of the lake, testing its depths. Her fingers stretch endlessly in front of her and when she finally returns to the surface she is disappointed to see that Simon is already heading for the shore, ploughing through the water in a perfect front crawl. She watches him go. Three years – it's a long time to be in unrequited love with someone.

Her hands are wrinkled and her skin is turning raspberry-pink when she finally drags herself from the lake and joins the others where they sprawl on the tartan picnic rug drinking warm beer in the shade of the trees. Kat lies back against the earth, her head resting on the cushion of Carla's thigh, and watches as patches of sky shift and dance through the latticed branches overhead. Beads of water drip from her hair onto her sunburnt shoulders. All around them is the low, soporific hum of insects.

'So who *does* it belong to, Mac?' Simon asks, gazing up at the blackened windows of the old stone cottage. 'It seems crazy that this place is just sitting here empty – abandoned.'

Mac shrugs. 'I guess it might have been an old shepherd's cottage,' he says, shielding his eyes from the sun.

'It looks as though it's been completely forgotten,' says Ben, exhaling a plume of smoke high above his head.

'Does it have a name?' asks Carla.

Mac shrugs again. 'I don't know.'

'*We* should name it,' says Kat. 'Claim it. Make it ours. We could come back here on this very day, every year from now.' She looks hopefully at Simon but he is gazing off towards the cottage.

'I'm going to take a closer look,' he says. 'Who's coming?'

Carla waves them away with a lazy flick of her hand and Mac declines too, content to sit with his arms wrapped round his knees gazing out across the water; so it is Kat and Ben who accompany Simon along the water's edge towards the ramshackle cottage.

From a distance the old place looked solid and sturdy, but as they move closer Kat can see how neglect has taken its toll. The gritstone walls are spotted with lichen and the roof appears to be missing several tiles. Closer still and she can see guttering hanging off at an alarming angle and birds' nests and cobwebs lodged under the eaves. In front of both ground floor windows, nestled amidst the dandelions and nettles are wild bursts of lime green seed heads, round and flat and translucent like paper. A woody vine climbs across one side of the house and beside the front door an old stone pot, cracked and empty, stands as a silent reminder of its past inhabitants. As they move closer still they see that the windows are black with grime and even though they press their faces up against the glass it is impossible to make out anything inside the gloomy interior. Kat hesitates but Simon is already at the front door, knocking loudly. 'Just in case,' he says, turning to them with a smile, but they all hold their breath anyway, listening to the dull echo as it resonates throughout the house. Satisfied, he reaches out and tries the tarnished door handle. It twists a quarter circle and sticks. 'Locked.'

'Well that's that,' says Kat with barely concealed relief.

'Hang on,' says Simon and he drags the cracked plant pot to one side.

'Yeah right,' laughs Ben, 'as if someone's just going to leave a front door key for us to find.'

Simon scuffs at the earth with his foot and there, nestled amidst the mud and the scuttling woodlice, is a hint of tarnished silver. He turns to them with one raised eyebrow, then bends and digs it out of the earth with his fingers. He wipes the key on his shirt then holds it up to them with a devilish grin. Kat tries to look pleased but she can't shake her trepidation. It feels wrong somehow – like they're trespassing.

The key turns easily in the lock and the door creaks open. The three of them stand there for a moment, framed within the dark rectangle of the doorway. 'Do you think we should?' Kat asks, but Simon is already across the threshold.

'Come on,' he says, turning to fix her with his gaze, 'don't be chicken. The place is ours.'

The temperature inside the building is much cooler than outside; the thick stone walls and echoing rooms, closed up for so long, seem impervious to the heat of the day and all around them the air is stale and heavy with a musty, damp smell. Sunlight filters through the grime-streaked windows, catching dust particles that shift and swirl, disturbed by their arrival. The room they enter runs the full width of the cottage and is virtually empty but for a long, low fireplace, a sagging brown velvet couch slumped beneath a window, an armchair and a steep staircase rising into the upper level of the cottage. Curtains hang from wooden poles, but they are old and faded, little more than tatty grey rags. Kat sees cobwebs slung between beams and and the droppings of an unknown animal scattered like pebbles across the dusty timber floorboards. She is careful to stay close to Simon as they move on through a low doorway into the second room at the rear of the cottage.

It comprises what must have once been the kitchen. There is another fireplace and an old-fashioned range, a wooden table and two long benches. On the chimney breast, hanging on hooks nailed into the stone, are the remnants of cooking utensils. Kat sees a black-bottomed skillet, a large copper pot and a colander stained brown with rust. Over on the other side of the room Simon twists a tap and releases a gush of water into the stone basin set beneath a window. 'There's running water.'

Kat nods and opens the door to a tall cupboard, shrieking as a small grey mouse scurries for cover. 'Christ,' laughs Simon, 'you made me jump.'

'Bit spooky, isn't it?' says Ben. He flicks an ancient-looking light switch on the wall. 'Electricity's off.'

'Are you surprised?'

31

'Come on,' says Simon, 'let's look upstairs.'

'Maybe we'll find a body.'

'Don't,' shudders Kat.

They head back into the front room and take the creaking stair-case leading up to the first floor, almost at the top when Simon puts his foot clean through one of the wooden steps. 'Watch it,' he warns, 'this one's rotten.' Kat and Ben descend into giggles as he struggles to pull his foot free from the hole. 'A little help would be nice,' he suggests and finally they manage to twist his foot out of the broken step and continue up the stairs.

As with downstairs, there isn't much to look at, just a tiny landing separating two basic bedrooms. Kat wanders into one and sees a mattress on the floor, grey with dust. There is a cracked mirror hanging above an old timber washstand, a large ceramic bowl and jug still standing on its surface. On the floor next to it is a china bedpan. Simon kicks it with his foot. 'I don't think much of the bathroom.'

In the second bedroom there is another old mattress, in only slightly better condition than the first. Beneath the window, lies the desiccated carcass of a dead bird, its scraggy bones gleaming white in the light slanting through the glass. Kat imagines the bird flying down the chimney and getting trapped inside the house; she thinks of it fluttering and bashing against the windows, imprisoned inside the cottage, then shivers at the thought and moves closer to Simon. He is fiddling with a window latch. He thumps violently on the frame until it springs open, bringing a welcome rush of warm air and light flooding into the small space. In the distance the lake glints seductively, no longer blue glass but darker now, like a sapphire gleaming in the late afternoon sun. Kat can just make out Carla lying in the shade of the trees and Mac seated beside her, his head turned towards the cottage. She lifts her hand in a wave but he doesn't seem to see her.

She moves across to the rear window and peers through the streaked glass at the overgrown garden below. She rubs at the dirt with her fingers and sees a small wooden shed. 'Let's check it out,' suggests Simon, following her gaze, so they make their way gingerly down the staircase, careful to avoid the freshly made hole near the top, and head outside to the back of the house.

It's not so much a garden, more a sprawling mass of vegetation and trees set into the lee of the hills, but there is evidence of the past occupants everywhere they look; a rusting old wheelbarrow, cracked earthenware pots, overgrown flower beds and fruit trees. The flat green seed heads she noticed growing at the front of the cottage are here too, growing in large clumps and mingling with fronds of fading purple flowers. 'Look at these, Ben,' she says, pointing to the translucent discs. 'This stuff is growing everywhere.'

'I know what it is,' he says, fingering one of the green discs. 'My mum has dried flower arrangements of it at home, but it's not green, it's white, like tracing paper. She calls it "honesty". Looks like it's reseeding itself all over the place.'

Kat studies the plant. 'Honesty, what a strange name.' Kat is no gardener, but looking about even she can see the shadows of a former vegetable plot; wilting bean canes and huge fronds of woody rhubarb sprouting from the ground like something from a Jurassic jungle, and higher still the first apples of the season forming on the fruit trees nestled into the shelter of the hill. 'Looks like someone once cared enough about this place to try to tame it,' she murmurs, but neither of the boys hears her. Ben is drifting further up the hillside, towards the apple trees, while Simon is wrenching at the door to the ramshackle wooden shed.

'It's a pit toilet. And there's an old tin bath propped behind.' He grins. 'Very rustic.'

'Who cares about a rusty old bath? Look what I've found,' cries Ben. They turn and see him bending to inspect a leafy green plant at his feet. 'Strawberries.' He pulls a scarlet berry from its stalk and crams it into his mouth. 'Delicious.'

Kat and Simon join him by the plants. She pulls a plump strawberry from its stalk and lifts it to her lips. He is right. They are delicious, warm and sweet and the three of them pick as many as they can, stuffing them into their mouths before returning to the others, carrying the rest cradled carefully within the folds of their shirts.

* * *

'I tell you what,' says Ben, his head resting in Carla's lap as she feeds him the last of the berries, 'if I died right now, I'd die happy.'

Kat stares out over the lake and sees that the sun is beginning to disappear below the surrounding hills; it hangs like a ball of fire in the sky, turning one lonely cloud a dazzling gold. Far away the sound of a pheasant echoes out across the lake.

'This is all right, isn't it?' agrees Carla, stroking the side of Ben's stubbled chin.

'I can't get over the fact that there's no one else here. What a waste.'

'I don't think I'd need much else in life if I had this view to wake to every morning,' agrees Simon.

'We should head back soon,' says Mac, scuffing the grass with the toe of his trainer.

'How about you just leave me here,' jokes Ben. 'Reckon I'd prefer to rough it here than go back with you lot. I can live without that job at my father's engineering firm.'

'At least you've got a job to go to,' says Carla.

'We'll be OK,' says Kat, plucking at the daisies dotted on the grass around her. 'I know the papers are full of doom and gloom but we're graduates.' She thinks of the endless application forms she's filled in, the numerous polite but firm rejections she's received back and swallows down her doubt. 'We've got valuable skills.'

Simon stifles a laugh. 'Valuable skills? You think? Unemployment's on the rise, taxes are going up, interest rates are increasing. This Thatcher woman's playing hardball. They're saying we'll be in recession soon . . . and then we'll all be screwed.'

'Wow, that's depressing.' Carla looks worried.

Simon shrugs. 'Only if you plan on becoming another cog in the machine.'

Kat studies Simon carefully. She can see the gleam in his eyes, the one that tells her he is warming to his subject.

34

'So tell us, oh wise one,' asks Ben from where he lies stretched out across the grass, 'what's the answer?'

Simon thinks for a moment. 'It's about getting back to basics . . . forgetting about the system and thinking about what you'd *really* like to do with your life, if money were no object. I don't mean engineering,' he says looking at Ben, 'or journalism,' and he turns to Kat. 'I mean that thing you *most* enjoy doing. The thing you always dreamed of doing when you were a little kid. Because I know as sure as hell that I didn't grow up wanting to be a lawyer.'

Kat pulls another daisy from the grass and pinches its stem between her fingernails. 'I like writing,' she says and then colours when she realises she's said it out loud. 'I mean, I always wanted to be a writer. That's what I wanted to be when I was a little girl.'

She's expecting laughter but Simon just nods. 'Exactly. Writing. You don't need money or a degree or a fancy house or car to write. Just a pen and a piece of paper. And you, Ben?'

'I like smoking weed,' he says, making them all laugh. 'And my guitar. I'd be happy if I could just hang out and smoke and make up daft tunes all day.'

'So no change then?' asks Kat.

Simon ignores her jibe. 'See, you both love doing things that don't require anything other than time and space. And yet that's the very thing you'll lose when you enter the workforce. Let's face it, all the past three years at university have really done is steer us towards joining a society based on commerce and greed, like lambs to the slaughter. I'll join a legal firm.' He nods at Ben. 'You'll get a job at your dad's engineering company, and you'll start on the bottom rung at a newspaper or magazine,' he says, turning to Kat. 'Mac here will get a little hippy job working with the environment and Carla here might pop out a few mini-Bens . . .'

'Hey,' exclaims Carla, 'I was planning on being a social worker first.'

'I know, I know,' smiles Simon holding up his hands, 'I'm just teasing . . . but a little further down the track we'll probably all sign ourselves up for mortgages and car loans and kids and then before you know it we'll have lost sight of the things that are most important to us, the dreams and ambitions we feel most strongly about. We'll be trapped in jobs we don't want to pay for lives we never really desired in the first place.'

'That's quite a speech.' Kat studies Simon carefully. She's seen him like this before, when he really begins to warm to an argument. She understands what he's saying; she can see the fundamental truth behind his words, but then it's easy to wax lyrical when you come from a position of money and privilege. They aren't all so fortunate.

'You're forgetting one crucial point: we all need money . . . an income,' says Carla quietly, mirroring Kat's own thoughts. 'We're all skint as it is.'

'Only because of the way the system works. It's a trap: live to work. Is that what you want?'

'So what would *you* have us do?' Kat asks. 'Live off the dole? Stay at university for the rest of our lives?' She shakes her head. 'It's not as if I want to leave next week . . .'

'It's simple. We just have to find a way to live our lives without relinquishing our freedom and our ideals for a few lousy pound notes. It's about making choices and taking control.'

'I think that's called Communism,' says Ben, letting out another quiet belch. 'Didn't work out so well for Stalin.'

Carla thinks for a moment. 'I do understand what you're saying but how do you take a stand when the rest of the world *is* the system? We don't all have filthy rich parents,' she adds pointedly, throwing Ben and Simon a reproachful glance.

Simon doesn't seem to notice her dig, or if he does he ignores it. Instead, he looks out over the lake, his eyes catching the sun and flashing amber. 'What if the answer is staring us in the face?' He turns and leans in towards them, lowering his voice. 'Look around you. This place is falling into ruin but someone could really make something of it. *We* could make something of it.'

Ben laughs. 'Sure, let's just move up here, drop out, stuff the future.'

'But that's my point,' says Simon, '*this* could be the future. This could be *our* future.'

'You mean we'd be squatters? Here?' asks Carla, the slightest hint of distaste in her voice.

'Ignore him,' says Kat, stretching out on the grass. 'It's the sunshine and the beer . . . they've gone to his head.'

'But why not?' continues Simon, unruffled. 'It's obvious no one else is using this place. Whoever owns this land, if indeed anybody does, is probably long dead. Why should these strawberries go uneaten or the lake untouched on a summer's day? Why should this cottage be left to fall into ruin? Why shouldn't we enjoy it . . . make something of the place?'

'I hate to be the one to burst your bubble, Simon, but what about money? What would we live on?' asks Ben. 'We'll need more than a few strawberries to see us through even a week up here.'

'You're not looking properly,' says Simon. 'Everything we need is right here: shelter, fresh water, produce from the land. There are fish in the lake, pheasants in the woods, enough firewood to keep us warm for the rest of our days. We could resurrect the vegetable patch behind the cottage and I bet there are ducks . . . and deer. We could live like kings. We could be self-sufficient, reliant on nobody but ourselves, free to choose our own pursuits.'

'Wow,' says Ben with jokey admiration, 'I never took you for the clogs and corduroy type, Simon.'

'I'm not talking about clogs and corduroy. I'm talking about control. I'm talking about escaping the treadmill and establishing our own rules. This isn't free-love-hippy-shit. This is the eighties – a whole new decade. We can submit to the system, or we can choose to live life our way – on our own terms. Think about it: up here Kat could write. Ben could make music, hell, he could smoke himself into a coma if he likes.'

Ben raises his beer bottle at the group. 'Cheers to that.'

Kat rolls over and props herself up on one elbow. She watches as Simon runs his hands through his hair. Soft shadows and sunlight dance across his face. There is the faintest trace of stubble on his jaw and a smattering of boyish freckles emerging on the bridge of his nose. The sight of him fills her heart with that familiar, bittersweet ache.

'Look at it this way,' he says, 'maybe the most radical thing we can do right now is to remove ourselves from a society that demands we sacrifice our desires for a salary. Here we can rely purely on what we can grow, make or forage. We could focus on the things we truly enjoy – the things that *really* matter. We could make a difference.'

'So we just leave the real world behind?' Kat asks.

Simon throws his arms wide. 'What if *this* is the real world?'

Kat feels the beginnings of a smile pull at the corners of her mouth.

'And what if some farmer or park ranger takes offence at us squatting here and turfs us out?' asks Carla. 'What if some little old lady appears out of the blue and asks for her cottage back?'

Simon shrugs. 'What have we lost? You've still got the rest of your lives to conform.' He sits up straight and eyes each of them in turn. 'We could try it for twelve months and see what happens? Think of it like an experiment. One year. I think we could manage that.'

Kat glances around at the others and sees them all staring at Simon with rapt attention. She knows how dangerously persuasive he can be when he gets in this mood and wonders where it comes from – this confidence, this swagger. Perhaps it's something innate, something in his genetic make-up; or perhaps it's taught at those expensive public schools? Maybe that's why wealthy families fork out astronomical fees each term – for classes in how to dazzle and persuade, how to unswervingly believe in yourself? Where it comes from she's not sure, but what she is sure of is that when Simon fixes you in his sights with a plan or an argument, he can be both formidable and almost impossible to resist.

'What do you say?' he continues. 'Twelve months out of an entire lifetime . . . it's nothing; and at least we'd have had fun trying.' He sits back on his heels and looks at them all, his eyes glowing black again in the faltering light, the faintest stain of strawberry juice on his lips. She swallows and drags her gaze away.

Finally, when no one says anything, he sighs and turns towards the still waters of the lake. 'Oh forget it. You're probably all right.

I'm being an idiot. Of course it's time for us to move on. We can't stay together like this for ever.'

Silence falls over them. Kat thinks about what he's suggesting; the five of them living in close quarters in a remote, tumbledown cottage, creating something from nothing, making a home together right here in the fresh air and the sunshine, beside this beautiful, shimmering lake. She thinks about having the time to read books and write – the time to think – the time to enjoy her friends' company; and then she thinks about the alternative.

Things aren't as straightforward for her as the rest of them. She has no parents to fall back on, no job assurances or promises of help in the family firm. The only person she has in the whole world is her sister, and Freya is busy now with her own life. But this place – this idea – would change everything. Compared to any of her other ideas for the future this place feels strangely solid and real and it comes with one shining promise she hasn't dared to imagine up until now: Simon, for another twelve months.

As she considers his argument she feels excitement spark like a warm ember in her belly. She takes a breath. 'I know I'll probably regret this . . .' she sighs, 'but I'll do it.' She says it so quietly she's not sure anyone will hear – but Simon is already spinning towards her, a smile breaking over his face.

'Kat,' he says. It's just one word, but the approval in his voice makes the smouldering ember flare to a white-hot flame. 'I knew *you'd* get it.'

She nods and tries to hide her smile.

'Anyone else?' he asks, looking around at the group.

Ben groans. 'Oh you . . . with your persuasive tongue and your honeyed words. You know my dad will kill me, don't you?'

Simon just shrugs.

'And there's not even any electricity. I mean, I don't think I'll survive without my record player and my vinyl. I might waste away.'

Simon just continues to stare at him.

'But I suppose the job could wait a while, while we explore this hare-brained scheme of yours.' He looks up at Carla and she tilts her head slightly. 'Twelve months, you say?'

Simon nods.

'Oh go on then,' says Ben, 'you've twisted my arm. I'm in.'

'Me too,' says Carla.

Kat smirks. They all know that when it comes to Ben and Carla, where one goes, the other follows.

'Great. So that just leaves you, Mac. . . you've been very quiet over there. What do you think?'

They wait. Mac sits with his knees pulled up to his chest, staring down at his dusty trainers.

'Come on, Mac, we wouldn't be able to do it without our *country boy*,' cajoles Ben, putting on a terrible northern accent.

'Yes, come on, Mac,' says Kat, 'you're the one who brought us here. It wouldn't feel right staying on without you.'

Mac looks at each of them in turn, peering at them through the shaggy curtain of his hair. He slaps at a midge on his arm then runs his hand across the pink stubble rash on his chin. 'You're all drunk,' he says.

The rest of them just stare at him, fixing him in their gaze.

'And it will be bloody hard work,' he adds.

Still no one says anything. A wood pigeon calls from high up in the trees.

'Christ,' he says at last, breaking into a crooked smile, 'it's not as if I can leave you lot by yourselves, can I? You wouldn't last five minutes alone out here.' He gives a small nod. 'I'm in.'

'Good man,' says Simon, reaching over and slapping him on the shoulder.

They seal the pact by clinking their beer bottles and drinking a toast and then, as the sun slowly begins to dip below the hills, they turn their thoughts towards the journey home, shaking out the rug and their towels and packing away the cool bag. Mac leads the way towards the dark copse of trees, the rest of them trailing at a distance, but Kat hangs back for a moment, standing at the water's edge, reluctant to tear herself away. The light is almost gone now, the lake a deep pool of ink in the murky twilight. They've agreed to return in a week, when they have packed up their house, secured a few essentials and waved goodbye to their student home, but now that the time has come to return to the city she finds she can't bear to go.

She hears the crunch of footsteps behind her, but she doesn't turn, not even when a second shadow joins hers at the edge of the lake, merging and stretching out over the dark mass of water, not even as a warm arm snakes around her shoulders. Hazy with sunshine and beer, she allows herself the luxury of leaning into the solid curve of Simon's body, resting her head on his shoulder.

'Don't want to leave, huh?'

'No,' she admits.

'Don't worry, we'll be back in a few days.' She nods and wonders if she is imagining the light, dancing motion of his fingertips on her bare skin. 'Twelve months,' he murmurs. 'No bullshit . . . just honest, hard work and the rewards that will come with it.'

For some reason, Simon's words remind her of the plant growing around the abandoned cottage, those green, papery discs shimmering in the faintest summer breeze. 'We must be mad,' she murmurs, but she feels it too; there is the promise of something good and real here, a life of simplicity and solitude. A life with Simon and her friends, removed from the distractions of the outside world. A life of honesty.

Simon stifles a yawn. 'Come on,' he says, spinning her round by the shoulders to face the grassy slope ahead, 'the others will be waiting.'

She nods and allows him to lead her by the hand through the lengthening shadows, all the way back to the car.

3

LILA

August

In the end it takes them three weeks to find both the time and energy to head up to the mysterious plot of land bequeathed to Lila, and when they do eventually drive out of London, any romantic ideas either of them may have privately entertained about a carefree summer road trip are quickly laid to rest. 'It's just as well we packed our coats,' says Tom, his jaw clenched and his knuckles white on the steering wheel as rain splatters loudly onto the windscreen.

'Yes,' agrees Lila, staring out at the distorted red smudges of brake lights ahead. 'Not exactly the day they promised, is it?' Another gust of wind hits the car and suddenly the wipers don't seem to move fast enough.

'Perhaps we should have waited. According to your map it's going to be quite a trek, some of it on foot. It's not going to be much fun in this weather.'

Your map. She can already feel Tom washing his hands of the day. 'You didn't *have* to come, you know.'

'I didn't mean . . .' He hesitates, trying to choose his words carefully. 'What I meant is . . .' He gives up. 'Look, I want to be here with you, OK?'

She nods and feels his glance in her direction but she still can't bring herself to look at him. She is worried that if she does the floodgates might open, that he might start talking about the terrible thing that hangs between them, the thing neither of them have discussed since the day she was released from the hospital. And she's not sure she can bear that, not today. The effect of the pills she swallowed with her breakfast is already waning.

'I'm trying, Lila,' he says. 'I really am.'

'I know.' She looks out at the traffic and twists the thin gold band of her wedding ring around her finger, considers reaching across to touch him, a small gesture of reconciliation. She wants to reassure him that she is trying too, that she still loves him; but the words stick in her throat and her hands remain folded in her lap, her face fixed upon the road ahead.

* * *

The first time she'd ever seen Tom was at a bus stop in Crouch End. He'd been leaning against the shelter, a battered leather satchel at his feet, his suit jacket flapping in the wind and a dog-eared paperback in his hands. She'd watched his eyes skimming quickly across its pages. *Never trust a man who doesn't read books*: it was a piece of advice once offered by her father – long-forgotten for she couldn't have been more than twelve or thirteen years old at the time – but standing there on the pavement, watching this unknown man with his slightly furrowed brow and his scuffed shoes, her father's words had come drifting back to her.

She'd watched him for a while, noting how his lips moved occasionally as his eyes traced the words on the page and when the bus had eventually arrived she'd sat at the very back and distracted herself with the shifting scenes outside the window, only once or twice allowing herself to search for a glimpse of him: the crease in his shirt collar . . . the curve of his jaw . . . that sticking-up tuft of hair on his crown that she imagined hardly ever lay flat.

The *reader*, as he had been labelled in her head, wasn't there the next morning, or the next, but on the fourth day he was back, leaning in the same position against the bus shelter, this time with a different book in his hands. As the bus arrived, Lila had followed him up the aisle and slid into the empty seat beside him, glancing down at the book lying in his lap. He'd smiled a crooked smile and held the cover up for her to see. 'Busted, sorry,' she'd apologised, flushing pink.

'No, I'm the same . . . always like to know what other people are reading.'

'Is it any good?' she'd asked, nodding her head in the direction of the hefty paperback with its shouty, gold-embossed title.

'It's OK. I borrowed it from a friend. To be honest,' he'd said, 'it's not really my thing, but I hate not finishing a book once I've started it.'

'Me too,' she'd agreed. 'That's why I never bothered with *War and Peace*.'

'Or *Moby Dick*.'

'Or *Anna Karenina*.'

They'd smiled at one another and by the time the bus had crawled through rush hour and reached Holborn they'd broken all of London's unspoken public transport rules and swapped names and phone numbers.

He was a design engineer, specialising in bridges. He'd told her all about it in the pub two nights later. His work took him all over the country but he was in London for a few more weeks, staying with friends in Crouch End while he inspected several constructions and drew up plans for a new design out near Stratford. 'It's all part of the plans to regenerate the area.'

She'd nodded and tried to decide if it sounded really interesting or really boring.

'It's not all hard hats and clipboards,' he'd said, as if reading her mind. 'The inspection stuff is OK, but what I really love is the design work. A bridge should never be boring, just a means of getting from A to B; it should be as appealing as the buildings surrounding it, as dynamic as the landscape it's a part of.'

She'd nodded, but she'd only been half listening, her attention caught by the intensity of his brown eyes as he spoke about his work and the jagged white scar across his right cheek that disappeared into a laughter line when he smiled. She'd reached out to touch it with the tip of her finger.

'My younger brother,' he'd said smiling, 'shot me with a pellet gun when I was eight. Siblings eh?'

She'd smiled. 'I'm an only child.'

'Well there you go, a lucky escape. I bet you carry a few less scars?'

Lila had shrugged. She knew she probably bore her own scars, in her own way. 'I always wanted brothers and sisters,' she'd confessed. 'It can be lonely being an only child.'

He'd eyed her over his pint glass. 'So what do *you* do, Lila?'

She'd told him that she was a designer too, of sorts. 'Interiors, property renovation. I work for corporate clients, you know, upgrading office spaces, usually creative industries, *media types*.' She said it with an affected drawl and they'd shared a grin. 'But I take on the occasional private client too; sometimes a house or a flat.'

'That sounds like fun.' He'd smiled at her and a crackle of static had hung in the air between them.

They barely knew one another but as he'd walked her home much later, their bodies swaying drunkenly, he'd pushed her against the shuttered side of a newsagent and kissed her in the strobing light of a faulty street lamp, neither of them caring who saw. They'd only stopped when the sky had exploded around them with sudden flashes of colour and noise. 'What the—' he'd said, looking up at the impressive fireworks display illuminating the night sky, a bank of grey smoke drifting high above them and carrying with it an acrid, sulphur smell.

She'd pulled him close again. 'Bonfire Night,' she'd said, her lips against his.

'Aha,' he'd grinned, 'no chance I can convince you I just arranged that little display then, for our first date?'

She remembered how her stomach had flipped at his use of the word 'first', the subtle implication that there might be a second, perhaps even a third? She'd leaned in to test him and when they'd finally pulled apart again, it had felt like the most natural thing in the world to invite him back to her place.

* * *

They drive north for several hours, stopping once at a grotty service station to refuel and ask for directions, then navigate their way through an urban sprawl before breaking out into open countryside. Cultivated farmland slowly gives way to a more unruly landscape and they find themselves driving through tangled woods and across open, shrubby moors. Eventually, they pull up onto the verge of a remote country lane, the car's hazard lights flashing urgently as they stare up a steep, unmarked track.

'It's got to be up there,' says Lila, turning back to the map in her hands. 'It's the only place it can be. We've driven up and down this lane three times now.'

Tom shakes his head. 'I don't like it, Lila. It looks really narrow and muddy. After all that rain . . . what if the car gets bogged?' He checks his phone. 'I don't even have mobile reception here.'

'So we're just going to turn around and go home?'

Tom doesn't answer.

'Come on,' she says, surprised to find herself being the encouraging one, 'we've got boots and coats. We'll survive. It's the Peak District, not Outer Mongolia.' She regards him with a sideways glance; he has definitely grown more cautious in recent weeks.

He must feel her studying him because without turning, he pulls a silly face at the windscreen that makes her smile in spite of herself. 'Come on,' she says again, a little more softly, 'we've come all this way; let's not give up now.'

'OK,' he sighs, flicking off the hazard lights and swinging the car up the overgrown track, 'but I'm warning you, it's you that's going to dig us out if we get stuck.'

'Deal,' she says and feels her grin creep across her face like a strange aberration. When was the last time she smiled?

* * *

In the early days, their relationship had been full of spontaneity and passion, born out of the intensity that a long-distance love affair can carry. Tom's job had meant a fair bit of back and forth; he'd travelled to visit her in London whenever he could but when a

46

project kept him in one place for a time, Lila would jump on trains or planes for illicit weekends in whichever city his work had taken him to. She'd loved the excitement of it all, the anonymous hotel rooms, the big white beds, the fluffy bathrobes and room service. It was a romantic way to start a relationship and the physicality of them – their ease with each other, the uncomplicated way they reached for one another, touched one another – seemed to form the very foundation of all that they shared.

Unlike other men she'd dated, Tom was a man who seemed consummately comfortable in his own skin. He communicated with his hands – and with his body; his fingers grazing the back of her neck, a hand resting lightly on her hip, an arm slung around her shoulders as they walked down the street. Whenever she thought of him in those early days it was always in a physical way – the curve of his bicep, the hollow of his collarbone, the early-morning stubble on his jaw – and it always evoked a tingle of lust.

They'd been together just over eighteen months when he proposed with an antique diamond ring in an intimate underground wine bar tucked down a one-way street off the Strand. She hadn't had to think about it; she'd shrieked her 'yes' and leapt into his arms and six months later they were married before friends and family at a small register office, the reception held afterwards in a flapping white marquee at the bottom of her parents' sprawling Buckinghamshire garden.

'I promise we will never lose this,' she'd said, pulling him close on their wedding night, and she'd thought of some of the other couples they were friends with who bickered and sniped publicly at each other, trying to draw the rest of them into their personal battles with jokey little barbs and asides designed to undermine or humiliate; and she thought of her parents, sitting there at the wedding breakfast, her father drunk on champagne and whisky, flirting outrageously with her maid of honour while her mother turned away from him with that sad, tight look upon her face. No, she'd thought, they would never be like that. They would never lose their closeness, their intimacy. They would never stop wanting each other.

'And I promise,' he had said, kissing her shoulder blade before trailing his lips all the way down to the crook of her elbow, 'that we will never go to bed angry at each other. There is nothing we won't resolve with a little compromise . . . or sex,' and he had grinned his crooked grin at her and tumbled her back onto the bed.

* * *

'Here it is,' she says, studying the map and then glancing back up to where the track widens out in front of them. 'This has got to be it.' Tom looks doubtful but he parks the car by a rotting wooden gate and they pull on their walking boots and coats before clambering over it and out across a boggy meadow. Using the map to guide them, Lila leads them through a densely wooded area and then out onto a high ridge where bruise-coloured clouds hang ominously low all around them.

She holds the map out again, wrestles it flat against the wind, and tries to gain her bearings. She looks up and points. 'I think it must be just over this ridge . . .'

Tom nods and eyes the darkening sky. 'Let's hope so because I think it's about to bucket down again.'

As rain streaks from the leaden sky they run the last few hundred metres, across the ridge, around a huge clump of blackberry brambles and then down a grassy bank towards an expanse of water, slate grey and choppy with rain. There isn't time to stop and take it all in; the rain lashes them, fierce and cold, stinging their skin. 'Come on,' yells Tom, but Lila can't keep up. She loses her footing and slides down the rest of the bank on her bum, shrieking as cold water seeps through her jeans.

He hauls her up and points towards the pencil-grey outline of a building, just visible in the distance through the curtain of rain. 'Over there,' he says and they run again, arriving on the doorstep moments later, soaked to the skin and gasping for breath.

'Is this it?' she asks.

'I don't know.'

She eyes the darkened windows of the tumbledown cottage. 'It's got to be it, hasn't it?' Now that she's here she's suddenly nervous. 'Try the door. Hurry.'

She pulls the silver key from her pocket and tries to turn it in the lock, but she is cold and wet and her hands are trembling. She can't do it. 'Maybe this isn't it,' she says. 'Maybe we've got the wrong place.'

But Tom takes the key from her hand and tries again. Within seconds the door has swung open with an ominous creak. He holds it ajar for her, ushering her in, before following her into the shadowy interior and shutting the door behind them with a bang.

She turns to look at him through the gloom, both of them soaking wet and breathless. 'We did it,' she says and then she looks around, drinking in her first impression of the old place. 'We're here.'

Tom reaches across to flick a light switch on the wall – more from habit than expectation – but they are both amazed when the bare light bulb overhead flickers, fizzes and then stays on. 'Electricity,' he says, 'well I never.'

Lila doesn't comment. She just stands there in the centre of the room, looking around at her surroundings, cast as they are in the light of a low-watt bulb. She sees a long stone hearth with its iron grate full of cold, white ash and beside it a wicker basket, presumably once filled with logs and kindling. Above the mantel is a dusty collection of candle stumps jammed into the necks of empty glass bottles, each melted into its own uniquely twisted form. There's a stack of old books and a curled pack of playing cards, a mildewed box of Scrabble, a chess set and a copy of Thoreau's *Walden* still splayed upon the surface, as if its owner has just put it down for a moment and walked out of the room to make a cup of tea. In the centre of the room is an upturned wooden crate. It forms a makeshift table and on its surface Lila spies a dusty oil lamp, empty beer bottles and a grimy ashtray. She lifts one of the bottles and holds it up to the dim light, sees the husk of a black beetle lodged at the bottom, long dead. Surrounding the crate are a low-slung brown velvet couch, several musty beanbags and one wingback armchair, stuffing bursting from its seat cushion.

'Mice,' says Tom, following the direction of her gaze. 'Probably using it for their nests.'

Lila nods and gives a little shudder.

'So here we are,' he says. 'It's kind of basic, huh?'

'I think the word you're looking for is *rustic*,' she says. She rubs her hands together, trying to get warm. 'If we had some matches we could light a fire.'

'I wouldn't. The chimney is probably clogged with birds' nests and soot. We'd set fire to this old place within minutes.'

'Oh,' says Lila, disheartened, thinking of her cold, wet jeans, clammy against her skin. The room gives off a strange, illicit air. She wonders if local kids have been gathering here, although judging by the thick layer of dust coating everything and the stale, damp quality of the air around them, it's obvious they haven't been back in a while. The only footprints visible are their own as they move about the room. She bends down and smooths her hand across the surface of one of the filthy floorboards and reveals a beautiful honey timber below the dirt. They could be polished, she thinks, restored. And those thick stone walls painted white again, to enhance the low-hanging wooden beams above. New curtains. New furniture. She can't help it. Even in the half-light of the rainstorm Lila's design instincts kick in and she can see the potential.

They move on into the second room where they discover a run-down kitchen with an old cast-iron range, one solitary saucepan still sitting on the hob. Opposite stands a long wooden table with two rickety benches drawn up and even more candles stuffed into the necks of old beer bottles. Three mugs are positioned on the table next to an empty rusting tin for a brand of powdered milk Lila knows is no longer available. There are more chipped mugs and a few dusty pint glasses lined up on a shelf, and above these, running the length of the ceiling, another low, exposed beam. Lila stares at it and notices a deep, splintered hole in the timber, an almost perfectly round indentation with the faintest trace of scorch marks at its edges. Could it be a gun shot? *Inside* the cottage? The thought makes her uneasy and she is just about to ask Tom to take a look when he calls out to her. 'Here, catch.'

A flash of colour wings through the air and Lila grabs at the object tumbling towards her. 'A Rubik's cube,' she says, holding it out on the palm of her hand.

'I haven't seen one of those for years. It's probably a collectors' item now. You should stick it on eBay.'

Lila gives it a couple of twists and then places it onto the shelf next to the pint glasses. 'Never could get the hang of them.'

As they climb the creaking staircase, Tom warns her round a perilous-looking hole in one of the steps near the top. 'Careful, some of these have seen better days.'

She skirts the hole and they arrive on a small landing with two rooms extending off it on either side. It's immediately obvious that while one is watertight the other leaks rainwater down the inside of the chimney breast. 'It probably needs new roof tiles and flashing up there,' she says, eyeing the water pooling on the floorboards. There are faded cotton curtains hanging at each window, the pink roses that once bloomed on the thin fabric only just visible. Mattresses lie on the floor in each room, a moth-eaten patchwork quilt still spread across one of them. A cracked mirror hangs at a drunken angle on one wall while another oil lamp and an empty drinking glass are perched on the seat of a wooden chair. Lila moves into the corner of the room to inspect what looks like a bundle of rags and realises it's a dusty holdall, out of which spill several items of clothing – a white cotton dress now yellowed with age, an embroidered smock, a pair of stripy woollen tights and a washed-out polo neck.

She moves to the other window where a ceramic jug stands on the sill bursting with the pale-moon seed heads of dried honesty. She reaches out to touch one of the translucent white discs with a fingertip and watches as it crumbles like ash next to the empty shells of long-dead insects. Something about the sight of the dried plant, the forgotten clothes, the oil lamp and empty glass perched on the chair beside the mattress, fills Lila with a deep and sudden sadness. This was someone's home. Someone once dressed in those clothes, cared enough to pick those stems of honesty, to place them there on the window sill in the pretty jug where they could catch the light. She wonders who they were and why they abandoned all this here – whether they expected their possessions to be here still after all these years, just waiting for a stranger to discover them.

Back downstairs she and Tom perch together on one of the wooden benches and drink coffee from the thermos flask they packed earlier that morning. Lila sips from her plastic mug and tries to put aside her emotions and survey the cottage with a detached, professional eye. She knows it will need a lot of work to make it habitable.

'It's pretty bloody desolate,' says Tom, as if reading her mind. 'Feels like we're in the middle of nowhere.'

Lila nods. He is right; there is no traffic noise, no dogs barking, no sirens – nothing but the soft pattering of the rain on the roof. The whole place gives off a strange, melancholy air. 'It's quaint,' she says, trying to raise a smile.

'I wonder who it belonged to.' He blows across the surface of his coffee. 'I'm not sure I can see your dad here.'

'No,' agrees Lila, looking around at the squalor. Her father was all about home comforts, good food, fine wines and expensive cigars. 'We both know he was no angel . . . he had his booze . . . his women . . . but this place?' She shakes her head. 'Even if he did own it, why would he leave it to me in such strange circumstances? Why wasn't it part of his will? Why all the secrecy? It doesn't make sense.'

'So who?' asks Tom.

Lila eyes him a moment. 'Someone he knew? One of his girl-friends? God knows there were enough of them . . .'

'A mistress, handing over the love nest?' Tom looks dubious.

'What else then?'

He shrugs.

Lila nods and stares around at their surroundings. 'It's a perfect mystery.' The sound of the rain eases slightly and she wraps her hands around her mug, warming them against its sides.

'Did you call the solicitors?'

'Yes. They were very cagey. Wouldn't tell me anything. Said they "had to respect their client's wishes". I could ask Mum, I suppose, when she's next back from France.'

'Yes,' he agrees, 'but tread carefully. If it's something to do with your dad's extramarital affairs you don't want to upset her.'

'No, good point.'

Tom takes another sip of his coffee. 'I suppose the main thing here is that it belongs to you now. Any ideas what you'll do with it?' He hesitates. 'I'm not sure this cottage will be worth much but the land will have value. We should get a surveyor out to take a proper look.'

'Mmmm . . .' says Lila, noncommittally. Something is niggling away at her, a feeling that has been growing ever since she walked through the door. It's the same feeling she gets when she begins a new work project: the possibility of the blank canvas, the thrill of creation. But how to even begin with such a project, she wonders? She tilts her head to one side. 'Listen,' she says.

'What?' asks Tom. 'I don't hear anything.'

She looks to the roof. 'The rain. It's stopped.'

The transformation is startling. As they step outside the front door, a shard of sun pierces the steel-coloured clouds and lands in a dazzling column upon the lake. The water is still choppy in the stiff breeze and dancing with dark shadows but the light at least makes it look a little less grey and forbidding. Lila gazes out across it. 'Oh,' she says, suddenly overcome by the strangest feeling.

She moves down the bank and stands by the tall reeds looking out over the expanse of water. A swift swoops low over the surface, then soars up and away again like a tiny fighter pilot banking into the breeze. Déjà vu – that's what it's called, isn't it? When you feel certain you have lived a moment before, stood in a place already. Shaken, Lila takes a step back and lowers herself onto a rotten old tree trunk slumped at an angle across the grassy bank; she perches on the makeshift seat and smooths her fingers across a gnarly old knot in the wood. It is a strange almond-shaped whorl with a dark teardrop falling from one corner. The closer she looks, the more she sees the knot's startling resemblance to a weeping eye, there at the very centre of the trunk. She shivers and turns away to look out over the lake. She knows she has never been there before but there is still something oddly familiar about it all, something raw and real, like the ache she feels deep inside.

And then it is upon her in a sudden, terrible wave and there is no holding it back. All that grief, all that pain, all that sadness and disappointment and anger. She can't hold it in any longer. With one dreadful sob the tears begin to fall and the silver lake disappears behind the veil of her sorrow. She senses Tom lowering himself onto the tree trunk beside her, feels him pulling her into his arms. 'It's OK,' he murmurs, holding her close. 'It's OK.'

But it's not OK. It will never be OK. She has lost their baby – their beautiful baby girl – and it is all her fault.

'I'm sorry, I'm so sorry,' she sobs. 'I don't know how it happened. The fall. I just wish . . . I just wish I could remember. It's killing me . . . the not knowing.'

'Shhhh . . .' he soothes. 'You have to let it go, Lila. It wasn't your fault.'

'But it was. I fell. I should have been more careful.'

'Lila, remembering isn't going to bring her back.'

She puts a hand to her mouth and bites down on the sleeve of her jumper, trying to stop her sobs.

'You have to stop blaming yourself. You were pregnant and you lost your balance. You fell down the stairs. There was nothing you – *anyone* – could do. I'm just so grateful that you're OK. I could have lost you both that day.'

Lila feels the tears sliding down her face but she can't stop them any more. 'She was so tiny . . . so perfect.' Their beautiful baby girl.

They both sit in silence as they remember the hardest, most heartbreaking moments in the hospital. Placental abruption, they'd called it, caused by the fall. She had come round in the hospital and been told that she had to deliver her baby then and there. 'It's too soon,' she'd cried. 'I can't do it.' But she'd had to – for their baby.

Lila sniffs and takes the tissue Tom is offering her and blows her nose. 'She had your eyes,' she says, with a sob.

'And your blond hair.'

'Her fingernails . . .'

Tom nods, remembering. '. . . perfect.'

Everything had been perfect: fingernails, toes, eyelashes; everything except their daughter's tiny lungs, still too weak to breathe on their own. The doctors had done their best . . . had reassured them that she stood a good chance. She was in the best place, with the most-experienced staff and the necessary equipment. Their baby had lain in the neonatal unit for three days and Lila hadn't left her side. She'd stroked her tiny, curled fingers through the hole in the incubator and willed her to live – begged her to hold on. She'd offered up every prayer she could think of, had plea-bargained for her daughter's safe-keeping but then complications had set in – pneumonia – and they'd been told her life hung in the balance. Two days after that the medical staff had switched off her life support and finally they'd been allowed to hold her. Tom had wrapped the body of their daughter in the soft knitted blanket Lila had bought for the nursery in a flurry of excitement only a week earlier and they'd held her then. She had been so pale and so terribly still, their beautiful, five-day-old baby girl. Milly, they'd called her.

Tom pulls her close. 'It wasn't your fault.' Lila can't look at him but he reaches for her chin and tilts her face towards him, forcing her to look at him through her tears. 'Say it. Go on. "It wasn't my fault."'

She eyes him for a moment then shakes her head.

Tom smooths a loose strand of hair from her face, strokes her cheek, leans in and kisses her. *Feel something*, she wills herself. *Feel it.* She kisses him back, presses her cold lips against his warm ones.

'We can try again,' he says. 'When you're ready.'

She nods and lets him kiss her again, lets his hands burrow beneath her coat, up under her T-shirt where he gently caresses the faded bruises on her ribcage, no longer purple but a ghastly yellow, trying not to flinch as his fingers graze the empty hollow of her belly.

This is us, she thinks. This is what we do. This is what we've always been about: closeness, intimacy. She leans into him a little more. *Feel it.*

Then his hands are moving up towards her breasts and he is pressing against her. She can feel his need and she gives in to it for just a moment. *Feel something.*

He is pulling her closer now, his mouth covering hers, his breath hot on her skin, but it isn't going to work. She can't forget . . . and she can't go back. In this moment she doesn't know how to live with her pain; it overwhelms all other feeling and sensation. Before she even really knows what she is doing, she has pushed him off. She stands and brushes angrily at her jeans. 'God, Tom, why does it always have to be about sex with you?'

He looks up at her, the hurt and confusion evident in his eyes. 'I . . . I . . . I thought you—'

'No,' she says, 'you didn't think. That's the problem.' And she turns and walks away from him, back towards the shadows of the cottage.

There doesn't seem to be much point staying any longer, so they pack up their things and return to the car in silence. The rain has stopped, but the drive home is still torturous, the atmosphere in the car claustrophobic with despair and disappointment. Lila can barely exchange more than a couple of words with Tom all the way back to London. She just sits in the passenger seat, gazing at the mottled sky as it turns slowly from grey to orange to dusky pink. *Red sky at night, shepherds delight,* she thinks, but even the dispersal of the rain clouds and the promise of a better day can't lighten her mood. *We can try again,* Tom had said, but Lila doesn't want to try again. How do you replace the irreplaceable? How do you bear the unbearable? She just wants their daughter back. She just wants this sickening, hollow feeling eating her up from the inside out to disappear. She thinks about the bottle of pills in the bathroom cabinet at home. She imagines unscrewing the lid and swallowing them all down, one by one, slowly giving in to oblivion.

She shifts in her seat, turns to gaze out of the window. She thinks about Tom and about the steep precipice their marriage teeters upon.

How quickly things have changed for them. A mere two or so years on from their wedding night and for all their giddy, whispered promises, she sees now how they were caught up in nothing but naive innocence – no, worse than that – arrogance . . . to think that they were special . . . different. She knows now that they aren't either of those things; they are just like everyone else – a couple of years of wedded bliss and here they are, flailing and floundering through the rocky terrain of their relationship.

She thinks of the cottage they have left behind – cold and lonely – standing beside that strange, shimmering lake and realises that is exactly how she feels: cold and hollow and empty. She had love growing and blossoming inside her, but now, perhaps like the cottage, it is gone; and the thing that scares her most of all, she thinks, glancing across at the grim face of her husband, is that she's just not sure if they will ever get it back.

4

AUGUST

1980

Kat lies in the tin boat, a fishing rod propped against the side of the hull, its float bobbing lazily somewhere out on the lake. Overhead, ephemeral white clouds drift across the sky, morphing into ever-changing shapes. She closes her eyes, giddy with the gentle rocking sensation of the boat – the wide-open sky – the freedom of it all.

It's only been a few short weeks since they moved to the cottage but already she has lost track of the days; they spiral away at the lake hazy and unchecked, the five of them falling into familiar patterns and routines, mostly revolving around sleeping, smoking and drinking, with the lake forming a focal point of sorts. In the mornings they bathe in the shallows, wring out T-shirts and bathing suits ready for the day ahead; at lunch, during the warmest part of the day, they float upon its mirrored surface, soaking up the sun's rays; and in the evening they build campfires down on the shingle, swat at midges and watch the sun set over the surrounding hills. So far, time spent at the cottage has felt like one, long, lazy holiday – one that no one wants to end. Kat has never felt so blissfully content.

Mac sits opposite her at the other end of the boat. She hears him pull on the oars, splashing them once, twice through the water, steadying their position. He has been fishing almost every day since they arrived, but for Kat it's her first time out in the boat and she likes the new perspective it gives her: the gentle rocking motion reminiscent of a hammock in the breeze, the cottage standing like a doll's house in the distance, the lazy clunk and splash of the oars, the low hum of a dragonfly skimming the lake. She reaches out and trails her fingers through the cool water. It is hard to believe that not so very far away there is a whole world out there bustling with life, while they wile away the days in isolated paradise. It's hard to believe that just a few short weeks ago they'd needed Simon to persuade them to give this idea a try. For despite their fears, no one has arrived to lay claim to the derelict cottage; no one has come storming over the hills and threatened to throw them off the land. They are all beginning to relax a little and entertain the thought that maybe, just maybe, this cottage has been lying here waiting for them to claim it all this time – waiting for them to make it their home.

'Look,' says Mac from the opposite end of the boat, 'that one looks like a shaggy dog. See, up there.'

She squints to where he points high above their heads until she sees the gliding wisp of cloud with drooping ears and feathery tail. She smiles and watches it drift and morph in shape until her vision blurs and she has to tear her eyes from the powder-blue expanse.

Mac's eyes are closed again, his own shaggy hair falling away from his face, his chin lifted to the sun. Kat watches him for a moment. Without the usual fringe of hair obscuring his eyes, she can see him clearly for once and something about him seems altered. He is still skinny, still kind of odd-looking. Unlike Simon and Ben, Mac remains caught somewhere in the awkward no-man's-land between man and boy, with a rash of spots blossoming on his stubbly chin and his tall, rangy frame yet to fill out properly; but compared to just a few weeks ago, he already looks different – a browner, healthier version of his former self. She supposes they all are now; three weeks of living outside in the fresh country air is transforming them all.

'What do you miss?' Mac asks, his grey eyes still closed to the sun.

Kat smiles. 'It's only been three weeks.'

'I know,' he says, 'but you must miss something.'

'But we've brought almost everything with us.'

Mac grins, his eyes still closed. 'True.'

'God,' laughs Kat, 'those first two days were nothing more than a back-and-forth march across that bloody meadow, lugging all that crap we brought with us. I nearly gave up on the whole idea then, to be honest.' She settles back against the warm metal hull. 'Thank God I didn't, hey?'

'It might seem like crap now, but we'll be grateful for it all soon.'

Kat shrugs. It had all seemed a bit pointless to her, the endless discussions about what they would need to survive up at the lake. She'd thought Simon had said that everything they required could be found up there, but the more they had thought about it, the more it had become clear that they would have to procure a fair few essentials if they were to get up and running. Their lists had included bedding and kitchen equipment, tools and groceries, firelighters, lamps and candles, batteries, matches, pen knives and fishing rods, a basic first aid kit.

'For people supposedly giving up the trappings of modern life we sure do seem to need a lot of stuff,' she'd half joked. 'I understand about your guitar, Ben, but do we really need all these old *Melody Makers*? There's a whole box of them here.'

'You're taking books aren't you?'

'Books are different.'

'Why?'

Kat had shrugged. 'They just are.'

'Not to me,' he'd sniffed. 'If I can't have my records then these are the next best thing.'

In the end it had all come with them. They bought practical walking boots and waterproof coats too and just when Kat had thought they might be drawing to the end of their list, Mac had started adding some very odd things: wire and nails, an axe, a hacksaw and a fierce-looking hunting knife.

'Bloody hell, Mac,' Carla had laughed, 'you're not going to get all *Heart of Darkness* on us, are you? What exactly are you planning to do up there?'

He'd shifted his weight and patiently explained. 'Chicken wire for the chicken coop we'll build. Copper wire for fixing snare traps.

A good knife for skinning and gutting rabbits.' They'd looked at him in amazement and he'd shaken his head. 'What did you think we're going to be eating up there? It's a long way to the nearest chippie.'

Simon had simply nodded and added everything to the list.

'Well if Mac gets wire I want toilet paper,' Carla had chipped in. 'It's going to be bad enough going in that outside pit. I don't want to have to wipe my bum on dock leaves as well.'

'What about a homebrew kit?' Ben had suggested, to everyone's murmurs of agreement, and so the list had grown. In the end the most sensible thing had seemed for them all to pool their savings and to stock up on the essentials that they needed. It had been a relief to see that even after they'd bought out half the local camping shop, they still had a healthy sum of money left in their kitty. Simon had reassured them that as long as they were careful with it they'd easily make it through to spring.

'I'm not sure I miss anything yet,' Kat says finally, eyeing Mac across the boat. 'Give it a few more days though and I'm sure I'll be sick of you lot and desperate for a hot bath and a bar of chocolate.'

Mac smiles. 'What about family? Don't you miss them?'

Kat thinks for a moment. 'I don't have a family. Not really. Just a sister – Freya.'

'Where are your parents?'

Kat shakes her head. 'God knows.'

Mac throws her a curious glance.

'Junkies,' she explains, looking out over the water. 'They fall into that category of grown-ups who never should've been allowed to have children. Dad left us first. Mum fell to bits after he walked out.' She swallows. There is so much more she could say but she doesn't want to release the ugly words into such a glorious day.

'Sorry,' mumbles Mac.

'It's OK. We were taken into care . . . raised by foster parents. *Peter and Margaret Browning.*' Both of them hear the slight edge in her voice. 'Don't get me wrong, they were nice, but I think they were ready to see the back of us as soon as we both turned eighteen. Sent us off to college with a pat on the back and a suggestion that

the odd letter might be nice; "just to let us know you're still alive".'
She looks at Mac. 'Twelve years I lived in their house and all they
wanted was the occasional letter. It stung a bit.' She tries to smile.

Mac stares at her. 'That must have been tough on you and
your sister.'

It had been tough, yes but it hadn't been nearly as tough as the
years that had preceded life with the Brownings. Kat shrugs. 'It's
just the way it was. I think our foster parents liked the idea of
"rescuing" us more than the actual job of parenting. Besides, Freya
and I were good at being independent. We learned pretty quickly
to rely only on each other. Freya's all I have in the way of family
but she's in London now, at art college.' She studies Mac a moment.
'She's great. You'd like her.'

'Are you very similar?'

'Me and Freya? Not really. There's only two years between us,
but we're really different.' She looks at Mac and smiles. 'Everybody
likes Freya. There's something about her.'

'Have you told her about this place?'

Kat shakes her head. 'What do you think? Tell no one, isn't that
what Simon said? But what about you?' she asks, deflecting Mac's
attention. 'Do you miss anything . . . anybody? Your family?'

Mac shrugs. 'No. It's just me and Mum now and she doesn't seem
to mind what I do, as long as I'm happy.'

'She sounds nice.'

Mac nods. 'She is. Dad was a lot older . . . a farmer. He used to
take me out on the land and teach me about farming and hunting,
about respecting the environment. He'd probably love what we're
trying to do here.'

Kat smiles. 'Is that how you know so much about the countryside?'

He shrugs. 'I guess so. He taught me a fair bit . . . until he died
a few years ago. A stroke. He always wanted me to go to university
though. He wanted me to have "options" so that's why I went. For
him, really.'

Kat studies the frayed coil of rope lying on the bottom of the
boat. 'Do you miss him?'

'Course,' he shrugs again. 'He was my dad.'

Kat hears the tenderness in Mac's voice and swallows down the ache in her throat. She's never spoken of her parents like that. Not once. She reaches down and touches the coiled rope, lets its thick hemp scratch against her skin. 'It's strange, isn't it? All that time sharing a house and we never once talked like this.'

Mac nods.

'We had to come all the way up here to find out a little more about each other.' She stares across at him and this time he holds her gaze until the solemn moment is broken by the sound of a splash. They both turn to see the float at the end of Kat's fishing line bob and then duck down below the surface of the water. 'Eh up,' says Mac with a grin. He stands carefully and slides across to sit beside her in the boat.

Kat seizes the fishing rod firmly in her hands then turns to Mac with a burst of helpless laughter. 'Is now a good time to tell you that I've got no idea what I'm doing?'

'Just reel it in, slow and steady. Like this.' Mac puts his hands over hers and shows her how to turn the handle on the rod. She concentrates, spooling the line, her tongue caught between her teeth, hauling it in until a huge silver perch lies flip-flopping on the bottom of the boat. Kat looks at it, half amazed, half repulsed. Its scaly sides heave in and out, its mouth gapes open and shut.

'What do we do now?'

'Stand back,' says Mac, and he bends down, removes the hook from the fish's rubbery mouth and then, before she can say another word, he grabs a heavy wooden stick lying on the bottom of the boat and clobbers the creature over the head. One sharp blow and the fish is still.

'Oh,' says Kat, horrified. 'Couldn't you have left it? It would have died soon enough.'

'Kinder this way,' says Mac with a shrug, and he looks up at her, his face transformed by the curve of his grin and the fish blood splattered across his left cheek and dripping like a crimson

63

tear from the corner of one eye. 'One more that size and we'll have supper sorted. Well done.'

Kat can't help it; despite her lingering revulsion at the violence of it all, she feels something else welling within her: a warm flush of pride.

* * *

The crickets are in full song as they gather around the campfire that evening. They fry the perch over the flames with wild sorrel Mac has uncovered in the woods and eat it straight from the pan, the fish melting like butter in their mouths.

Kat watches her friends hunched over their plates, cramming the fish she caught only hours earlier into their bellies and she can't stop her mouth twisting into a smile. 'What?' asks Ben, catching her eye. 'Is there something on my face?' He rubs at his scruffy goatee.

'No,' she laughs. 'It's just this.' She gestures around them. 'This place.'

Simon turns to her. 'What about it?'

'It's even better than I thought it would be.' Simon eyes her for a moment and then nods. 'I don't think I've ever felt so at home somewhere,' she adds quietly. 'It really feels as though it was meant to be, doesn't it?' and he nods again and returns her smile.

After they have picked the last of the fish bones clean, Simon leans back against the grassy slope and eyes them all. 'I think we should make some plans,' he says. 'Summer has been kind but the days are growing shorter already.'

'Uh-oh,' jokes Carla, 'it's time for a serious-Simon talk.'

He smiles, but he isn't deterred. 'Things are only going to get harder . . . and colder and if we're still here by winter – which I hope we will be – food will become more scarce.'

'What are you suggesting?' asks Ben, reaching for his pouch of tobacco and cigarette papers.

'We need to set up a food store. We could start with the garden. I know it hasn't been tended in a while and there's a lot that's gone to seed, but there are still things we can eat. We should harvest what we can now, before it spoils or the birds and snails get to it.'

'But what about everything we lugged up here when we moved in? I still can't see how we'll ever get through those huge sacks of flour, rice and sugar.'

'If we rely solely on that I can assure you we'll have nothing come October but really bad scurvy. We can't go running to the village shop every time we need a loaf of bread or a box of cereal. The less we do to draw attention to ourselves the better. Besides, if the weather turns bad – if a tree comes down across that track, or if we get snowed in – we wouldn't be able to go anywhere.'

'That's true,' admits Kat.

'And there are other things to think about. We'll need firewood, lots of it. We need to start stockpiling for winter.'

'We need chickens, too,' says Mac.

Carla laughs. 'Chickens?'

'Yes,' says Simon, 'we need chickens. For eggs, meat too, if we get desperate.'

Mac nods. 'I can make a chicken coop.'

'Is there no end to this boy's talents?' jokes Ben, putting the flame of a lighter to his roll-up.

Simon ignores him. 'And we need to start hunting and foraging. Every day. Some things we can store – apples, root vegetables, nuts – things that won't spoil. We can dry herbs. The supplies that won't keep we should consider trying to stew or preserve. I found a load of old glass jars stacked up inside the lean-to. We can use those.'

Kat looks at Carla and rolls her eyes. 'I suppose that will be our job.'

'Not necessarily,' says Simon. 'We don't have to fall into gender stereotypes here. *We* set the rules, remember?'

'So we really are going to live off the land?' asks Ben. 'I always just thought that was just a bit of a joke. I'm perfectly happy with my cornflakes and instant mash.'

'No,' says Simon firmly. 'I'm not saying we won't need to visit a shop once in a while, but our money isn't going to last long if we fritter it away on unnecessary groceries. No more boxes of cereal. No more biscuits and coffee and hair conditioner.' He looks pointedly at Carla. 'We need to adapt, make-do. We've been lucky. It's been three weeks and no one has found us yet but we shouldn't get cavalier.' He looks around at them all in turn. 'Agreed?'

There is shuffling and grumbling but they all agree.

'We could draw up a rota,' says Kat, 'allocate everyone a job or two. That might be most fair?'

Ben groans. 'Sounds to me like the holiday's over.'

'Maybe,' says Simon, 'but the most important thing is to lie low. We've been lucky. Let's keep it that way. I'm not ready to go home just yet, are you?'

They shake their heads and for all the mumbling and groaning, Kat can see that they're excited and up for the challenge that lies ahead. 'What about Mac's car?' she asks. 'It's just sitting out there on the track. Bit of a giveaway, don't you think?'

'Yes,' agrees Simon, 'I've been thinking about that. We could move it into a corner of the meadow, cover it with brush or branches. Only use it when it's absolutely necessary, ration our petrol.'

They all nod.

'What about the bedrooms?' Kat asks.

'What about them?'

She swallows. 'Well, we've never really allocated them. I wasn't sure . . .' She clears her throat, suddenly embarrassed. 'You know . . . Ben and Carla took one of the upstairs rooms and I'm in the other . . . but it seems a bit selfish, me there on my own and you and Mac squashed downstairs.'

Simon eyes her. 'What are you suggesting?'

'Nothing . . . I just . . .' She flushes pink, suddenly wishing she'd kept her mouth shut. 'I just wonder if we shouldn't draw straws . . .'

'But we're a couple,' says Carla. 'Ben and I need our own room.'

'I wasn't saying . . .' Kat swallows again. 'Perhaps Simon and Mac should share the second bedroom and I could sleep downstairs. It's just me, after all . . .'

Simon shrugs. 'I don't mind being downstairs. Do you, Mac?'

Mac shakes his head.

'Unless one of you wants to share with Kat?' adds Carla with a sly look.

Kat colours and shakes her head. 'And listen to their snoring?'

'So we're agreed?' asks Simon.

They nod again.

'Good,' says Simon, 'tomorrow we get to work.'

'Yes,' agrees Ben, 'tomorrow we work; but tonight . . .' he adds, with a grin, 'we party.'

He hands his still-burning roll-up to Carla then saunters to the jetty where he struts his way along the creaking boards, removing his T-shirt and shorts in an exaggerated striptease while Kat and Carla cat-call him from the shore. When he reaches the end he turns his back on them all and shimmies his pants to the floor, mooning them with his pasty buttocks in the half light. Throwing them one last glance over his shoulder, he acknowledges Carla's wolf whistle with a low bow then dives high out over the lake, bellyflopping onto the surface of the water with a loud slap and making the rest of them groan in unison. 'Ouch,' laughs Simon, 'now that's got to hurt.'

* * *

The atmosphere in the cottage changes overnight. Whereas before they lazed around, living hand to mouth, drifting between the house and the lake like spoiled children at a summer camp, now they begin to rise earlier, waking at first light and gathering around the long table in the kitchen before heading off to complete a long list of tasks Simon has drawn up. Kat knows that for all their grumbling they are excited to be making the place their own. At first they take it in turns, each trying out different jobs, but very quickly they fall into their preferred roles.

Ben, to his surprise – and everyone else's – assumes the role of cook. They each have a go but no one else has his deft touch with the feisty old range in the kitchen. After a few nights of sloppy stews and blackened loaves of bread still doughy in the middle, they agree it should be left to Ben. He's the only one who seems capable of stoking the fire and producing edible meals and they are happy to agree that the kitchen should be his domain. Kat grows accustomed to seeing him sitting on the back doorstep in just his boxers and one of his florid Hawaiian shirts, smoking his joints and stroking his goatee while he appraises his marijuana plants growing on the window sill or the vat of homebrew fermenting in the larder. Carla is never far away, more often than not out in the garden with a basket over one arm, hunting for berries, hunched over flower beds or pulling up oversized stems of rhubarb, hunting for anything edible she can find. 'You two are like a debauched Tom and Barbara Good,' Kat jokes one afternoon.

But Carla just smiles and turns back to the garden. 'I like it out here, it's so peaceful.'

While Ben and Carla busy themselves in the vicinity of the cottage, Mac ventures further afield. He proves himself to be the most resourceful of them all, roaming the countryside, hardly ever returning empty-handed. No one knows quite where he goes or how he does it – no one actually bothers to ask – but more often than not he returns with prizes foraged on his travels. One afternoon it's handfuls of earthy brown mushrooms plucked from the forest floor; another it's a basket of tender dandelion leaves which they eat in a salad; there are wild nettles and bilberries and plump rabbits caught in his carefully laid snares which they roast over the campfire. Another morning, he rises especially early and hammers away at a pile of timber, wrapping it in chicken wire until Kat can see the definite outline of a coop take shape. Before nightfall the next day he is back at the cottage with five laying hens scratching and pecking at each other in an old wooden crate.

'Where on earth?' asks Carla, peering at the disgruntled birds through the slatted wood.

'Don't ask,' says Mac, wiping his brow with the back of his hand. 'I know they seem scrawny but they're heavier than they look.'

'Ugly things, aren't they?' says Kat, staring at their beady eyes and scraggy feet.

'Doesn't matter what they look like,' says Mac, 'as long as they can lay.'

She looks at him in wonder. 'You were a wasted talent at university, you know that?'

Mac blushes at the compliment and they coax and then shove the flapping, protesting birds into their new home. Kat watches them unruffle their feathers and strut about the coop. Chickens, she thinks, whatever next?

With the other three focused on matters relating to food and provisions, Simon's responsibilities inevitably fall to the maintenance of the place. He spends hours up the old ladder they have found lying in the long grass behind the lean-to, patching up roof tiles or fixing the guttering. He moves Mac's car to a far corner of the overgrown meadow and covers it with an array of branches and ferns, until it is completely camouflaged from view. And every day he spends several hours collecting and chopping firewood, stacking the logs and kindling up behind the house into an ever-growing pile. Kat likes to watch him out by the lean-to; the wide swing of the axe in his hands, his shirt tied around his waist, the sheen of sweat shining on his tanned shoulders, the intense concentration on his face.

As the days pass, they each seem to fit naturally into the new set-up; it is just Kat who struggles to find her role within the group. Mac is a loner and she feels like a gooseberry in the kitchen with Ben and Carla. She'd happily spend her days with Simon but she isn't strong enough or practical enough to help him chop wood or fix the roof, so in the end she focuses on the more basic tasks, the ones she knows she can manage.

She starts with the cottage, sweeping and scrubbing the floors, washing the grime-streaked windows and wiping down walls until the place almost gleams. She brings firewood and kindling in for the range, hammers nails into a wall by the front door for them to hang their raincoats and drags the mattresses from the bedrooms, beating them outside until the last plumes of dust have wafted away over the lake. Each new job brings her in some way closer to the cottage, helps her to see the details of the place: a whorl in the old wooden floorboards, a loose brick in the chimney breast, the curve of an iron window latch upstairs. It is hard work but she doesn't mind it. She doesn't mind the calluses on her hands, the dirt beneath her fingernails, the splinters and the grime. All those hours spent in lecture theatres and pondering the abstract ideas and philosophies of the world, when really Simon had been right all along: none of that matters. It's the simple tasks, she realises, that fill her with the greatest pleasure. Laying a fire, boiling water, picking strawberries, making tea, scrawling words in a notebook or sitting upon the front step with her hands clasped around a mug and a hand-rolled cigarette dangling from her lips as the sun warms her face and the lake shimmers seductively before her. It's these moments above all others that tell her she has made the right decision coming here.

'This place suits you,' Simon tells her one afternoon, regarding her from the open doorway. She is down on her hands and knees with a bucket of water scrubbing at the muddy floorboards, her hair tied up in an old scarf, the hem of her T-shirt twisted into a knot above her navel. 'You're different here,' he adds.

She nods and watches as Simon uncurls his fist to reveal a cluster of blackberries lying on the palm of his hand, their juice already beginning to stain his skin.

'They're from the bushes up behind the house. They're just beginning to ripen. Ben says he's going to make a pie for Carla's birthday tomorrow . . . maybe even some jam.' He holds one out to her and she rises from the floor. 'They're sweet,' he adds as she accepts the berry he holds to her lips, opening her mouth and then biting down, enjoying the warm syrup on her tongue. Juice trickles from her lips, making her laugh, but Simon reaches out and catches it on his fingertip, then lifts it to his own lips, a gesture so intimate it makes her blush.

Something about the sweet taste of the berry, the warm sunshine falling through the open door, the loud drone of insects outside makes her feel peculiar, almost drunk; embarrassed, she turns away from him and returns to the half-scrubbed floor. It's only when she finds the courage to glance back towards the doorway that she sees he has gone.

* * *

For twenty-four hours she tells herself she has imagined it, that the look in his eyes in the cottage, the way he raised his blackberry-stained finger to his lips, was nothing but her own overactive imagination. She has fantasised about such moments far too many times to convince herself it was real. But later, out by the lake, under the stars, with the remains of Carla's birthday dinner still spread before them and Ben strumming quietly on his guitar, she feels Simon's gaze fall on her once more. His eyes blaze in the darkness, and his face, lit by the occasional flare of a cigarette, remains tilted in her direction. The thought of his eyes on her makes her dizzy. She tries to focus on the flickering stars overhead and remembers something Simon once told her, about how the lights glimmering up there in the sky are probably nothing more than the residual flare of stars burned out many millions of years before, beamed at them from light years away. She gazes up at them and wonders how something so lovely can be nothing but a lie – an illusion – a dark deceit. The thought doesn't help with her giddiness.

'So what *did* you tell them?' she hears Ben ask as she tunes back into the conversation around her.

'I told them I was taking a year off,' says Simon. 'I told them I wanted to experience a little of the world before I settled down to complete my legal training.'

'Did you tell them about this place?'

'God no.' Simon shakes his head. 'You think I'm crazy? The fewer people that know about this place the better – I thought we'd all agreed that?'

Ben nods.

'Besides,' Simon continues, 'I don't think squatting in a derelict cottage up north really fits with my parents' ideals of success and personal achievement.' He grins in the darkness. 'For all they know I'm halfway to Africa.'

Ben chuckles but Carla gives a low groan from where she lies propped against his leg. 'Don't jiggle like that,' she moans, 'you're making me feel sick.'

71

'Sorry, my love,' says Ben, putting his guitar down and stroking her hair.

Kat watches Ben's hand moving across Carla's curls, sees his fingers stroke the round curve of her cheek and sighs quietly. They are always together, always entwined.

'How did *your* dad take it?' Simon asks Ben.

'Oh you know,' says Ben, 'sat me down, asked me where my *drive* was, my sense of responsibility; told me I'd flushed his school fees and several perfectly good years at university down the toilet . . . threatened to cut me off. I thought it went rather well, considering.'

Simon gives a low laugh and Kat lets the soft sound of it wrap itself around her like a cloak. She gazes up at the sky and watches as dark clouds steal across the pale orb of the moon. Far out on the lake a fish jumps with a splash. Other than the light from the campfire and the occasional flare of a lighter or burning cigarette it grows increasingly black. She lies on the ground and gazes up at the emptiness.

The boys' talk of family stirs Kat's mind. Something about their conversation brings a memory floating up to the membrane of her consciousness. There she is, hunched inside a stale-smelling wardrobe with her little sister trembling in her arms while outside the flimsy chipboard door the shouts and thumps of her parents' terrifying fight rage on.

'I'm scared,' Freya whispers.

'Shhh,' she murmurs, holding her sister close. 'It will all be over soon.'

Their father roars. They hear the sharp sound of splintering wood followed by the soft whimpering of their mother. They wait until the front door slams, then creep out into the kitchen. Her sister accepts the milk and biscuits she offers her, but her blue eyes are still wide with fear.

'Do you want anything, Mum?' she asks at the open door to her parents' room.

'You're a good girl, Kat,' her mother slurs, sprawled like a discarded rag across the bed. 'Always looking out for your sister. You're a good girl.'

Kat shivers in the darkness. She'd thought perhaps she was alone in wanting to free herself from the weight of family responsibility, but as she lies on the damp grass listening to the chatter of her friends, it becomes clear to her that no matter what experiences they've grown up with – whether privilege or affection or neglect – they are each trying to escape the constraints of their history in some way. Perhaps that's one of the attractions of their life at the lake, she thinks; the freedom it offers them to explore who they are . . . and who they *want* to be . . . without the baggage of the past weighing them down.

'So who wants to go?' asks Simon.

'Go where?' asks Kat, rejoining the flow of the conversation.

'To the shop tomorrow.'

Carla offers up another groan from the darkness.

'Carla's going to be too hung-over to go *anywhere*,' says Ben cheerily.

'I'll go,' offers Kat, 'if no one else wants to.'

'Good' says Simon. 'Mac can drive you.'

'Actually, I was planning to—'

'No,' says Simon cutting Mac off, 'you'll drive Kat.'

'I can probably manage by myself,' says Kat lightly, not wanting to be the cause of discord, but Simon isn't having it.

'Mac, you'll drive Kat. End of discussion. Whatever *Swiss Family Robinson* plans you had will have to wait.'

Mac shifts uncomfortably and they all see the colour rise in his face, even though it is dark. Kat shoots him an apologetic look. Far out on the horizon above the hills a flash of late summer lightning zigzags across the sky. 'There's a storm coming,' she murmurs, but no one moves, not for ages, not until the first drops of rain begin to fall from the sky, sizzling and spitting onto the glowing embers of their campfire.

Upstairs, sprawled on her mattress, Kat can't sleep. It's not just the lightning strobing across the room or the thunder rumbling across the valley, it's fragments of the evening's conversation still niggling at the back of her mind. All their talk of family and responsibility has brought a wave of guilt crashing down on her.

Freya: she hasn't told her sister where she is. She's tried to justify her disappearance by telling herself that Freya will be caught up in her own life in London – busy with her own friends and her course; and she understands Simon's desire to keep their whereabouts secret, she really does . . . but Freya is her little sister and no matter how intoxicating it feels for Kat to be free of her past and free of any sense of duty or responsibility, she has *never* not been there for her. It doesn't feel right.

With a sigh, she slips out of bed, relights the oil lamp and rummages through her belongings until she finds her notebook and a chewed biro. She looks at the blank page before her and then writes in a careful hand: *Dear Freya*. She stares at the words, the biro poised at her lips, before she lowers the pen and continues to write. When she has finished, she reads the letter through then tucks the piece of paper beneath her pillow and turns off the oil lamp. She will slip it into the postbox when she goes to the shop. No one need know. Besides, she hasn't given an address, just a few sketchy details and reassurances that she is all right, that she'll be in touch again soon. It's enough to make her feel a little better as she slides back beneath the covers and turns off the light.

The storm is closer now. White lightning explodes again in the darkness and Kat squeezes her eyes shut and counts . . . waiting for the accompanying thunder, trying to calculate just how close the storm is: *one Mississippi . . . two Mississippi . . .* when the drumroll comes it seems almost to be upon the cottage. Kat wriggles down deeper beneath the covers. She thinks of Carla and Ben curled up together in the room next door, Mac and Simon slumped about the living room downstairs and feels very much alone. She wills sleep to come but moments later there is another bright flash, a white pulse of light. She opens her eyes and gasps. In the split second of the illumination she sees the outline of him in the doorway; then the room falls black again. Her breath catches at the back of her throat. Did she imagine him there? She peers into the darkness but it's no good; her eyes remain blinded momentarily by the flare as another loud rumble shakes the valley.

There is the unmistakable squeak of a floorboard, then the sound of footsteps moving across the room to where she lies. Her ears strain and she just makes out the soft *whoosh* of a T-shirt being dropped to the floor, the rasp of a zipper, the creak of another floorboard then the mattress shifting beneath a new weight. Kat closes her eyes, tries to breathe, her body tingling in the darkness. For a moment there is nothing and then she feels his hand on her hip bone, his fingers grazing the strip of bare skin just above the waistband of her pyjama bottoms.

'I know you're awake,' he says, his words warm against her neck. 'I can tell by your breathing.'

She doesn't move; she doesn't say a thing, but she drinks in the scent of him: beer, cigarettes, and the faintest trace of lake water still lingering on his skin. His hand moves and Kat has to force herself to breathe.

'You do want this, don't you?' he asks, one finger tracing the curve of her breast. 'You do want me?'

Kat wonders if she is in fact dreaming. Three years at university and not once did Simon make a move on her. Three years and never *once* did he indicate that she was anything more than a friend to him. Three years of longing and waiting and watching and now she can't find the words, so she turns and searches for his eyes in the darkness, trying to read him in the pitch black. He moves closer still, until they are chest to chest, breathing each other's hot breath and finally he presses his lips against hers. She can't help it; a sound escapes her lips, half whimper, half moan, and then she is kissing him back as the lightning flares and the thunder crashes once more.

He reaches for her T-shirt, pulls it up over her head then pushes her pyjama bottoms down until they are lost in the tangle of bedclothes. He threads his hands through her hair, pulls her head back so that he can kiss her neck. The room strobes white again then returns to darkness.

'What if the others . . . ?' she whispers.

'Shhh . . .' he says. Her eyes have adjusted now. She can see his face, the contour of his cheekbones, his eyes shining in the darkness. 'Not another word,' he says. 'Just this.'

Kat understands what he is saying: be here and nowhere else. Be here with him now. She rises up to meet him and loses herself in his touch.

5

LILA

September

Lila is lingering with a half-filled shopping trolley beside the deli counter when the woman's voice floats across the aisle towards her. 'Lila?' She feels a hand on her arm. 'Lila, I *thought* that was you.'

She turns away from the tubs of stuffed olives and sees a short, round woman with blond hair and clear blue eyes smiling up at her. Lila arranges her face into a greeting while trying to conjure a name from the soup of her brain. 'Hi . . .'

'It's me,' says the woman putting a hand to her chest, 'Marissa, from high school, remember?' She smiles encouragingly as Lila's brain slowly connects a series of faded memories: the flash of goose-pimpled legs and netball skirts, the musty smell of a school bus, giggling and passing notes at the back of an English class.

'Oh hi,' says Lila. 'Sorry, I was in another world.'

Marissa laughs. 'Don't worry, I do look a little different these days,' she pats at her waist, 'especially since this chap came along.' She gestures over to her trolley and for the first time Lila sees the chubby-faced infant strapped into the baby seat. 'This is Jack,' says Marissa proudly. 'Say hello, Jack.'

Jack gazes up at her, a thin trickle of drool spilling down his chin onto the plastic giraffe clutched tightly in his fist. Lila sees chubby, flushed cheeks, angelic blue eyes and a full head of curly blond hair, just like his mum's.

'He's teething,' Marissa says, somewhat apologetically. 'Hey,' she adds, with a broad smile, 'I bumped into Jen a few months ago. She told me that you were expecting too. Congratulations. And where is your little bundle of joy today? Don't tell me you've managed to escape for a few hours?'

Lila hesitates. A tight knot of dread forms in her belly. 'Yes,' she says quietly, 'I escaped.'

Marissa smiles. 'Lucky you. Love 'em to bits but it's nice to get a bit of time on your own, isn't it?'

Lila nods and tries to swallow.

'Boy or a girl?'

'A . . . a girl.'

'Ahh . . . lovely. Bet you're over the moon.'

Lila nods and looks around in panic.

'Her name?'

'Milly.'

'Lovely. Hope she's a good sleeper.' Marissa eyes her carefully. 'I've never been so tired in my life but these bags under the eyes are like a badge of honour, right? Just like those damn stretch marks.' Marissa grins and Lila swallows. 'We should get them together for a play date sometime. What do you think?'

'Yes,' says Lila, monosyllabic with shame. 'That would be nice,' she manages in a small voice.

'Great. I'll get your number off Jen and text you?'

Lila nods again.

'Lovely.' Marissa grins again. 'Now, don't waste any more of your precious time chatting to me. Go and have a coffee, get your nails done. Make the most of it while you can. You'll be back home changing nappies and mashing veggies before you know it.'

Lila tries to smile.

'Come on then, little man,' says Marissa, beginning to steer her trolley away, 'let's finish the shopping so we can get home to Daddy. He's taking Jack for his first swimming lesson this afternoon,' she explains with an indulgent smile. Then with an air kiss and a little wave, Marissa marches away down the nearest aisle.

Lila reaches out to place a steadying hand on the deli counter. She is dizzy with shame. Why did she just do that? Why did she *lie* to that woman? Why couldn't she tell her the truth? Marissa will hear what happened soon enough – probably from Jen – and then they'll both know that she has truly lost the plot. Lila shakes her head. Maybe Tom is right; maybe she should stop taking those pills. They take the edge off her grief but with everything so foggy all the time, making even the simplest decisions is proving hard.

'Can I help you, madam?' An obviously hung-over teenager in a stained white overall approaches from across the counter. She looks down at shiny slabs of pink meat and the marinated vegetables swimming in glistening pools of oil. For God's sake, she can't even decide whether to buy a pot of olives.

'I'm . . . I'm fine,' she mutters, 'thank you.'

She turns back to the aisles. People mill around her on all sides, a sea of bodies. Lila is overwhelmed, pressed in on all sides. Somewhere far away a child shrieks with indignation. The tannoy blares with a request for a cleaner to head to aisle eight. It's all too much. Without so much as a backwards glance, Lila ditches her half-filled shopping trolley beside a display of breakfast cereals and hurries towards the exit.

* * *

Her hands are still trembling as she lets herself in through the front door. She closes it with a gentle click and stands there for a moment, trying to compose herself. The sight of the carpeted stairs rising up in front of her and the small rug Tom has placed at the foot of them to neatly cover the bloodstain there makes her want to weep. She closes her eyes and forces herself to breathe. If only she could remember . . . how did it happen? *Why* did it happen? At that moment, she knows if she could find a way to crack open her brain and retrieve the memory of those lost hours she would do it. It won't bring Milly back, but at least it might help her understand.

Standing there, wrestling with her grief, Lila's ears slowly tune into the voices coming from the living room: Tom's low, earnest tones mingling with another, higher voice. What Lila would most like to do is head straight upstairs to collapse upon the cool, white expanse of her bed, but summoning her last reserves of energy, she pushes on the door and enters the room.

'There you are.' Tom leaps to his feet. 'And look who's here.' He gestures towards the sofa.

Lila stares at their visitor for a moment. 'Hi, Mum,' she says wearily, moving across the room to kiss her mother's cheek. 'What are you doing here? I didn't think you'd be back from France for another week or so?'

'Well that's not much of a welcome, is it?' her mother says with a bright smile. She envelops Lila in a tight hug before returning to the sofa, smoothing the fabric of her skirt. Her mother looks perfect, her blond hair styled into a neat bob, her make-up immaculate and an expensive-looking leather handbag settled at her feet. Lila turns to Tom and gives him a hard stare but he pretends not to see.

'Your mum changed her plans . . . phoned this morning to say she was back and thought she'd drop by for a cup of tea,' he says brightly.

She thinks of her husband's inexplicable rush to tidy the house earlier that morning and the penny drops. She turns back to her mother. 'Tom *asked* you to come, didn't he?'

High spots of colour appear on her mum's cheeks and she shrugs, caught in the web of their lie. Bloody Tom, thinks Lila. There is a pause as the three of them eye each other carefully.

'I brought you a cake,' says her mother finally, indicating the white cardboard box on the coffee table.

'How lovely. Here, let me.' Tom reaches for the box, clearly relieved to have a reason to leave the room. 'I'll put the kettle on. You sit down,' he urges, guiding Lila to the chair near the window. Then he's gone, leaving Lila and her mother to face-off across an expanse of cream carpet.

'The house is looking lovely,' her mother starts, gazing around at the room. 'Pretty tiles,' she adds, staring at the fireplace. 'I'm not sure I've ever noticed them before. Are they the originals?'

Lila shakes her head wearily. 'No, I found them in a salvage yard.'

'Well they go very well.' She looks around the room in admiration. 'It's hard to remember the wreck it was, when you first moved in here. You've worked your magic once again.'

Lila nods. 'How was France?'

'It's . . . it's been a comfort,' she says. 'I find the house out in Bucks so empty without your father. I rattle around there on my own but the gîte brings me solace . . . it reminds me of those holidays we used to take together. Happier times.'

Lila nods and an awkward silence fills the room.

'And how have you been?'

'Fine,' says Lila.

Her mother eyes her carefully. 'You look shattered.'

She gives a thin smile. Shattered: she supposes that's as good a word as any for how she's been feeling. 'I'm fine, Mum. I'm doing much better. I don't know why Tom called you.'

At least her mother has the grace not to bother with the pretence any more. 'He's just worried about you, darling. We both are. He said you were struggling . . . that you've been rather . . . depressed.'

Lila can't hold her gaze. She turns to face the window and allows the silence to swallow them up.

'Of course it's perfectly understandable,' her mother continues valiantly, 'after suffering such a . . . such a *terrible* loss . . . it would be natural to, well, to need a little time to process it all.'

Lila stares at her.

'Such a dreadful accident.' There is another pause. 'You still don't remember how it happened? The fall?'

Lila shakes her head. Why is she here? What does she want?

'Well, I suppose it's a small blessing.'

Her mother gives a little shiver and Lila nods and wills herself not to cry. A blessing?

'Have you been back to work yet?'

'No. It's quiet at the moment. They don't need me.' Christ, she was going to kill Tom. How desperate he must have been – or how at odds they are with each other now – that he could think this afternoon tea party might be the solution.

'Of course, since your father died . . . I've found it extremely hard too.'

At the mention of her father Lila softens slightly. 'I know, Mum.'

'There were days even just a few months ago when I couldn't get out of bed . . . when I really couldn't see the point of carrying on. He was such a presence in our lives and him not being here now, well,' she puts her hand to her lips, 'it's hard. I think that's why I prefer to be in France these days.'

Lila turns to look out the window again. She really doesn't want to be having this conversation – not about the baby and certainly not about her father. Outside, a boy flies past the bay window on his scooter. A little way behind his harried father follows, shouting at the child to slow down. Lila is aware that her mother is still talking at her, but she is struggling to tune in; it's as though the words are coming to her from down a long, echoing corridor. Sweat prickles in her palms. She's getting that strange, giddy feeling again too, as though her head isn't quite attached to her body. She wipes her clammy hands on her trousers and tries to concentrate.

'. . . I've found what helps me is to focus on the positives in my life,' continues her mother, oblivious to Lila's inner turmoil, 'and to remember those times we shared as a family.'

Lila bites her tongue. She could point out the insensitivity of her mother's words, that she wasn't given the opportunity to experience any 'happy times' with her daughter. She could point out how her mother's memories of their own family bliss seem to have been warped by time and grief. She could point out the endless lies, the whispered phone calls her father took in his study, all those nights he never even bothered to make it home. But there seems little point dredging all of that up in the face of her mother's visit, not now, not when Lila can't even summon the energy to make it round a supermarket.

'. . . like coming up to London today,' finishes her mother brightly. She smiles. 'Perhaps it's time you went back to work? Or found something fun to keep you busy, to get you out and about, back on your feet.'

Lila is relieved to see Tom enter the room with a rattling tea tray. 'The cake looks amazing,' he says. 'Thanks for bringing it.'

'Oh, it's nothing.' Her mother waves the offering away. 'I was just saying to Lila that a little project might be just what the doctor ordered.' She addresses Tom in a careful voice.

Give me strength, thinks Lila; these two are the worst actors in the world. 'There's a milk jug in the cupboard,' she says, eyeing the plastic bottle on the tray, but Tom just shoots her a look and places everything on the coffee table between them.

'I was telling Lila how when her father passed away, keeping busy was what got me through. That's when I took up with my walking group and signed up for a few evening classes. An activity or two might be helpful?'

'Yes,' says Tom, attacking the chocolate cake with a large bread knife. 'I've already suggested she try to catch up with a few friends socially.'

'And there's a proper cake slice in the drawer,' says Lila, watching him hack into the cake.

'This is fine,' says Tom.

'But you're making a terrible hash of—'

'It's *fine.*'

Out of the corner of her eye she sees her mother raise an eyebrow. Oh God, Lila thinks, we really have turned into *that* couple, arguing over milk jugs and cake slices.

'Of course I wanted to stay home, hang around in my dressing gown and feel sorry for myself,' continues her mother, 'but you just can't, can you? You have to carry on. You have to pick yourself up and soldier on.'

At that moment Lila feels like tipping the entire tea tray onto the floor and ordering her mother out of the house. Instead she counts to three. 'I'm not "feeling sorry for myself",' she says through gritted teeth. 'Our baby died. Milly: do either of you even remember her name?'

'I don't think that's—'

But Lila interrupts Tom. She won't let him speak. 'I'm grieving for *Milly* . . . our daughter. It's perfectly normal, or so the nurses at the hospital led me to believe.'

'Of course, dear,' says her mother in a soothing voice, 'I understand, I really do; I'm just saying that time heals all wounds . . . and you can always try again.'

Lila turns her face to the window once more. More platitudes. Can no one understand how she feels? Can no one see how it is – that she's been robbed of a very part of herself?

They had tried for twelve months to get pregnant before she had finally seen that thin blue line appear on the pregnancy test, and when she and Tom had peered down at the evidence, they'd turned to each other and giggled like little kids.

'Oh shit,' Tom had grinned, 'I guess that means I'll finally have to clear my snowboarding gear out of the spare room.'

She'd kissed him on the mouth and marvelled at how everything was about to change.

She had loved being pregnant – had loved the sensation of being filled with life. For almost seven thrilling months she had grown a baby inside her body. She had felt like a flower unfurling with its true, blooming potential. Every morning she'd woken early and just lain there in bed, moving her hands over her belly, revelling in the miracle of the tiny person growing inside her and the future that lay wide open. She'd taken to cooking and cleaning, enjoyed time with Tom, understanding that these were the last few weeks it would be just the two of them. She was high on hormones, high on life until – in an inexplicable moment, a moment seemingly erased from her memory for ever – the dream had been snatched from them.

Now, the only fragments she has left, the only evidence of her daughter's existence are the useless pile of maternity clothes stuffed at the back of her wardrobe, the few fading stretch marks left on her skin and the small white box of ashes they were given by the funeral director after the ceremony. She wants to shake her mother. She wants to shake Tom. She wants to scream at them both that this isn't the life she is supposed to be living. She isn't supposed to be sitting here eating cake and talking in this calm, quiet voice about grief and loss. They should all be living a new life, one transformed by love and joy and by the irrepressible, irresistible presence of a tiny, gurgling baby.

Outside, the small piece of London sky just visible through the window is a cool, empty grey. It mirrors exactly how she feels: blank and hollow, colourless. From seemingly nowhere an image flashes into her mind: a shimmering lake nestled within a ring of green hills and a small, ramshackle cottage glowing a pale honey-colour in the evening sunshine. She imagines herself back there, sitting upon that fallen tree trunk beneath a vast and shifting sky, staring out over the surface of the lake.

'Actually,' she says, the words tumbling from her mouth before she can stop them, 'I *am* thinking of taking on a new project.'

'Oh yes?' says Tom, licking chocolate icing from his finger.

'Well that's wonderful,' says her mother. She reaches for her cup and saucer. 'What is it? Another office revamp?'

'No,' says Lila with a shake of her head. 'A private job. A cottage renovation.'

Tom stares at her for a moment. 'You don't mean . . . ?'

'Yes,' she says, 'I do.'

'Are you sure?' he asks, that worried frown back on his face. 'It's a massive project.'

'Not *that* massive,' she argues. 'Besides, you're the one that's been telling me to *do* something.'

'Yes, but I didn't mean . . . it's just . . . well, it's miles away.'

Lila shrugs. Her mother remains silent, suddenly distracted by her cup and saucer and the careful stirring of a teaspoon through her tea.

'How would we make it work, you up there, me down here?' Tom continues.

'I can stay up there in the week, come back on weekends. Or you could come up there and help? It wouldn't be so different from how things used to be . . . in the early days.'

The furrow in Tom's brow deepens. 'This isn't exactly what I had in mind. I'm not sure you being so far away or so isolated is such a good idea. Besides, how will we afford it if it's not a proper, paying job?'

'I've got the money left to me in Dad's will, haven't I? If I do the place up I could sell it on, make a profit. Put the money into another project. It's what I've been talking about for ages now, setting up on my own. Maybe it's time to stop talking and start doing.'

'Well, this all sounds very positive,' says her mother, looking relieved. 'A little country renovation, how lovely.'

Tom shakes his head. 'I don't know . . .'

'You want me to do something don't you?' Lila eyes him. 'Well, here's the solution.'

He throws up his hands in defeat. 'I suppose it wouldn't hurt to see how it goes for a week or two.'

Lila nods and reaches for the teapot. 'So, who would like another cup of tea?'

*   *   *

Her mother leaves an hour or so later. She hugs Lila tightly then takes a step back and smooths the sweep of Lila's long fringe from her eyes. 'I'm going back to France next week. You two should come across on the Eurostar . . . come for a holiday? I'd love to have you both there with me.'

Lila nods and feels bad for having been so prickly. 'Mum,' she asks, seizing the moment, 'did we ever take any family holidays up north . . . in the Peak District?'

'What?' Her mother's eyes cloud with confusion.

'Yes . . . we never . . . Dad never . . . ?'

Her mother shakes her head then gives a light laugh. 'The Peak District? I don't think your father ever took us further north than the Watford Gap.' She eyes her carefully. 'Why?'

Lila shakes her head and backs away from the subject. 'No reason.'

Her mother fiddles with her handbag strap then clears her throat. 'I'll call you in a week or so. Take good care of yourself, Lila . . . and get some rest.'

Lila nods, hugs her mother one more time, then stands at the open door and watches her go, a slender, straight-backed, perfectly polished woman in her early fifties. She loves her mother but she knows there has been a growing sense of disconnect between them – something that stems not just from the recent loss of her baby and her own complicated feelings of grief, but that also revolves around her father and his death six months ago. It's been a difficult time for them both.

Earlier, watching her mother in the living room as she'd talked about her marriage and the loss of her husband, Lila had bitten her tongue. After all these years of course she'd have grown well practised at hiding it, but even Lila is surprised by her mother's ability not only to mask her pain, but now that he is gone, to actually re-create the story of her marriage and to draw things in a more favourable light. Lila had to peer closely beneath the mask her mother now wore to see the lingering pain that years of disappointment and disillusion had etched onto her face.

But Lila knows the truth, even if her mother won't admit it. Ever since Lila was a little girl, she'd known her parents' relationship was fraught with tension. It was there in the long silences on car rides when Lila sat in the back seat and felt the air hiss and crackle between them, and there on those late nights when her father had slung whisky down his throat and shouted hard, angry words at her mother about loss and pain and a life frittered away in lies and lost ideals. Lila had watched from the top of the stairs, not really understanding any of it . . . but understanding enough to know that it wasn't normal for your father to spend half the week in his London pied-à-terre shagging his latest *personal* assistant, or normal for your mother to spend the nights he was away lying in a darkened room weeping into her pillow. And yet he always came back, and when he did, her mother was always there waiting for him, her tears wiped dry, her face arranged into that bright mask of relief, ready to play happy families once more.

As she'd grown older, it had made Lila angry. She loved her father but she couldn't understand why her mother didn't *do* something . . . why she didn't stand up for herself? Why she didn't throw him out? But her mother never did and things were only drawn in even starker context after Lila had met Tom and spent time with his sprawling, rambunctious family. She'd watched Tom's easy interactions with his two younger brothers, the way he'd thrown his arms about his mother in the kitchen as she made supper, or how they'd all gently teased their father around the dinner table, and she'd marvelled at their candid, easy interactions. 'Don't you guys *ever* argue?' she'd asked.

'We have our moments.'

Lila had shaken her head.

'What?'

'It's just you all seem to really *like* each other.'

Tom had studied her for a moment. 'Why doesn't she leave him if he makes her so miserable?'

'I don't know. She loves him . . . besides, she makes it too easy for him to come back.'

'You're obviously very angry. *You* should have it out with him,' he'd suggested.

'Do you think?'

'If it's bothering you that much, yeah, I do.'

She'd thought Tom's advice through seriously and had just been summoning the courage to confront her father when she had taken the call at work: her father was dead – a heart attack while sitting at his desk going through the papers for a client's upcoming lawsuit.

Just like that, he was gone, leaving behind a mess of grief and hurt and burning anger. It was one of Lila's biggest regrets that she hadn't taken Tom's advice sooner and had it out with her father – before it was too late; because now, on top of everything else, she is stuck with her mother's increasingly rose-tinted version of the past – a version that doesn't seem to fit with her own memories at all. She watches as she climbs into her sleek blue car and with one last wave pulls away from the kerb. Lila shakes her head. Families: what a terrible, tangled mess they could be.

Tom sidles up beside her at the front door. 'Sorry,' he says, touching the sleeve of her jumper, 'I should have told you she was coming.'

'Yes. You should've.'

He hesitates before speaking again. 'Did you mean it about the cottage or were you just trying to get both of us off your case?'

'I meant it.' She holds his gaze. 'Don't look so worried. It'll be fine. I'll head up there for a few days and see what I can do. If it's a disaster I'll just come back.'

'But I *am* worried. You'll be so isolated and after what you've been through – what *we've* been through – I'm not sure it's a good idea.'

'But what if it's exactly what I need?' Lila remembers meeting Marissa in the supermarket, the excruciating scene that had played out. Suddenly, the idea of being tucked away in a place where nobody knows her really doesn't seem like the worst idea in the world. 'Think of it, that cottage and the lake . . . it's not just a project to keep me busy but it's also a change of scene. A retreat, a place to get myself back together. It seems to be working for Mum in France.' She studies his worried face. 'And it was very peaceful up there, wasn't it?'

He doesn't look convinced. 'I never thought you'd be drawn to a lake. You can't even swim, for God's sake.'

'Maybe I'll learn?'

He snorts. 'You? Swim . . . with *your* phobia? You won't even go near the lido.'

'I'm not going to throw myself in, if that's what you're worried about.'

He eyes her carefully. 'Of course not.' Silence hangs between them. 'I suppose it wouldn't hurt to try it for a week or so?' He thinks for a moment. 'But how on earth are you going to improve the place? You've got no proper access and it's already autumn. It's going to be one major headache.'

Lila shrugs. 'I don't intend to transform it into a five-star holiday home. Just tidy the place up, make it a little more comfortable, turn

89

it into more of an attractive proposition in case I do decide to sell it. I can probably manage a lot of it myself.'

Tom eyes her. 'You're braver than me.'

She smiles. 'Brave? Others might say stupid.' In the solemn afternoon light she can see the shadows under his eyes, the first hint of grey at his temples, the white scar on his right cheek.

He studies her for a moment. 'If I didn't know better, I'd think you were running away.' He doesn't need to add 'from me' – they both hear it in his voice.

She sighs. She doesn't have the energy to reassure him, not after her mother's visit. She'd like to put things right. She wishes they could return to the intimacy they shared just a few weeks ago, but it all feels too hard. Here she is, a woman skilled at aesthetics, at making things beautiful and there he is, a man who can build bridges and scale divides, and yet the chasm between them only seems to gape and grow more ugly as the days drift by. The irony is not lost on her. And now that she's had the idea of escape she just wants to be there up at the cottage, to be far away from London and their stalled life together – for a little while.

He reaches out and traces the curve of her cheek with a finger. 'We're OK, aren't we?'

'Course,' she says, although the word hangs heavily in the air between them, like the lie they both know it to be.

'When will you go?'

'Soon. You were right,' she says, not quite able to meet his eye, 'autumn's here. I should probably get started, before I talk myself out of it.'

He leans into her then and they stand there, two straight lines angled into each other, holding each other up for just a moment until she pulls away, leaving him alone at the front door as she heads upstairs to pack.

6

SEPTEMBER

1980

The grey heron stands motionless in the shallows of the lake. Kat pulls back the thin scrap of curtain to see it standing there in the early morning light, tall and elegant beside a clump of green reeds. It is perfectly still, craning its neck out over the water, waiting for a catch. Wrapped in a woollen blanket, she watches it for a moment, noting how every muscle – every tendon – every feather on its body remains static as the bird focuses upon its task. It is the very image of concentration and tenacity.

Behind her, Simon lies sprawled across the mattress; she can just make out his reflection in the windowpane. His body forms a lean curve beneath the sheets and for a moment she is tempted to throw off her blanket and slide under the covers again. She wakes most mornings now to find him lying beside her and yet the sight of him there never fails to surprise her, never fails to give her that thrill in the pit of her stomach. His very presence in the room, curled on the mattress around the still-warm indentation where she herself lay just moments ago is proof, she knows, of her own dogged tenacity.

She returns her gaze to the lake just in time to see a flash of movement as the heron bends its head and scoops a fat fish from the water in its orange beak. The silver perch flips like a worm caught on a hook. Kat watches as the bird gulps down its breakfast, then in one easy move stretches its wings and takes flight, soaring out over the lake.

She smiles. Breakfast: the thought makes her tummy rumble. She reaches for her jeans, a long-sleeved T-shirt and a knitted cardigan, then pulls on a pair of socks and makes her way down the staircase, treading quietly, careful not to wake the sleeping house.

Down in the kitchen she guzzles a cup of water and grabs a hunk of yesterday's bread, spreading a thin layer of Ben's too-runny blackberry jam across its surface. She eats standing up, eager to be outside in the cool morning air.

The hens are already scratching and pecking in the coop behind the house. She knows she could begin the usual round of chores – feeding the chickens, collecting the eggs, storing firewood beside the range – but something stops her. Perhaps it was the sight of the heron, easy in its solitude, but what she most feels like doing is striking out alone, heading off around the lake and mapping the perimeters of their surrounds a little more. Turning her back on the cottage and her slumbering housemates, she heads down the bank, following the trail of their footsteps now stamped into the flattened grass, towards the edge of the lake. She comes to a stop just a metre or so from where the heron had stood only moments ago and looks out over the valley.

The leaves of the alder trees are turning yellow and a slow brown-burnish is stealing across the hills; Kat can see that autumn's muted veil is beginning to settle. The intensity of summer has waned and it is a relief to be wrapped in a cooler, fresher climate. The mornings now require socks and sweaters and the clouds of midges that have hung over the lake for the last few weeks have drifted away on the breeze, to be replaced with low patches of mist hovering upon the surface of the lake. Down in their valley, she notices that the sun now takes a little longer to crest the hills and banish the early morning shadows, and in the evenings it falls just a little more quickly towards the horizon. As she looks about at the rich, earthy colours of the countryside, she is reminded of a line from a poem she once learned at school: *season of mists and mellow fruitfulness.*

Kat's plan is to skirt the lake and investigate the woodland surrounding the water. Until now she's been content to stay in the vicinity of the cottage, but the morning feels full of possibility. If Mac can roam the countryside and return with bloodied rabbits or armfuls of elderberries, then why can't she forage a little? How hard can it be?

Stepping away from the water's edge, Kat ducks her head and enters the wooded glade where leaves crackle beneath her boots and here and there brown alder cones litter the floor. Unlike the dry, grassy banks up near the cottage, the ground in the glade is boggy. She squelches through muddy ditches and jumps puddles, listening to the flitter of birds and the soft rustling of the undergrowth as she goes, careful to keep an eye out for anything that might prove edible or useful in some way.

She tells herself she just wants a little time on her own, away from the others, but the truth is she really wants time alone to think about Simon, to think about what's happening between them. She wants a chance to examine her thoughts, to pull them out like precious stones from deep within her pockets, so that she can hold them up to the light and polish them until they shine. As she walks, she thinks about his hands on her body, his lips on her skin, the way his eyes shine as black as coal as he moves over her in the darkness. She has loved him for so long, it seems, and yet she has never dreamed it could be like this. She's always felt too detached – too shut-off – to be wanted or loved. Her heart has been a locked prism, closed to emotion and pain, hidden from everyone except her sister, Freya. But now the seemingly impossible has happened. Simon has come to her. He wants her and she finally feels herself opening and transforming like the derelict cottage they inhabit. She has never felt so alive. She has never felt so vulnerable. It is both exhilarating and terrifying.

Kat still isn't quite sure what this *thing* is between them. It's more than sex, she's sure of it, for they've known each other so long; there is so much more beneath the physical intimacy they now share – an undercurrent of emotion that's impossible to ignore. But the ground they tread is new and unfamiliar, like the steep terrain rising up all around the lake. It's as though she's tiptoeing over it carefully, moving forwards but testing each footstep before she trusts enough to put her full weight down. And she is learning where the barriers are, where the rocks and crevices lie that she must negotiate. She's already learned not to be too affectionate during the day. The few times she has touched him, or put an arm around him, he has worn it with a wary smile, but she notices how he shrugs her off, or moves away. She understands; it's awkward for the others. They are a small, close-knit group; it wouldn't be good to parade their shifting relationship in front of them all. Ben and Carla have been a couple right from the start – something they've all readily accepted – but another couple in their midst, flaunting their closeness . . . well, it could destabilise things and it wouldn't be fair on Mac. She understands that.

Neither has she dared show her hand and tell Simon that she loves him. She knows it's only a matter of time, but she won't do it – not yet – not until she can be sure of his response. So while she waits, she clings to other certainties: the heat of his gaze following her around, the insistence of his touch in the pitch black of the bedroom and, perhaps most of all, the absolute conviction she feels now that they were *meant* to come here. This cottage – the lake – some strange serendipity brought them here that summer's day. In this place of simplicity and freedom they can make the love between them grow deeper and stronger. She is sure of it.

She stops at the base of a tree to examine several balls of puffy white fungus growing from the ground. She wonders whether she should pick them but decides against it. They could be poisonous and look suspiciously as if they might disintegrate at her touch. Instead she makes a mental note so that she can describe them to the others; she's learning quickly that sometimes the most surprising things around them are edible.

On through the woods and she comes across an old hazel tree, its bows laden with nuts encased in soft, downy leaves. She reaches up and shakes a low-hanging branch, sending a few scattering like raindrops at her feet, then stoops to gather them, shoving them deep into her pockets. She'll have to bring Ben here – he's the best climber among them – they could gather quite a stash if they claim them quickly, before the squirrels move in.

Further away she hears the sound of splashing out on the lake. Curious, she moves down closer to the water's edge and sees two mallards dabbling among the reeds. She watches them for a moment, imagines the look on Simon's face if she were to return to the cottage with two plump ducks and wishes she had a way to hunt them. As the ducks drift further away, Kat's attention is drawn by a tall, woody plant growing at the water's edge. Its stalks are thick and grooved like celery with tiny clusters of white flowers growing on top of spindly umbrella stems. She moves closer and pulls a stalk from the earth, wondering what it might be. Roots, thick and white, point like muddy fingers down towards the ground. To Kat they resemble pale carrots, or perhaps turnips; they definitely look edible. Encouraged by her discovery, she begins to pull handfuls of the plant from the ground, wholly absorbed in her task until from somewhere behind comes the snapping sound of twigs and a loud *chuk-chuk-chuk* as a pheasant flaps from the undergrowth.

Startled, Kat spins. Higher up on the wooded slope she sees the silhouette of a man, about ten yards away. She gasps and puts her hand to her chest. 'Mac, you made me jump. What are you doing sneaking up on me like that?'

He lifts his arm and shows her the three limp rabbits slung across his shoulder. 'Just checking the snares. They came good last night.' He nods towards the plant in her hand. 'What have you got there?'

'I'm not sure. It might just be cow parsley, but look at the roots.' She holds the plant up to him for inspection. 'They look like carrots, don't they? Turnips, perhaps? We could try them and see.' She beams proudly at him as he moves down the wooded slope towards her, the lifeless rabbits banging against his chest in time with his loping steps.

He peers more closely at the plant in her hand then rears away. 'Throw it back,' he says. 'It's water hemlock. Nasty stuff. Feed us that and you'll kill us all.'

She gives a half-laugh. 'Yeah, right.'

'I'm serious.' Mac shakes his head. 'Eat that and there's a good chance you won't wake up tomorrow. The leaves are poisonous but the roots are the worst. We had a cow eat some once. She was dead within the hour.'

Kat gapes at him, trying to read his eyes, obscured as they are beneath his straggly hair. 'Are you serious?' She stares down at the innocuous-looking plant in her hand. A thin, milky substance oozes from the wound of one woody stem where she has snapped it off. She gazes at it, both amazed and horrified that such a seemingly innocent landscape could harvest something so dangerous, then blushes at her stupidity. 'I'm not very good at this, am I? Perhaps I'd better stick to the laundry and the cleaning after all.'

Mac adjusts the rabbits over his shoulder and Kat sees a dark red stain on the denim of his jacket where the animals have bled. 'Come on,' he says, 'if you really want to forage I've got something to show you. Follow me.'

He leads her through the trees and down a steep wooded gully, jumping over rocks and bushy ferns until they arrive at a cluster of stumpy trees. 'Look.' He points towards their deep green foliage and as Kat draws closer, she sees clusters of blue-black berries nestled amongst the branches.

'What are they?' she asks, reaching out to touch their dusky skin with her fingertip.

'Sloes. We should pick them after the first frost.'

She looks at him, a little unsure. 'Do you eat them?'

He shakes his head. 'Ever tried sloe gin?'

'No.'

He gives her a crooked smile. 'You wait. It'll blow your socks off.'

*　*　*

They can hear talking and laughter in the kitchen as they draw closer to the cottage. Kat stamps her feet, loosening clumps of mud from her boots, then slides sock-footed through the back door, leaving Mac to deal with the rabbits outside. She's expecting a barrage of questions about where she's been, a little gentle ribbing about how everyone else has had to cover her jobs for her, but when she sees the scene in the kitchen anything she'd planned to say in her defence vanishes into thin air.

'You have a visitor,' says Simon. He is smiling broadly but she hears the edge in his voice.

'Surprise!'

Kat gapes at Freya. Her sister sits at the head of the table, flanked on one side by Simon and on the other by Carla. She beams up at her then turns to address the others. 'See,' she laughs, 'I told you her face would be a picture.'

Carla grins. 'You weren't wrong.'

Freya stands and moves towards Kat, pulling her into a hug. Kat breathes in the fresh, floral scent of her, feels the sweep of her long, blond hair brush against her face, but all the while they embrace her eyes never leave Simon's face. 'What are you *doing* here?' she asks finally, stepping back to hold her sister at arm's length. 'And how on earth did you find us?' The moment the question has left her mouth she regrets it.

'Your letter, of course.'

From the corner of her eye Kat sees Simon's eyebrows shoot skyward.

'I knew as soon as I read about this place that I just had to come and see it for myself,' she continues, then seeing Kat's face asks, 'You don't mind, do you?'

'Course not,' says Kat, finding her smile at last. She takes a step back and regards Freya carefully. She is taller than she remembers and thinner too, dressed in a colourful patterned silk dress that floats about her legs, knitted stockings and incongruous black boots. Her fair hair hangs down her back, a tangle of loose plaits threaded through here and there. Most striking of all though, is her skin; it's as pale as marble and sets off the blue of her eyes so that they shine like sapphires. As Kat studies her, she is reminded of the porcelain china dolls their foster mother Margaret had kept lined up on her bed – the ones they were allowed to look at but *never* touch. She smiles, understanding for the first time that her sister is a woman now, a very beautiful woman.

'Look at you,' she says, pulling her back into a hug, embracing her properly for the first time, 'you look great. But I still don't understand,' she adds warily, finally releasing her, 'how *did* you find us? I never told you where this place was.'

Freya taps her forehead with a finger. 'Not just a pretty face,' she grins. 'It really wasn't that hard. There was the postmark on your letter for one. And you mentioned a small lake, surrounded by hills, nothing around for miles. It didn't take long. The geography section in the college library is *very* well stocked with maps. Look,' she says, holding out a packet of chocolate digestives, 'I come bearing gifts. Your favourite, right?'

Kat nods, but she doesn't take one; she can still feel Simon's scrutinising gaze from across the room. She knows she's screwed up and silently kicks herself for not telling him about the letter.

'Freya was just telling us how she got here,' says Ben. 'Sounds a bit hairy.'

Kat turns back to her sister. 'Oh yes?'

'Yep,' says Freya, a hint of pride in her voice. 'I hitched a lift from London . . . at least as far as I could. Spent last night on a bench at a service station then ended up on the back of a tractor. I walked the last couple of miles. I'm bloody glad I guessed right. It would have been a long way to come for nothing.'

'You didn't tell anyone we were here, did you?' asks Simon, looking appalled.

'God no, just said I was out hiking. Probably seemed a bit odd, just me on my own with this bag,' she kicks her large holdall still lying on the floor, 'but no one asked too many questions.'

'You were lucky,' admonishes Kat. 'You could have been picked up by anyone . . . a rapist . . . an axe murderer. They still haven't caught the Yorkshire Ripper you know . . .'

Freya turns to the others with a grin. 'See, I told you she was the protective big sister.'

Kat refuses to be put off. 'But what are you *doing* here? What about college? Surely you start back any day now?'

'Well, about that,' says Freya, suddenly shifty. 'There was a bit of a kerfuffle at the end of last term. The head of my department thought it might be best if I deferred for a year.'

'A "kerfuffle"?'

'One of my lecturers—'

'You slept with him?'

'No! Course not. He's a randy old lech. I reported him for harassment. But somehow the story got out and the college seems to think it best I stay away for a few months while the whole thing blows over.' Freya reaches into the biscuit packet, pulls out a digestive and takes a bite.

'Best *you* stay away? They can't do that, surely?' Kat is indignant.

'I know,' says Freya airily, munching on the biscuit, 'I was going to fight it but when I got your letter I suddenly realised I didn't have to. It was the perfect opportunity to come and visit you up here instead.' She smiles sweetly at Kat, her eyes catching the light from the window and shining as blue as the placid lake outside. There are biscuit crumbs on her top lip and looking at her, Kat is suddenly reminded of Freya's uncanny ability of talking her way into or out of anything: a trip to the park, a packet of sweets, an extended curfew or a borrowed top. 'Simon's just been telling me all about this place. It sounds amazing,' she beams. 'I really love what you're all trying to do.' She hesitates then reaches down into her bag and pulls out a brightly-coloured object, which she throws at Kat. 'Here, I brought this for you too.'

Kat stares at the strange cube in her hands.

'It's a puzzle,' Freya explains. 'I nicked it from that old goat's office . . . figured he owed me.' She grins. 'It's the latest thing, apparently.'

'Cool,' says Ben, plucking the object from Kat's outstretched hands. 'A Rubik's cube. I've heard about these.' He gives it a few perfunctory twists but any further conversation is interrupted by the sound of boots stamping outside followed by the slam of the back door. Mac sidles into the room but stops dead when he sees Freya standing there in the middle of the group.

'Hello,' she says, stretching out a hand in greeting. 'I'm Freya, Kat's sister. You must be Mac?'

Mac shakes his hair from his eyes and reaches for her hand.

'Oh,' she exclaims, taking a step backwards.

Kat cranes her neck and sees the smears of blood on Mac's hands and wrists. Embarrassed, he pulls his hand back again.

'Well that's no way to greet a lady,' smirks Simon. 'You'll have to forgive our country boy, he's not very good with girls.'

'Sorry,' Mac mumbles, blushing bright red, 'I've been seeing to the rabbits. I should wash my hands.'

Freya swallows. 'I didn't . . . it wasn't . . .' She smiles uncertainly. 'Sorry, it's nice to meet you.'

Mac nods and moves across to the sink.

Kat still has half an eye on Simon and she watches how his gaze roves over Freya. She can see he is sizing her up, regarding her in that careful way he has, assessing, testing and she feels torn in two. On the one hand she feels protective; she wants to shelter Freya from Simon's judgemental gaze which she feels sure will be harsh; he will think her too naive, too girlish and fragile for this environment. *Scared of a little rabbit's blood*, he'll think. And yet at the same time she desperately wants him to like her sister – and for Freya to like Simon, too. They are the two most important people in her world but as she watches them talk, she realises that she has no idea what they will make of each other.

'What are you studying?' asks Simon.

Freya smiles winningly. 'Fashion and textiles. I've been learning about screen-printing techniques, designing my own fabrics. I'd like to get into fashion, one day.'

'An artist.' He nods and Kat can tell he approves. 'We've got a writer, a musician, a social worker, an environmentalist and a lawyer . . . but no artists . . . yet.' His face breaks into a broad grin. 'Well, I don't know about the others but I think you should stay.

I don't think we're in a position to turn down an extra pair of hands at the moment.'

'Of course,' says Carla, reaching over to give Freya's arm a little squeeze. 'It will be fun having another girl around the place. We've been outnumbered by the lads for far too long, haven't we, Kat?'

Kat lets out a breath she hadn't even known she was holding and smiles. 'It'll be a squash,' she warns. 'You'll have to share my room.'

'I don't mind,' grins Freya. 'It'll be fun. Like old times.'

'Yes,' she agrees and ruffles Freya's hair, 'just like old times.'

'Damn. This is hard,' groans Ben, looking up in exasperation from the Rubik's cube in his hands. 'Don't expect any dinner tonight, guys, not until I've solved this.'

'Come on,' says Kat, 'why don't I show you around? You're going to have to pull your weight, you know. This isn't a holiday camp.'

Freya's smile is bright enough to light up the entire kitchen.

* * *

Her sister's arrival is like a breath of fresh air wafting through the cottage. As she shows her around, Kat sees things as if for the first time again and she is surprised to realise just how much they have achieved in a few short weeks. There are freshly laid eggs nestled in a bowl on the table and jars of blackberry jam lined up on the shelf above the range, rows of pale grey mushrooms drying on trays in the larder and clean clothes flapping on the washing line they have strung-up between two trees out the back. Even the sunlight sparkling off the once-grimy windows gives Kat a sense of pride. All around them are signs of progress, signs that they are turning the cottage and its surrounds into a home and as she looks about at it all, she is filled with a deep feeling of satisfaction.

Freya, in turn, proves to be more than happy to muck in. She weeds the garden with Carla, or helps Ben in the kitchen by peeling vegetables, or laying fires or busying herself with washing-up or laundry. She starts a composting system for their scraps and very quickly makes herself indispensable by taking on the least popular jobs.

'You don't have to do all this stuff, you know,' says Kat, coming upon her in the kitchen, up to her elbows in greasy water as she scrubs at a burned pan. 'You don't have to play Cinderella.'

Freya shrugs. 'I like doing it. It feels a bit like playing house, doesn't it?'

'I guess,' says Kat.

'I can see why you like it here.'

'Oh yes?'

'Yeah.' Freya smiles. 'You . . . your friends . . . everyone here together . . . it's kind of like the family we never had, don't you think?'

Kat nods. 'I suppose so.'

Freya turns back to the sink. 'I thought I might try and make some new curtains for the front room,' she says. 'Maybe for our bedroom as well? What do you think?'

'Where will you get the fabric from?'

'I've got an old dress I could use. It's pretty . . . cream with gorgeous pink roses.'

Kat shrugs. 'I shouldn't bother.' Flowery curtains seems a little frivolous, even to her, and she can't help wondering what Simon would make of it. 'It would probably just be a waste of a perfectly good dress.'

'But the ones here are horrible – just old scraps of grey cloth that are practically disintegrating. It's such a little thing but it really would really make a difference.'

Kat shakes her head. 'Don't waste your time.'

But Freya isn't to be dissuaded. The following day Kat comes upon her sitting on one of the beanbags in the front room, surrounded by strips of cream fabric covered in cheery blooms of fuchsia-pink roses. She watches as Freya places two pieces back to back and then tacks them together along one edge, noting the neat, darting movements of her sister's slender hands as she pulls a needle and thread through the fabric. 'I never could do that,' says Kat enviously. 'I'm all fingers and thumbs.'

'It just takes practice,' says Freya.

'No, you've always been good at stuff like that. You've always been creative. Remember those clothes you used to make for that doll you loved? Painstakingly stitched, every one of them.'

Freya smiles. 'Well, you've always been the more practical one. You used glue and staples for yours and finished in half the time.'

Kat laughs. 'Just think, if you could take the best bits of both of us we'd virtually be Wonder Woman.'

Freya glances up at her. 'I already think you *are* Wonder Woman, Kat.'

'Oh don't be so ridiculous,' chides Kat, but she has to turn her face away from her to hide her blushes.

Later that evening, as they sit in front of the fire, sprawled across beanbags, sampling the first glasses of Ben's pungent homebrew, Kat looks about at Freya's handiwork. The new curtains have been hung and drawn, a jug of purple thistles placed on the window sill before them. She's even found a few candles and placed them into the necks of empty glass bottles, dotting them across the mantelpiece. Kat watches as a trail of molten wax drips down the side of one and forms a cloudy puddle on the stone surface. Freya was right, she thinks, it has made a difference. The room has taken on a cosier atmosphere, and she's not the only one who seems to think so.

'Something's different,' says Ben, looking up from the Rubik's cube still firmly attached to his hands. 'What is it?'

Carla rolls her eyes. 'Ignore him, Freya,' she says. 'He wouldn't notice if you'd knocked through a wall and built a huge extension out the back. It looks great.'

'It really does,' says Simon, putting his book down and staring across at the small jug of purple flowers in the window. 'It's the little things, isn't it,' he says. 'It's what we've been missing without even knowing it: the touches that really make this place feel like a home.' He smiles warmly at Freya.

Kat turns to Simon in surprise. She has never taken him for a man to be impressed by flowers and soft furnishings and she shakes her head and throws her sister a little wink of congratulation, pleased that Simon is accepting her sister's presence while at the same time trying to bury the tiny, irrational flicker of jealousy that has sprung from nowhere. They've been here nearly two months and she doesn't remember Simon ever praising *her* efforts in that way. She takes a sip of Ben's caustic homebrew and swallows it down with a grimace.

* * *

'So, is he like your leader or something?' Freya asks later that evening as she and Kat lie side by side on the mattress, staring up at the ceiling.

'Who?' asks Kat, already knowing the answer.

'Simon.'

Kat gazes up into the emptiness above their heads. 'No. What makes you say that?'

'I just noticed that you're all pretty quick to defer to him.'

'That's not true.'

'Yes it is. Whatever Simon says goes.'

'I don't think so.'

'Think about it, even me staying on here was his decision in the end.'

Kat considers her sister's suggestion for a moment then shakes her head. 'It's not like that. We decide things as a group. No one person is the boss here. We're a team.'

The silence stretches in the darkness. 'You like him though, don't you?' Freya says at last. 'You can tell me. I'm not a kid any more.'

'I know you're not.' Kat thinks about telling Freya. She wonders what it would feel like to say it out loud; to speak her desire for Simon and acknowledge it to someone other than herself for the very first time. The words burn on the tip of her tongue but she can't release them yet, not even into the darkness of the room, not even to Freya. 'Go to sleep,' she says, 'I'm tired.'

But Freya seems far from sleep. She wants to chat. 'Ben and Carla are fun, aren't they?'

'Mmmm . . .' agrees Kat.

'Have they been together long?'

'For ever. Three years or so.'

'And what's Mac like?'

Kat sighs. 'I don't know. Nice. He's quiet though . . . sometimes he can come across as a bit odd. He likes to keep himself to himself, but I think he's a good guy deep down.'

'He seems sweet. Maybe he's just a little shy?'

'Maybe,' agrees Kat.

Kat thinks Freya is falling asleep but a moment later she starts up again. 'It's OK, me being here, isn't it? You don't mind?'

'No,' says Kat, 'I don't mind.'

'Because I could always—'

'Shhh . . .' says Kat, 'go to sleep. We've got a lot to do tomorrow.'

Freya huffs but she rolls away onto her side and finally goes quiet.

Kat lies there in the dark on her back with her eyes open listening to the distant rumble of Ben's snores coming from the room next door. She feels the mattress holding her body, the quilt like a warm cocoon wrapped around her; but after a while the pitch black becomes strangely disorienting and she begins to feel that she is no longer lying on a solid floor, but rather floating – a tiny particle drifting through space.

She swallows and closes her eyes and tries to rid herself of the unnerving feeling. What she would really like is to have Simon's arms wrapped around her, to feel his skin pressed against hers, his breath on her neck. What she would really like is to anchor herself to his warm body. But she knows he won't come to her – not while Freya is there – so she comforts herself with her memories of him: the taste of warm blackberries on her tongue, hands moving across her skin, lips pressed hard upon hers, fingers tangled in her hair, until gradually she surrenders to the slow pull of sleep.

7

LILA

October

The baby is crying. Lila stirs beneath her woollen blanket as the piercing cries ring out. One more minute, she thinks from deep within her fog of sleep, just one more minute, *please* little one.

Another shrill cry breaks through the night air and then, as suddenly as if a bucket of ice-cold water has been tipped over her, Lila is awake. Her eyes snap open in the darkness. She lies still, hardly daring to breathe.

There is no crying. There is no baby. It's just a dream.

The empty feeling expands in Lila's gut, as cold and hard as stone. She wraps her arms around her body and blinks, searching for something to fix upon in the pitch black but it's too late; the panic is descending. She can feel it pressing down on her, squashing the breath from her lungs, filling her up. Take a breath, she tells herself. Take a breath. Slow it down.

She shifts slightly and the thin strip of canvas of her camp bed creaks beneath her. The sound tells her exactly where she is: upstairs in the musty old cottage beside the lake, lying on an uncomfortable camp bed, swaddled in a sleeping bag with a woollen blanket thrown over her for warmth. She nearly hadn't bothered with the bed or the extra blanket when it had come to lugging them across the meadow and down over the ridge but she's glad now that she did. The bed may not be luxurious, but she knows that it's a damn sight better than the floorboards would be. She tries not to think about Tom, sprawled across their bed at home, illuminated in the neon wash of a street lamp – tries not to think about how very far away from him she is at that moment. Instead, she shifts again on the thin canvas and tries to find a more comfortable position before turning her mind back to her dream.

She's always been a dreamer, always been one of those people connected to the shadows of her inner-consciousness, that mysterious part of the brain that takes over when sleep comes and the body shuts down. Since losing Milly, however, she's come to dread that sensation of going under. She lies in bed, teetering on the edge of sleep, then, just as her mind begins to numb and her breathing slows, she jolts awake, the sensation far too reminiscent of her sickening tumble down the stairs.

Even worse, when sleep does eventually come, it is fitful and disturbed, her dreams now escalating into full-blown nightmares. Sometimes it's the fall – she spirals through darkness, plunging endlessly towards the ground, waiting for an impact that never comes; sometimes, too, it's the lake – she wades out through its still, cool waters, moving beyond the shallows until her feet can't touch the bottom and she flounders and splashes until the dark water closes over her head; but tonight it's the baby – she dreams about her daughter's tiny curled hands and her navy blue eyes and she hears her heart-wrenching cries calling out for her in the night until she is filled with such an overwhelming need to hold her again that she could cry out loud in pain.

She'd thought getting away from London might help. She'd thought a complete change of scene would allow her to rest and relax, maybe even retrieve some of her lost memories. But something about the deep silence and the absolute black of night there beside the lake seem to create a fertile ground for her imagination. The cottage, it transpires, is a place for dreaming deeply and instead of getting easier, Lila finds herself even more troubled than before. She gulps at the cool night air. Breathe, she tells herself again, just breathe.

Gradually, her heartbeat slows. She takes another breath and closes her eyes. When the panic has eased a little, she takes a moment, lying there in the darkness, to do what she does every night now when sleep fails her. The doctor had told her that she might never fully remember the fall, but she simply can't accept that; she *needs* to remember so that she can understand and, perhaps, begin to let it go. She screws her eyes shut against the night and begins to run through the few, fragmented memories she retains.

She is back in her bedroom in London, sunlight streaming through the window, slanting onto the embroidered silk quilt spread across the bed behind her. She stands before the full-length mirror and reaches for a stretchy black top. She wrestles it on but it doesn't fit properly – it's too tight across her swollen belly and makes her feel even bigger than she is – so she pulls it off again, throwing it onto the growing pile of discarded clothes strewn across the bed. Impatiently, she reaches for another top and pulls it on, the pink silk fabric making her hair crackle with static. She turns back to the mirror and studies her face . . . her blue eyes shining with health and her cheeks plump with pregnancy hormones, a strand of blond hair falling free from her messy top-knot, the twisted gold earrings Tom gave her as a gift on her last birthday catching the light at her lobes. The details are all there, crystal clear . . . until they fade suddenly, like a mirror clouding over . . . and then there is nothing. Her mind is blank – nothing but blackness – until a connection rewires in her brain and she hears the steady beeping of machines, listens to fast footsteps slapping across a linoleum floor and breathes in the unmistakable disinfectant smell of a hospital ward. It's all she has.

Lila shakes her head and starts again. She replays the scene over and over, willing something new – *anything* – to surface until eventually tiredness creeps over her, threatening to draw her down once more. She shifts on the canvas bed, pulls her blanket up closer to her chin. She will sleep now, she knows it. She can feel its warm pull and she is just about to surrender to it when the silence around her is shattered by a loud, bloodcurdling wail.

Lila stiffens. The baby. It's the same plaintive cry, the same shrill sound as from her dream; only this time Lila *knows* she isn't dreaming. She is very much awake and the sound is not only very real, but also very *close*. Fear bucks in her belly as the cry echoes through the cottage then fades away into the night. Her blood runs as cold as the surrounding air.

Fighting the urge to bury her head beneath the blanket, she untucks an arm from her sleeping bag and reaches out into the darkness, fumbling for her phone. She unlocks the screen and sees that it is 02:34 and that she has no mobile reception. There are still hours of night to get through.

The cry comes again, closer now, echoing once more through the empty cottage. Lila stifles a whimper and thinks about her options. She could slide out of bed and grope her way towards the light switch over by the door. She could tiptoe downstairs and search for a weapon to hide beneath her pillow, something that would make her feel a little safer: a hammer . . . the bread knife . . . the metal poker from beside the fire? Or perhaps she should race out into the night and hurry up the ridge and across the meadow all the way back to her car. She could admit that she has made a terrible mistake and drive home to London and to Tom just as fast as she can.

In the end, even the thought of leaving the safety of her sleeping bag, of tiptoeing through the cold cottage, of navigating those creaking stairs and creeping through the empty, downstairs rooms is terrifying. She realises that she would rather lie there paralysed on a bone-jarring bed in a falling-down cottage in the middle of nowhere and await her fate at the hands of some eerie ghost-baby or crazed axe murderer than confront whatever it is that is making that blood-curdling noise. Lila swallows a hysterical laugh. Why is she here, alone in this deserted place? Why did she ever think coming *here* would be a good idea? This is it, she realises: she's finally lost it.

Another haunting wail rings out in the darkness. It is such a strange noise, so raw, so primal . . . so animal; and all of a sudden it hits her: of course, she has heard this sound before. It's not a newborn baby crying for its mother, but a fox shrieking out a warning: *mine, stay away*. She's heard them once or twice in London, seen their scraggy silhouettes slinking round the council rubbish bins, crying to one another in the orange glow of the street lamps. Thank

God, she thinks. Just imagine if she'd gone rushing home to Tom, all because of a fox. She lies there enjoying the sensation of relief washing over her. No need to leave, not just yet anyway.

She shifts once more on the camp bed. It really is horribly uncomfortable and she is wide awake again, adrenalin coursing through her veins. If she were feeling brave she would get up. She would light a fire, make tea, sit up and wait for the sun to rise. She'd forgotten all about Tom's warning of birds' nests and fires when she'd arrived back at the cottage and the past two nights she's enjoyed a roaring fire in the hearth and hasn't burned the old place down yet. Perhaps she could invest in an electric heater as well, if she's going to stay up here a little longer?

She thinks about the logs in the basket beside the fire and wonders how many were left before she retired to bed. She should have refilled it earlier. This is the way she must think now, she realises; she can't take anything for granted. Up here it's a different kind of existence and she is on her own. She must plan and organise. Nothing is going to just fall into her lap.

And then the thought is there, rattling with noisy insistence. The tatty wicker basket filled with firewood that had been standing so neatly, so conveniently beside the fireplace when she'd returned – had it been there that very first time, when she and Tom had visited the cottage together? With a shiver, she realises that she doesn't remember. Or perhaps, if it had been there, it had been empty? She can't recall. It is too confusing. She wracks her brain. They had been excited and distracted that first visit. She probably hadn't taken in half of the cottage and its state of disrepair – but surely she would have remembered a basket with a neat pile of tinder-dry logs and kindling, just waiting for her to lay a fire? And if the logs weren't there that very first visit, how on earth had they got there since? It's almost, she realises, as if someone has left them for her . . . as if someone has been expecting her.

The thought sends a shudder down her spine. Why was she sent the key to this cottage? Who is behind it and what can they possibly want from her? More to the point, why has she allowed herself to be led there, alone, in this strange and isolated place? First nightmares and crying babies, then foxes and mysterious gifts of firewood. Lila swallows and knows, beyond a shadow of a doubt, that she won't be getting any more sleep.

Braving the cold, she stretches out one arm again until her hand connects with the bottle of pills standing beside the camp bed. She twists the lid off and shakes two of them out into her hand, and then, before she can change her mind, she swallows them down and pulls the blanket up over her head. If she's going to be murdered in a random cottage in the middle of nowhere, she might as well be in a vaguely comatose state when it happens.

* * *

When morning eventually dawns it is cold and pale. Her breath hangs as a white fog in the air, reminding Lila of the cobwebs strung across the corners of each room. She is tired and her mind is still groggy from the pills, but there's a restless energy building in her limbs, too. She doesn't want to lie on that bed a moment longer. She wants to get cracking. There is so much to do.

She throws off her sleeping bag and blankets then sprints across the room to pull on jeans, woollen socks, two T-shirts, a fleece and a pair of sturdy leather boots, before descending the stairs and heading out the back door, across the grass frosted white like a cake, to where the horrible pit toilet looms. It would be nice to extend the cottage, to open out the kitchen and add a proper bathroom at the back. But those aren't jobs for now; they are for the future, *if* she decides to keep the place.

In the kitchen she slings cereal into a plastic bowl. As she wolfs it down, she looks around with a professional eye and begins to imagine the work she might do. There is no doubt in her mind that it is going to be an enormous project, but there are small things to celebrate already – the running water and the working electricity. She peers through the doorway into the front room and imagines the floorboards sanded and polished, the walls painted white and the windows gleaming in the sunshine, new curtains wafting in a summer's breeze. In the kitchen she visualises the oak table scrubbed and the long wooden benches repaired, the old-fashioned kitchen range polished to a shine. Yes, she can see it all now, sparkling and clean, cosy and warm, with green apples in a bowl and tubs of herbs growing on the window sill. The transformation in her mind's eye helps her to relax a little. This is what she does. This is what she's good at.

Above the range, she eyes the hole in the timber beam. She still can't think of a single, reasonable explanation why a bullet hole would be there *inside* the cottage – nothing, at least, that doesn't make her feel deeply uncomfortable – so she turns away from the shattered wood and focuses instead on the ancient cupboards and the blistered paint peeling from the window frames. The sight of fresh mouse droppings scattered across the floor gives her a moment's pause and between mouthfuls of cereal she grabs a pen and scribbles 'mousetraps' onto her growing shopping list. If she could be bothered to light the range she would; it would be nice to have hot water for tea, but she is keen to get outside and take a proper look at the exterior of the property, so she eats the rest of her breakfast standing at one of the front windows, looking out across the lake, lying like a sheet of grey steel in the autumn light.

* * *

Outside, a breeze has picked up. It sings across the water and whispers through the branches of the trees where leaves curl and crisp before tumbling slowly to the ground. She stares out over the lake and shivers. She just can't seem to shake the feeling that the old place is trying to tell her something. It's probably exhaustion, she thinks, but out here, all by herself, a person could definitely go a little crazy.

The leak in the bedroom is the most pressing of all the issues she faces so it's the roof she decides to look at first; until the cottage is watertight, there isn't much point addressing anything else. She starts by studying it from below. Visible even to her untrained eye are the few slipped tiles around the chimney. That, and a crack in the flashing would probably be enough to create the cascade of water running into the bedroom on a rainy day. She'll knows she'll need to get a proper roofer out but she eyes the tiles and wonders where she'll source a similar slate; she would prefer to restore the building to its original condition and use sympathetic, local materials where possible.

Next she turns her attention to the gutters, which don't seem to be in too bad a condition, although she can see that they are clogged with leaf-sludge and in one or two places have rotted through and will need replacing. Another thing to add to the list, she thinks.

Turning her back on the cottage, Lila moves towards the wooden shack slumped against the hillside like an old man catching his breath. She is hopeful she might find a ladder lurking within its shadows. Inside there are tools hanging from large metal hooks – a scythe, a shovel, large secateurs and a pitchfork. Nearer the door is a gnarly stump of wood – an old chopping block with a rusty axe still wedged into its surface. She investigates further and is delighted to discover running along one wall not just a huge pile of firewood, but also a stack of grey slate tiles, a perfect match for the ones on the roof. That will certainly save her some time and money. Her discovery is made all the sweeter by the sight of an old ladder lying in the dirt. She hefts it up onto her shoulder and carries it back to the cottage where she raises it up against the front wall and spends the next couple of hours scooping handfuls of slimy muck from the gutters. It is horrible work but she sets to it with a quiet determination, happy to lose herself for a while in the simple task. She feels better, she realises. Outside in the daylight, in the brisk fresh air, her nightmares fade away. It's always the way, she tells herself; everything always seems worse just before dawn.

With the last of the front gutters cleared, she begins to clamber down the ladder, balancing the bucket of debris on the rung beside her. From somewhere behind, she hears a fluttering of wings and leaves. She twists on the ladder, just in time to see a large magpie take flight from a tree down by the edge of the lake. *One for sorrow*, she thinks, remembering a line from a childhood rhyme. Lila watches the bird flit out across the water and fade into the backdrop of the hills before lowering her gaze to scan the line of trees closest to the water. The woods are dark and impenetrable but she gazes at them for a long moment and shivers. She can feel it. Someone is there. Someone is watching her.

She peers between the tree trunks, goose bumps prickling on her arms, but she can't make out anything in the gloom . . . there's nothing but waving branches and dark shadows. She shakes her head. Lack of sleep and the isolation of the place are definitely getting to her. There is no one out here – no one but her and the birds and the soft-sighing breeze skimming across the lake and rustling through the trees.

She climbs down the final steps of the ladder carefully. What with her nightmares and now this, she wonders if it's time she got away for an hour or two and acquainted herself with the local neighbourhood. She's surely earned herself a break? She will change and head to the nearest village – a place called Little Ramsdale just a few miles to the east, according to her map. She could do with a few groceries and someone there might be able to tell her more about her cottage and to whom it once belonged.

Behind the cottage a family of rabbits skitter out of her way, their tails flashing white against the long grass. She ducks beneath a drooping washing line hanging limply between two trees and on past the upturned chicken coop lying forlornly in the shade of a twisted apple tree, blown there, she presumes, by a violent wind. She stamps her boots, then slips inside to wash her hands and change into a clean pair of trousers.

Upstairs she stands at the cracked mirror, pulling faces at her distorted reflection as she pulls her hair into a ponytail. She's running through a list of building contacts in her head, wondering whom she should call about the roof and the rising damp, when her eye is caught by the reflected outline of something scrawled across the wall behind her. Puzzled, she turns and moves a little closer, trying to understand what it is she is looking at. She kneels and rubs a hand across the surface of the wall, removing a layer of dust, then gazes more closely and rubs again, watching in amazement as a faint but distinct image slowly reveals itself, like a picture drawn in invisible ink by a child.

'Huh,' she says, sitting back on her heels and staring at the wall. She has rubbed the dirt from a rectangle about half a metre high by two metres across to reveal six of them, six strange stick figures dancing across the wall in a faint, purple scrawl. They are naive representations but it's clear that three or four of the figures are male, the others female. In one stickman's hands dangles a large, conical reefer. No doubt about it, thinks Lila, kids have been here.

She decides she will leave the mural alone for a while; there will be plenty of time to come back to it when the more important jobs have been completed, and in the meantime the six dancing figures will stay. It's not as if she couldn't do with the company.

* * *

There is only one shop in Little Ramsdale, a small greengrocer's-come-post office in a quaint thatched building. Lila drives the length of the village but the only other places of note are a small stone church and a larger building that might have once been a pub, now converted into a private residence. Shame, she thinks; she could murder a pint. She turns the car around and parks in front of the village store.

A bell rings as Lila enters the shop and a middle-aged woman standing at the counter lazily flicking through the pages of a glossy magazine lifts her head and calls out a cheery, 'Hello.'

'Hi,' says Lila, realising that this is the first person she has seen or spoken to in a couple of days.

'Anything I can help you with, love?'

'Thanks, I'm just getting a few bits.'

'Righty-ho.' The woman smiles and returns to her magazine, leaving Lila to peruse the limited shelves. She chooses a packet of biscuits, a loaf of bread, a pint of milk, four apples and a couple of tins of soup and takes them up to the counter.

'That the lot?'

'Yes thank you,' says Lila.

The ruddy-cheeked woman rings the items up on the till. 'That'll be six pounds twenty, thanks, love.' The woman eyes Lila as she rummages in her wallet for the money. 'You holidaying round here?' she asks.

'Sort of. Well, no actually . . . I'm staying in the old stone cottage up near the lake. Do you know it?'

The woman thinks for a moment. 'That old falling down place, up near the moors?' she asks, eyeing her with interest.

'Yes.' Lila smiles. 'It was left to me recently,' she explains. 'I'm just up here checking it out.'

The woman nods and fills Lila's canvas shopping bag with her groceries. 'That old place has been empty for such a long time. I wasn't even sure it was still there, to be honest.'

'I don't suppose you know who it used to belong to, do you?' Lila's voice is hopeful, but the woman just shakes her head.

'No, love. I think it's been long forgotten.'

'Has anyone . . .' she doesn't know how to ask tactfully so she just blurts it out in the end, 'has anyone that you know of died round here recently?'

The woman gives her a strange look.

'You see,' continues Lila by way of explanation, 'it was left to me by someone, but I don't know who. I'd love to find out who it was.'

The woman looks puzzled. 'I'm sorry, love. I'd like to help you but I just can't think who it would be. No one that I know of has died in recent months, thank goodness.' She touches the wooden shelf beside her.

Lila nods and tries not to look disappointed.

'So you'll be sticking around for a bit then?' asks the woman.

'Yes, for a few more days definitely.'

The woman smiles. 'Well, you know where to come if you need anything. I'm Sally,' she says, offering Lila her hand.

'Lila.' They smile at each other across the counter.

* * *

Back in the car she thinks to check her mobile phone and sees she has missed three calls from Tom. Knowing that he will be worried, she dials his number then watches two lycra-clad cyclists flash past her window as she waits for him to answer. His phone goes straight to voicemail.

'Hi you,' she says, putting on her cheeriest voice, 'it's me. Everything's fine. I made it up here OK and the place isn't quite as bad as I remembered, although I might have to bribe Barry or some of his boys to come up and help with the roof and the damp in the kitchen. All in all, though, the old place has held up remarkably well.' She pauses, wondering what to say next. 'Anyway, hope you're OK. I just wanted to say hi.' She hesitates and wonders if she should invite him to visit at the weekend. 'So, I guess I'll say bye then. Oh,' she adds quickly, 'my phone reception is really patchy up here . . . probably best if I try to ring you again tomorrow . . . or the next day. Hopefully we can speak then.' She pauses. 'Bye.'

It's only after she's hung up and swung her car back onto the country lane and made it halfway back to the cottage that she realises she forgot to tell him that she misses him.

8

OCTOBER

1980

The morning they are discovered, Kat wakes to a freshly iced land-scape, everything pale and glittering, whitewashed overnight by the first sweep of winter's paintbrush. It is still the same familiar picture, but brighter, whiter, blinding somehow, as if caught in a photographer's flash. It takes her breath away.

'Wake up,' she urges Freya. 'You should see this. It's beautiful.'

'Mmmm . . .' mumbles Freya from deep beneath the bedclothes, 'later.'

'Suit yourself.' She pulls on a sweater over her pyjamas and heads downstairs, passing Simon curled beneath a blanket in front of the ash-filled grate. She stops and watches him for a moment, noting his parted lips and his breath forming tiny white clouds in the air above his head. She looks around for Mac and sees an indentation in the sofa, evidence of where he has slept, but no other sign or sound of him.

Unable to resist, she moves across the room and slides beneath Simon's blanket, pressing the length of her body against his. He murmurs, groggy with sleep, and then turns to her. 'Good morning,' she whispers and he nuzzles her neck. Breathless with her daring, she moves her hands down over his stomach and then under the waistband of his pyjamas.

'Oh God,' he says, with a groan and rolls on top of her. 'Kat,' he whispers, 'my Kat.' He smooths her hair off her neck and bends to kiss her, his lips grazing the skin above her collarbone. Then he moves over her and she raises her hips up off the floor, drawing him into her, moving with him.

'I've missed this,' she whispers into his ear, biting the lobe with her teeth until he shudders and goes still, leaning his full weight on her, pressing her into the hard floor. They are nothing but warmth and breath, his stubble scratching her cheek. 'You need a shave,' she murmurs and his laugh is hot against her neck.

She leaves him stretched before the fire and wanders into the kitchen to light the range. As she goes she can feel the sting and the scent of him on her skin. It was different this time; this time *she* went to him and she feels buoyed by his response, by his acceptance. She knows they should be more careful – that they should probably use contraception – but as she arranges kindling in the grate she wonders if it would really be so terrible to be pregnant with Simon's child? She imagines them at the cottage, happy and content, a proper family: her and Simon and a child with his eyes and olive skin and Kat's dark hair. No, she's not exactly in a rush to have a baby, but if it happened . . . well, would it be *so* bad? A child with Simon would be a connection to him for all time, something nobody could ever take away from her. And it would be a chance too, for her to prove that she had moved away once and for all from her own broken childhood. A baby with Simon would be a chance to do things differently – to bury the ghosts of her past. As she puts a match to the twigs in the grate, she hums a quiet tune. It might not be on either of their minds, no, but if it happened it certainly wouldn't be the worst thing in the world.

Within minutes she has got a crackling blaze going and a pan of water over the range readying to boil, but rather than stand there watching it, she slips through the back door and heads down the bank, her feet crunching on stiff white blades of grass, shattering them like glass.

The lake is still and serene, a low mist hanging in a diaphanous gauze above the water. One black cormorant skims the surface like a shadow before melting away into the fog. Higher up, just breaching the surrounding hills, the sun hangs like a pale moon in the sky, still gathering strength for the day ahead. Kat hugs herself and stamps her feet. The first frost; there's no denying that winter is on its way.

They are in pretty good shape. With Freya's extra help and a fair bit of luck they are making good progress. The larder is filling with jams and preserves, they've dried peas and mushrooms and begun to store root vegetables of every size and shape. Crab apples and plums have been retrieved from the trees up behind the house and several pumpkins discovered deep in the garden undergrowth. It's surprised her how much they've been able to salvage from the forgotten garden. They've hung onions, rosehips and the last of the garden herbs to dry, and taken care to top up on basic supplies of pasta, rice, tins of canned food, flour, powdered milk, oil and sugar purchased from stores located in a variety of far-flung villages, always careful never to visit the same one in too quick succession. Best of all, the chickens have proved invaluable with their daily egg-laying, providing them with some much needed protein when the fishing rods or Mac's traps have failed to produce. Mac's warned them that the hens will bunker down for winter soon, but with the larder growing increasingly full there is no reason, it seems, that life at the cottage can't continue unchecked into the winter months.

For Kat, however, the biggest blessing, she knows, is in feeling as though she is where she is supposed to be, with people who mean something to her. Not just Freya and Simon, but the others too. Freya was right: they don't just feel like a group of friends hanging out, playing house any more. They feel like a family – one unconventional, chaotic family – but *her* family all the same. She's never experienced anything like it before.

She bends down and trails her fingers through the water, no longer warm and inviting but crystal clear and skin-tinglingly cold. Pebbles glitter like pale gems in the silt. A strand of green weed undulates in the current. Their days of swimming in the lake, of sunbathing on the grassy bank, seem a lifetime ago. She shivers and thinks of tea, remembering the pan she has left boiling on the stove.

It's as she turns back to the cottage that she sees her: a woman, standing high up on the ridge, her silhouette in stark relief against the pale sky. Kat is frozen to the spot, her breath caught in her throat. She is too far away for Kat to see her face, but she can tell from the tilt of the woman's head and the stillness of her body that she is watching her. Kat stares back and for one interminably long moment the world slows, everything around them quiet and still, as they face off across the frosted ground.

Before Kat can react a golden labrador bounces over the ridge and stands panting at the woman's feet, its tongue lolling from its mouth. Kat glances towards the cottage, seeing it as if through the woman's eyes: the muddy boots scattered by the door, the ghostly outline of yesterday's laundry – stiff with frost – still hanging on the washing line, the thin column of smoke just beginning to curl from the chimney, all indisputable evidence of their occupation. She drags her gaze back to the woman on the ridge.

She doesn't know what she is waiting for. Angry shouts? Gesticulations? The waving of a loaded shotgun? Whatever it is, it's not the slow raising of the woman's hand in a hesitant gesture of greeting. Kat swallows and then, before she can stop herself, lifts her own hand in a half wave. The woman stares at her a moment longer, then seems to give the slightest nod before taking a step backwards, then another, and another . . . until she has disappeared over the ridge, the labrador melting away at her side.

Kat stands rooted to the spot a moment longer then turns and runs towards the cottage.

Simon is up and nursing a mug of tea at the kitchen table when she bursts through the back door. 'I made a pot,' he says, barely looking up.

Kat struggles for breath. 'I saw someone . . .' she gasps, 'outside . . . watching.' She can't get her words out.

'Slow down. Who saw you? What are you talking about?'

'A woman. She was just standing up there . . . watching me.'

Simon leaps up from the table and moves to the window. He peers out. 'Where?'

'Up on the ridge. She had a dog.'

He turns back to Kat. 'What did she do? Did she say anything?'

'No, she just sort of stood there and stared.'

'Not a word?'

'No.' Kat pauses. 'She waved.'

'She waved?'

'Yes.'

'What did you do?'

'I – I waved back.'

'You waved back?' Simon gapes at her. 'What did she look like?'

Kat shrugs. 'I don't know. Middle-aged.' She tries to think, remembers the woman's long wax jacket and stout boots, the sensible shoulder-length hair. 'She just looked . . . normal.'

Simon moves across the room and slumps back into his chair, then slams the table with his fist, sending Kat leaping backwards in alarm. 'Damn it.'

Kat doesn't know what to do. It feels as though it is all her fault. If only she hadn't gone out to the lake . . .

'What's going on?' asks Carla, appearing at the door with a yawn, wrapped in one of Ben's misshapen sweaters and with her frizzy hair sticking up at startling angles from her head.

Simon ignores her and turns back to Kat. 'Is she still out there?'

'No. She disappeared back over the ridge.'

'Go and wake the others,' says Simon to Carla, throwing the words over his shoulder at her.

'But what's going o—'

'Now,' insists Simon.

Kat sees the irritation flash across Carla's face, but she does as she's told and shuffles off to rouse the others from their sleep. After she's gone, silence fills the room. Kat waits, nervously chewing on a fingernail, willing Simon to say something reassuring; but he doesn't and the silence stretches on endlessly.

Finally, Ben appears in striped pyjamas and a bobble hat, shivering in the chill air. 'Christ, it's cold,' he says, hugging himself. 'Is there any tea?'

Simon pushes the pot across the table towards him.

'I can't find Mac,' says Carla re-entering the room, 'but Freya's coming down. Are you going to tell us what's going on?'

'Anyone know where Mac is?' asks Simon as Freya shuffles into the room, wiping the sleep from her eyes like a child.

They all shake their heads.

Simon sighs. 'OK. So here it is.' He looks about at them all seriously. 'It seems we've been discovered. Kat saw a woman up on the ridge, watching her.' Simon relays the rest of the events to the group then sits back and waits for their reactions.

'Why didn't the woman say anything to you?' asks Ben, turning to Kat.

'I don't know,' shrugs Kat, 'she was quite far away, I suppose.' She knows it could have been any of them standing there at the lake's edge but somehow, in Simon's retelling, she still feels as though she is being blamed for something.

'Bollocks,' says Ben.

Simon nods. 'Indeed.'

They are all silent as they contemplate the enormity of it. They have grown lax. They've begun to feel invisible, invincible. But nearly three months into their little experiment and reality has come knocking – or rather waving – over the crest of the hill and it suddenly feels as though their new life could come tumbling down around their ears. Kat feels like crying.

'So what do we do?' asks Carla, 'Start packing?'

'We're just going to give up?' asks Kat, panic-stricken.

'Hang on a minute,' says Simon, holding up his hands. 'Who said anything about giving up? We don't know who that woman was *or* what she wanted. She could have just been out for a stroll with her dog and stumbled upon us. She might have been a rambler, or a tourist, exploring the countryside. She doesn't necessarily know that this place isn't rightfully ours.'

Kat shakes her head. Somehow the woman hadn't looked like a tourist.

'She might be heading back to her car right now, driving far, far away and not giving us another moment's thought,' continues Simon.

Kat wants to believe him. His words and his confidence are soothing. She feels her heartbeat begin to slow in her chest.

'I vote we just hang out here and see what happens,' he continues. 'She may come back. She may bring others with her. And yes, perhaps we will be thrown out of the cottage. But let's wait to be asked, and then go peacefully. We've hardly trashed the place, have we?'

Ben nods. 'It's actually in better nick than when we first arrived. Who knows, the owner might be grateful,' he tries with a hopeful smile.

Simon looks around at them one by one. 'What do you say?'

Freya looks to Kat and shrugs.

Kat knows her answer. She's not ready to say goodbye to any of it just yet. 'Yes,' she says, 'we stay until we're asked to leave . . . or until we *want* to leave . . . whichever comes soonest.'

* * *

They're still gathered around the kitchen table an hour later when Mac returns, stumbling through the back door with rosy cheeks and mud-spattered jeans, the collar of his jacket turned up against the cold. 'Why so serious?' he asks, shaking his hair from his eyes. 'What have I missed?'

But no one answers. They are all far too interested in the wriggling and snuffling sounds coming from beneath Mac's denim jacket.

'What on earth?' asks Carla, looking at him with a mixture of fascination and horror.

Mac grins and reaches down to unbutton his jacket, revealing a pale pink snout and two chocolate-brown eyes.

'Oh my God,' whispers Freya, moving across to where Mac stands, 'she's divine.' She reaches out to undo his buttons further, revealing downy pink fur and four tiny trotters.

'She's a *he*,' says Mac, lifting the tiny piglet out from the warmth of his jacket and holding him up for them all to see. The pig gives a gentle snort.

'Can I hold him?' begs Freya. 'Is he hungry? What does he eat?' She looks at Mac, suddenly worried. 'We *are* keeping him, aren't we?'

'Yes,' says Mac, 'we are.'

Freya rewards him with one of her most dazzling smiles and Kat smirks to see Mac's cheeks flush even pinker.

'Where'd you get it?' Simon asks.

Mac turns to Simon. 'I took the runt. Doubt the old farmer will even notice he's gone.'

'You stole him?' says Carla in admonishment.

'I like to think I offered him a better life,' says Mac with a crooked smile.

Freya swoops up the snuffling piglet and cuddles him like a doll. Kat watches and is reminded of the Freya from her childhood, never happier than when playing house or dress-up with her dolls.

'He likes you,' says Mac, watching Freya with the piglet.

'He's pretty skinny . . . but I guess he might be good for a bacon sandwich or two.'

'Simon!' cries Freya, 'we're *not* eating him.' She turns to the pig. 'We're not eating you, don't worry. You can be our house mascot. Wilbur, that's what we'll call you. They didn't eat the pig in *Charlotte's Web*, did they?'

'"Our house mascot"?' asks Simon. 'That's assuming we still have a house to live in.'

Mac throws him a look. 'Have I missed something?' he asks, sensing for the first time the tension still lingering in the room.

Simon turns to Kat. 'Do you want to tell him or shall I?'

* * *

Although they've decided to brazen it out at the cottage, the morning passes in a state of uneasy limbo, each of them nervous and jumpy. None of them dare give voice to their fears but Kat knows they are all imagining a crowd of angry villagers rushing with pitchforks over the hillside towards them.

'I can't stand this,' says Ben, eventually, putting down his guitar. 'Let's do something.'

Mac nods. 'How about we go pick those sloes in the woods? There was a ground frost this morning. Now is a good time.'

Ben nods. 'Anyone else want to come?'

Carla and Simon agree to accompany them while Kat offers to stay back. 'You know,' she says, 'just in case.' No one seems to need any further explanation.

'I'll stay too,' says Freya, snuggling the piglet.

'I think somebody's in love,' laughs Ben.

'Don't get too fond of him,' warns Kat. 'We may have to eat him yet.'

Freya draws herself up. '*No one* is eating Wilbur.'

Simon glances between Kat and Freya, shakes his head in amusement.

'What?' asks Kat, catching his look.

'For sisters, you two are *very* different.'

'What do you mean?' she asks.

'Well you, Kat, you're tough . . . practical and rational.'

Kat nods, pleased.

'But Freya here,' he continues, 'am I right in thinking you're probably a little more impulsive, a little freer with your emotions?'

Freya shrugs her shoulders. 'I don't know. I guess.'

Simon shakes his head again. 'The proverbial chalk and cheese.'

Kat looks across at Freya. Her sister smiles and rolls her eyes, but Kat's own smile, when it comes, feels as tight as a mask. Practical is OK, she thinks. Rational is good.

* * *

'Don't you ever get bored here?' Freya asks, after the others have gone. She is slouched at the end of the sofa, picking at her split ends.

'No,' says Kat, glancing up from her notebook. 'Not really. Why,' she asks, 'are you bored?'

'No,' says Freya. 'But it *is* very quiet.'

Kat nods. 'I like that it's quiet. This place is supposed to be about getting back to a simpler way of life. We're forming a deeper connection with our environment and the landscape. Making time for the things that really matter.'

Freya looks up from her hair and eyes Kat.

'What?'

She hides her smile. 'Nothing.'

'What?' insists Kat, but Freya won't answer. 'It's not a load of waffle. It's true. Simon's right; we're so conditioned by society we've forgotten to appreciate our connection with the *real* world – where our food comes from, how to fill our days with honest, meaningful work. And when the work is done, there's more time for the fun stuff: reading and thinking, writing, engaging with each other. But you know,' she adds with a slight edge to her voice, seeing the smile still playing on her sister's lips, 'if you don't like it you don't *have* to stay. No one's forcing you.'

'I know that. I don't want to go . . . not yet. I like it here, honest. It's fun spending time with you again.'

Kat regards her for a moment and softens. 'How long do you think you'll stay?'

'A little while longer?' She hesitates. 'Maybe until Christmas . . . if that's OK with you? It's not as if I have anywhere else to go.'

'Sure,' agrees Kat. She turns back to the notepad in her lap and silence falls over them. She chews the end of her pen and scribbles a few more lines before she feels Freya's expectant gaze fall on her once more. She looks up with a sigh. 'What now?'

Freya shrugs. 'There was this girl at college, really pretty, amazing cheekbones – just like yours. I cut her hair for her, you know, short like a pixie. I reckon you'd look good with short hair.'

'Really?' Kat puts a hand up to her neck and feels where her hair hangs in a thick clump about her shoulders. It's greasy and could really do with a wash but bathing in the cottage is a laborious task now that the lake is too cold for swimming. She's not sure she can be bothered to heat the water and fill the old tin bath.

Freya waits for a moment. 'I could cut it for you, if you like?'

'You could cut my hair?' Kat stares at Freya a moment.

'Sure, but only if you wanted me to.'

Kat studies her through narrowed eyes. 'How short are we talking?'

'Short.'

'Like a boy?'

'Yeah, but it would look good, honest.'

Kat shakes her head. She's always worn it long.

'It would really suit you.'

Kat sighs and puts her notebook down on the arm of the chair. 'I'm not even sure we have any scissors.'

'I have some in my sewing kit.'

Kat considers Freya's offer. In her head she hears the echo of Simon's words: *so practical, so rational.* 'And you promise it will look good?'

'I promise.'

Kat thinks on it a moment longer. 'Come on then,' she says, 'it's only hair, after all.'

The piglet watches on as Freya dampens Kat's hair at the kitchen sink and then trots behind them as they head upstairs to the bedroom. Freya positions Kat in front of the cracked mirror and begins to hack. As she works she hums the tune to a favourite song and the pig snorts his encouragement from the corner of the room.

'Not too short,' says Kat, suddenly, seeing a long tuft of dark brown hair drift to the ground beside them.

'You can't say that now,' exclaims Freya. 'I've already cut one side. Trust me, it's all about short, asymmetrical cuts right now. Long hair is out, punk and new wave is in.'

'Why haven't you cut your own hair then?' asks Kat. 'You know, if it's so cool?'

'I don't have the right shape face for it, but you do. It's going to look great.'

Guided by her sister's hands, Kat tilts her head to one side and shivers as the cold metal of the scissors presses against her neck. 'It'd better.'

Freya cuts and cuts and clumps of dark hair drift down and settle like feathers at Kat's feet. '*Love will tear us apart*,' she sings, over and over.

'A little less singing and a bit more concentration, please.'

'Keep your hair on,' jokes Freya.

When she's finished, Freya stands back to regard her sister through narrowed eyes. 'Perfect,' she proclaims. 'I wish I had some gel to spike it up but it still looks good.'

Kat shakes her head to loosen the last of the shorn hairs then looks at herself properly in the cracked surface of the mirror. She stares for a moment, barely recognising herself.

'You look great, really different,' enthuses Freya.

'Do you think?' She turns this way then that. Freya has cropped her hair to the nape of her neck and styled it into an asymmetric sweep at the front. It is a dramatic change. Her eyes appear suddenly much bigger in her face and her cheekbones more pronounced. She tilts her head to one side and practises a smile. Freya is right; she really does look different. 'I like it, I think,' she says, a genuine smile beginning to pull at the corners of her mouth. She can feel the air moving against her skin where hair used to hang. 'It feels good,' she says, fluffing it with her hands. 'Lighter. Freer. It will be much easier to manage here too.' Freya nods and Kat squeezes her arm. 'Thank you,' she says.

Freya grins. 'I *told* you it would look good.'

'All right, Vidal,' says Kat, brushing herself off, 'no need to gloat.'

* * *

Carla is the first through the back door as the others return from the woods. 'Oh,' she says when she sees Kat's drastic new look. She dumps a basket of berries on the kitchen table and moves across to her. 'Look at you.' She reaches out and touches a strand of Kat's cropped hair. 'Turn around.'

'Do you like it?' asks Kat, suddenly nervous.

'I do. Did Freya do it? Isn't she clever?'

Kat peers behind Carla, anxious to garner Simon's reaction but it is Ben and Mac who enter the cottage next.

'Whoa,' says Ben, 'leave you girls alone for five minutes and you go and get all Twiggy on us.'

'It's not Twiggy,' corrects Freya, 'it's *new wave*. It's completely different.'

Simon enters the room and puts another basket of sloe berries onto the table before turning to them all. 'Any trouble?' he asks, and then stops short as he sees Kat's dramatic transformation. 'Oh,' he says, 'you cut your hair.'

'Yes.' She grins up at him. 'Like it?'

Simon regards her for a moment. 'It's very short.'

'Yes, Freya says short is in. It's all the rage in London. Do you like it?' she presses.

Simon smiles ambiguously. 'It doesn't matter if I like it, does it? You're the only person whose opinion really matters.' He turns back to the baskets of berries on the table.

'But I'm interested in what you think,' she presses.

'Well,' he says, 'if you really want my opinion, I don't agree with slaving yourself to trends. I preferred it long. I suppose I like a more feminine look. But as I say, my opinion really doesn't matter . . . as long as *you're* happy with it.'

'Oh.' Kat feels a hot sting of embarrassment flood her cheeks and an awkward silence fills the room. No one seems to know what to say.

'We got a good haul today,' says Ben at last. 'Shall we sort through them?'

'Yes,' agrees Carla quickly and the others turn to the table, clearly relieved for the distraction, leaving Kat to struggle with her rush of emotion. She feels Freya reach for her hand and give it a gentle squeeze. 'I think you look amazing,' she whispers, but Kat doesn't want her platitudes. She pulls her hand away. Why did she let her talk her into it? She glances around and sees Carla's high pineapple bouncing on her head and the tangle of Freya's long, blond locks and suddenly feels about as modern and attractive as a shorn sheep. She stares down at the blanket of purple-blue berries being spread across the table until they merge into a hazy, indigo fuzz behind her welling tears. Don't cry, she wills, not here, not in front of them all.

Ben continues his act of distraction by popping a sloe into his mouth and chewing. 'Christ,' he says, spitting the purple pulp straight out into the sink, 'they're disgusting. Remind me why we picked them.'

'They're for sloe gin,' says Mac patiently.

'What? We're going to ruin perfectly good gin with these things?'

'Trust me,' says Mac, 'you'll thank me when you've tried it . . . and any winter colds this year, well, it's the best medicine in the world; that's what my mum always said.'

'That's what *Mummy* said, is it Mac?' laughs Simon from the end of the table.

Mac lifts his chin and studies Simon for a moment across the table. 'Yes,' he says quietly.

'I'm sure there's more to those herbal remedies than we know,' says Freya, throwing him a careful smile.

'Well it'll certainly make a welcome change from the homebrew,' says Carla.

'There's nothing wrong with my homebrew,' snaps Ben.

'Nothing wrong with it? The last batch you made was virtually undrinkable.'

Ben turns on Carla. 'That wasn't my fault. I told you lot it hadn't had enough time to ferment properly but you wouldn't listen.'

'Now, now,' says Simon smoothly, 'let's save the lovers' tiff for behind closed doors.'

'Oh piss off,' says Ben, annoyed.

Kat takes a deep breath and moves closer to the table. 'So when will we be able to drink the stuff?'

Mac shakes his head. 'We have to make it first. Prick the berries. Steep them in gin and sugar and then let the whole lot ferment for a bit. It'll be a few weeks yet.'

Ben huffs. 'You know, just *sometimes* I wish we didn't have to wait for everything in this bloody place.'

'Oh come on,' says Simon, 'don't they say the best things in life are worth waiting for?'

'I thought it was the best things in life are free?' says Freya.

Kat sees Simon throw Freya an irritated look.

'I think it's both,' says Kat, finding her voice again.

Simon ignores her and reaches into his jacket pocket. 'Well you can forget the sloes for now. I think you'll find that *these* are both free and instantly more exciting than Mac's little berries.' He pulls his hand out of his jacket to reveal several stringy white mushrooms nestled on the flat of his palm.

Ben leans in for a closer look then lets out a long, low whistle. 'Where did you find these beauties?'

'Down in the meadow.'

'What are they?' asks Carla.

'Magic mushrooms,' says Mac, his voice flat.

'Magic mushrooms?' Carla leans in for a closer look.

'Oh yeah,' says Ben with a broad grin.

Kat glances about the group. Simon and Ben are grinning from ear to ear but Carla and Freya look less thrilled, and Mac, as ever, is hard to read, standing further back in the shadows now, allowing Simon his moment of glory.

'Are you sure?' asks Carla. 'You have to be careful with wild mushrooms . . .'

'Positive,' says Ben. 'They're liberty caps . . . the best kind. He rubs his hands together. 'Well this has just improved tonight's prospects somewhat.'

Simon beams at them all. 'So who's up for a little trip?'

* * *

'I'm not sure,' Freya says an hour or so later, eyeing the squares of mushroom Ben is carefully cutting up and laying out for each of them. 'How do we know they won't make us sick? You do hear of it, don't you? What if something goes wrong?'

'Cold feet?' asks Kat and the words sound more than a little unkind, even to her ears. She's still struggling not to blame her for Simon's reaction to her hair.

'Out of everyone here, I'd have thought our resident art student would be up for it.' Simon glances at Freya, the faintest edge to his voice. 'Anyone else having second thoughts?'

Kat takes a breath. She can feel the spectre of her parents there in the room with her and knows Freya feels it too. But this isn't heroin, cooked in some seedy den, sold on a street corner. These mushrooms are natural, grown in the meadow and picked by Simon's own hand. She can feel him watching her and she raises her chin slightly. 'Not me.'

Simon gives her a nod. 'Carla?'

She sighs. 'No.'

'Mac?'

Mac shakes his head. 'I'm in.'

Ben slides the pieces of mushroom across the table towards them in turn. Mac reaches for his and puts it straight into his mouth. Kat follows suit and chews quickly. It tastes horrible, like a mouthful of sweet, damp earth.

'Freya?' asks Simon.

Freya doesn't seem to hear. She sits curled on the sofa, her hands hidden in the sleeves of her cardigan as she watches Kat, as if anticipating an adverse reaction at any moment. Kat smiles back at her and chews carefully.

Simon swallows his piece of mushroom straight down then reaches for the Zippo and lights the roll-up between his fingers.

Freya continues to look around at them all nervously.

'You don't have to,' she hears Mac say to her sister, his voice low, '. . . not if you don't want to.'

Kat notices her own foot tapping restlessly on the floor and makes it go still. She's only ever smoked a bit of a weed before and she still has Freya's words ringing in her ears. What if things go wrong? What if she has a bad trip, or worse, the mushrooms poison them all? She looks across to Freya again. 'Go ahead,' she says, feeling Simon's gaze on her, 'it's fine. After all, you said you were bored . . .'

Freya gives Kat one final glance, then reaches for a piece of the mushroom and swallows it down with a slug of beer. 'So what happens now?' she asks, looking around wide-eyed at them all. 'How long does it take?'

'Dunno, really,' says Ben. 'We just hang out. We wait. We go with the flow.' He picks up his guitar and strums the opening chords to a Pink Floyd song. 'The most important thing is not to panic. Just enjoy the ride.'

Kat smiles at Simon. Go with the flow. Enjoy the ride. That shouldn't be too hard.

* * *

She's not sure how long it takes. One minute she is sitting next to Carla, talking about plans for the vegetable garden while Ben strums quietly on his guitar, then the next instant the evening has taken on a strange, shifting quality and nothing feels very fixed or real any more. Time bends and stretches in a new and curious way. Freya is lying on the floor in the middle of the lounge. Her hands are raised and she twists and turns them in the candlelight, as though they are the most fascinating things she has ever seen. Kat watches her, half listening to Carla's talk of pumpkins, watching the strange, swirling dance of her sister's hands. She turns to Carla and asks, 'Do you feel it?'

Carla gives her a wan, wispy smile. 'Yeah.'

'Kind of trippy, isn't it?'

'Uh-huh.'

Simon sits in the corner on one of the beanbags, his head tilted to the ceiling as he smokes a cigarette. Mac is on the sofa, watching Freya's strange horizontal dance. After a while Simon stubs out his cigarette and moves across to lie beside Freya on the floor. Freya turns to grin at him as he begins to copy her strange dancing movements. 'Isn't it amazing?' she asks.

Simon grins back and then clutches Freya's right hand and raises it to his lips before they continue their strange hand dancing together. Kat smiles to see them – her two favourite people in the entire world – and feels her love for them swelling to fill the room.

'Do you hear that?' asks Carla, leaning in towards Kat.

'What?'

'The music?'

Kat shakes her head. 'What music?'

'Listen.' Carla tilts her head to one side. 'Hear it now?'

Kat shakes her head again but then, from out of nowhere, she hears it; a sort of dull drumming noise, beating down on them from all around. 'The drums?'

Carla laughs. 'You hear drums?'

Kat nods, a little confused. 'What do you hear?'

Carla sighs and smiles beatifically. 'I hear rain.'

Kat stares at Carla, utterly confused. Rain? How can rain sound so rhythmic, so tribal? Suddenly Carla bursts out laughing. 'Come on,' she says, grabbing her by the hand. 'There's something I want to do, upstairs.'

* * *

It's a little like being inside a kaleidoscope. She is one fixed point while all around her scenes shift and slide in colourful new directions. Now she is up in Carla and Ben's bedroom. There is an oil lamp on the floor casting the room in a strange, flickering glow. She sits cross-legged on the mattress watching as Carla performs a crazy dance across the blank, white wall in front of her. As she watches, pictures take shape amidst the shadows, strange smudged images drawn in vivid purple paint.

'What is it?' asks Kat, peering at the wall, realising that the dripping purple paint isn't paint at all, but the smears of sloe berries.

'Look,' says Carla with sudden solemnity, 'it's us. I've drawn all of us here at the lake. See?'

Kat peers at the wall and slowly she sees the scrawls transform before her eyes until, yes, she can see it *is* them, not smudged at all but clear and precise, almost their exact likeness; the six figures are suddenly as identifiable as if drawn from a photograph. There is Ben, with his straggly goatee and smoking reefer in hand, and Simon with his broad shoulders and beautiful black eyes, a wide-eyed Freya with her tangled plaits and her arm linked through Carla's who wears

135

her fuzz of hair like a halo around her head; behind them comes Kat herself, skinny as a boy and with her short new haircut, while last of all, trailing in the distance comes the spindly shape of Mac. Kat is fascinated. She peers more closely and before her eyes the figures suddenly seem to come to life and dance across the wall in a jaunty, impromptu conga. Kat watches them and smiles. They all look so happy. 'You're really good at painting,' she says, turning to Carla, but Carla has gone.

* * *

The kaleidoscope turns again and Kat is lying on a mattress, watching the ceiling of the bedroom undulate like a huge piece of fabric. In a moment, she thinks, it will just lift off and there will be nothing left between her and that vast canvas of sky. And sure enough, as she watches, the roof of the cottage lifts up and floats away like a giant white sheet caught on the breeze. Kat stares at the fizzing stars dotted high up in the night sky; she watches as they move closer and closer, and fall one by one down into the room, exploding like fireworks all around her.

It's so beautiful, she thinks, so very beautiful.

* * *

He has come to her. Simon is there. He moves on top of her and she wraps her arms around his neck, feels his skin against hers, draws her nails down his back.

Simon, she says.

He stares into her, his eyes deep, black wells.

I love you. I love you. I love you. She doesn't know if she says the words aloud but she feels her heart expand and open until she is nothing but that one throbbing, beating organ, pulsing and alive.

She turns her head. Freya is on the far side of the room and Mac is there too, beside her, kissing her, one hand resting clumsily on her breast. She smiles. It's funny. Mac and Freya. Look, she says to Simon, look at them, and she closes her eyes and is carried away.

* * *

When she opens her eyes the kaleidoscope has shifted once more. Now she is alone . . . and she is cold. She reaches for the covers, pulls them up over her naked body, rolls over onto her side. In the darkness she sees that Mac and Freya are still there, Mac now curled away from Freya and Freya lying on her back, her long hair fanning out across the floor in a golden halo and her eyes closed. She looks like a doll. What Kat's brain can't understand, can't grapple with, is the image of Simon hovering above Freya. She watches him for a moment. What is he doing? She watches him move over her sister, his dark hair shifting in time as he moves forwards and backwards over Freya. Simon and Freya. Simon and Freya. Kat shakes her head and watches. She is frozen, her body ice-cold, but somewhere deep inside, right at her very core she feels something open up, something hot and acid, burning deep in the pit of her stomach. Simon and Freya.

No, she says. She looks up at the ceiling, where the stars no longer fizz and fall through the sky. There is nothing but darkness, looming over her, drawing her up into its cold abyss. No, she thinks, but the blackness still comes and it fills her up.

* * *

It is late when she wakes, the pale sun already slipping back towards the horizon. How long has she been asleep? The room is cold and empty and she can feel beneath the sheets that she is naked. A drum-beat begins somewhere deep inside her skull and slowly, in time to the dull thud of her headache, fragments of the night return to her. The rain. The music. The mural. The stars. Her and Simon. Simon and Freya.

Simon and Freya.

Kat swallows. Too late, she realises that she's going to be sick and she leans over and heaves a stream of hot bile onto the bedroom floor.

9

LILA

November

As the days shorten and winter descends over the valley, stripping trees of their last leaves and covering everything in a fine, white frost, Lila wonders if she has bitten off more than she can chew. She is making some headway with the cottage but she'd be lying to herself if she didn't recognise that every day since she started has been a struggle. She's still not sleeping well – still haunted by nightmares and desperately wracking her memory for details of her fall – and on top of that, she's beginning to miss the little luxuries of home she's always taken for granted: warm baths and carpet underfoot, wi-fi and proper espresso. More than once she's considered throwing in the towel and heading back to London, but whenever she's come close, it's the thought of admitting defeat to Tom and returning to their empty house that has kept her stubbornly in place.

If she is honest with herself, there is a small part of her that is becoming more accustomed to the place – to its strange, lonely atmosphere. At night, the creaking sounds of the cottage and the rustlings and calls of the wildlife outside are growing more familiar. No longer does she tense at the shriek of a fox or the echoing hoots of an owl; and while she's still a little spooked by the idea of who might have walked the floorboards or stoked the range or slept in these rooms before her, and still wrestling with the uncomfortable feeling that she's not always alone in the hidden valley, she can at least put her disquiet down to the extreme solitude.

Sometimes, when the weather allows, Lila downs tools and heads outside to sit beside the lake. The moss-covered tree slumped across the grassy bank is the perfect spot for contemplation. She likes to watch the reflection of the clouds drifting across the flat grey surface of the water and finds that the fresh air helps to clear her head. Even just stepping away for an hour or two helps to push things into perspective and remind her why she is there and what she is trying to accomplish. Someone watching her? It's laughable, really. Out there in the wilds it's far too easy to let her imagination run away with itself.

It's easy too, she's discovering, to lose track of the days. Lila finds she has no real need to keep pace with dates but it's as she's carrying an armful of junk up to the growing pile of rubbish at the end of the garden that it hits her: *Bonfire Night*. It's the fifth of November. She has been so distracted with her work that the significance of the date has almost passed her by. Tom is due at the cottage that evening and as Lila stands there in the shadow of the hills, gazing at the pile of detritus mounting up before her, it suddenly strikes her as nothing short of serendipitous that it should be today of all days that they are to be reunited. It has taken him several weeks but Tom has finally resolved a structural problem on a bridge down south and has called to say he will be joining her later that day.

Lila has always loved Bonfire Night, and it isn't just for those memories of her first drunken kiss with Tom. Ever since she was a little girl, she's loved the whole irreverent occasion of it. Her parents hadn't gone in much for committee meetings and garden parties, PTA meetings or dinner parties, but for some reason, when it came to Guy Fawkes Night, they'd pulled out all the stops. 'We're supposed to celebrate the fact that Guy Fawkes' gunpowder plot was foiled,' her father would say with a mischievous twinkle in his eye, 'but I prefer to think of it as a celebration for the man himself. Now there was someone who knew about breaking a few rules, about shaking things up, no matter what the cost . . . even if he did pay the ultimate price for his ideals.'

'The ultimate price?' she'd asked.

'Yes,' he'd nodded, 'hanged, drawn and quartered,' and she'd shuddered as her father pulled his finger across his throat and stuck out his tongue in ghoulish imitation of a corpse.

'Simon,' her mother had admonished, 'there's no need to terrify the poor girl.'

But Lila wasn't terrified. She'd grinned and shivered at the thought, but mostly she'd just been excited. Bonfire Night meant sausages and baked potatoes cooked in the glowing embers of the huge pyre lit at the bottom of the garden; her mother in her glamorous fur-collared coat and brightest lipstick and her father at the centre of it all, topping up drinks and handing out sparklers. With everyone bundled up in hats and gloves and the heady tang of wood smoke hanging in the air, she and her friends would whirl sparklers in mittened hands and write their names against the dark sky. It had always felt so illicit, so dangerous, one of the few nights of the year when she was allowed to stay up late and roam the garden, the heat from the bonfire warming her face, the cold night air at her back, everyone waiting for the moment when her father would light the fireworks and send them fizzing into the night sky; all of them *ooohing* and *aaahing* at the extravagant pyrotechnics while her mother just stood there, quiet and stern.

'Oh *darling*,' he would say to her in that way he had, like he was giving the punchline to some private joke they shared, 'you always *used* to enjoy a good party.' He'd throw his arms around her in a rare gesture of affection and urge her to 'live a little'. And he might get a smile from her then, in the warm glow of the bonfire.

Her father was in his element on those nights, charming and outlandish, foisting mulled wine and whisky on the fathers, flirting outrageously with the mothers. Like a dry piece of wood put to a flame, he would suddenly and miraculously whoosh to life.

Lila remembers it all, standing at the far end of the scruffy garden, and smiles. There is no way she can plan anything to match one of her parents' extravagant parties, but she has enough old wood, broken furniture, mildewed curtains and mouldy mattresses to give the bonfire a good run for its money. She decides it then: she and

Tom will set fire to the huge rubbish pile together. They will do it tonight, not just in honour of Guy Fawkes, but as a symbol of something else too, something unspoken. She imagines them standing side by side in the darkness, watching the heap catch alight, all of that detritus and decay disappearing into smoke and smouldering ash. It would be a shared moment for them, something symbolic.

Then, perhaps they will wander hand in hand back through the garden to open a bottle of wine in front of the blazing hearth. There will be no other distractions. For once it will be a chance for them to talk about Milly and about where they go from here. Yes, thinks Lila, hurling a rotten plank of wood onto the growing pile of junk, her mind is made up. This is exactly what they need after all these weeks of distance. This will be the start of making everything better between them.

She rummages through the pile at her feet, adds a broken balustrade, a chess board spotted with green mould, a mangy-looking sleeping bag and a sagging cardboard box to the bonfire. Her hands hover over an old Moses basket, an oval wicker thing, grubby and unravelling in places, with a moth-eaten blanket lying within. She'd found it with the rest of the junk under the stairs and had known instantly it was only good for the rubbish tip, but now that she has it up beside the unlit bonfire she hesitates. Chuck it on, she tells herself, get rid of it . . . declutter. But she can't. She fingers a corner of the knitted purple blanket and whether it's the idea of what the basket might have once contained, or thoughts of her own lost baby, she's not sure, but she places it to one side and when she has finished throwing the last of the rubbish onto the pile, she picks it up and carries it back into the cottage, stowing the grimy thing under the stairs where she'd found it. With one last, uneasy glance she slams the cupboard door shut.

* * *

'Hello again.' Sally greets her from behind the shop counter with a warm smile. 'It looks pretty wild out there. Is it raining yet?'

'Not yet,' says Lila, grabbing a plastic basket from beside the door.

'Won't be long,' says a tall man standing in front of the chilled foods cabinet, 'you can feel it in the air.'

Lila gives the man a small smile of acknowledgement, then heads to the shelf at the back of the shop where the limited assortment of wine and spirits are housed. She stares at the labels, clueless. She supposes it's a night for red, but she doesn't recognise any of the names on the bottles.

'How are you getting on out in the wilds, love?' Sally calls. 'Surviving up there?'

'Yes,' says Lila, 'just. My husband's coming up tonight – it will be nice to have some company.'

Sally gives a theatrical shudder. 'Don't know how you do it, all by yourself, day and night.'

'I'm getting used to it,' she says and tries to smile.

The woman turns back to her other customer. 'She's renovating an old place up near the moors, making it nice, you know, like one of those telly shows. She's quite mad, if you ask me. I'd need more than a chat with the old bat running the local village store every few days to keep me sane.'

The man turns to Lila with a polite nod. 'Is that right? Which place would that be?'

Lila smiles, embarrassed to have her news broadcast quite so publicly. 'It's about three or so miles from here . . . an old stone cottage beside a lake. I don't actually know if it has a name. Do you know the one?'

The man shrugs. 'Sounds like it could be an old shepherd's cottage. There's a few of them about.'

She hesitates. 'Do you have any idea who it might have once belonged to?' She regards him hopefully but the man just scratches his head. 'No idea, sorry. If it's the one I'm thinking of it's been empty for years.'

'Oh.' Lila turns back to the wine, disappointed. She reaches for a bottle, swayed by the pretty leaf design on its label, and adds it to her basket.

'It's been a shocking autumn, hasn't it?' Sally continues, turning her attention to the man now standing at her counter. He nods politely as he piles tins of dog food next to the till. 'My Stan says we might as well just give the livestock away at market if prices continue to slide like this.'

The man murmurs his response and Lila carefully tunes out their conversation, concentrating instead on the mental shopping list she has drawn up in her head. She adds a piece of Stilton, a packet of crackers, bread, cornflakes, coffee, biscuits, chutney and some ham to her basket, then throws in a bag of oranges and some milk too. She moves across to the till and stands patiently behind the man as he packs his own groceries into two large bags. His hair is grey and cropped short and he wears a long, wax jacket and heavy gumboots. She should invest in some proper outdoor gear like that, she thinks.

'Well you take care, ducky,' says Sally as the man turns to leave. Lila feels his sliding glance as he passes and looks up to smile but he doesn't quite meet her eye and is gone with a ring of the bell on the door. Sally leans in close to Lila and whispers, 'No idea why he's on his own, that one. Never found a decent woman, apparently. Shame, I hate to see a good man go to waste, don't you?'

Lila nods. She really doesn't want to get drawn into a long conversation about the dating restrictions of the rural Peak District. She is thinking, instead, of the muddy track she needs to negotiate back up to the cottage in her car and those low hanging clouds threatening to dump another downpour at any moment. She will have to hurry.

'So hubby's joining you later?' Sally continues, ringing up the price of the wine and placing it into a shopping bag for Lila.

'Yes, Tom,' she says, piling up the rest of her groceries onto the counter.

'No kids then?'

Lila takes a careful breath. 'Not yet, no.'

'Plenty of time for that. You're young, aren't you?'

'Yes,' says Lila, swallowing.

'Nice drop you've chosen,' Sally adds, indicating the bottle of wine again. 'You'll enjoy it.' Then she leans in close. 'You need anything else – chocolate, ice cream, *gossip magazines*,' she adds in a theatrical whisper, 'you come and see old Sally, OK?'

'OK,' says Lila, finding her smile at last.

Fat globs of rain are beginning to fall from the sky as she runs back to her car. They land on the road in front of her and mark the tarmac like giant ink blots. She slings her shopping across the back seat then jumps into the front, pushing her hair from her eyes. She's too late. The rain is coming. Her key turns in the ignition and Lila waits for the engine to roar to life.

Nothing. The engine sputters, clicks and then stops. She tries again but it doesn't even sputter this time, it just clicks and clicks then nothing. *Shit.*

She peers through the rain-spotted windscreen and spots the Land Rover parked on the opposite side of the road, the man from the shop just visible in the driver's seat. He fixes his seatbelt in place, then looks up and notices Lila watching him. Their eyes meet across the tarmac and she glances away, embarrassed. 'Come on,' she wills and tries the key in the ignition once more. *Click . . . click . . .* nothing. She slumps back in her seat in frustration. Now what? Call Tom and just sit here waiting for him to arrive God knows when to save her? Not exactly the self-sufficient, independent, coping-on-her-own image she has hoped to portray to him. She could call out a mechanic but in this part of the world that could take hours too, and worse, would probably cost an arm and a leg. Think, Lila, she wills herself, think.

She is jolted out of her reverie by a sharp rap on her window. Outside is the man from the shop, the rain teeming off his wide-brimmed hat and streaming in rivulets down his wax coat. She unwinds her window a crack. 'Trouble?' he asks.

'It won't start.'

'I'd offer to take a look but in this weather I think the most sensible thing to do is get you home. Can I give you a lift? You can come back for your car tomorrow.'

Lila hesitates, her city sensibilities kicking in.

'You said your husband was on his way up here?'

Lila nods.

'Presumably he can help you get the car going tomorrow?' He shivers and looks pointedly up at the sky. 'Getting a bit wet here . . .'

Oh screw it, she thinks, throwing caution to the wind. Sally in the shop had seemed to think he was nice enough. 'Yes please,' she says, quickly. 'Just let me grab my shopping bags.'

By the time she has transferred her shopping to the back of the man's Land Rover and settled into his passenger seat she is soaked to the skin and shivering.

'Brrrr.' The man removes his hat and starts up the wipers, directing the blowers of the car heater onto the windscreen to remove the fog building on the inside of the glass. 'We'll just give it a minute to let this clear . . . need to be able to see where I'm going.'

Lila nods. 'Thanks.' The Land Rover smells of wet dog. There are discarded mint wrappers on the floor by her feet, as well as clumps of dry mud and hay.

'Sorry about the state of the car,' says the man a little sheepishly, seeing her glance about.

'That's OK. And thanks for this. I doubt I'm anywhere close to where you're going.'

'No trouble,' he says, 'I think I know roughly where you're headed. You can direct me the rest of the way.' He turns the car around and guides them down the narrow lane that will eventually take them back towards the lake.

For a while, the only sound inside the car is the rain lashing against the windscreen and the swish of the wipers, travelling valiantly back and forth across the glass; they simply cannot go fast enough for the onslaught and the man has to slow the car and creep around hairpin bends, their visibility reduced to just a few metres. Lila waits a while, hoping he will say something else to break the awkward silence, but in the end it's her that speaks up. 'I'm Lila,' she says.

'William,' he replies, leaning right over the steering wheel to gain a few extra inches of visibility.

'Nice to meet you.' She pauses. 'You're a farmer round here then?'

'Yes.'

'What sort of farmer?'

'Sheep, mostly. But I keep a bit of game and poultry too.'

'That must be interesting.'

He glances across at her and nods.

Just shut up, Lila, she thinks. No need to be nervous. He seems perfectly nice – a little shy perhaps, a little reticent to make eye contact – but perfectly pleasant. Yet for some reason she can't relax and she sits tense and awkward, listening to the endless splash of puddles beneath the car's wheels. 'It's up here,' she says finally, pointing to the unmarked turn-off.

William nods and indicates left, peering to see the gap in the hedgerow, then begins to bump them up the muddy track.

'I hope your husband's got a vehicle with high clearance,' he says at last. 'He's going to need it to get up here tonight.'

Lila can see he is right. The recent comings and goings of the roofers had already churned the muddy track horribly, but now with the torrential downpour it's beginning to resemble a quagmire. They lurch along, occasionally dipping wildly into a ditch or puddle so deep a huge gush of muddy water surges up over the bonnet.

'Can you swim?' William asks and Lila gives a nervous laugh.

'I'm so sorry about this.'

'No trouble.'

'I don't actually think my car would have made it,' admits Lila, 'even if it had started back there. Tom should be OK though. He's got a four-wheel drive.' She points to the grass verge and reaches for her seat belt. 'Just here is great, thank you.'

William clears his throat, his hands still on the steering wheel. 'I have some old railway sleepers up at the farm. I could pull them down here with the tractor one day, if you like. If we sink them into the track they'll give you a bit more traction, stop it getting quite so boggy.'

Lila is embarrassed. 'It's very kind of you to offer, but I really wouldn't want to put you out . . .'

'It'd be no trouble,' he says. 'They're just sitting up at my place rotting.'

'Honestly, it's fine. This rain won't last for ever.'

He shrugs. 'Suit yourself.'

Lila reaches for the door handle, just as another huge gust of wind sends a barrage of raindrops splattering loudly onto the windscreen. The noise makes Lila jump. 'Goodness,' she says, 'it really has turned foul.' She knows she has to get out of the car but she just can't bring herself to leave the warmth of the vehicle.

'Come on,' says William, reaching over to the back seat for a bright orange plastic poncho, 'put this on. It's not pretty but it'll be better than that fleece you're wearing. I'll help you with the bags.'

'Oh – thank you, but it's still quite a long way from here,' she says, but William is already gathering her shopping, and so Lila does as she is told and pulls the poncho over her head and follows him out into the rain.

She stumbles across the meadow with William following and by the time they reach the copse of trees her shoes are filled with water and her jeans soaked up to her knees. There is little shelter among the near-leafless trees and as they troop down the ridge and reach the front door of the cottage she is not only soaked through but caked in mud too. She feels something akin to hysteria grip at her; for some reason she finds she can't stop laughing. What on earth is she doing in this remote, inhospitable place with this strange man? Another fit of giggles seizes her. 'Sorry,' she says, trying to compose herself, 'I don't know *what's* got into me.'

The man stands beside her on the doorstep looking somewhat bewildered and Lila can see from the expression on his face just how deranged she must seem. 'Please,' she says, putting her key to the lock, 'come in for a moment. You can dry off in here – maybe take a look around at my little project while you wait out the rain. I'll make us some tea?' It seems like the least she can do.

He hesitates again, seems about to say something, but then just nods and follows her silently into the dark interior of the cottage.

'Let me take your coat.' He is already sliding off his muddy boots and he hands her his dripping coat, watching wordlessly as she hangs it on one of the rusty nails set into the wall near the front door. 'I'll just change, then I'll get the fire going and put the kettle on. Make yourself at home, take a look around.'

He nods, but stays rooted to the spot.

'Or you could light the fire?' she suggests.

'Yes,' he says, obviously grateful for the suggestion. 'I'll do that.'

She points him towards the fireplace and the basket of logs then leaves him to it and heads upstairs where she strips off her wet jeans, socks, fleece and sweatshirt and replaces them with dry clothes, before heading back downstairs to boil water for tea. William is hunched before the hearth as she passes. She is amazed to see he already has a good blaze started and he leans into the grate, blowing gently, fanning the flames until the logs crackle and spit in the heat. 'I wish I could get it going that fast,' she says, wandering past and then on into the kitchen where she puts the kettle on. She tidies her groceries away, standing the bottle of red wine on the window sill, filling a bowl with the oranges and opening the packet of biscuits, laying a few out onto one of the few plates she has. She puts mugs and milk on the table, next to a jug of red berries she has picked from the garden, then adds the teapot.

'All set?' Lila starts at his voice. He is watching her from the doorway. 'The place will be warm in no time,' he adds.

She notices for the first time how weather-beaten his skin is, deep lines etched around his mouth and across his forehead, the impact of years spent outside in the sun and the wind, no doubt. His shoulders are broad and his arms strong, his hands red and callused. With his cropped grey hair and worn face he is hard to pin down in age, but she supposes him to be in his late forties or early fifties.

'I forgot to buy sugar,' she says, turning back to the table and fussing with the teapot, embarrassed to realise she has been staring quite openly at him. She's not sure why, but it feels strange to have him here in the cottage with her – her first visitor. There is something about the sight of him, a tall, strong man in a navy fisherman's jumper and socks, filling the doorway to the kitchen, that makes her feel a little odd. It's that strange déjà vu again. Perhaps it's the intimacy of it all, the two of them going about the domestic chores, padding around the cottage in their socks, their hair damp and their cheeks rosy from the cold. She shakes the feeling away and indicates he should sit on one of the long wooden benches, settling herself on the seat opposite.

'So how have your renovations been going?' he asks. 'Getting along all right?'

'More or less,' she says, pouring them both tea from the pot. 'It's hard going but I've done some of the tougher jobs now, with a bit of help. The damp proof course has been sorted,' she says, nodding to patches of plaster drying on the walls, 'and I've had the roof fixed, the electrics checked, the chimneys and the basic structure of the building gone over. It's old and neglected, but surprisingly sound. I was particularly worried about the old beams running through the property but they're relatively solid – a little sagging on the one in that front room but a column should help.'

He nods and takes a slurp of his tea. 'You seem to know what you're doing.'

Lila shrugs. 'It's my job, although I've never taken on anything quite like this before. You should see the pile of junk I've cleared out the back. I'm going to have a bonfire tonight with Tom, to get rid of it all. It's Guy Fawkes Night, after all.' She stops, realising what she's just said. 'Oh. We *were* going to have a bonfire . . .'

'Ha,' says William, 'I'd like to see you try and light it tonight.' As he smiles, his eyes crinkle beneath bushy grey eyebrows.

Lila is disappointed. The cosy image she'd entertained of her and Tom standing hand in hand at the top of the garden dissolves before her eyes.

'So what will you do with this place when you're finished?' he asks, taking a biscuit from the plate between them.

Lila thinks for a moment. 'I honestly don't know. Perhaps I'll sell it. I haven't quite decided yet.'

William nods, staring down into his mug, munching quietly. 'Nice to take your time,' he says eventually. He sits for a moment, then reaches out to touch one of the brilliant red berries hanging on the stems in the little jug.

'Pretty aren't they?' she says. 'I found them growing in the garden.'

He nods. 'Hawthorns.'

'Is that what they are? I didn't know.' The room falls silent once more. Lila clears her throat. 'So where's your farm? I hope I didn't bring you too far out of your way.'

'It's a few miles north of here. Quickest route by road is back down the way we came, past Little Ramsdale and then on through the next village. It's another mile or so from there by car.'

'You lived there long?'

'I've been running it for a few years now.'

Lila nods and takes a bite of her chocolate digestive.

'Have you been married long?'

'A couple of years. Tom,' she adds, feeling a sudden need to name the invisible figure hovering between them. 'His name's Tom.'

'He doesn't mind you being up here?'

Lila senses judgement in the man's tone and springs to Tom's defence. 'No. He's busy with work and it was good timing. It was my idea to come. I – I wanted to get away . . . ' Lila realises how bad that sounds. 'He understands.'

'And he's good to you?'

What a strange question, thinks Lila. 'Yes, I suppose so.'

William nods. Lila takes another sip of her tea, listens to the wind wrap itself around the cottage, before racing away again into the valley below.

'Any kids?'

Lila pauses, her lips on the hot rim of her mug, then shakes her head. 'You?'

'No,' says William. 'No wife. No kids. Never met the right woman. Often think I could do with a few strapping boys around the place though, to help me on the land.'

'Or girls,' suggests Lila.

'Pardon me?'

'Or strapping girls. To help out. Let's not be sexist.'

'Good point,' says William with a smile. 'You seem to be managing admirably here.'

For some reason Lila finds his praise brings a flush to her cheeks. 'To be honest I hadn't thought I had done much . . . but maybe you're right.' She looks around at the kitchen again then busies herself with pouring them both another cup of tea, eventually turning the conversation back to his work on the farm. As they chat, the sound of the drumming rain and the creaking timbers of the house create a cosy, intimate atmosphere inside the kitchen; it feels as if they are at sea in an old wooden ship. Neither of them notice the fading afternoon light as it turns from dark grey to an inky violet twilight; neither of them notice the sound of the rain as it eases slightly on the roof, but they both jump when the front door opens with a bang and the sound of boots stamping on the floorboards in the front room fills the house. 'Lila?' a voice calls.

Lila jumps up. 'Tom,' she says to William, 'my husband.' Her cheeks flush. 'I'd completely lost track of time,' and she grins.

'Lila,' Tom calls from the other room, 'are you here?'

'I'll be right back,' she says to William. 'I'll introduce you.'

William nods again and reaches for his mug, drains the last of his tea.

Lila finds Tom at the front door, shaking a huge golf umbrella out into the damp night air. 'You made it,' she says, going across to him and wrapping her arms about his waist.

'Hang on,' he says, pushing her away gently, 'I'm soaked. Let me get the door shut. I didn't know if you were here,' he says over his shoulder. 'I saw an old Land Rover but I didn't see *your* car on the track.' She backs away and watches as he props the umbrella up against the inside wall, slams the door shut against the wind, then removes his dripping coat and shoes. 'Christ, it's been bucketing down out there. Nearly didn't make it up the track. The car's filthy, absolutely caked in mud . . . and look at the state of me.' He holds out his arms and smiles, raindrops dripping down his face and staining the collar of his shirt dark blue. 'Brrrr,' he gives a dramatic shiver. 'It's lovely and warm in here though. Come and give me a hug. I've missed you.'

He looks so incongruous, standing there in a shirt and tie, like a piece of the outside world blown in unexpectedly on the storm. Lila goes to him and wraps herself around him, feels his warm breath in her hair. 'You feel good.'

'You too. I've missed you.' He bends to kiss her and she presses herself against him.

When he steps back he looks around at the tiny room in wonder. 'Wow, just having a fire going makes it seem a little cheerier than the last time we were here. Perhaps you'd better get me out of my wet things, before I catch a terrible cold.'

She catches the cheeky glint in his eyes but resists as he starts to draw her close again. 'Tom . . .'

'Oh come on . . .' he coaxes.

'Tom, wait, there's someone—'

There is a loud clearing of the throat and both of them spin round to see William standing at the open doorway to the kitchen. 'Hello,' he says, stepping forwards and holding out his hand to Tom.

Tom takes a small step back then turns to Lila with a puzzled look.

'This is William,' she explains. 'We met at the shops. My car broke down so he very kindly drove me back here.'

'Ah,' says Tom, relaxing, accepting the hand that's been offered. 'I see. That explains the missing car.' He hesitates, as if getting the measure of the man standing across from them.

'Yes,' she says, compensating for her husband's obvious appraisal, 'it was really very kind of him. I've taken him well out of his way home. We were just having a cup of tea. Would you like one? I can make another pot?'

Tom shakes his head and slings an arm over Lila's shoulder. 'I'm fine.'

The three of them stand awkwardly.

'Well,' says William after a moment, 'I should probably get going. Rosie will be waiting for me.'

'Rosie?' asks Lila.

'My collie,' he explains. 'She's very demanding, likes her dinner served in the kitchen at five p.m. sharp, every night.'

Lila smiles. 'Well we can't keep Rosie waiting now, can we? Will you be all right finding your way back to your car? It's dark already. I really should get some outside lights fixed out there.'

'Stop fussing,' says Tom, 'William's a grown man. He'll be fine.' He opens the door and Lila blushes at the abrupt dismissal.

William doesn't seem to mind. 'Yes, I'll be fine,' he says to Lila and pulls his coat collar up around his neck. 'Thanks for the tea.'

'Oh, anytime.'

He hesitates. 'You know, if you change your mind about those sleepers I'd be happy to come by.'

'Thank you,' says Lila, ignoring the tightening of Tom's grip on her shoulder. 'That's kind of you.'

'And you'll be all right picking up the car tomorrow?'

'I've got it covered,' says Tom.

William nods and turns away. 'Well nice to meet you both . . . goodbye,' he calls over his shoulder and disappears over the ridge into the darkness.

'Already mixing with the local country bumpkins I see?' says Tom, as soon as the door is shut.

She slaps him playfully on the arm. 'He's not a bumpkin. And you didn't have to make it quite so obvious you wanted him gone.'

'I didn't.'

Lila gives him a look. 'He was *my* guest.'

Tom shrugs. 'Can you blame me? I haven't seen you in ages.'

'It was just a cup of tea. I owed him, he came a long way out of his way.'

Tom nods but his smile is wary. 'You should be careful, you know, inviting strange men back here when you're all on your own.'

'It's fine. He seems like a good guy. A little shy, but nice enough.'

'You don't know him from Adam.'

Lila can read him like a book. 'You're jealous,' she says.

'Jealous?'

'Yes.'

He stares at her for a moment. 'Should I be jealous?'

'Of William?' She laughs. 'Come off it, he's old enough to be my father.'

He doesn't answer and Lila tries to laugh again at the ridiculousness of it all. 'You're being an idiot. He gave me a lift home – that's all. Come here.' She pulls him towards her by the loop of his belt and kisses his cheek, feels the scratch of his stubble against her skin. His scent is achingly familiar. 'How was the drive up?'

'Awful. Traffic at a standstill for three junctions on the M1.'

'You look exhausted,' she says, taking a step back and regarding him properly for the first time, noting his face pale and the bruise-coloured shadows under his eyes.

'Yeah,' agrees Tom, 'work's been horrible . . . and I've missed you.' He leans into her.

'I've missed you too.'

Tom studies Lila carefully. 'So when are you coming home?'

'Tom,' she warns. She doesn't want to have this conversation. Not yet.

'I mean it, when are you coming home? Have you got this hare-brained scheme out of your system yet?'

'It's not hare-brained. Besides, I think I'm starting to make some progress.'

Tom looks around the room. 'Really?'

'Yes,' she says.

'It kind of looks the same to me,' he says and yawns.

Lila swallows back her irritation. 'It doesn't look *any* different?'

Tom looks around again. He shrugs. 'A little,' but she can tell he's lying. 'Look, we've got two days together. Let's not argue. I've missed you. Isn't that enough?'

'Yes,' she relents. 'It's enough.'

He loosens his tie then undoes the top button on his shirt. 'I'm absolutely starving. Is there anything to eat?'

'Come on,' says Lila. She throws another log onto the fire before leading him into the kitchen where she lays out the bread and cheese and ham and opens the bottle of wine. They eat and drink in silence, listening to the wind howl around them and the rain splatter against the windowpanes. Seeing things through Tom's eyes now, Lila suddenly feels overwhelmed again. All the small changes she's made, the little things that she hoped would make a difference – the berries on the table, the bowl filled with oranges, the clean-swept floor and the fire blazing in the hearth – they aren't enough. She can only see all the things that still need fixing. Feeling irrationally cross with Tom for bursting her bubble, she shivers in the draught and pulls her sweater more tightly around her body. So much for her Bonfire Night celebration.

* * *

It's not the weekend with Tom that she'd been hoping for. They wake early on Saturday morning and even though she has given him the camp bed, he still seems tired and fractious. 'I don't know how you sleep on that thing,' he grumbles, 'it's like a prison bed.'

'I don't mind it,' she lies.

'We should get you a proper mattress at least, if you're really going to stay up here.'

'I really am,' she says and busies herself at the sink so she doesn't have to see the look on his face.

'So what did you have planned for us today?' he asks and Lila's heart sinks again, knowing that he's going to hate her.

* * *

It is more than twenty miles to the nearest home improvement store. They drive out in Tom's car, skidding down the muddy track and then on through the country lanes, passing through pretty stone-clad villages and on to more substantial A-roads until they finally locate the retail park on the outskirts of Glossop. It's still raining and it seems that everyone within a fifty-mile radius of the shops has decided to take refuge inside the cavernous shopping complex. The car park thrums with traffic. Tom has a stand-off with a man in a flashy sports car over a space near the entrance to the store then they race across the tarmac and in through the sliding glass doors. 'Christ,' says Tom, staring around at towering shelves stretching before them, 'where do we start?'

'Paint,' she says, grabbing a trolley and leading him through the aisles. She has a shopping list in her head and she systematically fills the trolley with paint and brushes, white spirit and rollers, checking it all off as they go.

'You know, this isn't how I'd hoped we'd spend the weekend,' he says, pushing the trolley a little faster then lifting his feet and gliding towards the checkouts like a little kid.

Lila sighs. 'It's just a couple of hours. I needed to get this stuff and an extra pair of hands *is* helpful.'

'OK,' says Tom, 'but at least let's salvage some of our day and go to the pub for lunch, shall we?' He hefts the contents of the trolley one by one up onto the conveyor belt.

Lila nods. 'Sure, we can do that.'

She feels the woman at the till glance at them both as she scans their items and Lila sees them suddenly, as if through her eyes: just another bickering couple in a DIY store on a Saturday morning. She can understand why Tom is annoyed.

They can't decide where to stop on the way home but eventually settle for a decidedly average-looking pub in a small market town. The food is bland and their conversation stilted and after a while Tom pushes his half-eaten burger across the table. 'Come on,' he says, admitting defeat, 'let's go and sort your car out.'

It's exactly where she'd left it the night before, parked outside the village shop. Tom takes her keys and tries them in the ignition. 'It's your battery,' he says, listening to the stutter of the engine. 'You probably haven't been driving it enough. I've got jump leads, we can get it started if you pull my car right up to your bonnet here.'

It takes them forty minutes but finally they get the engine going and she follows him back in his car to the cottage, relieved to see he manages to get her car to the top of the muddy track in one mud-splattered piece.

'Why don't you drive mine for a few weeks?' he suggests as she meets him round the back of his car to unload the shopping.

'Really?'

'Sure,' he says. 'Borrow it. Bring it home at Christmas.' He spoils the generous gesture with an eye roll. 'If that's the only way I'm going to entice you home?'

'Thank you,' she says, leaning in to kiss him, her lips meeting his chin as he turns back to the boot.

He shrugs. 'Come on. I guess we'd better start lugging this lot up to the cottage,' he says, indicating Lila's purchases with a shake of his head. 'It's going to take us long enough.'

* * *

By the time they retire to bed that night they are too tired for anything more than a perfunctory kiss goodnight. Tom offers Lila the camp bed but she declines. 'I'll be fine, you have it.'

He hesitates a moment. 'Are you sure?'

'I'm sure.'

Still he doesn't move. He stands there in a T-shirt and tracksuit bottoms and watches her for a moment. 'I wish we could both fit.'

'Ha,' she says, 'I'd like to see us try,' and she moves away and distracts herself by arranging her own nest of blankets on the floor, secretly grateful that they won't be sharing a bed that night. Her physical bruises may have healed but she can still feel her emotional scars deep inside. The thought of sleeping with him terrifies her – she doesn't even know if that side of her exists any more: the one all about need and desire and intimacy – and she certainly doesn't know what she will say if he presses her.

'Goodnight then,' he says, switching out the light and settling onto the creaking bed.

Lila breathes a silent sigh of relief. 'Goodnight.'

Silence fills the darkness.

'Lila . . .'

'Yes?'

There is a pause. 'Nothing.'

She holds her breath but Tom remains silent. 'Tomorrow will be a better day,' she says eventually, 'I promise.' But he must be asleep already because he doesn't reply.

* * *

'Lila!' Tom is shaking her in the dark. 'Lila, wake up.'

'What?' she asks. 'What is it?' Her heart hammers wildly in her chest.

'You were screaming.'

'I was?' She props herself up on one elbow, tries to focus on the outline of him in the darkness.

'Yes.'

'Oh,' she says, putting a hand to her sweaty brow, 'I was.'

'Are you OK?'

She thinks for a moment, tries to calm her thudding heart. 'I'm OK. It was just a dream.'

'You frightened the living daylights out of me.'

'Sorry.'

'It's OK.' He hesitates, then sits down next to her and puts his warm hand on her shoulder, strokes the curve of her neck with his fingers. 'What were you dreaming about?'

Lila swallows. 'The fall.'

'Oh.' In the darkness she can see his head droop slightly. 'Do you dream about it much?'

She nods.

'Have you remembered anything new?'

'It's strange. Tiny fragments are coming back to me but there's still this huge hole. Every night now it's the same. I'm in my bedroom, trying on clothes. The sun is shining through the window. I look in the mirror.' She swallows again. 'That was all I could remember for a long time but there's a little more now.'

'What?' asks Tom.

'My memory jumps – like a stuck record – and it's the strangest thing . . .' She hesitates. 'You see, I'm *running* down the landing at home and I reach the top of the stairs,' she swallows, 'but then I'm just falling – plunging into darkness.'

Tom is quiet for a moment. 'Perhaps you're confusing dreams with memories?'

She shakes her head. 'No. It feels real.'

Tom reaches out to smooth a loose strand of hair away from her face. 'Don't you find this place spooky, out here on your own?' he asks quietly.

'Spooky how?'

'I don't know.' He shivers in the cold night air. 'It's hard to explain. There are just some places that feel . . . that feel as though something has *happened* there. I think this cottage might be one of them.'

She understands: the logs in the basket . . . the bullet hole in the kitchen . . . the abandoned possessions . . . the inexplicable sensation of being watched; ever since she arrived at the cottage she hasn't been able to shake the feeling that the old cottage has been trying to tell her something.

'Don't you find it unnerving?' he persists.

'No,' she lies, 'not really.'

He sits with her a while longer, stroking her hair until sleep's creeping tendrils wrap themselves around her once more. 'Tom,' she murmurs.

'Yes, Lila.'

'Go back to bed.'

'OK, Lila.'

* * *

It is her suggestion to hike up onto the moorland the next morning. It has finally stopped raining and looking out over the blue eye of the lake, she is desperate, suddenly, to offer Tom a different side to her life in the valley. She wants to show him how beautiful it can be there, how peaceful and still. 'Come on, it's your last day. You should get a good look at the place.'

'But what about the painting? I thought you wanted my help?'

'It can wait. Let's go, while there's a break in the weather . . .'

Tom nods. 'Come on then,' he says, the slightest challenge in his voice, 'show me what you *love* about this place.'

At first she thinks she'll lead him through the woodland circum-navigating the lake, where the trees shiver in their near-leafless state and throw long, spiny shadows out over the water, but then she remembers the rain and how boggy it will be, so instead she turns to strike out across the meadow and up the steep track leading over the hills. The higher up they go the more stripped-back the land becomes until soon they are walking across open moorland. For a while they walk in silence, their arms swinging at their sides, a metre or so apart all the way.

'Where are we going?' he asks.

'I don't know,' she admits, unwinding her woollen scarf, letting it dangle from her hands, 'just rambling.'

He nods. 'OK.'

Eventually they come to an old stone wall. 'Shall we sit for a bit?' she asks.

They perch together on the weathered wall and gaze out at the vast sky. 'Isn't it beautiful?' she says. 'Look, that must be the cottage, all the way down there.' She points to a thin plume of smoke rising in the distance, evidence of the fire they have left smouldering in the grate. 'Don't you feel a million miles away from London right now? From the rest of the world?'

'Yes,' says Tom, but the way he says it doesn't make it sound like a good thing.

Lila wonders if now is the time for them to talk, up here, in the clean air, away from everything that is familiar or real. Geographical change is good, she knows, it's a distraction, but she's also coming to understand that Tom is right; she can't outrun her grief. As much as she wishes she could leave it far behind, like a sprinter taking off from a start line, she sees that no matter how fast she runs, she is on an oval track, and she only ever comes back to the beginning, back to the pain she hasn't yet worked out how to live with. So perhaps she should discuss the baby with him. Perhaps she should discuss her strange and disturbing dreams in more detail, but every time she thinks to bring it up she loses her nerve. The only thing it seems Tom wants to talk about is *when* she will give up the cottage and return home.

He sighs and shifts on the wall next to her. 'It's so remote, Lila. I'm worried about you, that's all.'

'I'm OK. I like the space . . . the freedom. I like waking in the morning with that ache in my muscles that tells me I've done a real day's work.'

'And *I* like waking in our bed with you beside me.'

'I just don't want to be there right now. I can't explain it.'

'You mean you don't want to be with *me* right now?'

'No. I didn't say that. It's not you. It's just this feeling of . . . of—'

'Of what, Lila?'

'I can't explain.'

'Well try.'

Lila sighs.

'It wasn't my fault,' says Tom eventually, so quietly she almost doesn't hear.

'I know that,' says Lila, shocked. 'Why would I think losing Milly was *your* fault?'

He shrugs. 'Sometimes it feels as though you're blaming me.'

Lila is baffled. The only person she has been blaming in all of this is herself. 'I'm not blaming you . . . but it might help if you talked to me about it . . . if you opened up a little. Sometimes *I* feel as though I'm the only one who's grieving for her.'

Tom shakes his head. 'How can you say that?'

'Well, for one thing you could talk about her . . . you could say her name.'

Tom stares at her.

'You never say it. Milly: you never say your daughter's name.'

'I do.'

'No,' Lila shakes her head firmly, 'you don't.'

Tom is silent, his head lowered. When he speaks next his voice is so quiet she has to lean in close to hear him. 'I say it in my head . . . sometimes it feels like she's *all* I have in my head.'

She nods, understanding, but still can't help noticing he hasn't said their daughter's name out loud. 'Look,' she says after a while, softening her voice, 'why don't you take some time off work and come and stay here for a little while? Two pairs of hands will be much quicker than one. It will be a chance for us to be together. It could be good for us.'

'You know I can't just drop everything.' He runs his hands through his hair and then gazes out across the horizon. 'It's not a good time at work.'

'I just think—'

But he cuts her off. 'Lila, I don't know what's going on with you but we can't go on like this. Come home, please. I need you.'

She looks at him, stung. He doesn't know what is going on with *her*? Does he not remember what they went through – together – just a few short months ago? The agony of the labour, the terrifying sight of their baby – too small – too pale – being whisked away by the nurses and hooked up to a scary array of tubes and machines in the neonatal unit. Does he not remember the tears, the bruises, the heartache of losing their daughter? The loss of all they'd dreamed of? Of course the physical signs of the pregnancy and the fall have gone: her body has shrunk back in on itself, the cuts and bruises have healed . . . but her heart . . . her heart is another thing entirely, still damaged, still broken. Does he really not remember *any* of that?

'And I need this,' she says finally. She looks across at him, tears in her eyes, imploring him to try to understand, but he keeps his gaze fixed on the blank sky overhead, his eyes trained on a kestrel wheeling and turning on a thermal high above their heads. 'Tom?'

He doesn't turn and staring at him she feels an anger spiral up from deep inside. *This* is their problem, she thinks, this disconnect they just can't seem to get beyond.

Leaving him on the wall, she jumps down, turns on her heel and stomps off across the boggy terrain, the cold wind drying the tears in her eyes before they can spill down her cheeks. Let him find his own way back to the cottage, Lila thinks; she doesn't care.

* * *

When they say goodbye later that evening, a small part of her is relieved to see him go. It hasn't been the romantic reunion either of them had been hoping for. With Tom there, Lila has seen the place differently again, through his eyes, noticing every flaw and every imperfection, every job that needs doing, big and small; but rather than make her want to leave, it has fired up that stubborn part of her that won't let it go. It has made her impatient to keep going, to fix things before she can lose heart.

She heads upstairs to the bedroom, eyes the camp bed where Tom lay just a few hours before. She reaches for his blanket and folds it into a neat square then perches on the bed frame and gazes, unseeing, at the dusty old fireplace across the other side of the room. She can feel her grief there with her still; like a well-worn garment that she has unpacked from her bag, shaken out and hung neatly on the clothes rail in the corner; a permanent, physical fixture hanging silently, waiting for her there no matter where she goes.

She gazes into the empty hearth and wonders how on earth she and Tom will ever reconnect across the chasm of their grief. She churns it over and over in her head until her mind turns outwards and her eyes begin to focus on a strange shadow upon the brickwork of the chimney breast. It's probably just soot but she moves across the room and reaches out to touch the stone with her fingertip. The brick slips slightly and she sees that if she pulls a little she can remove it completely from where it is lodged. She tugs on it gently and the brick comes away in her hand, and there, beneath it, is a folded piece of paper, grey with dust and grime.

Quickly, she unfolds it and reads the first words of a handwritten scrawl. *I can't stop thinking about it . . .* it begins.

Lila feels her heart begin to hammer in her chest. She thinks about the funny mural in the other room, the bullet hole downstairs, the pile of junk waiting to be burned at the top of the garden and then looks back to the piece of paper in her hand. Somebody was here. Somebody committed these words to paper and stashed them behind this stone. The goose bumps are back on her arms. She glances around, trying to rid herself of the echo of Tom's words spoken in the very same room only hours earlier: *something happened here.* She shakes her head and then, with trembling hands, she smooths out the crumpled sheet of paper and begins to read.

10

NOVEMBER

1980

> *I can't stop thinking about it. That night - that awful, bloody night. I don't want to but it's inside my head and I'm going crazy with it. Of course we were all off our heads but still - some would say that's when we become our true selves, let our real instincts take over. Why did they do it? How could they do it? I was right there!*
>
> *Everyone's acting as if nothing happened, but they all know. I see it in their eyes. Everything feels different. And worst of all is that he is acting different. He barely looks at me - barely touches me now. It's killing me. I love him. I felt sure, deep down, that he loved me too. Oh, this is agony. I can't lose him. I would rather die. I would rather*

'Kat!'

Kat slams the pen down and slides the notepad she has been scribbling on beneath the bedclothes.

'Kat, didn't you hear me calling you?' Freya stands in the doorway to their bedroom with her hands on her hips.

'What?'

'Are you coming? We're waiting for you.' Freya eyes her. 'What are you doing, anyway?'

Kat edges the paper deeper beneath the bed covers. 'Nothing. Just having a lie-in. Is that OK?'

Her sister shrugs. 'Of course. It's just we thought you wanted to collect chestnuts with us. You said last night—'

'Who else is going?'

'Carla, Ben . . . and Simon.' The faintest blush spreads across Freya's pale cheeks.

'I'll come,' says Kat quickly. 'Just let me get dressed.'

'OK.' Freya hesitates a moment.

'What? What is it?'

Freya doesn't move.

'Are you just going to stand there?'

Freya swallows. 'I'll leave you to it.'

Kat watches as her sister turns and leaves, listens to the sound of her footsteps retreating down the stairs, before falling back onto her pillow with a sigh. The notepad crackles beneath her. It's not much, but it feels good to release some of her anger, to scratch out those ugly, bitter words onto a sheet of paper, to see them there in stark black ink. It's a release, of sorts, a salve on the hot furnace of anger that burns inside her.

Ever since that stupid night when they took the mushrooms Kat has felt it gaining strength. She can't help it. In the cold light of day she knows it was madness, all of them tripping, off their heads, but she just can't get that image of Simon and Freya out of her mind. She's tried and tried to banish it but every time she thinks it's gone, it explodes like a firework, hotter, fiercer, brighter than before.

It wouldn't be so bad if Simon was acting normally, but there is a distinct shift in their relationship now. She doesn't know if it's her – her anger driving a wedge between them – or if it's him pulling away, acting more distantly towards her. It's hard to gauge and she feels as if she's second-guessing his every move, his every word, until she is crazy with suspicion and desperation. She just wants life to feel easy again.

But nothing is easy any more. It's cold. She's sick of eating pasta and rice and root vegetables. She wants to lie in a warm bath or eat buttered toast popped straight from a toaster, not half-burned offerings she has had to watch and turn on the smoking hearth. She wants to drink hot chocolate from an unchipped mug and snuggle up in front of an old movie on the television. She wants to flush a toilet, not sit shivering on that rough wooden seat in the earth closet, her eyes darting around in the gloom for spiders and beetles. She's tired and she's irritable and she wishes things would return to how they were just a few short days ago. Or better still, she wishes they could leave, that Simon would declare their little experiment over and announce that it's time to go.

More than once now, Kat has fantasised about that woman returning – the one she saw last month standing up on the ridge with her dog. She's imagined her coming over the hill with a cluster of angry villagers in tow. There would be shotguns and angry words and Kat and the others would throw up their hands, pack their belongings and drive away from the cottage, back to their old lives. Mac could drop them all in the city. They would shrug, say they'd had a good stab at it and then move on – her and Simon – to somewhere new, somewhere different. Just the two of them.

But even thoughts of abandoning their project fill her with anger. Whenever she finds herself thinking of it she gets mad; it should be Freya who leaves. Freya is the interloper, the uninvited guest. She should be the one to go; but Freya hasn't yet given voice to her plans to leave and the others seem happy enough that she is there.

'Kat!' It is Simon's voice now, loud and impatient, rising up the staircase. 'Two minutes then we're going without you.'

'Coming,' she yells and throws back the bedclothes, dressing quickly. She pauses before the mirror and grimaces. Her hair is still desperately short and sticks up at alarming angles from her head. She smooths it down as best she can then turns to leave and is almost out the door when she remembers the incriminating piece of paper still hidden beneath her sheets. She hurries back to the bed and pulls the notepad out, studies it for a moment wondering where on earth she can stash the sheet of paper where no one will find it. She should destroy it really, burn it so that no one can ever read her words – but there is no time so she rips the top sheet from the pad then moves across to the empty hearth and casts about desperately. There must be somewhere she can hide it? Not in her clothes. She and Freya are always rummaging through each other's belongings, borrowing things. But then she sees it, a darker shadow around one of the worn stone bricks next to the fireplace. She tugs at it and sure enough the entire stone comes away in her hand, leaving behind it a perfect, dusty hole set into the wall. She folds the paper hurriedly into a tiny square and presses it into the space, then places the stone back into place. Perfect, she thinks. It looks almost exactly as it had before. No one will ever find it. She'll come back to it tonight and burn it on the fire when the others are distracted.

'Kat!' Simon bellows.

She steps out of the bedroom and glides down the stairs, arranging her face into a picture of calm.

'There you are,' says Simon, turning to glare at her. 'You took your time.'

'Sorry,' she says, fixing him with her brightest smile. 'Shall we go?'

As they head out the door and down the grassy bank she falls carefully into step beside Simon, pleased to note Freya keeping her distance from them all, trailing behind with her gaze fixed upon the ground.

* * *

It had been Simon's suggestion to forage once more for sweet chestnuts but Mac had warned them that they would struggle. 'The squirrels will have had them all by now,' he'd said, 'and any left on the ground will be too damp. We got the best of them last month.'

'What's a little damp?' Simon had asked, clearly annoyed that Mac wasn't impressed by his plan. 'We can dry them out. *Chestnuts roasting on an open fire*,' he'd crooned in a bad Bing Crosby impression.

The others had laughed but Mac just shook his head. 'They go mouldy. Fine for Wilbur but no good for us.'

They'd only half believed him but as they make their way through the woods it is all too clear that Mac had been right. They wander aimlessly among the twisted trunks of towering trees and the few chestnuts they do find hidden among the wet leaf litter bear the telltale signs of deterioration. After three hours they admit defeat and return cold, hungry and empty-handed, bar a cluster of grub-infested nuts, which the piglet hoovers up hungrily from the flats of their palms. Kat's stomach twists at the sight; she is more hungry than she knew.

Unfortunately, it's becoming a common occurrence. Gone are the heady days of plucking velvety blackberries from brambles or scooping fish out of the lake. The hens' laying has grown erratic and even Mac is struggling; more often than not he returns empty-handed, no longer the lifeless body of a rabbit or a pheasant swinging over his shoulder. The countryside is pulling down its shutters for winter.

'There's only one thing for it,' Ben says, spooning out the remains of their rice later that night. 'We're going to have to start eating less, ration our supplies to get us through the winter. I think it's time to tighten our belts.'

'I've already tightened my belt two notches,' says Carla, lifting up her sweatshirt to show them her pale, flat stomach. 'This is the best diet ever; I've never been so slim.' Kat glances at Carla and notes the hollows of her once plump cheeks. She's right, she's losing her curves; she supposes they all are.

Simon nods. 'Ben's right. It'll be a long, cold winter otherwise . . . and Wilbur will be in for the chop a little sooner than we thought,' he adds, jerking his head in the direction of the pig sitting in Freya's lap.

'No, you can't,' she says, horrified.

'We've still got some savings, haven't we?' asks Kat.

'Yes, but we can't keep dipping into them. We need to hold some back for emergencies.'

Ben looks worried. 'But we need more milk powder and sugar. We're getting low on salt and flour too.'

Simon holds his hands up. 'I'm not saying we can't buy essentials. Next year we'll be far more prepared. We started too late this year.'

There are murmurs around the table.

'Look,' Simon continues, 'I know it's getting hard. I know we miss our home comforts. Personally, I would kill for a pint and a packet of salt and vinegar crisps. But let's not give up, just because it's getting a little harder. We always knew these next few months were going to be the toughest. But we've come so far. We've been here four months already. No one has kicked us out yet. Let's see it through into the new year. Come on,' he says, looking at each of them in turn, 'I'm up for it, aren't you?'

Kat glances across at Freya. Her head is bowed; she isn't looking at any of them. Maybe she will leave, thinks Kat. Maybe she's had enough too. As if sensing her gaze, Freya raises her head and meets her eye. The two sisters stare at each other for a moment.

'So who's going to make the next trip to the shop with Mac?' Simon asks, looking around at them all.

'I'll go,' says Freya, and there is the slightest tilt of her chin as she says it.

'Good. Tomorrow, then.'

Kat turns away from Freya. She can't help it; part of her hopes she will go and just not come back.

* * *

Unfortunately she does come back. She bursts through the back door with Mac, her eyes glittering with excitement, her pale cheeks a rosy pink from the cold winter air. 'You'll never guess what we found,' she says, placing two shopping bags filled with groceries onto the kitchen floor.

'What?' asks Carla, drying her hands on a tea towel.

'This.' Mac steps forwards and holds up a plump bird with reddish brown plumage and a stumpy tail.

'A red grouse,' says Simon. 'A big one too. How on earth did you catch it?'

'We didn't. It was just lying there at the side of the road,' says Mac. 'Must have been hit by a car. Freya saw it as we were driving along.' Mac throws Freya a smile. 'I reversed up the road and she jumped out and grabbed it, didn't even hesitate.'

'Yuck,' says Kat, irritated by the boys' admiring glances. 'We can't eat that. It's road kill.'

Mac shrugs. 'What does that matter? Look, it's fresh, you can tell from the colour of the blood here . . . and its eyes are still bright too. Can't have been dead more than an hour or so.'

'Well done,' says Simon to Freya, low and quiet, but Kat still hears and bristles.

'What do we do with it?' asks Carla.

'We eat it, you fools,' cries Ben. 'Haven't any of you ever tried grouse before?'

The girls shake their heads.

'Well you haven't lived.' He throws his hands out in a wide, theatrical gesture. 'Tonight we feast like kings.'

Kat slinks away, leaving Ben and Carla to the unenviable job of plucking and gutting the bird. She wants to be alone – to think and scribble in her notepad – but no sooner is she lying on her bed when she hears the creaking approach of someone ascending the staircase. She hopes it might be Simon and feels a spiralling disappointment when Freya pokes her head round the door. 'Sorry,' she says, 'did you want to be alone?'

Kat nods but Freya shuffles into the room and just stands there in her floaty silk dress and a pair of ridiculous red velvet slippers. 'I think we should talk,' she says.

Kat shrugs but she doesn't say anything. Fine, if she wants to talk, let her talk.

'I know you're angry with me. Is it – is it about the other night?'

Kat doesn't move; she hardly breathes.

'I know you like Simon. You won't say it but it's obvious – to me, to everyone.'

Kat feels her cheeks colour but still she doesn't speak.

'I just want you to know,' continues Freya, 'that whole night was crazy. I don't think you understand how . . . well . . .' She struggles with her words. 'How Simon and me . . . it wasn't something—'

'Just don't, Freya.' Hearing her speak his name is enough to enrage her. She holds up her hand. 'You've said enough. You've just admitted you knew how I felt and yet you still did it, didn't you?'

'But—'

Kat laughs. 'But *what*? You didn't sleep with him? Nice try, Freya. I was *right there* in the room with you. I saw you. So don't try to tell me that you didn't. OK?'

Freya's face flushes crimson. Kat can see tears welling in her eyes. 'It wasn't like that,' she implores.

But Kat is too angry for excuses. 'I don't want to hear it, Freya. It's time you grew up. Don't be like Mum. Don't ride roughshod over other people's lives, never taking responsibility for your actions. Don't go down that road.'

Freya stares at her, tears streaming down her face.

Kat sighs. 'Just go, will you? Leave me alone.' She turns back to her notepad and tries to ignore her sister's sobs.

'I don't want it to be like this,' says Freya, so quietly that she almost doesn't hear. 'It's not as if I can undo what happened . . . no matter how much I wish it, I can't.'

'No.'

'So can't we just go back to how things were?'

Kat shrugs. She just wants her gone.

'I'm sorry, OK? I never meant to hurt you.'

Kat lowers her gaze and is relieved when she hears the creak of Freya's footsteps leaving the room. She leans back against her pillow and sighs. From somewhere downstairs drifts the smell of frying onions. The scent makes her stomach twist. She puts her hands on her belly and registers the dull cramping sensation that has been building there all day. Her period: well that puts paid to *that* little fantasy for another month, she thinks with a grim smile.

A few hours later they all gather round the kitchen table. Ben ladles the rich game stew into their bowls and, as they sit down to eat, Simon raises his glass. 'I propose a toast – to Freya – for finding the grouse and bringing it to our table.'

'Hear, hear,' join in the others, 'to Freya.'

Kat is silent. The overpowering scent of the stew is doing strange things to her empty belly. She would dive straight in but it seems Simon has more to say. 'This just goes to prove my point,' he continues, 'that if we have faith in the land, the land will provide. This is nature's way of telling us we are in the right place. This is where we are meant to be. Who wants to go home now, hey?'

Kat waits for someone to laugh; Simon is beginning to sound more and more pompous and evangelical. But nobody does laugh, for the truth is there is something quite awe-inspiring about him seated at the head of the table, his face intense and serious, his dark eyes shining in the candlelight, the high angle of his cheekbones exaggerated in the dim glow. She watches his face and it comes to her again just how much she loves him.

He's right, she thinks; this is where she is supposed to be, sitting next to Simon, in this cottage, beside this lake. This is her family now. They just have to get to Christmas and then Freya will leave as planned and everything will return to normal. She lowers her head and reaches for her spoon and the room falls silent as they all turn to their bowls and begin to eat.

11

LILA

December

Every morning, Lila wakes to the remnants of her dreams: running down a landing, a sickening plunge, a shattering impact. It's always the same until one ice-cold morning she wakes to the haunting fragment of something else, something new, something echoing from deep within the shadows of her sleep. She's still running, she's still falling, only this time there are three distinct words tumbling down behind her into the void: *just like her.*

She lies in bed staring up at the ceiling, half of it now painted a bright white, the other half still soot-stained and grey. *Just. Like. Her.* What can they mean? As she ponders this new detail the words beat drum-like in her head. *Just. Like. Her.*

She's hot. She pushes off the covers and presses the flat of her hand to her forehead. It comes away clammy. Her pyjamas are sweat-soaked too. She swallows, registers the blade lodged deep in her throat and stifles a groan. She can't get sick, not now. Not when there is still so much to do.

She staggers off the camp bed and makes her way through the cottage to the earth closet outside where she releases a stream of pee into the dark hole in the ground. The winter air is a balm on her skin, cooling her down, but by the time she has made it back inside the cottage she is shivering uncontrollably. She fills a glass of water at the kitchen sink, takes a sip, then stares out of the window. What should she do? She had planned to paint the other half of the bedroom ceiling today, but common sense is telling her that she should light the fire and crawl back into bed for another hour or so.

A movement outside the kitchen window diverts her attention: something red-gold slinking through the dull winter landscape, sliding between the papery-white honesty seed pods. Lila watches, her eyes slowly joining the dots as the creature moves through the foliage, until she can see the outline of a fox. It stops near the collapsed frame of the rotten chicken coop and lifts its nose to the wind, puffs of its breath fogging in the air; then slowly it swings its head round towards the window. Lila doesn't breathe. Can it see her? Is it watching her? For a moment the whole world is still. It is just Lila and the fox, its ears pricked skywards and those tiny clouds of air frosting above its head. A bird startles in the tree overhead and with a flash of red, the fox darts back into the undergrowth and is gone.

Lila's brain is slow to catch up. She eyes the empty space where the fox stood just seconds ago, as if the air still holds the imprint of the animal, molecules slowly shifting and closing over the void once more. She shakes her head. She really doesn't feel good.

Back in the bedroom she notices how her breath fogs in clouds, just like the fox's. She touches the electric heater standing in the corner of the room and realises it is stone cold. She flicks the ON-OFF switch then turns the temperature dial. She unplugs and plugs it back in at the old wall socket, then kicks the broken appliance in frustration. She can't be bothered to carry firewood upstairs; nor can she be bothered to carry her camp bed downstairs to the lounge where the basket of logs stands next to the grate. Instead, she crawls back into her sleeping bag and lies on the creaking canvas, hauling the blankets over her. Just a few more minutes in bed, then she'll make tea and find some paracetamol. Lila closes her eyes against the slow drumbeat in her head and the too-bright light flooding through the window. Just a few more minutes' sleep.

* * *

When she opens her eyes next, the light outside her window has changed; it's no longer a brutal white but a strange dusky grey. Twilight or dawn, she isn't sure, but she is drenched in sweat again and shivering uncontrollably. She knows she must get up, get changed and get warm.

She creeps around the room like an old lady, pulling on tracksuit bottoms, a long-sleeved T-shirt, two sweaters and an old pair of hiking socks. She goes downstairs and gives the fire a good go. She lays kindling and firelighters and watches them catch, but she doesn't have the patience to tend it as she should; she smothers it with logs too quickly and after one smouldering effort and a nasty coughing fit she gives up and creeps back to the relative warmth of her bed. Outside, in the half-light, a lace curtain is falling over the valley. She watches it for a moment, wondering what it could be, until the curtain draws close enough for her to realise that it is snow, falling all around, cloaking the cottage and the lake in a thick veil of white. It is strangely beautiful and she finds herself thinking of Tom and wishing he were there with her.

The veil moves closer until snowflakes flurry at the windowpane, like feathers whirling through the air after a pillow fight. She watches for a while until her eyes tire and she closes them in sleep once more.

*　*　*

Delirious with fever, the night passes in a terrifying, dream-filled state, a steady stream of scenes and images spinning round the carousel of her mind. At one point her father is there; he sits beside her and smooths her brow. *You're just like her,* he says and she sits bolt upright in the darkness and calls out to him. *Like who? Who am I like?* But he simply smiles and draws his finger across his throat in a macabre gesture before disappearing like a wraith in the night.

Then it is Tom's turn. He is standing in the shallows of the lake, beckoning for her to join him. She wanders down to the lake's edge and watches him for a moment. She wants to step into the water. She wants to be with him but she knows she cannot enter the lake because she is afraid. She cannot swim. Tom holds his arms out to her, pleading with her to come to him, but there is nothing she can do. Sadly, she shakes her head then turns and walks away.

Back in the cottage she hears the shrill wail of a baby. She stops and listens, tries to place where the sound is coming from. Upstairs, she thinks, so she races to the bedroom but finds nothing but dust and cobwebs and that strange shadowy mural painted across one wall. It is some kind of trick because the crying is downstairs now, and louder. She checks the living room and then the kitchen, but it's only as she looks out the window that she sees her: a tiny baby swaddled in an oval Moses basket and a red-gold fox standing over her, sniffing. *Get away!* she cries. *Get away from her!* But the fox just turns and bares its teeth and Lila watches on helplessly as the animal snatches up the blanketed bundle in its jaws and drags it away into the woods. *No*, she cries, *no. Don't take her from me.* She can't bear it: the feeling of losing her all over again. Hot tears stream down her cheeks.

Somewhere far away, she hears boots stamping by the front door. There is a knock and a man's voice calling out, 'Hello?'

She is too tired to respond and burrows deeper into sleep.

'Hello? Lila, are you there?'

She knows she should wake but she can't open her eyes, not even when she hears the front door open and heavy footsteps moving across the floor and up the creaking staircase towards her. A shadow falls across her bed and then a rough hand is laid on her brow. 'Lila. You're burning up. Can you hear me?'

She tries to open her eyes. She tries to tell him that she's OK but everything is so jumbled and confusing and the wrong words leave her mouth. 'There's a fox,' she says. 'He's taken my baby.'

'Shhh,' says the man. 'Shhh. You're not well.'

Suddenly she is airborne, lifted like a snowflake eddying on the breeze. She is carried out into bright daylight, but it is too much and she buries her head in the man's shoulder. He holds her close and transports her over a vast, white plain, as though she's flying, a feather whirling in the cold, white air.

When Lila eventually wakes, it is to a warm weight lying across her legs and a raspy, wet tongue slobbering at her face. Alarmed, she tries to push herself up to a seated position.

'Rosie! Rosie, get down!'

Through bleary eyes she sees a black and white dog bound across the room and wheel in circles around a pair of cord-clad legs.

'Sorry about that. She gets a bit excited around strangers.' William comes into view by the open door; he has the dog by the collar now. 'We don't get too many visitors up here at the farm. Rosie's my old working dog – retired now – and I'm afraid she's thoroughly spoilt, aren't you girl?' The dog beats her tail on the floor.

As she props herself up against the bedhead Lila sees a beautiful grey cat stretch languidly at the end of the covers then, disgruntled to have lost her warm sleep spot, jump down off the bed. Lila gives a weak smile and adjusts her pillows.

'How are you feeling?' William asks, hovering in the doorway.

'I'm – I'm not sure.' She puts a hand to her temple: her skin feels cool and dry. 'Better, I think.'

'Good.' William nods. 'The fever must have broken.'

'Where am I?'

'God, sorry,' says William, looking horrified. 'You're at my farm.' He shifts his weight from foot to foot, rubs his arm. 'You must have thought I'd kidnapped you.' He swallows and can't quite meet her eye. 'You were in a bad way and I just thought it would be better – warmer – and easier too, if we needed the doctor.'

'You called a doctor?'

'Yes. You were delirious.'

'I was?'

William nods. 'A nasty case of flu. Apparently there's a lot of it going around. Doc says you'll be fine in a few days, though. You need rest and plenty of fluids.'

'How long have I been here?'

'About twenty-four hours.'

Lila stares at him. 'I've been asleep for twenty-four hours?' She shakes her head. 'I should call Tom.'

'It's OK. I rang him last night. He wanted to come straight away but the doc recommended bed rest so I told him you'd call as soon as you were awake. Now, how about a drink? A cup of tea?'

Lila nods. 'Yes please. Can I . . . where is . . . the bathroom?'

'Second door on the left, just before the stairs. I'll bring your tea up.'

'No, that's OK. I'll come down. I think I'm feeling strong enough.'

'Well don't rush. Take your time.'

'Thank you.'

William steps out the door and Lila can't help herself; she lifts the sheets and is relieved to see she is still fully clothed, still wearing tracksuit bottoms and her old university T-shirt. Well that's something, at least.

Looking around, she sees that she is lying in a single bed in the corner of an attic room with a low, sloping ceiling and a dormer window. A radiator clanks and creaks on the far wall opposite. Spread upon the floor is a colourful, knotted rug, while curtains adorned with pretty blue and green butterflies hang across the window. She pulls one back and is amazed to see the landscape stretching out before her, snow-covered fields and moorland rising up to meet the pale white sky. They must be high in the peaks because it feels as though she can see for miles and there is snow everywhere, a thick layer of it clinging to the hedgerows and bare branches of the spindly silver birch trees standing like ghosts on the horizon. Directly below the window she sees the roof of William's Land Rover and a series of farm buildings dotted around a yard, muddy boot marks stomped here and there through the snow. As she gazes out at the scene, a low wind sweeps across the ground, picking up a dusting of snowflakes and tossing them about like shreds of torn paper.

Turning her gaze back into the room she sees her mobile phone on the bedside table. She pulls up Tom's number and is relieved when he answers almost immediately.

'Lila, are you OK?'

'Hi, yes.' Her voice is croaky. '. . . I think so. I'm at William's.'

'I know. He called me from your phone last night. Are you OK? How are you feeling?'

'I . . . I don't know. I've just woken. I'm a bit shaky.'

'I want to come and get you.'

'Um . . . I – I don't know.' Her brain is still foggy. She tries to think. 'I have your car here.'

'Forget the car, I'll come up there right now. You shouldn't be there. You should be here at home.'

Lila thinks for a moment. 'There's snow. Lots of it. I don't know if my car would manage it. Don't do anything just yet. Give me an hour or two. Let me see how I'm feeling first. I'll call you again in a bit. OK?'

There is silence at the other end of the phone.

'OK?'

Tom sighs. 'I'll be waiting.'

* * *

It's a strange sensation, padding through the quiet interior of an unfamiliar house. Lila feels as though she has been dropped, like Alice, down a rabbit hole. She creeps along a carpeted landing and pushes the latch on a wooden door that she hopes is the bathroom. Behind it she finds another small room with a sloping ceiling, an old rocking chair, a knotted rug and a long wooden desk, across which is strewn a dusty array of beads and wire, pliers and cutters and other fine implements she has no idea about. Definitely *not* the bathroom.

She backs out hurriedly and tries another door, relieved to find the right room this time. She shuts the door and turns the lock then spins to look in the shaving mirror above the sink. Her face looms ghostly white – as white as the snowy landscape outside – her eyes red-rimmed and bloodshot, her hair greasy. She eyes the bath enviously and wonders if William would mind. It's been so long since she's had a proper soak in a tub.

For the time being she satisfies herself with washing her face and scrubbing at her teeth with a finger of toothpaste, before tucking her lank hair behind her ears. It feels like a tiny improvement as she heads back out onto the landing and takes the stairs carefully, one at a time, her hand on the banister, distrustful of her balance after two days lying horizontal in bed. She can see the dog – Rosie – waiting for her at the bottom and when she reaches the final step Lila reaches out to pat her. The dog's fur is warm and silky beneath her fingers. 'Hello, Rosie,' she says and the dog thumps its tail at her in greeting.

It's Rosie who leads her down the flagstone hallway towards the sounds of clinking china and rattling cutlery. She enters through a low wooden doorway and finds herself in a cheery farmhouse kitchen, warm and bright. William stands at the kitchen sink rinsing mugs. A copper kettle sits on top of the Aga, billowing steam. Lila clears her throat.

'There you are,' says William, turning around to greet her. 'Find everything you needed?'

She nods. 'Yes thank you.'

'Good.' He stares at her for just a little too long and Lila flushes pink, embarrassed at her dishevelled state and fiddles with a strand of her greasy hair. He seems to catch himself and directs his gaze to somewhere just behind her. 'Now,' he says, 'let me introduce you to Evelyn.'

Lila turns to the long oak table and notices for the first time the elderly grey-haired lady sitting in a wooden chair at the far end.

'Mum,' continues William, 'this is Lila.'

The woman beams at her. 'Hello, dear. Awake at last. I hope you're feeling a little better.'

'Hello,' says Lila. The woman's face is wrinkled like a wizened crab apple but the likeness between mother and son is still obvious; she and William share the same grey eyes and long, straight nose. There is a ginger cat in her lap and a tangle of wool and knitting needles on the table in front of her. 'Thank you, I'm feeling much better.'

The woman nods. 'Good.'

Lila stands awkwardly in the middle of the room. It seems more than a little bizarre that she is here, in a virtual stranger's kitchen. She looks about and sees the warm honey-coloured flagstones, the buttercup-coloured walls, the pretty striped curtains, the earthenware mugs hanging from hooks beneath a long shelf, checked tea towels drying on a radiator, a knitted tea cosy and a dog's bed pushed up in a corner beside the warm Aga, everything practical but homely.

'Take a seat,' says William. 'Make yourself comfortable.'

Lila pulls up one of the wooden chairs and sits opposite Evelyn. Something warm presses against her legs and she looks down to see another cat, this one black and white, weaving about her, arching its back. She reaches down and obliges by stroking its fur.

'That's Fred,' says William, carrying mugs and a teapot to the table. 'Ginger's over with Mum.' Lila smiles as Fred jumps up onto her lap, turns once, twice then settles into a warm circle. 'Hope you're not allergic? We've got a bit of a menagerie.'

'No, it's fine. I like animals.'

'Would you like something to eat . . . some toast?'

Lila shakes her head. Her throat still feels like sandpaper. 'Just tea, thank you.'

'Put some sugar in it for her,' says Evelyn, eyeing Lila carefully. 'Poor thing looks as though she could do with it.'

Lila smiles. 'I said I'd call Tom back . . . let him know when I was coming home.'

'Of course, although I hope you know there's no need to rush off,' says William, fetching teaspoons and milk. 'I was just listening to the radio and it looks as though this snow will be with us for at least another twenty-four hours. Stay as long as you need to. Get your strength up.'

'Thanks, but I really don't want to be a bother.'

Evelyn squeezes Lila's hand. 'No bother,' she says, smiling up at her with her cloudy grey eyes. 'It's nice to have the company.' Lila nods her thanks and wraps her arms around her body. 'We're just glad you came back to us, aren't we, William?'

Lila smiles weakly and shoots William an uncertain look.

He intervenes, placing the mugs onto the table before them. 'Sorry, I should explain, Mum gets a bit confused sometimes,' and then, when Evelyn has returned to her knitting he mouths at her: *dementia.*

'Oh,' says Lila. 'Oh, I'm sorry.'

William nods. 'It's hard – for her mostly,' he says in a quiet voice. 'She can get very distressed.'

Evelyn casts a stitch or two, then feeling their gaze, looks up and smiles. She holds a neat, pink square up for them to see. 'For the baby,' she explains.

'How lovely,' says Lila, and tries to smile.

William throws her another apologetic look. 'I'll pour the tea.'

* * *

Even though she protests, Lila stays with William and Evelyn for two more days. She is too weak to think about moving on before then and the truth is that there is something peaceful about the remote location and the farmhouse's easy comforts.

'I'm being a burden. You don't need me here,' she says more than once, but William just shakes his head.

'You're not going anywhere until you're a bit stronger,' he says, gruff but firm.

Tom had struggled with her decision, but when Lila had explained about the snow and reassured him that she was fine and that she would be back in London as soon as she was feeling stronger, he had relented. 'Look at it this way,' she'd added on the phone, 'I'll be able to return with your car and you'll have me home for the entire Christmas break. That's what you want, isn't it?' She'd been relieved when he'd agreed.

She passes the days curled up on William's sofa before a roaring fire, with Rosie settled at her feet and cats of varying shades taking shifts on her lap. William brings her homemade soup to eat and books to read, even a glossy magazine with photos of a celebrity wedding splashed across its cover. 'The books are mine,' he says, handing her the well-thumbed pile of Thomas Hardy novels, 'but the magazine is from Sally down at the shop. She says to say "hi" and "get well soon".' Lila takes the bath she has been craving and for the first time in a very long while, she sleeps a deep, dreamless sleep in the little bed under the eaves while the wind moans outside and rattles at the windowpanes.

'Thank you,' she says, 'for all of this,' and she wonders if she will ever be able to bring herself to leave the charm of the farmhouse and return to the cold, bleak cottage down beside the lake. Although she barely knows them, there is something easy about being in William and Evelyn's company. Watching the way he interacts with his mother, she sees a softer side to him, less gruff and awkward. Whether it's the way he settles her before the fire each night with a favourite radio show and a patchwork quilt across her legs, or how patiently he sits across from her holding his hands out to catch the wool she untangles from a pile in her lap, he surprises Lila with his tenderness.

'Mum's always loved making things,' he explains, nodding at Evelyn's knitting. 'Quilts, cushions, curtains and jewellery . . . her talents were probably wasted as a farmer's wife, although she was pretty good at that too.'

Lila can hear the pride in his voice. 'Is that what all the stuff is in that room upstairs?' she asks, thinking of the strange tools she'd stumbled upon in the tiny room, on her very first morning at the farm.

'Yes, she used to make and sell jewellery. She doesn't do it any more though. It's too fiddly with her arthritis.'

'That's a shame,' says Lila. 'Life can be so cruel, can't it?'

William nods and turns to stare into the crackling hearth.

* * *

On the third day, Lila wakes to weak sunshine filtering through the bedroom curtains and a landscape transformed once more. There are snowdrifts scattered still across the highest parts of the moors and on the roofs of William's barns and outbuildings, but much of the snow is melting, falling from the gutters in a steady drip-drip-drip, forming muddy puddles in the farmyard. The sight of the bare brown earth emerging through the white tells Lila that it's time to return to London. She joins her companions in the kitchen and asks William if he will drive her back to the cottage after breakfast. 'Of course,' he says, cracking the top of his boiled egg with a teaspoon. 'Whenever you're ready.'

'You've been so kind. I could stay another week, but I really should be getting back to London – and to Tom. Thank you, though, for everything.'

'Why don't you stay a little longer?' says Evelyn suddenly, reaching out to grip Lila's hand across the table. 'I haven't shown you my jewellery yet. Don't leave us again, not yet.'

'Now, Mum,' says William, 'Lila has to go.'

Evelyn's face is crestfallen.

'I'm sorry, I really must go home, but I will come and visit you again . . . in the new year.'

Evelyn pats her hand with her own warm one. ' Well just don't leave it so long next time. Promise?'

Lila plays along. 'I won't,' she says and smiles across at William, who nods his thanks.

He drops her on the track next to Tom's parked car, all trace of snow now gone, just the churned mud of the trail stretching away down the hillside and the rickety old gate casting a long shadow in the pale winter light.

'Thank you,' she says and she doesn't know whether to hug him or shake his hand, but in the end it's impossible to do either because he turns away from her to pat Rosie in the back seat.

'Drive safely,' he says.

'I will. Have a happy Christmas.'

'And you.'

She lets herself out of the car and squelches her way through the meadow and out along the ridge until she is back in the cottage. It is exactly as she has left it: a pair of muddy trainers by the front door, a jug of shrivelled berries on the kitchen table, a half-filled glass of water standing beside the sink. Upstairs the bedroom still sports a half-painted ceiling, tins of white paint standing on a dust sheet in one corner of the bedroom, while in the other is her camp bed, a tangle of discarded blankets cascading off the canvas sling onto the dusty floor. After the warmth and hospitality of the farm, the cottage feels very cold and very empty and Lila doesn't waste any time packing up her things, throwing a few clothes and other basics into a bag.

She's not giving up, she tells herself, she's just heading home for a little while to rest and recuperate, but for some reason she can't rid herself of the lingering feeling of failure and when it comes time for her to leave, she walks through each room, gazing around as if imprinting it onto her memory. *Something happened here.* She shakes her head. Maybe she'll never know.

12

DECEMBER

1980

Kat sits beneath a slate-grey sky at the far end of the jetty, her boots swinging in the empty space between the wooden platform and the dark surface of the lake. There is a ghostly stillness to the scene. No birds, no insects, no fish flipping on the water. Just her, and her thoughts; although she isn't so distracted by them as to be unaware of the romantic picture she paints: a young woman sitting in solitude at the edge of the lake; so when she hears the boards creak behind her she isn't wholly surprised. She plays a quick, silent game with herself. Is it Simon? Or perhaps Mac with a fishing rod? They haven't caught anything for several weeks now, but that doesn't stop him trying.

She doesn't turn, she just watches the empty space on the boards beside her, hoping for a glimpse of Simon's worn leather boots; but it isn't Simon. Or Mac. Instead she sees a pair of stripy tights and her sister's red velvet slippers appear beside her on the jetty. 'Can I join you?' she asks.

Kat shrugs. 'Sure,' she says, but they both hear the 'no' in her voice.

Freya slides down onto the boards beside her. She still wears her long white nightie, but she has added the woollen tights and slippers as well as a polo neck and heavy wool overcoat to the ensemble. On anyone else the outfit would look ridiculous but on Freya it looks like the costume of an ethereal, tragic heroine. The two sisters sit in silence, looking out over the plain of water. There is no sound but the rustling of the brown reeds and the gentle *plip-plip-plip* of water sloshing up against the rotting posts of the jetty.

'I'm going to leave.' Freya speaks with her chin buried into the neck of her jumper so that Kat has to lean to catch her words. 'At the end of the month. I'll wait until after Christmas and then go.'

Kat nods. If Freya has been hoping for an argument she isn't going to get one.

'I have a friend in London,' she continues after a while. 'I'll look her up . . . see if I can sleep on her floor for a few weeks, just until I get some work and can pay my own rent . . . before I go back to college next September.'

'OK.'

Silence falls over them. Freya clears her throat. 'I never wanted—'

'Don't,' says Kat. She can't bear it.

'But that night – can't we at least—'

Kat turns on her sharply. 'I said *don't*. I don't want to talk about it. I think it's best we just forget it.'

Freya looks down at her lap. She flushes red and there's that look on her face, the one Kat knows well, the one that means she is about to cry, but she bites her lip and visibly tries to fight the tears. 'OK,' she says, 'we'll just forget it.' For a moment it seems as if there is something else she wants to say, but it must be too hard because eventually she stands and walks away, the jetty creaking her progress all the way back to the shore until Kat is left with nothing but her solitude.

She knows it's the best they can hope for right now: an uneasy truce until Freya finally leaves. She'd like to reach out to her sister and tell her it's OK, that it's been forgotten – forgiven, but the truth is it hasn't. She still feels speared by her sister's betrayal. It hurts like a blade lodged in her heart because for so many years she's been the one to look out for her, to protect her and care for her, but now it feels as though Freya has pushed all of that to one side and turned around and stabbed her in the back. And for what? A stupid fling? No. No matter how many times she's tried to tell herself it doesn't matter, that it was just a silly mistake, it always comes back to that one night, that one image of Freya and Simon – together. It's time Freya grew up. It's time she understood that there are consequences to her actions and that some situations can't be made better with a simple fluttering of her big blue eyes and a half-hearted apology. Some situations require time . . . and distance. Yes, she thinks, it is best that Freya leaves the cottage. As soon as possible.

Kat bends down over the jetty and watches the water for a while. It lies deep and still before her and in its clear surface she sees the reflection of her own pale face, a gaunt version of herself, her eyes almost black and sunken into deep sockets. She barely recognises herself. She is translucent and hollowed-out, like an empty husk.

When it gets too cold, she returns to the cottage, making a stop at the chicken coop to check for eggs. The pig is there too, snuffling and scratching at the ground where the chickens have spilled their grain. She reaches in and nudges the warm birds out of the way but there is nothing to collect – again – so she returns to the cottage with Wilbur trotting along at her heels. It's only as she steps through the back door and into the kitchen that she realises she has walked into a full-blown row. Carla stands with her hands on her hips, her frizzy auburn hair standing in an untamed halo about her head and a furious scowl on her face. To Kat, she looks like a wild banshee woman. 'I told you we had to space them out. They need air to circulate around them. This box is completely spoiled. Look!' Carla shakes a cardboard box of crab apples in Ben's face. 'Ruined.'

'Calm down, will you? I don't know why you're going on at me. You never told me we had to store them in a particular way.'

'Yes I did.'

'No, you didn't. Anyway, if it was so important, why didn't you do it yourself?'

'I would have but you never let anyone else get a look in. You run this kitchen like it's your own private domain. Don't you think I might like to cook something once in a while? Or Kat might like to?' Kat ducks her head at the mention of her name. 'Or what about Mac or Freya?' Carla continues.

'You know what,' says Ben, hurling a tea towel at the sink, 'be my guest. I didn't ask to be your personal chef. I'd like to see the rest of you try to find anything better in that bloody pantry.'

Like a protective parent, Kat scoops up the pig and carries him into the lounge where Simon lies sprawled on a beanbag before the fire, a cracked paperback in his hands. 'Here,' he says, seemingly oblivious to the argument drifting from the kitchen, 'listen to this: "The mass of men lead lives of quiet desperation".' He glances up at her with a meaningful look but she just stares back at him, her face blank. 'OK. How about this bit.' He flicks forwards through the pages. 'Here it is: "Rather than love, than money, than fame, give me truth. I sat at a table where were rich food and wine in abundance, and obsequious attendance, but sincerity and truth were not; and I went away hungry from the inhospitable board."'

'What is that?' Kat asks, settling the pig beside the fire before perching opposite Simon on the edge of the sofa.

'*Walden*. Written by Henry David Thoreau in the 1850s. Now there was a man ahead of his time.'

She nods and picks at the threads of stuffing bursting from the armrest. 'So you're saying it's OK we're all hungry because we're living a life of sincerity and truth?'

Simon shakes his head, visibly irritated. 'That's not what *I'm* saying, it's what this guy's saying. Thoreau.' He shakes the book. 'But you have to admit, it strikes a chord, no?'

Kat nods and turns her head towards the kitchen from where another round of angry shouts explodes. 'Do you think we should intervene?' she asks, watching the piglet stretch out its trotters and then close its eyes to sleep.

Simon shakes his head. 'Let them have it out. It's been brewing between them for days. Probably do them good to let off a bit of steam.'

'It sounds like we've got more food issues,' she says. 'Apples this time.' She studies his face looking for traces of concern.

'Oh yeah?' he says but his attention is back in his book.

'Yeah,' says Kat. She doesn't need to mention the potatoes or the sack of flour that have already spoiled. They are all aware of their dwindling supplies. She hesitates then decides she has nothing to lose. 'I'm worried, Simon. I think everyone's sick of living off nuts and rice. Morale's pretty low, don't you think?'

Simon sighs and puts the book down onto the floor beside him. 'You worry too much, Kat, you know that?'

'But everyone's so hungry.' It comes out like a whine and Kat sees the irritation flash across his face.

'What would you have me do, Kat? Magic up a fat goose and an enormous trifle for your consumption? I didn't *force* anyone to come and live here. Everyone understood the reality. If we're struggling now it's because we didn't work hard enough a few months ago. We'll learn. There's nothing more motivating than the ache of hunger in your belly, is there? Anyway,' he adds, 'it's not as if I'm keeping anyone here. Go and join the rest of the world in their "lives of quiet desperation". Hell, go and stuff your faces with TV dinners and takeaways for all I care.'

Kat blushes. She has never heard Simon speak so harshly towards her and instantly regrets being the one to raise the problem with him.

'WELL IT'S A BIT LATE FOR THAT NOW, DON'T YOU THINK?' yells Ben, his words echoing around the cottage.

Kat sighs. Simon can deny it all he likes, but morale *is* low. In the last few days everyone's tempers have frayed and the hunger isn't helping. Last night they barely uttered a word as they sat at the kitchen table chasing baked beans around their plates and with Christmas just a couple of weeks away she knows their thoughts will have turned towards the home comforts and family traditions they are missing out on.

The volume in the kitchen drops. Kat hears conciliatory murmurs followed by the sound of quiet sobbing. Simon gives her a knowing look. 'See,' he says, 'told you they just needed to have it out with each other.'

* * *

He must have been listening to her though, because it is Simon who suggests another store-run to the group later that evening. 'Go,' he says, 'get a change of scene, why not. We can stock up for Christmas.'

The five of them gape at him. 'What?' he asks, all innocence. 'We are going to celebrate, aren't we?'

Carla smiles. 'Will you come, Kat? There's room in the car for one more.' but Kat shakes her head. She would like to go; she would like to wander around the aisles of a supermarket, to run her hands across the myriad packets of food and marvel at the vast extravagance of it all, but if Simon doesn't want to go then she won't either. As much as she would like to re-enter the outside world, she knows she would rather spend the time with him, alone.

They leave the next morning and Kat watches them go, four loping silhouettes heading up over the ridge and out towards the trees. Carla and Ben seem to have forgotten their row; Ben's arm is slung across Carla's shoulders, her hand jammed into the back pocket of his jeans. The sight of them, connected at the shoulders and hips, reminds Kat of the paper chain dolls she used to make when she was a kid. Mac and Freya follow slightly behind. She sees Mac say something to Freya and her sister toss her long blond hair and laugh up into the sky. Mac watches her for a moment then grins, his pale face transformed by the smile. It surprises her. Mac isn't usually one for jokes.

As soon as they have disappeared from view, she turns back to Simon. 'I have an idea,' she says.

'Oh yes?'

'Fancy a walk?'

He nods. 'OK, but where?'

'I'll show you. Come on. We'll need the axe.'

She leads him out of the cottage and down to the wooded area beside the lake. As they enter the dusky glade she summons her courage and takes him by the hand; it feels warm and solid in her own and she squeezes it tightly and is glad when he doesn't pull away. They thread their way through the spindly trunks of alders and silver birch trees until eventually they arrive at her intended destination. 'Look, there,' she says, pointing into the dense undergrowth.

Simon doesn't see it at first, but when he does he smiles. 'A Christmas tree?'

Kat nods and smiles. It is a solitary pine, standing at least six feet high with its generous branches tapering to a tall point. 'Is it too big? Do you think we could get it back to the cottage?'

Simon nods. 'Easy.' He turns to look at her then. 'Well if this doesn't cheer them up I don't know what will.'

She smiles and it feels like the most natural thing in the world to take a step towards him and press her lips against his. She tries not to think about Freya, tries not to think about the two of them together. She banishes the image by pressing the length of her body against his, chest-to-chest, hip-to-hip, showing him her full desire. He takes it and reciprocates with his own body before seizing her hands and moving her backwards, one step then another until she can feel the rough bark of a thick tree trunk at her back. He lowers his head and kisses the bare skin at her neck, runs his hands down her body and undoes the buttons on her jeans. Kat closes her eyes and lets the sensation of him overwhelm all other thought or feeling.

* * *

When Simon eventually pulls away he pushes his hair out of his face and smiles down at her, his gaze not quite meeting her eyes. 'I suppose we should get cracking if we're going to get this tree back in time to surprise the others.' He turns away and buttons his fly and she nods and tries not to feel disappointed that it is all over so quickly. It happened, after all. In some small way she feels as if she has reclaimed him, made him hers and it's a relief to know that he still wants her.

Simon retrieves the axe from where they've left it lying on the forest floor and begins to hack at the trunk of the pine tree. Kat watches, admiring his strength, the easy way he swings the blade through the air and takes the full impact as it connects with the wood, bark chips flying like sparks around him. Within minutes the tree comes crashing down and they pull it back through the undergrowth and into the cottage where it fills the space before the front window, its spiny apex bending slightly where it grazes the ceiling. Kat breathes in its fresh, pine scent and feels a surge of happiness. 'They're going to love it,' she says, seeing it standing there just as she'd imagined.

* * *

The others don't arrive back until late, long after the sun has slunk below the hills and the cottage is wrapped in a cloak of darkness. 'It's the most awful thing,' exclaims Carla, bursting through the door first, her cheeks flushed and her eyes red-rimmed as though she's been crying. 'John Lennon's been shot.'

Kat gapes at her. 'Is he . . . is he dead?'

Freya, standing behind Carla in the doorway, nods.

'I just can't believe it,' says Carla.

'That's . . . God . . . that's awful.' Kat swallows and then Carla does start to cry, tears streaming down her face. Kat moves across the room to hug her and is enveloped in a heady haze of alcohol.

'I just . . . it doesn't . . .' She turns her face up to Kat's. 'Why would someone *do* that?' Carla moans.

'It was some lunatic,' says Ben. 'It's in all the papers and they're playing "Imagine" over and over on the radio.' He shakes his head. 'I still can't believe we didn't know.'

'One of the blessings of being so removed, I guess,' says Simon. He sinks onto the arm of the sofa. 'Man, the modern world is *so* fucked up.'

Mac arrives through the door and places several shopping bags down on the floor. 'Nice tree,' he says, eyeing the pine standing in the corner of the room.

Kat nods. 'We found it in the woods. I thought we could all decorate it, you know, make it feel a little more festive around here.' She shrugs. There is nothing festive about the atmosphere at that moment, just sadness and a strange, lingering tension.

Simon turns to Mac. 'You've been gone ages. What took you so long?'

But Mac doesn't answer. Ben does and Kat gets the sense it has already been decided he will tackle the thorny question. 'The girls were pretty upset. You know . . . it's been a real shock. We thought a stiff drink was in order.' He tilts his chin slightly and holds Simon's gaze.

'You've been to the pub?'

Ben nods. 'Yeah, is that a problem?'

Simon eyes him. 'Hope you didn't spend *all* our money?'

Freya moves across to the grocery bags and starts to unpack things. 'No, look, we got lots.' She holds up a bag of oranges, a box of cherry Bakewells, peanuts, dates, potatoes, carrots, Brussels sprouts and three bottles of cheap-looking wine.

'What on earth is that?' asks Simon, poking the last item to emerge from the shopping bags . . . a long plastic-wrapped object. He peers down at it. 'Turkey roll? What the hell? I've never seen a turkey that shape before.'

'It was cheap,' says Freya. 'We were *trying* to save money.'

'And that's why you went to the pub is it? Money-saving?'

They at least have the decency to look a little ashamed. Kat studies the results of the shopping trip and knows their haul won't last them long, no more than a few days at best. She sighs and sidles across to Simon. 'Well you're back now,' she smooths, trying to banish the atmosphere from the room. 'Who wants to help decorate the tree?'

* * *

In the end, it doesn't matter about the meagre Christmas supplies or the covert pub trip or even the revolting-looking turkey roll. In the end they get something much better. It's waiting for them on the doorstep, early on Christmas Day morning. Ben discovers it as soon as he steps outside and his yelp of joy rings out across the valley, bringing the others racing downstairs. 'So it looks as though Santa found us last night,' he says, holding a giant, plucked turkey aloft in his hands.

'What the hell . . . where did *that* come from?' asks Carla.

'It was right here, on the doorstep. Look.' He points to the large wicker basket laden with fresh vegetables, homemade mince pies, a bottle of brandy, a small urn of cream and a white ceramic bowl wrapped in a cheery checked cloth which Kat knows can only be Christmas pudding. 'Someone has delivered us a feast.'

Simon steps outside in his bare feet and glances around. 'Who is it from? Is there a note?'

Ben shakes his head. 'Who knows? Who cares? Whoever they are, they obviously like us.' He throws back his shaggy head and howls, 'Thank you,' to the sky.

Carla beams and hugs Mac. Freya is on her hands and knees, rummaging through the goodies. She holds up a box of chocolate Matchsticks, the smile spreading across her face. 'Yum.'

Only Kat and Simon seem worried by the anonymous donation. Its arrival at their doorstep means that someone knows they are there. No, not only knows they are there, but has crept up to their back door and left it for them to discover on Christmas morning. It's hardly the most sinister of gestures, but it makes Kat nervous, all the same. Who knows they are here? She thinks of the woman on the ridge, the one she saw all those weeks ago. Could she have returned with this gift for them? It seems unlikely after all this time, but what's the alternative? That someone out there is watching them?

'Come on,' says Ben, scooping up the basket, 'let's not stand here getting cold. We've got a Christmas meal to prepare.'

Kat looks out across the horizon, her eyes searching the ridge and peering into the line of trees for evidence of anyone watching from the shadows. When she turns back to the cottage she sees Simon's equally worried look. She can tell he doesn't like it either, but it's also clear that none of them are prepared to turn down a free meal, not on Christmas Day.

* * *

It's something akin to a Christmas miracle: all the sniping and the grumbling and the bitching forgotten in just a few hours. How simple, thinks Kat, how easy to turn their spirits around; all it takes is one basket of food and they are all smiles and joviality and efficiency. Carla and Kat peel the vegetables while Ben stands at the kitchen sink wrangling with the turkey. Simon and Mac fetch the wood and pile it up by the range before Simon takes up Ben's guitar and serenades them all with Christmas carols from the bench nearest the window. Ben and Carla break into a boisterous duet of 'While Shepherds Washed Their Socks By Night' and, as they sing, Kat thinks about how it suddenly feels as it did at the beginning, when they first moved to the cottage and were filled with the thrill of freedom and possibility. Only Freya seems to set herself apart from the group. She busies herself out in the garden, feeding the chickens and then wandering the grassy slopes behind the cottage while the pig trots loyally at her heels.

'What's she doing?' asks Carla, glancing out the window as she scrubs the dirt off a creamy-white potato.

Kat shrugs. 'Beats me.'

Carla pauses to watch her for a moment. 'She looks like a Christmas angel out there with all that long blond hair streaming behind her in the breeze.'

Kat thinks of her own shaggy haircut, now growing out over her ears and swallows back the jealous lump in her throat. 'She must be cold in that nightie and cardigan. Silly girl.'

Carla smiles. 'Sometimes you sound more like her mum than her sister.'

Kat frowns. 'She can be so dreamy . . . so childish . . . someone has to look out for her.'

'Isn't it funny how that pig follows her around like that? They're quite the pair, aren't they?' Carla continues. 'You're lucky too, you know, having a sister. I always wanted one.'

'Yes,' says Kat drily, 'I'm lucky.' She wonders whether she should tell Carla about Freya's plan to leave, but Carla has already moved away to watch Ben wrestle with the turkey giblets so Kat stays at the window, scrubbing the potatoes, watching Freya as she drifts about the garden.

Simon is singing again, softly crooning the lyrics to one of her favourite Christmas carols.

Snow had fallen, snow on snow, snow on snow, in the bleak midwinter, long ago.

Kat hums along as she watches Freya. She does look like an angel, so pale and waiflike. Her face is almost the same milk colour as her nightdress but there are high spots of colour on the apples of her cheeks and her hair shines a lustrous gold in the pale light. Kat sees the scissors in her sister's hand and watches as she reaches out to one of the shrubs. She cuts a stem of red berries from a bush while a disgruntled redwing hops from bough to bough in the tree above, upset to see his winter store depleted. Then she bends and pulls something else from the ground: shimmering seed heads of honesty, no longer green but transformed to opaque-white tracing paper, as round and pale as tiny moons.

Angels and archangels may have gathered there, cherubim and seraphim thronged the air.

As Simon's words wrap themselves around her, another gust of wind shivers its way across the garden and rattles the window frames of the cottage. Kat looks out to see Freya pull her cardigan tight across her body.

But his mother only, in her maiden bliss, worshipped the beloved with a kiss.

'This bird's going to need a good few hours in the oven,' Ben says from somewhere behind her, but Kat isn't listening any more, not even to Simon's low crooning. Instead, she is transfixed by the sight of Freya, the strange shape of her; the gentle slope of her belly now visible beneath the taut fabric of her cardigan. Kat peers through the glass and wonders if she is seeing things. It's not possible, surely? Her sister is rake thin, her arms and legs pale and skinny like the spindly silver birch branches outside. She shakes her head and looks again; but there it is, the rounding of her stomach, a slight swelling which she knows for certain wasn't there a couple of months ago and has no right to be there now. None of them have put on any weight since they arrived at the cottage – the exact opposite, in fact. Dread grips her.

Kat watches as Freya makes her way down through the garden. She appears at the back door moments later with sprays of berries and the shimmering honesty lying across her arms in a delicate bouquet.

'Brrrr,' she says, stamping her feet, 'it's freezing out there. Look what I found. I thought they would make nice decorations. The honesty can go in our bedroom. The berries are for the living room.'

'Very festive,' says Carla, but Kat can't find any words.

'What?' asks Freya. 'What's wrong? You look awful.'

But Kat just shakes her head and turns on her heel.

* * *

Kat still doesn't have an appetite by the time it comes to sit down and eat but she chews carefully on her roast dinner and joins in with the clinking of glasses as they toast the chef and their mysterious benefactor with the first bottle of sloe gin, opened with ceremony by a proud Mac. The afternoon shadows have drawn in around them and Freya has lit candles, the flickering light catching on their glass tumblers and making their eyes shine like the lush berries now hanging over the mantelpiece.

'Told you it was good, didn't I?' says Mac with a wide, sloe-stained grin.

They drink the syrupy gin and Kat watches as Freya joins in, knocking back a glass of the stuff, laughing at something Ben says. She tries to concentrate on the meal and the conversation but she can't help herself; every so often she steals sideways glances at Freya across the table, wondering if she could have got it wrong – if her eyes had in fact deceived her. But she knows she is right. She knows what she saw.

After dinner, half drunk and full of good cheer, they retreat to the living room for a game of charades. Kat tries to join in but after weeks of such a plain diet the rich food is too much. Making her excuses she leaves the others to their game and moves into the kitchen where she props open the back door, allowing a draught of cold air to wash over her. She takes a few deep breaths and tries to rid herself of the churning feeling in her belly. It is pitch black outside but as her eyes adjust to the night she notices pale shapes falling from the sky and settling in a delicate grey blanket where the light spills from the open doorway across the ground.

'It's snowing,' says Freya quietly.

Kat hasn't heard her enter the room. She glances round at her sister then returns to gaze to the darkness outside.

'Isn't it beautiful?'

Kat swallows back her anger but Freya, oblivious to Kat's inner turmoil, reaches for her hand.

She sighs softly. 'So lovely . . . a white Christmas,' and she raises her glass to her lips and drinks deeply.

Kat can't help herself. She snatches her hand away and turns to Freya with eyes blazing. 'Do you really think you should be doing that?'

'Doing what?' asks Freya, startled by the tone of her sister's voice.

'Drinking.'

'What's wrong? It's Christmas, isn't it? Since when were you so square?' She puts her hand to her mouth. 'Oh, sorry . . . if you're thinking about Mum . . . about her drinking and stuff, you don't—'

'No,' says Kat, 'this isn't about *Mum* . . . it's about *you*. I would have thought . . . in your condition . . .' Kat stares meaningfully at Freya's belly then raises her eyes in defiance. Freya can pretend all she likes but Kat won't stand there and be lied to.

'What do you mean, "in my condition"?' Freya stares at Kat in confusion, and then, like sand trickling through a timer, Kat watches as confusion shifts to self-doubt, and doubt shifts once more, her sister's eyes widening now with a growing and terrifying understanding. Freya's hands dart to her belly, her mouth opens in a small 'o' and suddenly Kat realises something else, something astounding. *Freya didn't know.* She had no idea that she is pregnant.

Poor, dumb Freya, thinks Kat. She would laugh if it didn't hurt so much.

13

LILA

January

The Christmas tree is still up. It leans like a tired drunk against the bay window, spilling pine needles all over the cream carpet. The sight of its sad, brown-tinged branches and drooping decorations is immensely depressing and yet Lila still can't summon the energy to take it down. She knows it's bad luck to leave it there but the thought of packing away all those baubles, the tinsel, unthreading the ribbons of tangled lights and dragging the tree out into the garden all just feels too much. Even so, as she stands at the mirror over the fireplace applying her make-up, she feels its reproachful gaze out of the corner of her eye. Tomorrow, she thinks, brushing mascara onto her lashes, she'll take it down tomorrow. Today there are other things to face.

Lila takes a step back and studies her reflection. It's strange seeing herself in make-up again. She's still pale from her bout of flu and it doesn't sit quite right on her skin – too obvious, too artificial. She squints through critical eyes then rubs the blusher and lipstick off with a tissue. No need to make the war paint quite so obvious. She reaches for her pills and swallows two down quickly. Just for luck.

It was her mother's idea to meet for lunch. She'd pitched it as a *girls' day out* – a chance for a little mother–daughter bonding before she returned to France, but Lila knows all too well that it's another clumsy attempt for her to check up on her daughter and after sharing such a gloomy Christmas day with her, she hadn't felt able to say no.

For once, the public transport system seems to be on her side. A bus driver spots her racing down the pavement and waits at the stop. 'Thank you,' she gasps, swiping her card. The man gives her a wink and closes the doors behind her. Lila stumbles to the back of the bus and slides into an empty seat, her lungs burning with the effort of her run. She rests her handbag on her lap – the new one her mother has given her for Christmas – and turns to the window, watching the bustle of the city pass outside.

They slide past a Turkish greengrocer, a Halal meat shop and a colourful Italian deli. Above a railway bridge hangs a huge advertising hoarding urging passing commuters to *FIND PARADISE*. A taxi blares its horn at a pack of laughing kids scampering across the road. A group of men gesticulate outside a betting shop while a scruffy black dog, tied to a lamp-post, barks encouragement at them. As the bus pulls in to the next stop, Lila averts her gaze from a heavily pregnant woman waddling up the steps and concentrates instead on two lads with matching facial hair, black skinny jeans and Wayfarer sunglasses. They slouch onto the bus and slide into the seat in front of Lila's, both of them hunched over their mobile phones, tapping furiously at the tiny keyboards. Somewhere far away a siren shrieks. A baby cries. The city is an endless grey but everywhere she looks humanity springs, bold and colourful, like flowers rising up through asphalt cracks, stretching out towards the space and the light.

It's what she's always loved about London – the pace, the life; but as she watches her hometown drift past the window, she finds her mind turning in on itself and drifting back to the tranquillity of the lake. It is such a contrast, the valley a place impervious to the rise and fall of the economy, a place relatively unscathed by time. Indeed, the only forces the lake submits to are the shifting of the seasons and the wind racing down from the moors, or the shoreline adjusting with the varying sunshine and rainfall – influences as inevitable as they are natural.

As she ponders the lake, her mind meanders on to William and Evelyn. She thinks of their simple life on the farm; the pleasure derived from feeding livestock or walking a dog, making a bracelet or knitting a blanket. It's strange: she's always thought of London as a city pulsing with life and energy, a place where everything is tangible and real; but as she looks around at the frenzy, she wonders if *this* is the illusion. Could it be the cottage and its valley, the wide-open moors and the glassy eye of the lake that are most real to her now? Looking around at the concrete city towering all around her, Lila is suddenly overwhelmed by the sensation that it is nothing more than a flimsy set that could come crumbling down around her at any moment. She looks up into the small patch of grey above and forces herself to breathe.

* * *

They've arranged to meet in the bar of a chic boutique hotel located just off Regent Street. Lila enters via a revolving door and is directed by the concierge through the lobby and into an elegant room decked out with stylish armchairs, gleaming chrome surfaces and flamboyant wallpaper. There is no sign of her mother, so she perches on a bar stool and eyes the drinks menu.

Lila hasn't seen her mother since Christmas Day and she is feeling nervous. The day hadn't gone well. She and Tom had driven out to her old family home in Buckinghamshire – to the Gothic mansion belonging to her parents and set within the exclusive cul-de-sac in the commuter-belt village. There they had attempted to make it a special day, despite the dusty, boarded-up air of the house after weeks of standing empty and the grief lingering over them all.

They'd visited her father's grave, laying white lilies beside the polished headstone, before returning to the house to warm up with red wine and a roast dinner far too big for just the three of them. She'd tried, but Lila hadn't been able to snap out of her doldrums. Even the Christmas carols playing on the radio as Lila had peeled potatoes in her mother's kitchen had lost their cheerful, nostalgic sheen. Somehow, to her ear, they had sounded sad and gloomy. Lila had gazed out at the blank grey sky – an overcast nothingness. *In the bleak midwinter*: she couldn't have put it better herself.

'The turkey is delicious.' Tom had smiled across at her mother but it seemed that the empty seat at the head of the dining table was too stark a reminder.

'Don't cry, Mum,' Lila had tried gently. 'It's Christmas, after all. He wouldn't want you to be sad.'

Her mother had nodded and held her napkin to her lips. 'I know. I'm sorry. It's just so hard. This year has been so difficult and here we are now, the first Christmas without him . . . and without . . . without your beautiful baby.' She'd sniffed and gazed down into her wine glass.

Lila had reached across for her mother's hand. She looked so shrunken in on herself. Christmas was always difficult for her mother, she knew that much. It always seemed to bring out a morose side of her.

'Why does Mum get so sad at Christmas?' she'd asked her father once, as he tucked her in on Christmas Eve. 'Isn't it supposed to be a happy day?'

He'd nodded and looked a little downcast. 'Christmas does that to some people . . . it's full of memories . . . it can make them feel quite lonely.'

'But Mum doesn't have to feel lonely – she has us,' Lila had offered.

'Yes,' her dad had smiled and smoothed her fringe off her forehead, 'she has us.'

Although Lila can see now that her mother never really quite *had* her father, not all to herself. Even on Christmas Day, after the carols were sung and the turkey eaten, the pudding flambéed in brandy and the chocolates opened, her father would retreat, either to drink himself into a stupor in his study, or to conduct intense, hushed phone conversations with whichever woman was keeping him busy at the time. She and her mother would sit up in front of the television, Lila watching a stream of saccharine Christmas programmes while her mother just stared unseeing out of the window, lost in her own private thoughts. No, Christmas had never been a particularly jolly affair in her family home.

But if her father had been the ghost of Christmas past hanging over the day this year, then the ghost of Christmas yet to come was there too – in the looming absence of their baby girl. Not since her due date had come and gone had she felt her loss more keenly than on that day. Her mistake, she knew, had been daring to imagine it while still pregnant and blooming with hope. As her baby had grown inside her, she'd jumped ahead in her mind and imagined her and Tom and their little girl building their own family's Christmas traditions and memories. So on that day with her mother, while none of them hardly dared address the absence, it was obvious to them all that she should have been there, a four-month-old baby girl, bouncing on their laps, grinning and gurgling. There should have been colourful presents to open, toys and baby clothes to coo over and everyone softened by the presence of a new life and the hope that came with it.

Instead, everything felt wrong – the whole day steeped in grief and sadness, both for her father and her daughter. To cope, Lila had knocked back too many pills with a large glass of wine and then continued to drink steadily as the day wore on. It was only as she'd stumbled and spilled red wine all over her mother's pale grey carpet that they'd realised quite how much she'd had to drink. 'I think I should take you home,' Tom had said as dusk crept over the house. He'd guided her gently out to the car and driven her back to London, her head pressed against the cool glass of the window all the way. 'Promise me something,' he'd asked, reaching out to stroke her thigh with his warm hand. 'Promise me you won't go back to the cottage – not until we've sorted this out.'

She'd nodded, but she hadn't turned her head because she hadn't wanted him to see the tears in her eyes. He'd carried her upstairs, pushed aside the expensive silk underwear still lying in its pink tissue paper at the end of the bed where she'd unwrapped it earlier that morning and tried to lay her down. 'Sh-shall I try it on now?' she'd slurred, winding her arms around his neck. 'I'll put it on for you.'

'Try it in the morning,' he'd said gently.

'Oh come on, make love to me,' she'd taunted. 'Go on.'

He'd held her close for a moment, one thumb stroking the smooth curve of her collarbone and she'd seen the heat flare in his eyes.

'Make me *feel* something,' she'd urged and she'd seen it then in his face – desire but something else too: a mingling of confusion and pain. Gently, he'd untangled her arms from around his neck, undressed her and pulled the covers up over her naked body. Her tears had fallen silently, as he'd turned off the light and left her there in the darkness; both of them under the same roof and yet still so far apart.

* * *

She sees her mother winding her way through the armchairs of the hotel bar, chic as ever in a camel coat and knee-length leather boots, her hair freshly styled at the salon. 'You look nice,' Lila compliments.

'Thank you.' They kiss each other on both cheeks.

'Doesn't look like I'm the only one to think so either,' nudges Lila, tossing her head in the direction of a grey-haired man seated a few tables away whose eyes are fixed firmly on her mother.

She blushes. 'Don't be silly.'

'I'm not. He's definitely checking you out.'

The colour deepens in her mother's cheeks. 'Oh stop it.'

Lila smirks. 'What are you drinking?'

'I'll have a glass of white wine . . . Semillon, if they have it. You?'

Lila studies the list of drinks in front of her. The prices are eye-wateringly expensive and the memory of her Boxing Day hangover still lingers. Besides, she took those two pills not so long ago. 'I'll just have a sparkling water, I think.'

Her mother's head swings towards her and, too late, Lila realises her mistake. 'Oh Lila, are you—?'

'No,' says Lila quickly, cutting her off. 'I'm not pregnant, no.'

'Oh.' Her mother's face falls. 'Well I'm sure it won't be long.'

Lila doesn't reply. She doesn't feel any desire to share the sparse details of her love life.

The barman appears with a deferential flourish. 'Ladies?'

Her mother orders a glass of wine from the list and at the last minute Lila changes her mind and orders a vodka and tonic. 'Might as well, right?' she says a little too brightly.

'So how are you?' her mother asks.

'I'm OK.'

'You're over your nasty bug?'

'Yes.'

'Not working too hard?'

Lila shakes her head. She wonders for a moment whether to tell her about the cottage but her mother has already moved the conversation on again.

'And everything's all right between you and Tom?'

She eyes her carefully. 'Yes.'

'Are you sure? It's just . . . at Christmas you both seemed a little . . . well, after what you've both been through it would be perfectly understandable if—'

'We're fine, thank you.' Lila cuts her off. She can't bear the thought of marriage guidance advice from her mother, but she doesn't seem to take the hint.

'You know, marriage is a long and rocky road, Lila. It's important you spend the time reconnecting when things get harder between you . . .'

Lila takes a gulp of her vodka and feels it burn all the way down the back of her throat. She takes another big swig and then tunes back into her mother's words.

'. . . there's no shame in admitting when things aren't going so well and even talking to someone – a professional – if necessary.'

Lila takes another large gulp of her drink and decides she can't take much more of her mother's pseudo-counselling. Words that have sat burning on the tip of her tongue for months tumble out in a rush. 'Didn't you ever get sick of the pretence?' she blurts. 'Didn't you ever think of leaving Dad?'

Her mother's eyes narrow. 'Why would I have done that?'

'Come off it, Mum. He was my dad and I loved him, but I lived in that house too. I wasn't blind. I knew what he was up to. All those nights he didn't come home. The phone calls he took in his study. He even flirted with my violin teacher, Ms Wade. Do you remember her? I'd stand there on her doorstep with my violin case bashing against my legs, feeling like a spare part. He was an out and out womaniser.'

'That's enough,' says her mother sharply. 'I don't like hearing you speak of your father that way.'

'But why not, Mum? Don't you think it's time we spoke the truth to each other? Laid it all out there?'

Her mother shakes her head. 'Do we really have to go here again, Lila?'

'*Again?*' Lila stares at her mother. 'As far as I'm aware we've never once discussed Dad's infidelity, have we? It's never once been acknowledged. We all carefully and politely tiptoed around it.'

Her mother's cheeks flush red. She reaches for her wine glass and twirls the stem between her fingers. 'No, of course, what I meant is I had this out with him a long time ago. It was between us. I'd rather not revisit it all with you. Not now.' She reaches into her handbag and pulls out a tissue. She blows her nose and then busies herself with the clasp of the bag. Lila is surprised; her mother seems so flustered.

'I'm just trying to understand,' Lila says more gently. 'If you really want to know the truth, I'm angry with him.'

'You're *angry* with your father?' Her mother looks astonished.

'Yes. I'll never get a chance to say this to his face now, but I *am* angry. I think he was selfish . . . and cruel to you. I don't think he made you happy.'

Her mother stares for a moment then shakes her head. 'You think I was a victim?' She gives a small smile and shakes her head. 'You don't understand. Your father made difficult choices – for you . . . and for me. He gave up so much to give us the life we had – more than you will ever know.'

Lila shakes her head in frustration. 'So tell me about it. Help me to understand.'

Her mother eyes her. 'You know he was a man of principle.' Lila raises her eyebrows but her mother ignores her. 'And he was very charismatic, very persuasive. That's why he made such a good lawyer.' Lila sees the softening in her mother's face. 'He believed life should be lived a certain way . . . he didn't believe in handouts. He believed in hard work and the rewards that came with it. He didn't give up on things easily . . . and he hated compromise.'

'You mean he was stubborn as a mule,' adds Lila with a dry laugh.

'Not all the time. When you were born we didn't have very much of anything. It almost killed him having to take a job in your grandfather's firm.'

'Is that why things were always so tense between him and Granddad?'

Her mother sighs. 'You're young, Lila. Life doesn't always go the way you plan it. You work hard, you fight for what you want – what you think is important – but sometimes the life you hoped for can still escape you.'

Lila stares at her mother, confused. Who is her mother talking about – herself? Her father? Lila? Because she's wrong; she understands better than most about having hope snatched away.

The words from her dream come back to her in a rush: *just like her*. Lila looks across at her mother, hunched over her wine, twirling the stem of the glass back and forth. She sees then that she is probably more like her mother than even she knows, both of them united and paralysed in their grief. Is that what her dreams are trying to tell her? She reaches across the shiny chrome bar and takes her mother's cool hand in her own, tries not to watch as her mother's tears splash down onto the silver surface between them, then hands her a tissue and waits for them to pass.

When her mother has regained her composure, Lila looks around the room, searching for distraction. Her eyes fall upon the grey-haired man dining alone in the corner once more. 'He's still staring at you,' she whispers, trying to lighten the sombre mood that has swept over them both. 'Do you want me to go and give him your phone number?'

Her mother manages a half laugh, half sob. 'Why would you do that?' she asks.

'Because you're still young, Mum . . . still attractive. You don't have to be on your own.'

Her mother shakes her head. 'No one will ever replace your father, Lila.' She twists her glass again between her fingers. 'He was one of a kind.'

Lila takes a large swig of her vodka. 'Well he certainly was that.'

* * *

They eat lunch in a small French bistro nearby. It is quiet and the waiter is too attentive, his hovering presence preventing them from returning to the emotional subjects raised earlier and by the time the bill has arrived Lila has already decided that she will claim a headache and cry-off from their shopping trip. 'You don't mind, do you? We can meet again another time. When you're next over?'

'Of course I don't mind,' says her mother lightly, turning her cheek for Lila to kiss. 'You must look after yourself. You're still so pale.'

Lila nods. 'Bye, Mum.'

She leaves her at the tube station and wanders down through the crush of shoppers swarming along Oxford Street, elbows and bags filled with January sale bargains jostling her on her way. She submits herself to the flow like a leaf caught in the current of a fast-moving stream, until eventually she spills out onto Tottenham Court Road where the crowds thin slightly. The LED display at the bus stop says she still has eleven minutes to wait so she distracts herself with a nearby shop window crammed with home wares. There are large Moroccan bowls painted in bright clashing colours, patterned rugs and a scattering of colourful cushions. Two indigo cushions in a striking ikat fabric catch her eye; she imagines them nestled on a white-painted window seat up at the cottage and in a moment of sheer impulse dashes into the store to buy them.

She holds the cushions on her lap all the way home on the bus. Just thinking of them propped in the window of the cottage brings the valley and the lake back to mind. She's promised Tom that she won't return to the Peak District until things are better between them, but she feels the pull of the place now; it's there inside her, as if an invisible cord stretches all the way out to connect her to it. Even though she knows it will be cold and desolate, that the warmth and colour of spring is still a long way off and that the place echoes with the shadows of its former inhabitants, she yearns to be back in the valley, working on the cottage or walking out across the emptiness of the moors, the huge sky swallowing her up until she is nothing more than an insignificant dot on the barren landscape.

Lila sighs and shifts in her seat. She gazes out at a boarded-up shop . . . a car being towed . . . a little girl in a pink bobble hat pedalling furiously on a tricycle . . . and as the bus wends its way through the creeping traffic, Lila knows that she won't be able to keep her promise to Tom.

14

JANUARY

1981

Kat and Mac sit huddled inside the beached rowing boat beneath a heap of old blankets. A thin layer of ice lies like glass upon the shallows. Further out the water rests as flat and still as a pond and the same pale grey colour as the sky overhead. It is cold. Kat is wrapped in an old coat with a scarf wound all the way up to her ears, while Mac wears a hat pulled down so low all that's visible between the brim and the blanket he shivers beneath is the thin gleam of his eyes and the occasional puff of his breath. Kat's eyes are fixed on the centre of the lake where two Whooper swans skim slowly across the water. As she watches them her stomach gives a low growl. 'What do you think they would taste like?' she asks, her eyes never leaving the lake.

Mac follows her gaze out to the birds. 'I don't know . . . chicken?'

'Or maybe duck?' She thinks for a moment. 'There's got to be a fair bit of meat on them. How do you think we'd catch one?'

'Are you serious?' Mac looks at her in astonishment.

'We'd have to wait for one to come closer to the shore,' she continues. 'Then we could grab it.' Kat watches the birds as they drift across the grey lake. She imagines her hands around a long white neck, squeezing and twisting, the ruffling of feathers and the sharp crack of bones snapping beneath her fingers.

'They can be very aggressive. I wouldn't want to get too close.'

'Yes,' she says, 'a gun would be better.'

Mac pushes his hat up slightly with a wry smile. 'You do know it's against the law to kill a swan, don't you? They're protected. They belong to the Queen . . . or something.'

'Fuck the law. Fuck the Queen,' says Kat.

Mac stares at Kat, his face half concern and half amusement. 'Are you OK?'

'No, I'm not OK. I'm bloody starving.'

Mac thinks for a moment. 'We could kill one of the chickens.'

'No. They might start laying again soon and we'll need the eggs. They're our only reliable source of protein.' Kat cups her hands around her mouth and breathes into them. She thinks for a moment. 'There's always Wilbur. He's bigger now.'

'Do *you* want to have that conversation with Freya?'

Kat shrugs. 'I doubt Freya will be here much longer.'

'What?'

She feels Mac's head snap up to look at her again but she doesn't return his stare, she just keeps her eyes fixed on the lake. 'Yeah, she says she wants to go back to London.'

Mac continues to stare. 'Oh,' is all he says, eventually. It's just one flat syllable but she can hear the confusion and disappointment in his voice, like a child opening the wrong gift at Christmas.

'Christ, not you too?'

'What?'

Kat shakes her head. 'You like her.'

Mac swallows. 'Course I like her. We all do.' He turns to stare out over the water.

'No,' says Kat, 'you *really* like her.'

He doesn't say anything for a long time and as they sit in silence on the shingle Kat wonders whether to tell him about the baby. A spiteful part of her would like to burst his romantic bubble. In the end though, it's Mac who speaks. 'Do *you* want her to go?'

She keeps her gaze fixed on the lake. 'I think Freya should do what she's got to do.'

Mac sighs and shakes his head. 'Why leave now though? Spring isn't so far away. She hasn't seen this place at its best.'

Kat shrugs but doesn't say anything.

'You should be nicer to her, you know,' he says quietly. 'It's not her fault.'

'What's not her fault?' She eyes him carefully now but Mac can't hold her gaze.

'You know,' he mumbles. 'Simon. The way he acts.'

The way he acts. So Mac has noticed it too; Simon's gaze following Freya around the cottage, the too-familiar way he brushes his hand against hers or squeezes a shoulder as she passes by. Kat turns back to the lake to hide the blood rising in her cheeks.

'You could stick up for her more,' he continues, then shakes his head, clenches his fists. 'No, you know what, *we* should stand up to *him* more.'

The swans are drifting away now, their elegant forms vanishing behind a thin veil of mist, nothing but a trace of silver wake fanning out behind them on the lake. 'I don't know what you're talking about,' Kat says and watches as the ripples flatten and fade on the surface of the water.

They wander back up to the cottage, Mac holding out his hand to help Kat across the slippery mud of the bank, before they both grab a couple of logs from the woodpile by the back door and enter the warmth of the kitchen. They are greeted by the sound of a terrible, hacking cough. It spirals down the staircase and echoes around the cottage. Kat catches Carla's worried glance. 'No better?'

Carla shakes her head.

'Did you talk to Simon?'

'Not yet.'

Kat sees the anxiety written all over her face. 'Let's do it together, now.'

'Really?' Carla looks relieved.

'Yes. How long's he been like this?'

'Over a week.'

Kat nods. 'Come on.'

She leads her through the kitchen into the other room where a fire crackles in the hearth. Simon lounges before it, his long legs stretched out so that his socks almost touch the warm grate. He is whittling thin branches of saplings into sharp spikes with a penknife, a smouldering cigarette balanced in the ashtray beside him, a long column of ash wilting precariously. Kat looks around and is relieved to see he is alone. 'Ben's really sick,' she says.

'I know. I can hear, poor bugger.'

'We think he needs to see a doctor.' She looks across to Carla who nods. 'He might need antibiotics.'

'It sounds like the cough has moved to his chest,' Carla chips in.

'Who says we need a doctor?' says Simon with a small smile. 'You both seem very capable with your medical diagnoses.'

'But we'll need a prescription,' continues Kat calmly.

Simon sighs and stretches his arms up to the ceiling, rolling his shoulders. 'We've got aspirin and those rosehips are full of vitamin C. We have honey too. Have you tried making a herbal tea?'

Carla wrings her hands. 'Yes. And steam inhalations too but nothing seems to help.'

Simon shrugs and slices another piece of bark off the stick in his hand. 'Ben's a big boy. I'm sure he can fight it. Our matron at school used to tell us we relied on antibiotics too readily. If you can get rid of the infection on your own, your immune system will be that much stronger the next time. Cold baths and fresh air, that's what she used to prescribe us . . . and we've got both of those in abundance here.'

Carla refuses to be put off. 'But listen to him, Simon. He sounds terrible. I'm worried. He's really sick. He hasn't eaten anything for a couple of days now, and he's barely drinking.' She shakes her head. 'He could get dehydrated . . . pneumonia. I really think he should see a doctor.'

Simon's hands fall still, the blade of the knife held against a thin curl of bark hanging from the stick. 'So what would you have us do, Carla? Drive him to the local GP? Register his name and address with them?'

Carla shrinks at Simon's tone, but she holds her ground. 'I think you're being a little paranoid. A local doctor isn't going to care where he's living. Besides, we could make something up, pretend we're just passing through.'

'Sure we could, but I'm afraid it's not that simple. We have to think about the cost too. Our money is a finite resource now. We need to keep it back for emergencies.'

'But it's just a prescription . . . a few pills. It would hardly cost anything.' She looks at him, amazed.

'Come on,' cajoles Kat, trying to talk him round, 'Ben's really ill. This might be one of those emergencies.'

Simon shakes his head. 'Ben's a big boy. He'll be OK. He'll be up on his feet, strumming his guitar and annoying us with his lame Jimi Hendrix renditions before you know it.'

Carla eyes him. 'So if I used a little money . . . if I took him on my own . . . would you stop me?'

Kat sees a steely glint enter Simon's eyes, hard and cold like flint. She remembers Mac's words down at the water's edge: *We should stand up to him more.*

'Would it really hurt if we just—' she tries to intervene but Simon holds up his hand to cut her off, the blade of the knife glittering like a flame in the light cast by the fire.

'Enough,' he says. 'I've given you both my answer. Let's wait another twenty-four hours and see if he can pull through by himself.'

Carla stares from Simon to Kat then turns on her heel and stalks from the room.

'Simon,' Kat begins, 'I really think—'

'Not now,' says Simon with a world-weary sigh. 'Why don't you go and calm her down?' He throws her a conciliatory look. 'You know, make her see sense. You're good at that.'

Kat wants to argue with him but the words won't come.

'Have you seen Freya?' he continues, casually.

'No.' She can't quite meet his eye. Always bloody Freya.

He shakes his head. 'She could help out a little more round the place, don't you think?'

Kat nods dumbly.

'She's odd, isn't she, your sister?' He says it with a thin smile.

'Yes,' says Kat. She is torn. A small part of her feels as though she should defend Freya, but deep down she is pleased to hear the displeasure in Simon's voice. Kat has noticed Freya's growing absence, of course she has, but frankly she doesn't care where her sister goes. She's just grateful to have her out from under Simon's feet, grateful not to see her moping about the house, or sneaking outside to the pit toilet, green-faced with nausea. They haven't talked properly since Christmas Day – just polite exchanges about the logistics of the jobs to be done around the cottage – but the new year has come and gone and Kat is *still* waiting for Freya to announce her departure. If she doesn't go soon the others might start to get suspicious.

'Well, see what you can do with Carla, will you?' Simon continues. 'I don't know,' he rolls his eyes, 'all these over-wrought women about the place . . . this is supposed to be a bit of fun.' He glances up at her. 'Maybe we should all just pack up and go our separate ways?' He shakes his head and returns to the stick in his hand and Kat, feeling the panic lurch in her guts, nods and leaves the room.

She finds Carla at the kitchen sink, muttering over a pan of water. She spins at the sound of Kat's footsteps. 'Who does he think he is?' she asks. 'Who made him lord and master of us all? I don't remember taking a vote.'

'I know.' Kat shifts uncomfortably beside the table, wondering how to placate her. 'But you know what it's like, we all fall into our roles, don't we? Simon's a natural leader. We certainly thanked him for it at the beginning, didn't we, when things were easier?'

Carla slams the pan against the sink, sending water sloshing to the floor. 'It's not even as if it's about the money, is it? It's about Simon wielding his power.'

Kat shakes her head. 'Let's trust him. Things will be better again before long. Ben will get well and it will be spring soon. I think we should trust him.'

Carla turns to face her. 'Which role do you fall into then?' she asks, eyeing Kat carefully.

'Pardon?'

'Which role are you playing? Kingmaker?'

'Don't be like that. I'm just trying to help.'

Carla sighs. 'Sorry. I'm just sick of it all. This place. The cold. The lack of food. It's all too hard. If Ben wasn't so ill I'd be tempted to throw in the towel right now and go home.'

'I know,' says Kat gently, 'but we're doing the hard yards now. It will get easier again. Remember how it was last summer? Swimming in the lake . . . picking blackberries . . . drinking beer . . . all of us hanging out, having fun?'

Carla slumps back against the sink.

'Let's try another steam inhalation,' Kat suggests gently. 'If he's not any better in twenty-four hours we'll take it up with Simon again. Or we'll just take the money and do it anyway. OK?'

Kat really hopes it won't come to that and is relieved when Carla nods, pulls herself up again and moves to place the pan of water on the range. Morale is slipping so low she knows the last thing any of them need is a full-blown argument; it could be enough to fracture the group once and for all. 'You'll see,' she says, in a voice more reassuring than she feels, 'everything's going to be fine.'

Carla nods once more and they don't speak of it again, but later that night, while the rest of them sleep, Kat creeps out of bed and down the stairs, heading into the kitchen and to the shelf where she knows Simon keeps the money. She reaches into the old tin canister and pulls out a wad of notes. In the light of a thin crescent moon she counts them out at the table, relieved to see that there is over one hundred and fifty pounds left; more than enough to help Ben . . . more than enough to see them through the winter. She sits back on the bench and looks at the money spread across the table. Simon wants her to play the peacemaker, to smooth things over? Well, maybe they will all have to make a little sacrifice, for the sake of the group. She sits there for a while, mulling over the options, and by the time she returns to bed, her footsteps feel a little lighter upon the floorboards.

* * *

Kat wakes Freya early, before any of the others have stirred. 'Freya,' she says, shaking her gently, 'Freya, wake up.'

Freya mumbles incoherently and rolls away beneath the covers. 'Come on,' she says, 'budge up, it's cold.'

Reluctantly, Freya shifts across to make room for Kat. 'What are you doing?' she mumbles. 'What time is it?'

'Still early.'

'God, your feet are freezing.' She scoots up closer to the wall, her back still turned to Kat.

'Shush,' says Kat, 'don't wake the others.'

Dawn hovers on the horizon. Its pale light filters through the thin rose-covered curtains and stretches in a triangle across the ceiling. 'Do you remember how we used to do this?' Freya murmurs from under the covers. 'You hated that top bunk.'

Kat can't help smiling. It's been years since they lay like this in the same bed but somehow it feels familiar, two warm bodies lying on a skinny mattress, the slow rise and fall of their breathing. 'I didn't hate it,' she says. 'I just said that so that you wouldn't feel so bad about being afraid. I always climbed back up the ladder as soon as you were asleep.'

'Oh.'

Silence settles over them both as they remember.

'It was hard, wasn't it, those first months, with Margaret and Peter . . . in their home,' says Freya quietly.

'Yes.' There is no need for either of them to say anything else. Freya has put her finger on it with those two simple words: *their home*. A neat little terrace with double-glazed windows and a trimmed square of grass out the back; it couldn't have been further from the chaos of the life they'd been removed from. They'd been well cared for by the Brownings; warm baths and healthy packed lunches, fruit in the bowl and freshly pressed school uniforms. Their shoes had always fitted and not once did either Margaret or Peter raise a hand to them or steal their pocket money for booze and cigarettes. Suddenly all the things that marked the dysfunction and chaos of life with their own parents – the mornings when their mum hadn't been able to get out of bed or had lain on the sofa in her own vomit, or the evenings her dad had walked out, disappearing for days on end – had vanished, to be replaced by a cooler, cleaner, more sterile kind of parenting.

The Brownings were a wholesome couple, big on self-improvement and philanthropy. *Charity begins at home* was an expression they used a lot, yet it always made Kat squirm because it had seemed to prove that rather than being taken on by a desire to create a family, they saw the sisters as projects, two disadvantaged girls they could offer up to the world as symbols of their own benevolence. She'd heard Margaret talking about them at their late-night dinner parties, Kat seated at the top of the stairs in a freshly starched nightie, as she'd talked about social responsibility in that bleeding hearts voice of hers. She'd heard Margaret's self-congratulatory tone and known then that they were little more than symbols, a way for the Brownings to measure their worth against the rest of society.

But for all their flaws, they were responsible and steady and they were kind to the girls. Sure, Margaret would have rather ironed a basket-load of washing than had a conversation with Kat about the boys she liked or the confusing things happening to her body through puberty; and the day Kat had summoned the courage to tell Peter about the mean girls bullying her at school Peter had just crouched down on one knee so that their faces were level and told her: *Don't come to me with a problem, my girl, come to me with a solution*. It was one of his favourite sayings. Kat understood; he wanted them to be independent, to learn to stand up for themselves, but what he didn't get was that they were already independent, that they'd had to be on the days their parents couldn't rouse themselves from bed or the nights when they didn't come home at all. If they'd sat an exam to test them on some accepted code of parenting, the Brownings would have passed with a steady B-, but she supposed it was better than the resounding 'fail' her biological parents would have received.

In the end it was inevitable that Kat had played the mother figure to her younger sister and to a certain extent she'd enjoyed it. She'd been happy to be the one Freya ran to when she grazed a knee or got her first period; it was fun to be the one taken into her confidence about first crushes, the one Freya had wanted to celebrate her exam results with . . . enjoy her first legal drink with. Back then, she would have done anything to protect or help her little sister. So what's changed, Kat wonders? Why does she find herself lying there on the mattress in the still-warm indentation of her sister's body, feeling so full of rage and resentment?

Simon.

It all boils down to Simon. Kat has finally opened her heart to someone, finally trusted herself to fall in love and Freya has swooped in and stolen him away. She could have put up with many things from Freya, but sleeping with Simon is the worst thing she could have done. Freya could have had anyone. Why did it have to be him?

Her sister is still lying with her back to her, but she can tell from the rhythm of her breathing and the slight tension in her body that she is properly awake now. She swallows and realises she's going to have to speak. 'What are you going to do?' she asks at last, breaking the silence. 'You can't ignore it, you know. It's not going to just go away.'

Freya sighs and rolls onto her back. 'I wish it would.'

Kat sees the single tear sliding down her sister's pale face. It drops onto the pillow between them, hitting the fabric with a faint thud. 'That night. It was early October . . . you're over three months along.' Kat has worked it all out in her head.

'Don't you think I know that?' Freya asks, turning to her at last.

'So what are you going to do?'

'What *can* I do?'

'You could leave. Get an abortion. Get rid of . . . it.' Neither of them wants to use the word *baby*.

It makes sense in Kat's head, but Freya just gives a bitter laugh. 'Yeah? And where would I go?' She shakes her head. 'I've got no money. No home. I can't go back to college in this state and it's not as if I can return to Margaret and Peter either. Imagine.'

Kat does imagine; she sees the shame blooming on Margaret's cheeks and Peter's cold, hard stare. *Don't come to me with a problem, come with a solution.* Freya is right. There is no way she can go there.

'And I know *you* don't want me here.'

Kat remains silent.

'Face it,' says Freya, 'I'm out of options.'

'What if I could get you the money . . . you know, so you could go somewhere nice, a private clinic . . . just enough to pay for the procedure and to help you get back on your feet again afterwards? Enough for transport, a few weeks' food and rent?'

'And where would you get that kind of money from?'

Kat swallows. 'The tin.'

Freya goes quiet for a moment. 'But that money belongs to everyone. What would you guys live off? We're barely scraping by as it is. What would the others say?' She hesitates. 'What would Simon say?'

Kat shrugs. 'We'd manage. We'd have to. Besides, by the time anyone has noticed, you'd be long gone. I'd take the blame.'

Freya studies her for a moment. 'You'd do that for me?'

No, she wants to answer. I wouldn't do it for you, not this time. She'd be doing it for her and Simon; to return things to the way they were just a few short months ago, before Freya ever arrived at the cottage. 'Yes,' she says, convinced at last about what she's offering, 'I'd do it . . . on one condition though: if you promise me you'll go . . . and never come back. If you promise me you'll leave Simon alone.'

Freya's gaze snaps back to Kat's. There is a fire in her eyes but her words, when they come, are like ice. 'Me leave *him* alone?'

Kat nods.

'You think *I* seduced *him*?' In the pale morning light, Kat sees her sister's eyes blaze. 'You think *I* stole him from you?'

Kat swallows. 'I understand. Believe me, I understand better than most. He's a charismatic guy. I saw the effect he had on girls at university when he turned his spotlight on them. Honestly, I don't blame you for getting swept up in that.'

'You don't *blame* me?' Freya is wide-eyed with incredulity and shock. She shakes her head. 'Kat, I didn't seduce him.' She swallows and looks up to the empty space above their heads. 'He *raped* me.'

Kat stares into Freya's perfect blue eyes. She waits for them to crinkle with amusement, for that smile to creep across her pretty china doll face. *Got you!* But Freya's eyes stay fixed and still, staring at the ceiling. 'Come off it,' she begins, 'I really don't think—'

'Don't!' says Freya. 'Don't tell me I'm wrong. Don't take *his* side.'

'Freya, I'm not taking sides. I just think you're wide of the mark here. That night was crazy. We were all off our heads. But saying Simon *raped* you? Come on. We'd all seen the way you'd been flirting and flitting around him.'

'What? I was being friendly. Trying to make your friends like me. To accept me. I was no different with Simon than I was with Ben . . . or Mac.'

'So you were flirting with them all? Throwing yourself at them like some cheap tart? Simon . . . Mac . . . Ben too, eh? When Carla wasn't around?'

'What are you talking about?' Freya looks genuinely confused.

'Don't play the innocent. You knew what you were doing . . . flicking your long blond hair, fluttering your big blue eyes. You just couldn't help yourself. You knew how I felt about Simon and yet you still went ahead and slept with him.' Kat is struggling to keep her voice to an angry whisper. 'You took him from me.'

'I took him from you? Oh yes,' Freya gives a bitter laugh, 'I lay down, passed out on the floor, off my head with mushrooms and spliffs and beer and just *stole* him away.' She hisses the words at her. 'Kat, I'm sorry to burst your bubble but none of this is about you. This is about Simon. About his power trip. He's loving lording it over everyone here. Don't you see that?'

Kat shakes her head. 'Just for once in your life, Freya, would you not play the victim?'

'But I *am* the victim. He took advantage of me that night. I came round and there he was—' Freya bites her lip. 'It was horrible.'

'Is that right?' Kat shakes her head. 'Well excuse me if I just can't quite believe you when you seem so happy to stay here . . . to spend your time with someone so forceful, so manipulative.' She gives a low, bitter laugh. 'You with your flirting and your fawning over him.'

'Is that what you see?' Freya shakes her head. 'God, Kat, open your eyes. Why do you think I leave the room or move away, whenever he comes near? Why do you think I spend so much time out of the cottage now? I can't stand it. He's always watching me, touching and pawing at me.' Freya lowers her voice to a low whisper. 'He's not a nice man. I really think – I think he could be dangerous.'

Kat bursts out laughing, a high-pitched sound that makes her clap her hand over her mouth as soon as it is released into the room. Dangerous? Simon? No. Freya is just lashing out. She's in denial, can't face the truth of the situation she has got herself into. 'Why don't you leave then? If it's so awful here, just go. Take the money I'm offering you. There's your way out.'

Freya glances about the room. 'There is – there is another complication.'

Kat raises an eyebrow.

'Mac.'

'What about him?'

'I can't be sure . . . it was such a strange night . . . I don't think we, you know. But everything is so mixed up in my head.' She turns to Kat, spots of colour burning on her cheeks. 'It might have been him. The baby could be his.'

'Well there you go then,' says Kat with relief. 'Of course you can't be sure. That's exactly what I was saying. We were all out of it. You slept with Mac. You slept with Simon. You don't even know who the father is.' Kat can't hide the disgust in her voice. 'Freya, trust me, just take the money. Go. Get an abortion. Get on with your life. It's your best option.'

'But I need you to believe me.' Freya looks close to tears. 'I need you to know that I wouldn't do that to you, Kat.'

Kat studies her sister's face. She can't believe her. She won't, because if Freya wouldn't do that to her, it means her story about

Simon is true, and she knows in her heart he would never do that. Not to Freya. Not to her sister. Kat turns to study the vacant space above their heads. The silence that hangs over them is her answer.

'OK,' says Freya, finally. 'I'll go. Get me the money and I'll leave. Right away.'

Kat nods. 'Fine.'

They lie there beside each other a moment longer, but the camaraderie of earlier has dissipated. There is no sisterly feeling any more, just the cold light of day creeping through the curtains and a bitter taste burning at the back of Kat's throat. Rape? She won't believe it of Simon. She just won't.

* * *

Kat is agitated for most of the morning. Rain splatters on the windows and everyone is stuck inside the house, bored and fidgety. Freya stays huddled upstairs on her bed and the biggest excitement of the morning comes when Ben croaks hoarsely down the stairs that the roof has started leaking, sending Kat and Simon scurrying upstairs with an array of plastic bags and saucepans in a vain attempt to stem the flow. It really is the worst kind of day.

After another measly lunch, Simon and Mac sit together on beanbags, playing chess while Carla flits about the house, up and down the stairs, carrying hot drinks and blankets to Ben. They can all hear his coughing but it sounds different, somehow looser, easier. Simon, more than once, throws Kat an *I-told-you-so* look. For Kat, though, the day is torture. She sits curled by the window re-reading a well-thumbed copy of *Pride and Prejudice*, her eyes glazing over the same few paragraphs, her attention drifting frequently to the kitchen doorway. She thinks of the money in the tin and of Freya's whispered promise to leave if she steals it for her, and knows she will have to pick her moment carefully.

'Checkmate,' says Simon at last, breaking the silence of the room. He topples Mac's king over and it falls onto the chequerboard with a loud clunk.

Mac gives a small nod. 'You win . . . again.'

'Come on,' Simon says, stretching like a cat. 'I've had enough of this.'

'You want to go out in this weather?' Mac asks, incredulous.

'What's the problem? Scared of a little rain?'

'No . . . it's just . . . well, where are we going?'

'Get your coat. I'll tell you on the way.'

Mac raises an eyebrow at Kat but she just shakes her head; she doesn't know what Simon's up to, but she watches with relief as they gather their boots and coats and minutes later step out into the blustery day. It will be easier now, with them gone.

She waits for a minute or two, wanting to be certain they have gone, watching the rain streak across the windows and obscure the lake completely from view, until eventually Carla appears on the stairs with an empty tray in her hands. 'Is Freya OK?' she asks. 'She's been in bed all day.'

'Yep, I think so,' says Kat, turning from the window. 'Probably just got her period.'

Carla looks worried. 'I hope she's not coming down with Ben's bug.'

'Mmmm,' murmurs Kat. 'He sounds a bit better.'

'Yes,' agrees Carla, but she won't meet her eye and Kat knows she's still angry with her for taking Simon's side.

Carla heads for the kitchen. Kat hears her clattering around, then the slam of the back door as she heads outside to use the toilet. She thinks of the money and seizes her chance.

It's quiet in the kitchen. As she tiptoes across to the shelves she justifies what she's doing. With Freya gone things can carry on as before, as if she'd never even been there in the first place. They'll find other ways to raise money. They could sell eggs, or vegetables in the spring, when things begin to grow again. Yes, she thinks, get rid of Freya and everything will return to how it was before.

She is just reaching for the tin when the sound of footsteps behind her makes her start. 'Oh!' she exclaims, jumping around, one hand to her heart, to see Ben standing in the doorway in his bobble hat and pyjamas with a blanket draped across his shoulders, his face pale beneath his wild, ginger beard. 'You made me jump.'

'I can see that,' he says, shuffling into the kitchen. 'Are you OK?'

'Yes,' says Kat, flustered, 'although shouldn't I be asking *you* that? What are you doing out of bed?'

'Water,' he says, shaking his empty glass at her.

'Here, give it to me.' She takes the glass from his outstretched hand, fills it and returns it to him, watching him down the contents in several large gulps.

'Steady on,' she says and waits, hoping he will take himself back upstairs but instead he pulls out a chair and slumps at the kitchen table.

'I'm so sick of lying up there staring at the ceiling. There's only so many times you can count the cobwebs or read back issues of *Melody Maker*. I wish we had a few more books. Or some music. Anything.'

She smiles and waits, thinking of the tin on the shelf behind her. 'Want some aspirin?'

'No thanks, Carla has been force-feeding them to me. I swear if you shook me I'd rattle.' He runs his hands across his straggly beard. 'I feel like a piece of crap.'

'You don't look much better,' admits Kat.

'Probably don't smell too good either,' he grins.

'Want a cup of tea?' she relents, and when he nods she knows the money will have to wait a little longer.

'None of that rosehip shit though. Just give me a proper brew.'

Kat nods. 'Coming right up.'

* * *

A little later the rain stops. Freya ventures downstairs – still in her nightdress – and curls into a ball on the sofa by the window, as if trying to make herself as small as possible. Soon after that Simon and Mac return with a vigorous stamping of boots and flapping of raincoats outside the door. They all turn in anticipation, waiting. Simon bursts in first, his cheeks ruddy from the cold and a devilish grin across his face. Kat has been hoping for groceries – perhaps fresh vegetables, some meat, or even an illicit bar of chocolate – but there aren't any shopping bags. What she sees instead, displayed proudly in Simon's outstretched hands, makes her suddenly and inexplicably afraid.

'The hunters return,' he crows.

Out of the corner of her eye, Kat sees Freya recoil, turning her face to the window.

'Where on earth did you get that?' croaks Ben.

'Oh, hello, mate. You're up. How are you feeling? Better?' Simon gives Carla a knowing wink but she just throws him a filthy look in return.

'Awful. What is that?'

'Mac and I went to see a man. About a gun.' He waves the rifle around the room like a trophy. 'It's a .22. Isn't she a beauty?'

'Careful,' says Carla, flinching. 'Is it loaded?'

'It's OK,' says Mac, stepping out from Simon's shadow, 'the safety's on.'

Ben is fumbling with a roll-up and reaching for a lighter when Carla turns on him. 'Don't you dare,' she says, pulling the dangling cigarette from his lips. 'Honestly, you've got a chest infection. Smoking is the worst thing you could do right now.' She sighs and shakes her head. 'You boys . . . you're no better than little kids.' She spins back to Simon. 'So where did you get the money from?'

'The savings.' Simon's voice carries an airy nonchalance but Kat notices how he can't quite make eye contact with Carla.

'Nice,' says Carla. 'So we've got enough money for guns and cigarettes, but not for medicine? I didn't realise that's the kind of place this was.' Simon just shrugs but Carla won't let it lie. 'It looks expensive. Shouldn't we have voted on it or something?'

Simon shrugs again. 'I was right about the doctor, wasn't I? He's up and about.' He turns to Ben. 'You're feeling better, aren't you, mate?' Ben gives an obliging nod, followed by a hacking great cough. 'Besides, this little beauty,' he shakes the gun again, 'will pay for itself.'

'And just how do you figure that?'

'We've been struggling to bring in enough food. Now we can hunt our own meat. Deer. Pheasant. Ducks. They're all out there; we just haven't been able to catch them – until now. We'll have food . . . a better diet. It will stop the rest of us getting sick. Prevention is better than cure.'

Kat thinks of her conversation with Mac about the swan and wonders if this was his idea but somehow she can tell from his face that it wasn't.

Simon beams around at them all. 'God, I thought you'd all be pleased.'

No one says anything. 'Suit yourselves. Mope around in here if you want but I'm going outside to get some shooting practice in. Feel free to join me.' When the door slams shut, it sounds like a bullet being fired out across the lake.

* * *

In the end, the lure of something new and different is too much for them to resist. All of them, bar Freya, traipse out into the faltering light and watch as Simon, Mac and Ben take it in turns to aim at random targets. An old wooden crate. A moss-covered stump at the end of the jetty. A discarded beer bottle now filled with rainwater. They miss every time and no one seems to worry about the whip-crack noise of the shots echoing out around the valley. Carla rolls her eyes at Kat. 'Boys and their toys.' Kat nods and, sensing her chance, slips back inside the house.

Freya is still sitting by the window. She turns to Kat as she enters the room and it's there in her face, an *I-told-you-so* look that makes Kat's blood boil. 'We have to feed ourselves,' she says, but she quickens her pace into the kitchen anyway and notices the slight tremble of her hands as she reaches for the tin. There is a nagging worry at the back of her mind and it won't go until she has checked the kitty.

She can see instantly that there isn't enough but she still counts it out anyway, her hands trembling as she handles the notes. Twenty.

Thirty. Forty. Fifty Just over fifty pounds left after Simon's latest shopping spree. It's hardly enough to get them through the last few weeks of winter, let alone to offer Freya an escape.

Another shot rings out, this time followed almost immediately by the sound of splintering glass. Everyone cheers.

Kat shakes her head. Fifty pounds. Surely no way near enough to get Freya safely away from the cottage and set up somewhere else? She stands and stares at the money, willing it to magically multiply before her eyes, to offer her a solution. She is so tired. She is so fed up with worrying about her sister, with trying to solve her problems. With a sigh, she neatly folds the remaining notes back into a wad and returns them to the tin, placing it carefully back into the dusty imprint marking its place on the shelf.

When she turns around she is startled to see Simon standing at the back door, the rifle resting in the crook of his arm. Dusk hangs over the hills behind him, and the muted light throws his shadow into the room, pointing like a finger of accusation towards her. 'What are you doing?' he asks, his eyes glittering just a little too brightly in the dim light.

'Nothing.'

'Checking up?'

'No.' She blushes. 'I – I was just interested to know how much you'd spent on the gun. Is that a problem?'

Simon shakes his head. 'The money belongs to all of us, doesn't it?'

'Yes,' she says. 'Yes, it does.'

They face off against each other for a moment and Kat sees the stubborn, little-boy tilt of his chin, the way his hair – now long and shaggy – curls beyond the nape of his neck.

'Carla's still got the hump,' he says at last, breaking the silence.

'She's just worried about Ben.'

'And Freya? She's in a foul mood too.'

Kat shrugs her shoulders but she can't meet his gaze.

They stand there in silence for a moment longer until, finally, he opens his arms to her. 'Come here,' he says and she can't help it. She moves across the room, into his embrace, the cold metal of the gun pressing against her shoulder blade. He smooths her hair with his free hand then kisses the top of her head. 'My Kat,' he says. 'My reliable Kat. Everyone else is so damn emotional, so unpredictable. You know you're the only one I can count on, don't you?'

For just a moment she leans into his embrace, breathes his warm scent, allows him to support her. Then gently, he spins her around, so that her back is against his chest, his arms still around her as he lifts the rifle and wraps one of her hands around the butt, the other around the trigger. 'Here,' he shows her, 'like this,' and he places his hands over hers. Together they lift the gun and settle its sights on an old saucepan hanging on a hook on the stone chimney breast. Kat closes her eyes and enjoys the sensation of his body pressed against hers, the strength of his shoulders, the taut muscles of his arms. She feels it more clearly than she ever has before: home. *He* is her home now and she won't lose this, she thinks, not for anything.

'Pow!' he says, jolting her out of her reverie, mimicking the ricochet of a bullet, rocking her back into the curve of his body. 'See,' he says, 'you and me together. There's no way we can lose.'

15

LILA

February

Lila is growing experienced in the art of distraction: which cotton to use for tacking hems onto a pair of curtains; the careful dip of a brush into a paint pot; the rhythmic rasp of sandpaper scraping across a blistered window frame; the *tap-tap-tap* of a nail sinking into wood. They are all small jobs and yet each one serves its purpose: while her hands are busy, her mind doesn't seem to churn so much and the anxiety remains at bay. Besides, every day that she stays put, she can see the cottage improve in some small way and she takes a glimmer of satisfaction from that too. Even though Tom is angry with her for leaving again, there is no doubt in Lila's mind that she had been right to return.

The cottage still echoes emptily all around her, but she must be getting used to it because she doesn't have that eerie sensation of being watched quite so often and she's learning other strategies to cope with the loneliness too. She walks every day now, rain or shine. At a certain point each day she downs tools, pulls on her coat and boots and stomps out across the moors or down through the forest ringing the lake, breathing in lungfuls of frosty air, enjoying the sensation of the blood moving around her body.

The days are short and bitterly cold but the faintest promise of spring hangs like a whisper over the countryside. Lila notices catkins growing high up in the thin canopy of the alder trees and thick clumps of snowdrops springing up almost overnight across the woodland floor. Out on the lake she sees a flock of wild geese take flight and once she even stumbles upon an old, grey heron, standing as still as a garden ornament among the reeds. As she walks through the landscape, the pale sun at her back, she notices the subtle changes occurring all around her. Winter is still very much in residence but she can't help hoping she has weathered its worst.

* * *

She is dragging a huge shard of wood out of the trees, puffing and panting with exertion but determined to claim it as her own, when she hears the excited barks of a dog. Surprised, she spins to see William clumping his way down the ridge with Rosie bounding at his heels. 'You're back,' he says, raising a gloved hand at her in greeting.

'Yes,' she says, dropping the piece of wood, pushing her hair out of her eyes. 'Hello. Happy New Year.' She bends to pat Rosie, tweaking the dog's ears. 'I was going to come by . . .'

He nods. 'That's OK. We thought we'd come and check on the place for you, just in case.'

'Thank you . . . and thank you for the track . . . and the firewood. I assume that was you, putting the sleepers in and topping up my woodpile?'

William nods sheepishly. 'I know you said not to, but I couldn't see how you would get your car back up here, if you returned.'

She'd had the exact same thought halfway up the motorway just a few weeks ago. Taking off on the spur of the moment, she'd only remembered the muddy track and how her car would struggle when it had been too late to turn back; but she needn't have worried. Jolting and bouncing her way up the steep trail in her car, it had been clear that William had been busy in her absence. Old railway sleepers were buried at intervals up the route and when she'd arrived at the back door of the cottage she'd seen her dwindling supply of firewood had been generously replenished. As she'd let herself in through the door she'd offered up a silent prayer of thanks for his kindness. 'I wish I could say you shouldn't have, but it really has made a big difference. I hope it wasn't too much work?'

William shrugs. 'No trouble.'

They stare at each other. Lila can see he hasn't shaved in a few days. The stubble on his chin gleams the same silver colour as his eyes. 'How's this place coming along?' he asks.

'I've been busy,' she says. 'Want to take a look around?'

'Sure.' William whistles for Rosie and the dog comes racing.

'Come on then,' she says, 'you can help me with my treasure.' She points to the large piece of wood lying at her feet.

'What's this for?'

'A coffee table.'

William shakes his head and smiles, lifts the wood easily at one end and drags it back to the cottage with Lila and Rosie following close behind.

* * *

They step out of their muddy boots and slide into the kitchen. 'Goodness,' says William, looking around, 'you weren't kidding. It's transformed.'

She smiles. 'So you like it?' It has taken her nearly two weeks of solid work, but she has washed down the walls and painted them a soft white, sanded all the wooden cupboards and painted them a duck-egg blue. The old cast iron range has been polished until it shines and she's replaced the rusting pots and pans with a new set of gleaming copper ones that hang on the hooks upon the chimney breast. She's scrubbed the kitchen table, mended the wobbly benches and added cheery curtains to the windows. The thing she is most pleased with, however, is the seat she has built into the bay of the window, where her two ikat cushions, purchased in London, now sit amongst a scattering of other colourful vintage cushions requisitioned from junk shops. On the table is a tin jug bursting with snowdrops, while several of the less chipped blue patterned plates from the cupboard, the ones that were salvageable, now hang along the wall facing the range. It's a simple but highly effective transformation.

'It looks great – very cheerful,' he adds.

'It is, isn't it?' Seeing it through his eyes, she can appreciate at last how much she's achieved. She bends to stoke the smouldering range and adds another log to the flames. 'Would you and Rosie like to stay for dinner? I was going to make pancakes. It is Shrove Tuesday, after all.'

'Is it?' William scratches his head. 'I had no idea.'

'Stay,' she urges. 'I'd like the company.'

He hesitates.

'Please.'

He gives her a nod. 'OK.'

She mixes the batter and heats butter in the frying pan, all the while stealing sideways glances at William where he sits in the new window seat looking out across the tangled garden. He isn't exactly handsome, at least not in an obvious way, but there is something undeniably attractive about him. His face is solid and kind-looking, weathered by a life lived on the land, and his frame strong and muscular from physical labour. When she first met him he'd seemed shifty and awkward but today he exudes a different air – a sort of quiet, calm confidence, like a man who knows that he is exactly where he is supposed to be. Rosie lies at his feet, blissed-out, craning her neck as he scratches beneath her chin, and as Lila cooks they talk about her work at the cottage and William's hopes for the upcoming lambing season. 'Here we go,' she says, laying a plate stacked with pancakes onto the table between them. 'I made extra for Rosie.'

'She shouldn't,' he says, 'she's getting fat,' but as they tuck into the pancakes, drizzled with lemon juice and sugar, William feeds Rosie pieces from his fingers under the table. 'I thought you'd stay down south a little longer,' he says after a while, 'you know, wait for it to warm up a bit before you braved this place again.'

'No.' She hesitates. 'I wanted to come back.'

'Getting under your skin, is it?'

She tilts her head at him.

'This place, the lake, the land. It's got to you, hasn't it?'

She nods. 'It's peaceful . . . and it feels like a refuge.' He throws her a curious glance and she sighs. 'Things haven't been easy between Tom and me recently.'

William looks down at his plate and doesn't ask for further explanation, but for some reason Lila finds herself offering it. 'We . . . we lost a baby . . . last summer.'

He swallows. 'I'm sorry.'

'Thanks.' She hesitates then surprises herself by continuing. 'It was my fault. I was supposed to be going shopping for baby things with Mum. I was rushing to get ready and I took a really bad fall down the stairs. I don't remember how it happened . . . but I fell all the way. I was twenty-seven weeks pregnant.'

William winces.

'Mum arrived at the house to pick me up and when I didn't answer the doorbell she peered through the letter box . . . saw me lying there at the bottom of the stairs, unconscious . . . blood everywhere, apparently.'

'God,' murmurs William, 'that must have been awful . . . for all of you.'

Lila nods. 'Mum called the ambulance and I was rushed to hospital.'

William nods carefully but doesn't interrupt, as if sensing Lila's need to keep talking.

'When I came round they told me the trauma of the fall had meant the placenta had separated. There was no time to wait. There was no other choice. I had to give birth to her there and then.' She swallows. 'It was the hardest thing I've ever done, knowing she was coming – too early – knowing it was my fault.' Lila falls silent, staring at the empty plate before her. 'She was born on the twenty-third of June and she lived for five days. She fought hard, our little girl. She clung on.' A tear rolls down Lila's cheek and drips onto the scrubbed surface of the table. She smooths it away with the tip of her finger. 'I held her hand through the hole in the incubator. I willed her to be strong, to make it, but it wasn't enough. I couldn't save her.'

'What was her name?' William asks, not quite meeting her eye.

'We called her Milly. It means "brave" – because that's what she was.'

He smiles. 'Milly. That's lovely.'

Lila's not sure if it's a trick of the light but it seems as though William is fighting tears too. She swallows and takes a breath, but still the words come. 'It's been so hard. Ever since, I've been so sad . . . and angry too. All I wanted to do was wake up from the nightmare, to return to the life we had been living just a few days before, when everything stretched before us, a future of possibility. I just wanted to rewind, to go back to the hospital and scoop my baby up and take her home and be a mother to her. I wanted to keep her safe, but I couldn't do it.'

William nods.

'Now every day I wake up and the first thing I think is that she isn't with us.' She sighs. 'I wish I could go could back to that one day. I wish I could live it again. I wouldn't rush; I wouldn't worry over the stupid things . . . which top to wear, which shoes look right. I'd take things slow, appreciate the pregnancy, the life growing inside me.' She wipes at her eyes. 'I ask myself over and over, how could I fall? I should have been more careful, should have fought harder. I should have found a way to save her, to keep her with me.'

She sees the shake of William's head from the corner of her eye. He clears his throat. 'Some things – precious things – escape you, no matter how much you might want to keep them close.'

She glances across at him, hearing the emotion in his words and realises that he too has lost something or someone important. She wonders about his lonely existence up at the farm. A woman, she thinks – the one that got away.

'Sometimes the real fight is what comes after the event, when you face what you are left with,' he continues. 'How you live with that. That's the real battle.'

She nods in understanding before cautiously reaching across the table. She gives his hand a gentle squeeze then draws her own back again, laying it in her lap.

'But that's the fight that makes you stronger,' he adds. 'Makes you a better person. At least,' he says, running a hand across his chin, 'that's what I think.' He seems embarrassed to have spoken so openly. He clears his throat again. 'It doesn't sound to me as though anything that happened that day is your fault though. It was an accident.'

She shakes her head. 'It's the not remembering . . . I can't let it go until I know *exactly* what happened . . . and I just can't shake this feeling that there's something missing . . . something I've forgotten. Until I remember it all I don't think I can move forwards.'

William eyes her sadly. 'What if you never remember?'

She shrugs. 'I think that's why I like being up here. There's something about it – an escape, something to focus on that stops me from going completely mad. Patching this place up, well,' she says, letting out a harsh laugh, 'I don't suppose it takes a genius to work out what I'm *really* trying to fix.'

William nods. 'And what about Tom?'

Lila looks at him, confused.

'He must be struggling too. Why isn't he here with you? Why aren't you doing this together?'

Lila shakes her head. 'Like I said, things haven't been so good between us since the accident. It's as if we're on completely different wavelengths with our grief. I've been poleaxed but Tom's way of coping is to bury it all inside and focus on his work. He won't really talk about the fall and he doesn't seem to want to face what we've lost.'

William shakes his head. 'You two shouldn't let this fester, you know.'

'I know, but every time we try to draw close again it's as though there's an insurmountable wall between us. Sorry,' she says, shaking her head, 'I didn't mean to get all heavy on you.' She pushes her plate away, suddenly embarrassed.

'That's OK.'

'I shouldn't have gone on like that.'

'No,' says William, 'it's OK. I'm glad you told me.'

She leans back and eyes him for a moment. 'Thank you,' she says.

'For what?'

'For listening . . . for being so kind.'

William shrugs. It is his turn to be embarrassed. He looks about the room, searching for something to distract. 'I could help you with that,' he says, his gaze settling on the huge piece of timber propped in the corner of the room.

'Oh that's OK. I can probably manage.'

'What were you going to do with it? A coffee table? You'll need to dry it out, then cut it to size and plane it smooth.'

She nods. 'I wasn't going to bother with the drying stage. A little warping or splitting will just add character, right?' She doesn't want to wait. She is impatient to get going, to see her changes take shape in the rest of the cottage.

'Well OK, but let me do it for you. I'd like to.'

'You must be so busy . . .' she protests.

'To be honest, it's pretty quiet up at the farm this time of year. There are only so many fences to mend . . . you'd be doing me a favour.'

She thinks for a moment and then nods. 'OK. You're on.'

'Great.' He stands and carries their empty plates to the sink. 'Now, let me do the washing up and then I really must get back to Evelyn. She'll be worrying.'

Lila nods.

'But I'll come again tomorrow, if that's OK? I'll start on the timber then.'

Lila smiles. 'Thank you.'

William does the washing up while Lila stands beside him at the sink, taking the rinsed dishes from his soapy hands and drying them on a tea towel. Once or twice their fingers meet on a cup or a plate and they smile, embarrassed, but there is something else between them now too, a warm understanding that hasn't been there before.

When they are finished, she lets him out into the night, Rosie sloping away by his side. 'Good night,' she calls after them, her words ringing out over the lake, watching as their outlines melt away into the darkness.

After they have gone she turns back to the cottage and eyes the echoing front room. The kitchen may be an improvement but there is still so much to do. She feels an impatience to keep going. *Don't let it fester.* That's what William had suggested about her relationship with Tom but it applies to the cottage too. *Sometimes the real fight is what comes after the event, when you face what you are left with . . . how you live with that. That's the real battle.* His words make sense on so many levels. Everything has been so cloudy. She's felt as though she's been sleepwalking these past few months. She doesn't want to be in that fog any more. She wants to see and think and *feel* things clearly and suddenly she knows there is something else she must do.

She runs upstairs and grabs the bottle of pills from her washbag and by the light of a torch she tiptoes out to the earth closet, unscrews the lid and, before she can change her mind, tips the whole lot into the darkness below. There, she thinks, staring down into the black pit, it's done. There is no way she will *ever* get them back now.

*   *   *

William, true to his word, arrives the next day with his tools and turns the huge branch of wood into a beautiful, smooth, misshapen plank, perfect for what Lila has planned. The following afternoon he is back again, this time hauling a trailer behind his Land Rover. 'They were just going to waste up at my place.' He hovers in front of a dusty mahogany bed frame and double mattress with his hands thrust deep into his pockets. 'I've had them in the barn for a while. I know it's not the most beautiful bed but it's comfortable and it will be a damn sight better than that camp bed you've been sleeping on.' He's wrong. It's a beautiful bed. Lila can tell from the quality of the wood and craftsmanship that it is an antique. 'We'll have to carry the frame and the slats across the meadow and down the bank but I think we can probably manage between us, don't you?'

She is about to protest at his generosity when he holds up a hand. 'Please, they're just cluttering up my place. Take them.'

'But—'

'Please.'

She eyes him for a moment, thinking of the narrow camp bed back in the cottage. 'OK,' she relents, 'thank you.'

They carry the frame into the cottage first then return for the mattress, which proves to be rather unwieldy and so heavy Lila has to keep putting her half down for a rest and it's not until late afternoon as the light disappears over the hills that they finally get it inside the cottage. 'Now for the final push,' she says, eyeing the stairs. 'Do you think we can manage?'

'Come on,' says William, 'I'll take the top half.'

They half push, half pull it up the first few stairs and have just managed to wedge it firmly between the wall and the banister – William stuck at the top with Lila further down near the bottom – when a voice calls from the doorway. 'Lila, are you here?'

She peers down between the balustrades and sees Tom standing at the open door, an overnight bag on his shoulder and a huge bunch of white freesias in his hands. 'Tom!' she exclaims. 'What are you doing here?'

He moves across the room, the flowers held out before him in offering. 'It's Valentine's Day,' he says, eyeing the mattress on the stairs. 'Christ, you're not moving that by yourself, are you? Here,' he says, slinging his bag onto the floor and placing the flowers on the stone mantelpiece, 'let me help you.'

'It's OK,' calls William from the top landing, 'I've got the other end.'

Tom takes a step backwards then cranes to peer up the stairs. 'Oh, hello, William, isn't it? Sorry, I didn't see you up there.' He shoots Lila a look.

Lila feels her cheeks flush pink. 'What are you *doing* here?' she asks, sounding more defensive than she'd intended.

'I thought I'd surprise you.' Tom hovers at the bottom of the stairs. 'Do you want a hand?'

'Yes,' says Lila. 'My end could do with a shove.'

Tom shrugs off his coat and then moves to the stairs, and between the three of them they manoeuvre the mattress up into the bedroom where the wooden frame has already been assembled. Tom eyes the bed carefully and then turns back to Lila, one eyebrow raised, before the three of them lift the mattress and position it onto the base.

'Well,' says William, brushing his hands off, 'I'd best get going. Leave you two in peace.'

Lila can feel hostility radiating off Tom where he stands beside her. 'OK, mate.'

'Thank you, so much,' scrabbles Lila. 'I really appreciate it.'

'No trouble. Like I said, it really was just cluttering up my place.'

He gathers his coat, whistles for Rosie and then he is gone.

Tom waits a beat then turns to her. 'A bed?' he asks, incredulous. 'He's given you a bed?'

'What?'

Tom shakes his head. 'I have to hand it to the guy: that's a pretty slick move if ever I saw one . . . and on Valentine's Day, too.'

'Tom,' says Lila, blushing with embarrassment, 'it's not like that. He's a friend. He brought it all the way up here in his trailer. It's incredibly kind.'

'Hmmm . . .' says Tom.

'What?'

'You might think it's the platonic gesture of a friend, Lila, but he's a man. A lonely old man. He wants to get in your pants.'

'He does not. Anyway, he's not *that* old.'

Tom shakes his head. 'I don't like it, Lila. Why is it every time I come here there he is, hanging around you, making himself useful? I can guarantee he's got an ulterior motive.'

Lila sniffs. She wants to argue. She wants to tell Tom that not everyone has sex on the brain, but there is a part of her that doesn't want to even mention sex at that moment, not with the vast double bed standing between them like the proverbial elephant in the room.

Tom seems to soften slightly. 'Don't I get a hello then?'

'Sorry.' She moves around the bed frame towards him. 'Hello.'

He wraps his arms around her and for just a moment she forces herself to stop thinking and to just enjoy the sensation of being encircled in his arms. 'I'm glad you're here.'

'Are you?'

'Yes. How long are you staying for?'

'Just a night or two. I was lucky to escape. The Stratford site is keeping us flat out at the moment.'

She looks up and sees him properly then. His olive skin. His clear brown eyes. The two-day-old stubble on his chin. She reaches out and gently traces the jagged silver scar across his cheek. He lets her fingers caress the mark and travel down the side of his face before he reaches up and catches her hand, pulls her into a kiss. As their lips meet she feels the twist of something warm inside, something she hasn't felt in a long time, and she leans into him. It's a relief to know she still wants him – but she is scared too.

As if reading her thoughts, he pulls back. 'Come on then,' he says, 'you'd better show me what you've been up to. Prove to me this isn't all just a lovely holiday up here.'

She nods, grateful he isn't rushing her, and leads him by the hand down the creaking staircase.

*   *   *

At bedtime, they cover the mattress with old blankets and lie side by side in their sleeping bags, staring up at the ceiling.

'It's quiet here, isn't it?' Tom comments.

'Yes.'

'Cold too.'

'Yes,' she says again.

'Not too bad, is it, this mattress?'

'So you're not cross with William now?' she asks, unable to resist a dig.

'I still think he's got an ulterior motive.'

Lila doesn't say anything and the silence between them deepens.

'We should huddle together for warmth,' he suggests finally, a smile in his voice. 'You know, like penguins.'

She waits a beat. 'We should,' she agrees.

Tom seems surprised by her answer. He doesn't move, and so to prove that she means it, Lila unzips her sleeping bag. Finally Tom follows suit and they move together and spread both sleeping bags over them. Tom pulls her close and wraps his arms around her waist. She nestles into the warm curve of him. As she lies there she remembers that hot flame from earlier. His arms tighten slightly. She can feel the tiniest movement of his fingers on her ribcage, stroking the skin beneath her T-shirt. Slowly, she turns, her lips finding his in the dark. His hands move up under her top, across the curve of her breasts then trace a line to her hipbone. She sighs into his open mouth, inhales his breath.

'I want you,' he says.

She answers him with her lips. His hands move down to the tie on her pyjama bottoms and fumble with the bow until she reaches down, impatient with desire, and pushes them off herself. He does the same and then they are warm and naked and moving together in the darkness, the pattern of their tangled bodies suddenly as familiar as her own skin. There is no talking. No thinking. Just skin on skin and hot breath and the steady beating of their hearts.

* * *

In her dream she is back in London, upstairs in their bedroom, sunshine falling through the window, clothes discarded across the bed. She is rushing, impatient and frustrated; she knows she is going to be late. First the black top. Then the pink. The dream jumps and suddenly it isn't impatience she feels any more but anger. It pumps through her body like hot acid. Her fists are clenched. Fight or flight? She turns on her heel and races down the landing, towards the stairs, towards her escape.

Another jump and she is nearing the top step. A new detail emerges: far below the front door comes into view, white light pouring through its frosted glass panel. Then something else: footsteps, echoing down the landing behind her. *Lila!* The shout is distorted, an audio soundtrack played at the wrong speed. She is at the top of the stairs when she feels them: hands upon her, grabbing, pulling, tripping her up . . .

She teeters there for a moment, frozen in time, her heart rising sickeningly into her mouth. She reaches out for the banister but there is nothing to grab but empty space and then she is tumbling over the ledge.

Down, down, down she goes, plunging into the abyss with nothing to save her but the cold, hard reality of impact.

In the darkness she jolts awake. Beside her she can feel Tom's still, warm weight upon the mattress. She remembers where she is and the thudding beat of her heart gradually slows. She swallows and tries to breathe.

It was so real.

It was so real.

Lila knows then. She knows that she wasn't alone in the house when she fell.

Someone was there with her. There had been an argument. She had run. They had reached out for her, their hands at her back and she had gone tumbling down the stairs. The thought makes her heart rattle against her ribcage. She shivers and turns her head to seek out Tom in the pitch-black. All she can see is the hump of his back turned away from her, the slope of his broad shoulders, rising and falling with his slow breathing. She studies him for a moment, then slides out of bed. It's freezing, but she knows she can't lie there a moment longer.

Downstairs in the kitchen, huddled in a blanket, she sits at the table and tries to remember. Someone was with her, in her home on the morning she fell, she's sure of it. But who? She thinks and thinks but all that will come to her are the words Tom spoke to her up on the moors last November: *Sometimes it feels as though you're blaming me.*

His words had seemed odd, even then, but now, as she scrutinises the new fragments of her dream, she wonders if they have a more sinister meaning. Had he been there with her? Had they argued?

Could Tom have had a hand in her fall? Could his words be the sign of a guilty conscience?

She shakes her head. It seems impossible. Tom wouldn't have left her like that at the bottom of the stairs, unconscious and bleeding, would he?

But the dream had felt *so real*. And there isn't anyone else it could have been. It was her mother who had seen her through the letter box and called the ambulance. No one else could have been there with her *inside* the house besides Tom . . . Tom, who won't talk about the fall . . . Tom who can barely bring himself to utter their daughter's name . . . and who wonders if Lila is *blaming* him for something.

Lila shivers and wraps the blanket more tightly around her shoulders. Over and over she turns the details in her head, until dawn's pale fingers have crept over the surrounding hills and reached out to her with a cold embrace.

16

FEBRUARY

1981

Menacing grey storm clouds form above the valley over the course of a day and when night arrives it comes armed for violence. The gale has fixed them in its sights. It buffets the cottage, howls through cracks in the windows and slams any door left ajar. Everyone gravitates downstairs, drawn to the smouldering fire and the unspoken comfort of being together in number. Kat surveys the dwindling fire and directs a kick at the near-empty log basket. 'Whose turn was it to fill this up?' she asks.

'I did it this morning,' says Ben.

Simon and Mac just shrug so Kat turns her glare to Freya who sits hunched at the far end of the sofa, her face turned to the window. 'Freya?'

She looks round, startled. 'Yes?'

'Were you supposed to fill the log basket?'

'The what? The basket?' She looks distracted.

'Yes, was it your turn to fill it?'

'I – I don't know. Maybe.'

Kat sighs. 'Oh forget it. I'll do it myself.'

She stomps into the kitchen, past Carla who stands with her arms in a sink of washing up. 'You're not going out there, are you?' she asks, eyeing Kat as she pulls on Simon's heavy coat.

'Someone's got to. We need wood.'

'Aren't we supposed to be rationing what's left?'

Kat nods. They'd all thought they'd chopped enough wood to see them through to spring but winter has been harsh and their stocks have depleted rapidly. What's left on the ground is too damp to make a satisfactory fire – it smokes and spits and fails to catch. Kat isn't quite sure what will happen when the last of the logs have been burned – no one seems to want to talk about that – but she gazes at Carla and raises an eyebrow. 'You want to spend tonight of all nights without a fire?'

Carla turns back to the sink. 'Fair point.'

The wind snatches the back door out of her hand, nearly blowing it off its hinges. She shuts it firmly behind her then heads across to the dwindling woodpile stacked beneath the eaves of the house where she fills the basket quickly, heaping up enough logs to see them through the night before dragging it back to the house. She finds Wilbur snuffling and snorting at the door and opens it a crack to let him into the kitchen, then pulls it shut again and turns her face into the wind. There's something in the air – a crackle of electricity – the scent of violence – that speaks to her. Kat decides she wants to experience the full power of the storm, just for a minute.

Leaving the basket, she steps out from the shelter of the house and battles her way down towards the lake, where the wind whips across the surface of the water, billowing the reeds and bending them flat against the shore. She keeps walking, leaning into the gale with her arms outstretched until she is in the marginal shelter of the trees. Closing her eyes, she stands for a moment and listens to the storm roar like a jet engine across the lake. The cold air stings her cheeks and burrows deep into her marrow. All along the bank the trees creak and groan, branches crashing together like warring swords. She throws her arms wide again and howls into the night, filling her lungs with its icy breath, her cry instantly tossed away like a tumbling paper bag. In the face of such power she feels tiny and insignificant, but she feels alive.

A memory comes to her from somewhere, as if blown on the violent storm. 'I'm just popping out, Kat. You be a good girl. Look after your sister . . . I'll be back soon.'

'Yes, Mummy,' she says and tries not to cry as her mother shuts the door behind her, turning the key with a *click* in the lock.

For two days and two nights they roam the flat, filthy, hungry and abandoned. There's the remains of a packet of biscuits and a box of cornflakes in the lowest cupboard with a handful of crushed cereal dust at the bottom of the polythene bag. Kat tips it out and they eat the crumbs straight from the floor. They are thirsty too, but Freya's milk bottle is soon empty and they can't reach the taps at the sink. Her sister's nappy begins to smell bad. She takes it off and tries to clean her, but the mess goes everywhere. She wipes her as best she can with an old blanket and they huddle in their parents' bed, cold and hungry. 'Don't worry,' she says. 'Mummy will be back soon.' All that's left to do is sleep.

The banging and shouting sounds like a gale when they come, a terrifying rattling at the doors and windows. 'Open up, Mrs Thomas. We have a warrant.' When she opens her eyes there are two strange, suited men standing in her parents' room, staring down at them from the end of the bed. She snaps her eyes shut again in fear. 'Shit, Mark,' she hears one of them say, 'the stupid cow's only gone and left her kids.'

One of the men comes closer. She squeezes her eyes shut more tightly. 'Are you OK, little one?' he asks. 'What's your name?'

She doesn't tell him, she knows better than that; she just screws up her eyes and wishes Mummy would come back, but when the cup of water is held out to her she can't resist and she drinks it down quickly as the man smiles his encouragement.

'You're a brave little mite, looking after your sister like that. You're a survivor, you are.'

There is an ambulance ride and clean white beds in a shiny hospital that smells of the cream she remembers once rubbing onto her sister's grazed knees. When the nurse with the freckles comes back Kat asks, 'Is Mummy in trouble?'

'Ach,' the nurse says, 'don't you worry about her. She'll be just fine. We have to get you and your sister well first.'

As the wind tears at her skin and clothes, Kat remembers it all. She closes her eyes and another huge gust nearly knocks her off her feet. She staggers backwards a couple of steps, struggling to keep herself upright. From somewhere to her right she hears a loud splintering sound, as if a ship's hull has ploughed across the lake and beached itself among the trees. Kat looks up and sees one of the tallest alders lean out of the gloom towards her. It is a giant pointing finger, teetering and groaning. She takes another step backwards and then watches in horrified fascination as the tree begins its long descent towards the ground, until it crashes at her feet like a huge white ghost conquered in battle.

Kat stares at the fallen tree. Just a few feet more and she would have been caught beneath its branches. She stares at it for a moment and then, exhilarated by fear and by the sheer extraordinary violence of the storm, she lifts her chin to the wind and laughs into the night sky. The man had been right; she *is* a survivor.

*   *   *

'I was just beginning to get worried about you,' says Carla as Kat enters through the back door, dragging the log basket behind her. 'Survived out there then?'

'Yes,' says Kat with a slight smile. She's already decided to let them discover the tree for themselves in the morning.

'Did you find Wilbur?'

'Yes. I let him in earlier.'

Carla nods. 'Good. He's probably stretched out in front of the fire with Freya, the lazy little pig.'

'Let's hope he doesn't get too close. He'll be crispy bacon if the boys have anything to do with it.'

'Not if Freya is there.'

Kat nods. 'Freya always did like a waif or a stray. She used to collect baby birds in shoeboxes and expect us to perform miracles on them. She didn't understand that once they'd fallen out of the nest it was too late; better to leave them for the cats.'

Carla studies her. 'You're one tough cookie, did you know that?'

Kat shrugs. 'It's just nature, isn't it? Survival of the fittest. That's the way the world works.'

Carla reaches for a tea towel and dries her hands. 'Kat, do you think Freya is OK?'

'Sure.' She waits a beat, her heart in her mouth, wondering if Carla has guessed.

'She just seems so . . . so down. She's like a different person to the one who arrived a few months ago. Have you noticed?'

Kat isn't sure what to say. 'She's always had a tendency to be a little moody.' The lie feels like a betrayal but she knows she has no choice.

'Oh.' Carla hangs the tea towel on a spare hook. 'I guess I don't know her as well as you. I suppose if she weren't happy here she could always leave. No one's forcing her to stay.'

'No,' says Kat and swallows down the lump in her throat. 'So,' she asks, trying to move the subject on, 'if it's not crispy bacon, what *is* for dinner tonight?'

'Beans.'

Kat groans.

'I know. It's that or rice.'

Kat thinks for a moment. 'Have we got any sugar or powdered milk left?'

'A little of both.'

'Jam?'

'We're down to the last two pots.'

'How about we make rice pudding?'

Carla breaks into a smile. 'You're on.'

* * *

The wind snarls and claws at the house all night. Kat lies awake upstairs, tossing and turning, mulling Freya's predicament over and over in her head. The more she thinks on it, the more she is eaten up by a creeping panic. They have left it too long. Carla already seems suspicious and soon Freya's growing bump will be obvious to everyone. It doesn't matter how many billowing nighties or floaty dresses she drapes herself in, soon there will be no hiding the pregnancy – not from Carla, not from anyone. Most importantly, Freya must be nearing the cusp of being able to have an abortion.

Kat has been wracking her brain trying to think of other ways to find the money to get Freya away from the cottage. Even if she can get an abortion for free she'll need money for food and lodgings somewhere, at least until she's back on her feet. But short of robbing a bank nothing has come to her. She's sick of worrying about it; sick of trying to come up with a plan. Part of her wishes she would wake up one morning and find her sister gone but Kat knows that isn't going to happen because Freya has nowhere to go. Meanwhile, time marches on and the baby inside Freya grows bigger by the day. Kat is terrified of them noticing – of Simon noticing – but she just doesn't know what to do.

Bloody Simon and that *bloody* gun. If only he knew how one stupid decision might have jeopardised their entire future at the cottage. As she gazes up into the darkness she thinks of Simon and about how he might react when Freya's secret is revealed. He will see more clearly than anyone how a baby will ruin everything. A crying, crawling, wailing, real-life baby – it will be nothing short of a disaster and the very thing that will fracture their life at the cottage. They will go their separate ways, back to the city, back to jobs and family. Simon will leave her without a backwards glance, heading to the safety of his affluent family with their big house and their fancy cars and Kat will be left with nothing; no job, no home, no Simon.

It's as she turns it all over that the idea explodes in her mind. Simon. His family. She has been so afraid of him finding out, but why? What if he did know? What if he could help? If he borrowed the money from his parents, Freya could leave and the rest of them would be able to continue as before at the cottage, unimpeded. She plays the conversation out, over and over in her head and although she knows he won't like it, she thinks she can convince him that it's the only way for them to keep the cottage. Surely he owes them that much after the part he's played? She can't carry this on her own any more. She needs his help.

Kat listens to the raging wind and rehearses her argument over and over in her mind, sleep only coming to her as the ailing wind lowers its snarls to a low, faltering moan.

* * *

It is Ben who discovers the tree. His crow of delight wakes Freya, who shuffles to the window, still wrapped in her bedding. 'Come and look at this,' she says from the window sill.

Kat is groggy from lack of sleep but she joins her sister at the window and looks out across the vista to see Ben standing with one foot resting on the massive trunk, his hands clasped above his head in the victorious stance of a hunter claiming his kill. The tree looks even more impressive in the cold light of day. She shivers and turns to face Freya. 'How are you feeling?'

Freya blushes and reaches down to finger one of the white stems of honesty in the jug on the sill. They never openly talk about the pregnancy but she seems to understand what Kat is asking. 'I don't feel sick any more.'

Kat swallows. The morning sickness has passed which must mean the pregnancy is progressing. They are running out of time. She knows she must talk to Simon – today.

* * *

'Shame we don't have a chainsaw,' says Simon. 'We'll never get a handsaw through this trunk, but at least there are all these dead branches we can remove. There must be enough wood here to see us through to summer.'

Kat stands beside him and eyes the tree. She can still hear the echo of its deafening descent. She circles it slowly and notices the gnarled knot halfway up the huge trunk where the bark has puckered into an unusual oval shape, with another darker whorl inside, reminiscent of the iris of an eye. Hanging from one corner is a dark teardrop stain marking the bark. She traces the imperfection in the wood with her fingers, marvelling at how closely it resembles a weeping eye. She would point it out to Simon but he is still talking. 'If we move as much of it inside as possible it will dry out pretty quickly,' he adds. Kat nods and he turns to her. 'Are you OK? You're very quiet. One of the others can help instead if you're not feeling up to it.'

'I'm fine,' she says. It's rare for them to be on their own and she wants to enjoy this time with him for just a few more moments, before the spectre of Freya rises up between them again.

The sky is a grey sheet hanging over them as they snap and pull at the smaller branches of the tree, gradually working their way into the centre of the canopy where they hack at the thicker stems with the axe and a small handsaw. As the pile of firewood begins to grow, Kat's muscles warm with the exertion. She feels sweat bloom on her skin and slips off her sweater, the cold air making her bare arms tingle. It feels good to do something physical and for a while she loses herself in the rhythm of the task. 'Let's take a break,' Simon suggests finally, and he hands her a cold flask of water. She drinks deeply then hands it back to him and watches as he tips it back and swallows, his Adam's apple sliding up and down in his throat. 'So are you going to tell me what's bothering you?' he asks, wiping his mouth on his sleeve. 'You've hardly said a word all morning.'

Don't make me do this, she wills. Don't make me ruin this. But she knows she must. With a sigh, she pats the tree trunk and indicates for him to sit. 'There's something I need to talk to you about and I don't think you're going to like it.'

Simon eyes her evenly. 'Out with it then.'

'It's Freya.'

'Go on.'

He really doesn't have a clue, she thinks. She takes a breath. 'She's pregnant.'

Simon's eyes visibly widen. 'Pregnant?'

'Yes.'

'As in . . .'

'. . . going to have a baby? Yes.' Kat is annoyed to find that she is the one blushing. Does she really have to spell it out to him?

'It was that night,' she continues, 'you know, when we took the mushrooms, when everything went a bit crazy.' She tries to smile, tries to show him that she understands, that she forgives him. Simon stares at her then has the decency to drop his gaze as embarrassment flares on his cheeks. She takes a small kernel of satisfaction from witnessing his shame.

'Oh,' he says.

'Yes. Oh.'

Simon raises his head and shakes his hair out of his eyes. 'Kat, I don't know what . . .'

Kat shakes her head. 'It happened.'

Simon eyes her. 'You're not . . . cross?'

She holds his gaze. Cross? She's not cross? Is he serious? Of course she's cross. She's livid. She's destroyed. Her heart is no longer a warm, beating thing of heat and beauty but fragments of broken glass scattered across her ribcage. He will never know what he has done to her, but she won't tell him. She won't show herself to be weak or needy. She knows how he operates. Instead, she shakes her head. 'No,' she says lightly, 'I'm not cross. It was just one stupid night, right?'

Simon lets out a slow breath. 'Shit . . . she must be what . . . four . . . nearly five months along?'

Kat nods.

He shakes his head and they sit together in silence on the log for a while until Kat can't stand it any longer. 'She wants to have an abortion . . . but she's got no money and nowhere to go afterwards. That's why I was checking the tin the other day.'

'Oh.'

'We need money, quickly . . . so that she can go to a clinic, you know, I was thinking somewhere private . . . somewhere nice. And she'll need to find somewhere to stay for a while, until she can get back on her feet and return to college.' She is talking quickly, almost tripping over the words.

Simon shakes his head. 'An abortion?'

'Yes,' says Kat. 'I really don't see she has a choice.'

Simon rubs his hand across his stubbly chin. 'How much?'

'I don't know exactly. I was thinking a couple of hundred pounds, maybe a bit more, enough for the procedure and a month or two of rent.'

'We don't have that kind of money. You know as well as I do how much is left in the tin.'

'I know.' She hesitates. 'I thought – I thought perhaps you could talk to your parents.'

Simon's laugh surprises her. 'My parents? Oh they'd love that. The prodigal son turning up out of the blue and asking for a handout to abort his bastard child and set his floozy up in some love shack.' He shakes his head. 'I don't think so.'

She eyes him for a moment. 'Freya is hardly your *floozy*. Besides, if it's the abortion they'd disapprove of you could always lie about what the money was for.'

Simon's eyes narrow and when he speaks next his words shock Kat to the core. 'Why can't she keep it?'

'Because . . . because she – she just can't,' Kat blusters. She shakes her head. 'Of course she can't. She's only twenty.'

'What does age have to do with it?'

'Everything.' Kat gapes at him. 'She's too young. She wants to go to back to college.'

He gives a thin smile. 'We can't always do exactly as we please in life, can we? Maybe she has different responsibilities now.'

'So she'd raise the baby on her own, a single mother with no money and no home?' Kat gives a bitter laugh. 'I don't think so, do you?'

'But she's not on her own, is she? She's got us and *this* is her home.'

Kat tastes acid at the back of her throat. She swallows it down and tries to focus her thoughts into one logical argument. 'OK,' she tries calmly, 'so say she has this baby; what about doctors, hospitals, regular check-ups?'

Simon shakes his head and smiles again. 'You're so conditioned, Kat, so ready to accept what society dictates to you. Hasn't our time here taught you anything? Having a baby should be the most natural thing in the world. And isn't that what this place is all about . . . putting our trust in nature, accepting the outcome and making the best of what we're given? Freya will have you and Carla to help her, women who love and support her.'

'But we're hardly professional midwives.' Kat can't believe what she's hearing. 'Anyway, what about nappies, baby food and clothes? We're not set up for any of that here. How would we afford it? It's impossible.'

'What do you think women did years ago? Race off to Mothercare and fill a shopping trolley with disposable nappies and baby lotion? If you think about it, the most important things that the baby will need are already here: milk, shelter and more than enough adults to nurture and care for it.'

'But a baby?' She is incredulous. 'We can't raise a baby *here*.'

Simon rubs his chin again. 'I think you're coming at this all wrong, Kat. Maybe this isn't the problem you're perceiving it to be.' He is visibly warming to his idea; she can see a faint gleam of excitement in his eyes. 'Maybe this is an opportunity. It's new life, Kat. It should be embraced. It was meant for us, as part of our challenge here at the cottage. This baby might be the best thing that happens to Freya, to you, to me. We can raise the child in a new kind of family. We'll learn from our parents' mistakes and do things differently.' He smiles and puts a hand out to touch her arm. 'We'll do it together.'

Together? Is he dreaming? Kat wants to shake him. 'You won't help us?'

Simon looks out across the still waters of the lake. 'Of course I'll help . . . but not with money for an abortion.'

Kat's cheeks flare an angry red. 'It should be Freya's decision. It's her body.'

'Yes, but what decision can she make if she is already more than four months along and there is no money?' He jumps down off the log and offers a hand to Kat. She doesn't want to accept it but he holds it there and in the end she takes it, unsure whether he even notices the tremble of her own hand. He is rocking backwards and forwards on his feet with impatience. 'Let's get back to it. There isn't too much more to do. Then I'll talk to Freya.'

Kat turns crestfallen to a branch as white and brittle as bone. She snaps it from a larger limb and hurls it onto the growing pile of kindling. She is filled with fury. She can't believe Simon's reaction. She looks across at him wrestling with a huge branch and sees that he is visibly buoyed by the news, his chest puffed up like a cockerel. Every so often he glances up at the house, shakes his head and smiles. As she watches him she realises with a creeping horror that keeping the baby – something she hasn't even considered until now – is the worst possible thing that can happen. A living, growing baby will be a physical connection that will exist between Simon and Freya, for ever. Something she will never be able to break. As she wrestles with the tangled branches she feels the seed of bitterness lodged in her core take root; it grows and spreads, hidden inside her like the sleeping vegetation all around, just waiting to spring into life and roam across the landscape. She eyes the huge trunk sprawled before her. Maybe it would have been better if it hadn't missed her after all.

* * *

Kat removes her boots to enter the kitchen and finds Freya at the range, filling a pan with water. Simon enters the room behind her then moves on to Freya, reaching out to squeeze her shoulder. 'Good girl,' he says, eyeing the bread and jam lying on the plate beside the sink, 'you've got to keep your strength up now, haven't you?'

Freya spins, her panic-stricken gaze darting from Simon to Kat. In her sister's eyes Kat sees one shocked question: *He knows?*

Kat nods slowly and with a heavy heart, she turns and leaves the room. You win, she thinks. You have him. I can't do this any more.

17

LILA

March

Lila has just reached the end of another back-breaking day in the cottage when she decides enough is enough. She can't let this thing between her and Tom fester a moment longer.

The morning after Valentine's Day, when she'd sat up until dawn turning the shocking, new detail of her fall over and over in her head, she'd been incapable of anything but complete withdrawal from him. He'd tried to pull close, tried to gather her up into his arms after their night together but she'd remained cold and distant and had ushered him out of the cottage just as soon as she'd been able to. She'd seen his look of confusion and he'd asked her what was wrong, but she'd had no reassurances for him and frankly she'd been glad to see him go, terrified that if he didn't, she'd blurt out the fears running riot in her head.

But it doesn't seem to matter; whether he is there at the cottage with her or not, the fear remains. She has to know the truth about the fall. She has to know the part he played. Grabbing her phone, she stomps out over the ridge and across the meadow towards her car.

The evening is drawing in as she hurtles down the track and drives the twisting country lanes, searching for a spot where her mobile phone has reception. She is halfway to Little Ramsdale when a couple of bars spring to life on the screen. She hits the hazard lights and pulls onto the verge, scrolling for Tom's number.

It rings and rings and she is about to give up when his voice floods through the receiver. 'Hello,' he shouts. 'Lila?'

'Yes, it's me.' She can hear raucous laughter, music blaring and the clinking of glasses in the background.

'Is everything OK?'

'Where are you?' she asks.

'In the pub.'

'Oh.'

'What's up? Are you OK?'

'Yes, I just thought . . . I wanted . . .' She takes a deep breath. 'I don't know.' She is suddenly unsure. She hadn't imagined the conversation playing out like this.

'Hang on,' shouts Tom, so loudly she has to hold the phone away from her ear, 'I can't hear you. I'm going outside.'

Lila hears Tom's muffled words followed by the teasing reply of one of his friends and gradually the background noises fade away until there is nothing but the low thrum of London traffic.

'Are you still there?' he asks. 'Sorry, the football's on and it's bloody noisy in there.'

'I'm here.'

'Everything OK?'

She swallows and stares out through the windscreen into the darkness. How does she say it? How does she ask if it was *him*? If he was there with her on the day she fell? If he was the one she remembers chasing after her, his hands at her back, tripping her up and sending her toppling down the stairs? How does she say it out loud?

'Lila?'

'I'm still here.'

'What's wrong?'

The faraway roar of a crowd erupting at a goal filters through the phone. The sound makes her feel not just a couple of hundred miles away but a million. Here she is agonising about the worst thing that's ever happened to her and there he is enjoying a lads' night out in the pub. 'Nothing,' she says, 'I was just phoning to say hi.' She curses her cowardice.

'Oh.' He sounds surprised. 'Right.' Silence hangs between them. 'I thought maybe you were calling to say you were coming home.'

She shakes her head. 'No, not yet.'

'I see.'

Lila takes a breath. 'And you're OK?'

'Yep.' He sounds so brusque – suddenly not a bit like the Tom she knows. There is another pause and then Tom is speaking again, his words coming in a rush. 'Look, I wasn't planning on saying this tonight but as you've called . . . I think you should know that I've decided to stay away. It's clear from the way things were left after Valentine's Day that you don't want me there so I'm not going to keep racing up there and bothering you. The way we said goodbye that last time . . . well, it hurt, Lila. I can't keep doing this. You know where I am, when you're ready . . .'

Lila bristles. *Tom* is hurt? Isn't she the one who's supposed to be hurt and angry here? Silence extends across the telephone line. She wants to say something. She wants to ask him about the fall but the words still won't come.

'I should probably get back to the boys. It's my round.'

'Oh.'

'You know where I am. I'll be waiting.' There is another pause. 'Take care of yourself, Lila.'

The dial tone comes before she can say another word.

Lila sits there on the verge a while longer, the orange lights of her car flashing on and off, alternately illuminating then hiding one small patch of hedgerow. She doesn't know how long she stays watching the undergrowth appear and disappear, flash orange to black, orange to black, but eventually she turns the key in the ignition, spins the car around and takes the track all the way back to the cottage.

* * *

It's the first night in a while that she wishes she hadn't thrown her pills away. She tosses and turns, fretting over her conversation with Tom and eventually, when sleep does arrive, it is filled with

261

a reel of disturbing dreams. The images flicker and race across her shuttered eyelids.

She dreams of her father, seated beside her at the kitchen table, his face twisted with frustration as they pore over her homework. 'You have to dedicate yourself to this, Lila,' he says, banging his fist on the table, his dark eyes flashing. 'You have to commit.' And the words well up in her: *What about your dedication . . . your commitment, to your wife . . . to your family?* But he has gone and her words are lost like dust on a breeze.

She dreams of a woman drifting through the cottage crooning soft lullabies, accompanied by the papery rustle of honesty seed heads, caught in the waft of a current as she passes by.

She dreams of running down an endless landing, the sound of footsteps chasing her and the shock of hands at her back, tugging at her, sending her tumbling down into a void of indescribable loss. *Just like her.* The words echo through the corridors of her sleep, making her twist and turn, so that she wakes in the morning still tired and with the taste of grief lying heavy on her tongue.

She lies there for a moment, curled in the antique bed, and knows that she can't face another day of hard physical labour or paint fumes. She needs a break. She wants to walk. William has been inviting her for weeks, even drawn a map of how to find his place on foot, but she's always found another job to prevent her from visiting. But now she imagines sitting in William's warm, creaking kitchen with its shining copper pans and pretty check curtains, Evelyn knitting at the table with a warm cat curled in her lap and Rosie stretched at her feet, and knows it's where she wants to be. She's sick of her own company and fed up with worrying about Tom and the fall so, after wrapping herself in a warm jumper and a woollen hat and scarf, she strikes out up the hillside, her head down, her feet stomping across the claggy terrain, only once in a while lifting her head to check her bearings against William's hand-drawn map.

It's a day for being outside, the air damp and cool, the sun a yellow orb still low in the sky. The bluebells are late to bloom in the Peak District and she notices their lush green stems and drooping blue trumpets as she walks, stooping to pick a handful before continuing on over the moors.

Higher up, she stops for a rest on an old stone wall, removes the hat which is too hot now and making her head itch, then presses on and is surprised when she makes it to the farm in just over an hour. She is greeted on arrival by Rosie's delighted barks and a pretty ceramic sign on one of the gateposts welcoming her to *Mackenzie Farm*. As she walks through the yard, bursts of cheery yellow daffodils wave at her from their flowerbeds. The scene is a far cry from the snowy vista she remembers on her last, unexpected visit.

'Well, well,' calls William, appearing from behind a large green tractor, wiping his hands on a dirty, oil-stained cloth. 'So you decided to pay us a visit after all?'

She smiles. 'Is that all right?'

'Of course. Just wait till Evelyn sees you.' Rosie wheels in circles at her feet. 'Come on, Rosie, let's get the poor girl inside. She's probably desperate for a cuppa.'

They find Evelyn in the kitchen where she greets Lila like an old friend, tears springing in her pale grey eyes. 'Oh my dear girl,' she says, gripping her arm, 'you came back.'

'Of course I did. I brought you these,' she adds, holding out the small bouquet of bluebells. 'Besides, I told you last time . . . I had to come back to see your jewellery.'

Evelyn beams at her and accepts the small bouquet. 'They're lovely. Thank you. I'll take you upstairs, just as soon as we've had that cup of tea.'

'I'm on it, Mum,' says William, reaching for the blue and white striped teapot.

After tea and a little small talk, Evelyn leads her up the creaking wooden staircase then pulls her into the tiny room where Lila had first seen the desk of strange tools and implements. Evelyn ignores the table and moves instead to a low wooden chest in the far corner of the room. 'I keep my treasure in here.' She blows a thin layer of dust from the lid of the trunk then opens it to reveal two wooden jewellery boxes nestled amongst piles of old photographs, postcards, letters and trinkets. 'I haven't looked in here for such a long time . . .'

As Evelyn pulls out the boxes, Lila can't help herself; she reaches for one of the nearest photographs and studies the faces in the picture. 'Is this you?' she asks, pointing to a dark-haired lady in a patterned housecoat.

Evelyn looks at the photo, her eyes clouded with confusion. It takes her a moment but eventually her face breaks with a warm smile of recognition. 'Yes, that's me . . . and that's my Albert,' she says, pointing to the tall man in a flat cap and baggy corduroy trousers at her side.

'You made a very handsome couple.'

'Thank you, dear. He was a good man.'

Lila peers more closely at the smaller figure to their right and tries to identify the outline of William in the faded image of the skinny boy squinting up at the camera, with his dark hair and impressively flared jeans. She laughs. 'Look at William. Doesn't he look different?'

'Yes, doesn't he?' says Evelyn glancing across at the photo. 'He was a funny-looking boy back then. So skinny . . . all ears and legs. Ah, now here we go. Here's my treasure.' She passes the first box to Lila and watches as she rummages with excitement through the silver bangles and brooches and necklaces contained within.

'You made these?' Lila asks in disbelief. 'But they're gorgeous, Evelyn. You have a real talent.'

'Oh, I don't know about that.'

Lila holds up to the light a necklace with a tiny, silver forget-me-not flower pendant hanging from the chain. 'Well I think they're absolutely lovely.'

Evelyn's papery cheeks blush a delicate pink. 'Thank you, my dear. You can keep that one if you like?'

'Oh, but I couldn't. They're yours.' She returns the necklace to the jewellery box then turns to meet Evelyn's gaze. As their eyes connect the elderly woman reaches out and strokes her cheek with the rough palm of her hand and Lila has the strangest feeling that it's not her she's looking at but someone else, someone far beyond her skin.

'I'm so glad you came back,' she says. 'We did miss you.'

* * *

'Before you go,' William says, leading her from the farmhouse towards one of the barns, 'I thought you might like to see the lambs. There's a newborn I'm handfeeding.' He gives her a sideways glance. 'Want to help?'

'Sure,' she says. 'I'd love to. What do I do?'

'Follow me.'

William opens the door to the barn and Lila enters its warm, earthy interior. Inside she can hear the soft shuffling and bleating of sheep. 'She's over here,' he beckons, moving past pens of ewes and lambs to a corner of the barn where a white fluffy ball lies alone in a heap of straw.

'Poor thing,' she says, 'she's so tiny. Why do you have to feed her by hand?'

'The ewe died in labour.'

'Oh,' says Lila, 'that's sad.'

He shrugs then reaches for a bottle and Lila watches as he fills it with milk and twists the lid on, giving it a good shake. 'Here, I'll show you how to do it.'

Lila is nervous but she follows William's instructions, kneels down in the straw and lets him place the front legs of the animal over her thighs. At the sight of the bottle the lamb seems to know what to do. She head-butts Lila, eager to get to the milk and almost knocks her over. Lila laughs and lowers the teat to the lamb's muzzle and soon the animal is tugging and sucking away happily with greedy slurping sounds. 'This is amazing,' she says in hushed awe.

'Isn't it?' agrees William.

Lila holds the creature in her arms, closes her eyes and breathes in the sweet scent of straw and the animal's warm, musky fleece. The lamb is so small and so fragile and it occurs to Lila that the last time she held anything this new and precious had been at the hospital . . . only then there had been no wriggling, warm, life-filled body . . . no heart hammering palpably just beneath her fingers.

She can't help it. As Lila remembers, she begins to cry. The tears stream down her cheeks and embarrassed, she tries to bury her face in lamb's fleece so that William won't see, but it doesn't work. 'Oh, Lila,' he says. She feels him shift beside her, awkward in the presence of her grief.

'I'm sorry,' she sniffs, 'ignore me. I'm an idiot.'

'No you're not. Don't say that.' He reaches for the lamb and returns her gently to the straw, then pulls Lila to her feet. Before she knows it she is in his arms, William patting her on the back helplessly, over and over. 'There, there,' he says, soothing her as if she were a distressed animal, 'there, there. Let it out. It's time to let it all out.'

18

MARCH

1981

It's another interminably wet evening as they gather round the fire. Mac and Kat are playing a game of chess. Ben sits in the old wingback chair, tuning his guitar as a roll-up coils smoke into the air beside him. Carla sits at his feet lost in a book while Freya is curled in her usual position at one end of the sofa darning holes in a pair of tights. Simon appears in the kitchen doorway and clears his throat. No one knows what he is going to say until the words are out of his mouth, cast like pebbles into the stillness of the room. 'I think you should all know that Freya is pregnant.'

Kat's hand hovers over her queen. She daren't look up. The whole room is frozen, not a single breath taken.

'The baby's due late June,' he continues.

The silence stretches on. Kat feels Mac's gaze shift towards Freya but she can't look at any of them; instead she keeps her eyes fixed on the black and white squares of the board stretching before her.

'It's an exciting time for all of us,' continues Simon, 'and she's going to need our support.' He hesitates. 'Any questions?'

No one says a word. Carla shifts on her cushion, then closes her book. Kat is focusing so intently on the chessboard that the chequered squares begin to blur into a sea of grey. Finally Ben clears his throat. 'Are you feeling OK, Freya?'

'Yes thank you,' she answers in a small voice.

Carla sighs. 'Wow, a baby. I had no idea.'

Kat feels Carla's gaze move in her direction and she lifts her head and meets her stare head-on, tilts her chin ever so slightly. She won't have her feeling sorry for her.

Only Mac is yet to move. She can feel tension radiating from him, his body a coiled spring ready to decompress and when she does find the courage to glance at him she can see that his face has flushed an impossible red. Without uttering a word, he rises from their game and leaves the room, pushing roughly past Simon where he stands in the kitchen doorway. Kat sees Freya's gaze follow him out of the room, her flinch as the back door slams. Simon moves across and takes the seat at the other end of the sofa to her. 'See,' he says, 'it's fine. I don't know why you were so worried.'

Freya gives the slightest nod and Kat understands then that the announcement had been planned. Simon and Freya had discussed it in advance. They were in it together.

* * *

It really feels as though winter is never going to end. The cottage is cold and damp and filled with the unpleasant smell of mouldy trainers and laundry that has taken too long to dry. Everyone is sick of being cooped up in such a small, dank space. By now they'd hoped for spring vegetables and sunshine, primroses and puffy white clouds, but the sky above the valley is an endless sea of grey, continually lashing rain, and nothing much remains in the pantry but some rice and a few jars of dried beans. Even worse, everyone is tiptoeing awkwardly around each other now that the news of Freya's pregnancy is out in the open. The revelation has rocked them all in different ways and altered the dynamics of the group trapped inside the cottage.

Kat can barely stand to be in the same room as Freya but whenever she comes across her, she finds her eyes drawn by some twisted force to her sister's growing belly. The sight of it horrifies her, and yet she can't seem to stop herself. Freya is at pains to hide it, wafting around in her baggiest dresses and flowing scarves or some days not even bothering to change out of her nightie, but it's no use; her clothes grow tighter by the day and it's visible to them all now, the swell of her baby bump jutting out to stretch the fabric taut across her body.

What's worse, they are all treating Freya differently. It's as though overnight she has sprouted fairy wings and a golden halo. Simon is the worst, as though she's been elevated in his eyes to something superior and untouchable: the mother of his child. But the others play along too; they tiptoe around her in respectful deference. *Is there anything I can get you, Freya? Here, have my seat, Freya. Let me make you some tea, Freya.* To her face they are all politeness and awe, although Kat has heard the whispers, she knows what they are really thinking; she has heard Carla and Ben talking late at night when they've thought everyone else asleep.

'It's just bloody odd, if you ask me,' Carla had whispered to Ben with the tiniest trace of salacious glee. 'I thought he was supposed to be with Kat, but now this. Perhaps they're *both* sleeping with him? No wonder he's strutting around like he's cock of the walk.'

'If I'd known we were advocating a polygamist model here I might have made a move myself.'

She'd heard Carla's low chuckle followed by the thump of a pillow connecting with flesh. 'We could go,' she'd heard Carla whisper a moment later, 'pack our bags and leave.'

'Leave? You want to leave now?' Ben had murmured. 'Just when things are getting so *interesting* . . .'

Kat had turned away from the half-open door and tried to block out the sound of Carla's sniggers, but she'd been sure to give them both a little less rice at dinner the following night – petty perhaps, but satisfying all the same.

And then, just like that, the sun peers tentatively over the crest of the surrounding hills and they wake to a crisp, clean day. They step out into the pale sunshine like lambs tottering out on unsteady legs.

'There's frogspawn in the lake,' says Ben, pointing down at a glutinous, speckled jelly lying just beyond the jetty. 'We could be eating frogs' legs in a few weeks,' he jokes. 'They're supposed to taste like chicken, right?'

Carla leads Kat up into the garden where they pick the tips of young nettles for soup and pull the first leaves of their spring greens from the ground. 'I never thought I'd be so glad to see spinach,' she jokes. 'After all those carbs I'll be glad of a few vitamins.'

Kat nods.

'This stuff will be good for the baby too,' she adds. 'Where has your sister got to? She was here just a minute ago.'

Kat shrugs. 'I'm hardly her keeper.'

No one seems to know where Freya has gone and she doesn't return until sunset, by which time Simon is brooding with quiet fury. 'Where the hell have you been? We were worried sick.'

She eyes him carefully then pushes past. 'I went for a walk.'

'All day? What if something had happened to you . . . or to the baby?'

'It didn't.' Her voice is flat, uninterested.

Kat takes in her sister's appearance in one sweeping glance: her ruddy cheeks, her plaited hair, her mud-spattered clothes; if anything she looks even more beautiful, like a pale spring flower coming into bloom. Kat sees Simon's fists clench at his side as he takes a breath. 'Perhaps you could do us the courtesy of telling us where you are going next time?'

Freya pours herself a drink of water and leaves the kitchen without answering. Kat is surprised. It's almost as though Freya has wrested some power from Simon and the next day she goes out again, and the next, never once telling any of them where she is going, but always returning just before sunset, until Simon eventually drops the subject. He doesn't like it but he seems to know that he can't stop her.

Kat is pleased to see her go. She has no patience for her sister's gloomy face. Freya is acting like a trapped animal, but Kat knows that really *she's* the one without options. It's like some terrible game: everyone on tenterhooks waiting to see what will happen next. Some mornings, when she wakes early, she lies in bed and wishes she were brave enough to leave the cottage – to leave all of them behind – but she just can't bear to be without Simon. Her heart is still full of him.

Besides, there are moments of hope. Whenever she has just about convinced herself it's over between them, he surprises her by taking her to one side, singling her out, giving her shoulder a gentle squeeze, or her back a rub or once or twice leading her upstairs while the others are distracted with their chores outside, where he pins her down on the mattress and makes love to her with a ferocious intensity. There's something about it she hates – the lack of time and tenderness – but she consoles herself with the fact that it is, at least, something and she holds the memory of him on her bruised thighs and in her dishevelled hair like precious secrets.

* * *

In the end, it's the smallest detail that creates the biggest drama: a ball of purple wool unspooling in Freya's lap. Kat watches it unravel from across the room, listens to the rhythmic click-clack of the knitting needles as they twist in Freya's hands and the longer she watches, the hotter her rage burns. Simon must have bought it for her with the money from the tin. *Their* money. Since when are Freya's sewing materials considered essential for the maintenance of the cottage? One rule for Freya and another for the rest of them. Kat takes a breath and tries to steady her voice. 'What are you doing?' she asks.

Freya doesn't bother to look up. 'Knitting.'

'I can see that. What are you making though?'

'A blanket.'

Understanding dawns: a baby blanket. She studies Freya for a moment. 'Where did the wool come from?'

Freya remains silent and Kat feels her anger burn more brightly. She knew it. 'Did Simon buy it for you?'

Freya shakes her head, her tongue caught between her teeth as she counts a row of stitches.

'But it's for the baby, right?' There is nowhere else she could have got it from.

'I had the wool already, OK? I brought it with me.'

Kat shakes her head. 'No you didn't.'

'How do you know?'

'Because I would have seen it before now.'

Freya sighs. 'Just leave it, Kat. It's not important.'

But it is important; if Simon has been buying gifts for Freya – if they have been discussing the baby, making plans, spending what little cash they have left on the child – then Kat wants to know.

'Just tell me where it came from.' She tries smiling, softening her voice. 'It's no big deal.'

But Freya shakes her head then ignores her sister, focusing purely on the needles clacking between her fingers.

'God dammit, Freya, why won't you tell me? Just admit that it was Simon.'

Freya's hands fall still. She looks up from the tangle of wool in her lap. 'You may think you know everything about this place, but you don't. You don't know anything.'

Kat bristles. 'What's that supposed to mean?'

Freya shakes her head and returns her attention to the knitting in her lap.

'Come on,' says Kat, well and truly goaded. 'What did you mean by that? Spit it out.'

'Forget it,' says Freya, and Kat can tell from the determined set of her sister's jaw that she won't get another ounce of information from her. Bloody Simon, it has to be him.

She finds him in the kitchen, just moments later. He sits at the table, parts of the rifle disassembled and spread before him. 'Why have you been buying Freya gifts?' she asks, unable to stop herself.

'What?' He looks up, bemused, black grease smeared across one cheekbone. Even in her rage, she feels her heart twist at the sight of him. 'What are you talking about?'

'The blanket . . . the one Freya's making for the baby.'

'What blanket?' He gazes at her, his eyes like charcoal in the fading light. He shakes his head. 'I don't know what you're on about,' and he returns his attention to the gun.

'Sure you do.' She sidles over and stands beside him, her shadow falling across the table. 'You bought her wool.' She says it with a smile in her voice, even though her guts are still gripped with anger. 'With our money.'

He throws her an irritated look and sighs. 'What wool? Can you move, you're in my light.'

He returns his attention to the gun barrel in his hands and Kat feels heat simmer in her belly. In one smooth movement he slides the bolt back into the receiver. Kat shifts closer. She reaches out a finger and rolls a cartridge across the table, forwards and backwards, forwards and backwards.

'Don't,' he says, grabbing the cartridge from her, snapping it into place.

'Can't you leave that alone for one minute while we talk about this? It's important.'

He won't even look at her. 'Is it?' He sounds doubtful.

'It's important that we all have a say what we spend our money on. I didn't think there was room for personal indulgences. It's only fair.'

'I've told you,' he says, his voice grim now, a warning. 'I don't know what you're talking about.' He pushes the bolt handle down locking the round in place and lifts the gun experimentally to his shoulder.

She reaches out to bat it away. 'God dammit, Simon! Put the gun down.'

It's not exactly clear what happens next. Kat's hand pushes against the barrel, but at the same time, Simon's finger must catch inside the trigger, because a split second later a loud shot rings out in the kitchen, sending a shower of dust and splinters from the overhead beam raining down upon the flagstone floor. Kat leaps back, startled. She can feel the thud of her heart in her ribcage and a burning sensation on her neck. She reaches up to touch her skin where it stings and her fingers come away red. As she stares at the blood on her fingertips, the room begins to swim.

'Fuck.'

She reaches out a hand to steady herself, the blast still ringing in her ears.

'What the hell?' Mac appears in the doorway.

Kat stares at Simon. 'It was an accident,' she says weakly.

'I thought the safety was on.'

'Damn it, Simon,' says Mac, moving into the room, 'you could have killed her.' He takes the gun from Simon's hands and clips the safety into position, lays it carefully on the table and then turns back to Kat. 'Are you OK?'

She nods and leans heavily against the table.

'Oh God,' says Carla, appearing in the kitchen. 'You're bleeding.' She moves across to Kat. 'Sit down,' she urges and then leans in to inspect her neck. 'I need a cloth.' Mac throws her a clean tea towel and she begins to dab at the wound.

'It's nothing,' says Kat through gritted teeth. 'Just a scratch.' She reaches up and pulls something thin and sharp from the wound. 'Look, just a splinter . . . off the beam.' She holds the black shard of wood out to them on the tip of her finger.

'What's happening?' It's Freya, standing in the doorway, looking horrified. 'Kat? Are you OK?'

Kat looks at her sister and sees her shocked face, the firm swell of her stomach and the ball of purple wool still in her hands, unfurling at her side. 'Will everyone stop fussing? I'm fine.' But she eyes the shattered wood on the beam above the range. An inch or two to the right and things would have been very different.

19

LILA

April

William is throwing sticks for Rosie. He curves them out low over the surface of the lake, like boomerangs that don't arc back. Rosie waits for the sign – a splash of wood hitting water – then explodes off the bank and into the shallows, spray rising up to hang suspended, for just a moment, as a string of pearls in the sunshine. When the water gets too deep to wade she doggy paddles on, seizes the stick between her jaws and swims back to William, dropping her prize at his feet and yapping like an excited puppy until he throws it out again.

'Doesn't she get tired?' asks Lila, perched beside him on the sagging tree trunk.

'She'd do this all day if I kept throwing them. Not bad for an old girl.'

'She's smiling, look,' says Lila, pointing down to where Rosie grins at their feet.

'Who can blame her. It looks inviting, doesn't it?'

Lila looks out across the lake and shrugs.

'You don't think so?'

She shifts on the log. 'It looks all right.'

'Only all right?'

She holds up her hands. 'OK, I confess: I can't swim.'

'You can't swim?'

She shakes her head.

'Seriously?'

'Yep.'

He eyes her. 'Your parents—' he says and then stops.

'*My parents* what?'

'Your parents should have taught you. It's a good skill to have. Could save your life.'

'Oh they both tried but they just couldn't get me near the water. From when I was very little, apparently, one look at the sea, a pond, a swimming pool and I would scream and scream. A bath is fine now but anything deeper . . .' She shakes her head. 'I've always been afraid of it. '

William studies her with interest. 'Why?'

'Beats me. Some irrational fear. Why does anyone have a particular phobia?'

He nods. 'And yet here you are.' He indicates the proximity of the lake.

'Yes, here I am.' She smiles. 'I'm OK, as long as I don't get too close.'

'It doesn't have to be like that, you know. You could learn.'

'Oh, I think it's a bit late for that, don't you?

'Why?'

'You know the saying: old dog, new tricks.'

'The only old dog around here is Rosie. You'd be fine.' William thinks on it a moment. 'I could teach you.'

Lila laughs. 'I don't think so.'

'Why not?'

'I'd sink like a stone. This body,' she says, indicating herself with a self-deprecating wave, 'isn't made for swimming. Besides,' she adds, 'it's freezing. I'm happy sitting right here, letting Rosie have all the fun.'

'You'd get used to the temperature pretty quickly.'

'Is that right? You know what they say: talk's cheap.'

'Is that a challenge?'

'Might be.'

William stands and pulls off his jumper. 'OK, if I go in, you accept a swimming lesson? Deal?'

Lila smiles. 'You won't go in, I know it.'

'Deal?'

'You're not going in.'

'Do we have a deal?'

'Deal,' she relents.

William places his sweater on the tree trunk then removes his shirt and vest before reaching for the buckle of his belt. Embarrassed, Lila averts her gaze to the distant grey clouds gliding over the furthest hills. When she looks back he is wading into the shallows in just his boxer shorts. She watches the slope of his pale, broad shoulders as they get closer and closer to the water. 'I know you're bluffing,' she catcalls.

He turns around to face her and then, with a huge smile, opens his arms wide and launches himself backwards into the water, disappearing completely from view. The lake closes up behind him until all that remains is a trail of bubbles rising to the surface with the faintest popping sound.

She waits for him to reappear, and when he does he surprises her by being at least another ten metres or so out from where he went down. He bursts through the water like Rosie, shaking his hair and gasping for breath and the collie dog, not wanting to miss out, leaps in after him. Lila sits on the rotting tree stump and squints into the sunshine, watching them play together in the lake as she picks at flecks of furry moss growing on the fallen tree trunk. Even she has to admit it looks like fun.

'So,' he says, when he finally emerges, his skin pink and covered in goosebumps, 'first lesson tomorrow?'

Lila laughs and shakes her head. 'We didn't shake on it.'

'Oh come on.'

'Honestly, I wouldn't be any good.' She eyes the darker water further out and can't help a little shudder.

'What is it you're worried about?'

Lila thinks about her dreams. Falling. Drowning. She doesn't imagine there is much difference between the two. 'I – I . . .' But she can't explain it. 'It's too cold for me.'

'Well,' says William, drying himself off with his vest, 'if you change your mind, you know where I am.'

'Thanks.' She smiles with relief. 'But I don't think there's any chance of that.'

* * *

She sees the swimming costumes hanging on a rail in the supermarket just a couple of days later. They swing limply next to shelves of summer sandals and plastic sunglasses and are cheap at only ten pounds each. Lila eyes them, circling the rail once, then moves on to the next aisle before she can do anything so foolish as to put one in her trolley. She's not going to learn to swim. No way.

It's only as she queues at the checkout that she has a sudden change of heart. There is a memory stuck in her mind, of Rosie bursting through the water, grinning like an idiot with that big stick in her mouth.

'I'll be right back,' she says apologetically to the woman waiting in line behind, and she runs to the swimwear display, grabs the first one she can find in her size, and flings it onto the conveyor belt behind the rest of her groceries. What the hell, she thinks. It's only a tenner.

* * *

They start the following week. Lila is still reluctant but the weather is surprisingly mild for April and the sight of the sun playing upon the surface of the lake helps to dampen her fear a little. 'We'll start slow, here where it's shallow,' reassures William. 'Just a few basics. You can practise putting your face in the water, blowing bubbles, a bit of doggy paddle. I'll be right here with you, OK?'

Lila nods and tugs self-consciously at her swimsuit. She feels like a little kid with her goose pimples and her knocking knees.

William guides her out into the lake. Through the clear water she sees tiny pebbles glistening on the bottom and fronds of green weed undulating in the wash from their feet. She squeals as the cold water rises up around her thighs. 'You lied. It's freezing.'

'You'll be all right once you're in.'

She gazes out at the dark centre of the lake and tries to swallow down the fear rising like bile in her throat. 'I don't think—'

'Don't think, just do as I say.' They step out further until the water is up to her chest. It is so cold she's not sure she can feel her feet any more. 'Now, we're going to lean forwards and blow bubbles through our mouths. Put your face right in the water and blow. OK? On three. One. Two. Three.'

She feels like an idiot, like a little child being instructed by her father, but she does it anyway, copying exactly what William does.

'Good,' he says. 'When your face is in the water, you blow out, not in. That's the first lesson mastered. See, it's easy.'

She tries to smile through chattering teeth.

'Now let's move on to basic doggy paddle. You need to scoop the water with your hands, long arms. See.' He holds out his hands to show her what he means and she copies him again, scooping through the water with long pulling movements. 'Excellent.'

The lesson continues until Lila can't feel her face, let alone her feet. 'I'm so cold. I have to go in.'

William nods.

'OK. Let's see if you can put it all into practice. I want you to swim for the shore.' She gives him a look. 'Go on. Just launch yourself off the bottom, kick your legs and pull with your arms. Keep your head out of the water. Think about how Rosie does it.'

She shakes her head. 'I c-can't.'

'You want to get out, don't you? Well, that's the quickest way, trust me.'

She eyes him, then, before she can chicken out, she kicks up off the bottom and flails madly through the water. All she is thinking about is getting out of the godforsaken lake and getting warm and dry. Somewhere in the back of her mind she hears William's instructions, scoop the water, kick with her legs, knees together, not too much splash, and before she knows it her knees are grazing the bottom of the lake. She has made it back at least three metres towards the shore, unassisted. She staggers out of the water and wraps herself in a towel, watching from the bank as William swims a little longer. By the time he emerges her teeth have stopped chattering.

'You did really well,' he says. 'You swam all by yourself.'

'I just wanted to get out.'

'Well it worked.'

She shakes her head. 'Tom will never believe it.'

'You must tell him,' insists William, 'tonight.'

'Yes,' says Lila, doubtfully, drying her hair.

'You can't keep avoiding him like this,' says William, pulling a sweater on over his head. 'It's none of my business,' he adds, his face appearing again through the neck hole, 'but my advice would be don't let whatever it is that's going on between you two drag on. It's not good for either of you. You have to talk.'

'We are talking,' she says.

He eyes her carefully and she can see he isn't fooled.

She sighs. She thinks about her dreams. She thinks about her certainty now that someone was with her when she fell. That *Tom* was with her. She knows she needs to talk to him. She knows she can't keep shutting him out. She just doesn't know how to speak aloud the sheer awfulness of what she is thinking. 'It's not that simple,' she says finally.

'Of course it's that simple,' says William, surprising her with his vehemence. 'Look at you. You were terrified of the water and now you can paddle yourself along unaided.'

'Only a couple of metres.'

'Three metres and it's three metres more than you could manage an hour ago. How good does that make you feel?' He swallows. 'You can't spend your life hiding in shadows.'

'I don't know,' says Lila, shaking her head.

William gazes out over the lake. 'Don't wait too long, Lila. You might lose the one thing that's most important to you.'

She is surprised by the emotion in his voice and wonders if they're still talking about her and Tom. 'Are you OK?'

William shakes himself then stoops to pick up his damp towel. 'I'm fine.'

Lila gives him a worried glance but he is already whistling for Rosie and turning away, making for the grassy ridge that will lead him back to the track and his Land Rover.

'I'll try to swim six metres if you come again tomorrow?' she calls after him. He turns on the crest of the hill and raises his hand, then disappears from view.

*   *   *

It takes three weeks and William coming almost every day to teach her, but by the end of those weeks, Lila has not only conquered her phobia but also mastered a passable breaststroke. She can dive down below the surface for pebbles and even float on her back spread-eagled like a star. Gradually, whether William comes or not, it becomes part of her daily routine to end each day with a splash in the lake to wash away the dust and dirt of her work. After a hard day sanding and painting or hammering and polishing, she likes to lie upon the water – not too far out, but just far enough to feel a detachment from the cottage and the land around her, to feel herself weightless upon its surface. For just a moment, surrounded by the vast bowl of land, the valley rising up all around her, she feels her insignificance. She is nothing: a dandelion seed floating on the surface, a drifting water bug, the reflection of a cloud.

She uses her hands to make tiny sculling movements in the water, just as William has shown her, to hold her position. She slows them and brings them to rest on her stomach then inhales deeply and closes her eyes. One more minute and she'll return to shore. She feels the chill now, feels the goose pimples prickling across her skin. She moves her hands over her belly, her skin cold and her abdomen firm to the touch. Her fingers slow. Then her eyes snap open.

Her body has felt like this before. Her skin taut, her bones tired, her breasts aching and full. She recognises the sensation and her breath catches in her throat. Pregnant?

Unable to hold the floating position while a maelstrom swirls in her mind, she flips over and begins to swim back to the shore, making a beeline for the pile of clothes she has left near the fallen tree.

Valentine's night with Tom: could it have happened then? She tries to recall whether she's had a period since. She's been so distracted with the cottage, with getting everything in order, the swimming lessons . . . could she *really* be pregnant?

She hauls herself out of the shallows and reaches for her clothes, carries them back to the cottage, dripping and shivering, doing the calculations rapidly in her head. When she's finally dressed and sitting at the kitchen table, a cup of tea before her, Lila tentatively explores her emotions; she tests them like someone walking across a creaking lake of ice, taking each step slowly, not quite daring to put her full weight down until she is certain it will hold.

When Milly died, well-meaning friends and family had told them how sorry they were and a few had added, *You're young – you can always try again.* To Lila the sentiment had seemed both thoughtless and cruel, as though they were trying to sweep her grief – her daughter – beneath a carpet. It took away from what they were feeling, what they were going through.

Ever since then, Lila hasn't allowed herself to think about getting pregnant again – and not just because of the state of her and Tom's marriage, the absence of their sex life. Deep down, she's known there can never be a replacement for her first child. The loss will always be there – a void that will never be filled. She supposes the truth is that she just hasn't known if she is brave enough to put herself through it all over again – to try again.

But now there is this. She sips her tea and looks out across the darkening lake. *She could be pregnant again.* The thought fills her with trepidation and a spiralling fear and the tiny flicker of something else too – is it excitement? She shakes her head. She isn't sure. The only thing she can know for certain is that her world may have just tilted in a terrifying new direction.

2 0

APRIL

1981

The water is still cold, but after months of washing with icy flannels or laboriously heating water on the range, it's a relief to be able to throw themselves into the lake and swim again. It's bracing stuff but they can't resist the lake's lure.

Kat's routine now is to wake early every morning and wade into its depths. She pulls herself across the surface with a strong front crawl, enjoying the sensation of her muscles working, the exhalation of air from her mouth, the twist of her head followed by the quick inhalation, the oxygen recharging her body, flowing through her blood. It's almost meditative, nothing but her and her breath and her limbs ploughing through the water. She can feel herself getting stronger, fitter, leaner – like an animal, all muscle and sinew and skin.

In contrast, Freya is softening and ripening. Nearly seven months pregnant and she swells with promise, growing plumper by the day. She still seems ashamed to reveal the changes to her body, but like the rest of them, she can't resist the water. Often she joins Kat in the lake but unlike her sister's gruelling laps, Freya prefers to splash around until she has acclimatised to the temperature and then float upon its surface, the pale hump of her body rising up out of the water. 'I feel weightless,' she says. 'I feel like nothing.' Her voice is wistful. 'It's as if I could just float away.'

Kat doesn't look at her. She finds her sister's belly and the plump curve of her breasts grotesque. She pretends she hasn't heard and dives back beneath the water, pulling herself away from Freya, back towards the shore.

* * *

Kat is careful to leave the water first that morning. It's been a week or so since Freya has taken one of her long, solitary walks and she can sense her restlessness building. She is certain she'll be leaving again soon on one of her mysterious outings and this time, when Freya leaves, Kat is determined to follow.

She shivers her way across the damp grass and dresses quickly in jeans and a jumper then towel dries her hair. Up near the cottage she leans over a clump of spindly nettles and carefully picks a few young shoots, before heading into the kitchen where she makes a cup of bitter nettle tea. As the leaves steep, she stands at the window with her hands wrapped around the warm mug. She can hear Ben and Carla hooting with laughter somewhere upstairs but she pays them no attention. Instead, she watches as Freya wades from the water, drying herself with a towel then leaning awkwardly, trying to wrap her long, wet hair in the fabric. It doesn't look easy, the bulge of her belly constricting her movements.

Mac approaches from over near the lean-to. He says something to Freya that Kat can't hear then holds his hand out for the towel. Freya nods, passes it over and turns her back to him. Kat blows across the hot surface of her tea but her eyes never leave the couple down by the lake. She watches intently as Mac reaches up and takes her sister's long, damp hair between the folds of the towel. He rubs and rubs and Kat notices how Freya leans into him, just a little, how his hands hover for a moment over Freya's shoulders, as if wanting to touch her but afraid to. Summoning his courage with a visible breath, he lowers them, finally, then spins her around to face him. Freya smiles up at Mac and their eyes lock for what feels like a very long time. Kat watches it all from the cottage and understands: Mac and Freya. How *sweet*, she thinks with a twist of resentment. Is there anything – or anyone – Freya won't try to take?

An hour later, Freya slips out of the back door just as the yellow sun strikes the tops of the alder trees. Kat gives her a couple of minutes' head start then follows her out in the direction of the meadow. She breaks through the copse of trees just in time to see Freya heft herself awkwardly over the gate before turning right up the overgrown track. Kat hangs back for a moment then marches on in pursuit.

The endless spring rain has made the track boggy. Kat slips and splashes her way up the hill, following her sister's footprints through the claggy mud. Overgrown verges burst with dandelion flowers and white tufts of cotton grass. The hedgerows rustle with life. As she goes an inquisitive blue tit flits in and out of the thicket, urging her on with a cheeky staccato chirrup.

Higher and higher they climb until the landscape changes, opening out from enclosed hedgerows and fields to scrubby moorland. It is harder for Kat to stay hidden. She drops back even further, keeping an eye out for the distant flash of Freya's billowing white dress, but she needn't worry; Freya doesn't turn round once. Typical, thinks Kat, so trusting, so naive.

It's colder the higher up they go, the air clearer and crisper. The sky gapes wide open. Kat feels as though she's walking right into it. It's a barren landscape – nothing much but scrubby heather and bilberry bushes yet to flower and here and there a lonely rowan tree pushing up towards the sky.

Freya strides on, no longer following a visible walking track, but still confident in her direction, as if guided by some inner compass. Kat follows behind doggedly, determined not to lose her.

A little further on and Freya startles an unsuspecting red grouse from a clump of heather. As it takes flight, she reaches out a hand to the crumbling stone wall beside her, her other hand coming to rest for a moment on the swell of her belly. Kat hangs back, her heart in her mouth, waiting for her sister to walk on but Freya doesn't move and Kat wonders if she has been spotted. But it's not Kat that has brought her to a standstill. Up on the moor, only twenty metres or so from where her sister stands, a red deer comes into view. Kat's eyes widen. It is startlingly beautiful, yet to shed its elegant antlers, which point to the sky like the twisted branches of the rowan trees. Freya stands stock-still, facing off against the stag until a gust of wind catches the fabric of her dress, sending it billowing out around her legs. The movement spooks the animal and it rears away over the crest of the hill. Kat holds her breath, only releasing it when Freya begins to walk again. She can't believe she hasn't been up here before. It's too easy, at the cottage, to forget about the beauty all around them. She's become lazy. She's forgotten to appreciate their wild isolation.

They walk and walk until gradually the landscape shifts once more, assuming a more cultivated feel with stone walls and stretches of barbed wire fencing, tufts of ratty sheep's wool locked onto the spikes and flapping in the breeze like tiny white flags. Kat spies a field of gambolling lambs and then further, in the distance, a grey stretch of gravel road leading towards a thin plume of smoke wafting high into the air, below which Kat can just make out the chimney stack it drifts from. She understands, at last, what it is they are heading towards: a farm, nestled high up on the moors.

She hangs back even further now. Having come so far, the last thing she wants is to be discovered by someone working in the fields, but when Freya draws near to the sprawling stone farmhouse, she realises she is in danger of losing sight of her altogether, and so she speeds up again and is just in time to hear the barking of a dog as it greets Freya in the yard. Kat peers round a crumbling wall and sees a golden Labrador bumping against her sister's legs.

Alerted perhaps by the sound of the dog, a dark-haired woman opens the front door and stands there, looking out. She wipes her hands on a checked tea towel and when she sees Freya playing with the dog, gives an exclamation of surprise. Kat watches open-mouthed as Freya steps up to the doorway and into the arms of the woman. They greet each other like old friends before Freya is drawn into the warmth of the farmhouse and the weathered door closes behind her, shutting Kat off from the unfolding scene within.

Kat stands frozen in her hiding place. She doesn't know what to make of what she's just seen, but she knows who the woman is, she's sure of it; it's the same woman who waved at her that morning all those months ago, from up on the ridge. Kat's brain clicks into gear and things quickly begin to fall into place: the lavish Christmas Day basket . . . the purple wool. Freya has been making friends with the locals. Freya has been *cheating*. While the rest of them have been toughing it out, sticking to the rules, trying to live frugal lives of self-sufficiency, Freya has been indulging herself with social outings and home comforts. Kat's smile is grim. It's hardly the image of independence that Simon has extolled and Kat knows he would class it as a betrayal, not least because Freya has potentially jeopardised their entire project. Simon didn't even want them visiting local pubs or shops too often. What on earth would he make of Freya befriending a local farmer, visiting her regularly for cups of tea and cosy chats?

It's a long walk back to the cottage and once or twice Kat isn't even sure if she is following the right path, but she picks her way across the moorland and then down the hillside until she rejoins the track leading to the meadow and the lake, buoyed by the knowledge that she has something that shows Freya in a less than perfect light. Finally, she has ammunition to use, when the time is right. Kat knows there is no way Simon will forgive Freya for this and she smoulders with indignation and anger the whole way. But there is something else there too, lurking in the hot furnace of her belly: a spark of relief.

*　*　*

Simon is waiting. He appears in the doorway of the lean-to and beckons for her to join him. Kat walks across the trampled grass, taking the moment to observe him from a distance. Living together in such close proximity, she's grown used to seeing him up close; she has forgotten to see the full shape of him. Now she regards

287

him as a stranger might: a tall, lean man with dark hair curling to his shoulders and a faint shadow of stubble on his chin. He is thinner than he was at university, but somehow he looks stronger, more muscular and powerful, his body honed by physical work. His face is changed too – all angles and shadows in the half light of the shed, like a cubist painting – and yet still the familiar curve of his lips, the high cheekbones, the dark, brooding eyes. She feels his beauty – and her desire for him – like a hot ache.

She is expecting him to ask where she has been but his mind is on other matters. 'Come here,' he says ushering her into the shadows of the lean-to.

She throws him a playful smile but as soon as she is inside she sees the bucket, rope and hunting knife laid out upon the wooden crate and a little further away, the rifle propped against the wall where it gleams ominously in the gloom. 'What's all this?' she asks, the smile beginning to fade on her face.

'It's time for Wilbur to meet his maker.'

Kat stares at him. 'But . . . Freya. . . she'll be devastated.'

Simon shrugs.

'Does Mac know?'

'I hardly think we need his permission, do we?'

Kat clears her throat. 'Shouldn't we wait for him though?'

'Why?' asks Simon, a tight smile playing on his lips. 'You think Mac's the only one who knows how to do anything remotely useful around here?'

'No, of course not,' she backtracks. 'I just thought . . . you and him together . . . it would be easier, surely?'

'Don't worry; I'll hold the pig. *You're* the one that's going to shoot him.'

Kat swallows. She searches his eyes for a spark of humour – hopes to see that he is just toying with her – but his face is set with grim determination. 'One shot through the head. Then we hang him up, skin him and remove the entrails. How hard can it be?'

Kat swallows again. 'I don't know . . .'

'What don't you know, Kat?' Simon looks at her, his head tilted to one side. 'Isn't this what it's about? Growing and rearing our own food . . . being responsible for death as well as life?'

'I don't think—'

'He's been royally pampered all the time he's been here. Probably eaten better than us most days.'

She can't return his smile. She can't get Freya out of her head. Her sister loves Wilbur. She thinks about the way he follows her about the cottage garden, or trails her by the lake, the affection she bestows upon it as she would a spoiled child. Kat is agonising over the decision when the hapless pig wanders into the barn. He snuffles and snorts his way through the dirt, then stares up at them longingly, hopeful for a dry crust or a handful of scraps.

'Look at him, so spoilt, so fat. He's not a pet. It's time he played his part.' Simon reaches out and touches her arm but Kat can't help it; silently she wills the pig to run away, to turn and leave the barn . . . but Wilbur, oblivious to the fateful conversation taking place above his head, just trots a little closer, still hopeful for some food.

'Here little piggy,' croons Simon. He bends down with his empty hand outstretched and Wilbur trots obediently forwards. When the pig is close enough, Simon grabs him around the neck and wraps the rope like a noose about him. The pig bucks and squeals but Simon ties him tight to one of the wooden posts in the shed and then straddles him, holding him still between his knees. Wilbur doesn't like it. His squeals rise in pitch. 'Quick, Kat, fetch the gun.'

She moves on autopilot, takes up the gun in her hands, feels the cool metal beneath her trembling fingers.

'Take the safety off. Good. Now point it at the front of his head. There. Slightly above and between the eyes.'

Wilbur falls silent. It's as if he knows what's coming. He gives one last half-hearted buck but Simon wrestles him back between his knees and secures the noose more tightly against the post. 'OK, slowly now; I'll move away, you shoot.'

289

'I don't think . . . I can't . . .' Kat is filled with panic. 'What if I miss?'

Simon's gaze bores straight into her, his eyes like flint. 'Don't.'

She presses the rifle to the pig's forehead. Wilbur gazes up at her, his blue eyes wide with terror. Kat tries to stare him down then looks away. She can't do it.

'Come on,' says Simon, egging her on. 'Do it. Shoot him.' Slowly, he backs away, leaving Wilbur tied to the post, the gun pressed to his head.

She thinks about Freya. She thinks of her sister lying upstairs in the cottage while Simon made love to her. She thinks of the baby, Simon's child, growing in her sister's swollen belly. She thinks of Freya and the way she had gazed at Mac only that morning down by the shores of the lake . . . the sight of her walking purposefully out across the moors . . . of how she'd been welcomed by that stranger with open arms.

'Now,' whispers Simon.

She thinks of all Freya's betrayals and she closes her eyes and squeezes the trigger.

The sound is deafening. The impact ricochets up her arms and lodges in her shoulders. She feels the explosion deep in her chest, as if it is *her* that has been shot, not the pig. Something warm and wet splatters onto her hands. She feels it on her face too. She moans at the horror but gradually the ringing in her ears stops and she hears footsteps running towards the barn.

'What the hell?' It is Mac, standing breathless in the doorway. He sees the pig lying on the dirt between them and he races forwards. 'What have you done?'

A pool of pig's blood is spreading at her feet. Kat steps backwards, so as not to tread in it.

'We thought it was time for some roast pork.' Simon is smiling but Mac's face is a picture of horror.

'You don't do it like this!'

'Why not?'

290

'You don't do it on a whim, in the dirt with the animal half scared to death. You do it with preparation and respect.'

The smell of blood fills the air. Its cloying metallic tang fills Kat's nose and lungs; it makes her feel sick.

'We were prepared,' Simon says coolly.

Mac shakes his head. 'No,' he says firmly, 'not like this.'

Simon rolls his eyes at Kat but Mac doesn't seem to notice. He is too distracted by the pig. 'We've got to get it off the ground. Raise it up. Slit its throat. If we don't remove the stomach and intestines quickly the meat will spoil.' Mac stares at the pig and shakes his head. Kat is shocked to see tears in his eyes.

'I do know all this,' says Simon through gritted teeth. He takes a step towards Mac and Mac, sensing the movement, swings his head up in surprise. They face off across the dead animal, tension radiating from both of them. Kat sees Simon's hands clench at his side, a flash of silver – the hunting knife – held in one curled fist and Kat knows this isn't just about the pig any more.

She would intervene. She would tell them to stop being such macho idiots and just butcher the pig before the entire exercise is wasted, but she doesn't have time to worry about that now. The sight of the fleshy pink pig, lolling on the ground in the dirt, and the coppery smell of the blood makes her guts heave violently. She turns and runs to the doorway, only just making it out of the barn before her stomach clenches and a stream of watery vomit splatters onto the dirt outside.

* * *

Freya returns late, to a cottage still simmering with tension and filled with the sickly-sweet aroma of roasting pork.

'What's that smell?' she asks, shrugging off her cardigan and hanging it by the door. 'Has someone been shopping?' She puts her nose to the air.

Ben glances across at Kat, clearly not wanting to be the one to tell her.

Kat swallows and then clears her throat. 'It was . . . it was time . . .' She can't finish her sentence and she looks to the floor instead.

Freya stares from Kat to Ben and then back to Kat. 'What?' she asks. 'What was time?' Slowly, her smile fades. 'You didn't,' she says, her voice barely a whisper.

It's hardly a question but Kat finds she doesn't have the answer anyway. All she can think of is the pig's terrified blue eyes staring up at her, just before she pulled the trigger.

'Wilbur?'

Ben nods.

Freya's cheeks flood with colour. She turns on Kat. 'Who did it?'

Before she can answer, Simon sidles into the room in bare feet, his hands wrapped around a chipped mug of tea. 'Oh, hello, Freya,' he greets her with airy nonchalance, 'back from your walk? And just in time for dinner, good.' He stops and looks between the three of them. 'What?'

'Who killed Wilbur?' Freya's voice is ice. 'Was it you?'

Simon gives a small smile and shakes his head. 'I had no idea your sister was such an excellent shot. We'll have to take her out hunting with us next time.'

Freya spins back to Kat in disbelief. 'You?'

Kat drops her head. The look in her sister's eyes is worse than she had imagined.

'You should be thanking us,' says Simon from the doorway. 'You could do with a little more protein in your diet . . . for the baby,' he adds unnecessarily.

Freya stares at him, her eyes like daggers, but she has no words. Instead she pushes past him and stomps up the stairs, the sound of her sobs echoing behind her as she goes. Simon shrugs. 'I don't know why she's so upset. It was going to happen sooner or later. We always told her he wasn't a pet.'

* * *

It's a miserable meal. They sit round the table pushing charred pieces of meat about their plates while Freya's seat remains glaringly empty.

'She's remarkably stubborn, isn't she?' says Simon to no one in particular.

Kat spears a piece of meat with her fork and puts it to her lips. She isn't hungry but she forces it into her mouth and chews slowly. It is tender and sweet, a little smoky where the fat has charred, but all she can think about is the creeping pool of blood on the dirt floor of the barn and the terror in Wilbur's wide blue eyes. The meat slips down her throat like a hard marble and lands in her guts where it churns sickeningly for the rest of the evening. She feels, in Simon's approving gaze, that she has won something, but she's not sure if Freya will ever forgive her for what she's had to do to claim her prize.

21

LILA

May

Lila has just towelled her hair dry, pulled on a clean dress and headed downstairs in bare feet to boil the kettle when there is a loud rap at the front door. 'Coming,' she yells. The excited barks accompanying the knocks tell her who it is before she's even thrown the door open.

'Oh good,' says William, standing on the doorstep wearing a freshly ironed shirt and a tentative smile, 'we were hoping to catch you.'

'I don't leave until the morning.' She steps back. 'Come in, please. I was just going to make tea. Or perhaps you'd like a glass of wine? There's a bottle in the kitchen.'

William hesitates. 'Thank you.' He slips his boots off by the door then follows Lila into the kitchen, Rosie trotting at his heels. The dog curls up in her favourite spot by the range while William perches on the wooden bench, stretching his long legs in front of him. Both he and Lila see the hole in the toe of his sock at the same time and William grins and folds his feet back beneath him.

'Want me to darn that?' Lila teases.

He blushes. 'No, thanks. I can manage it myself . . . just.'

She holds up a bottle of red wine for his approval then fiddles with the corkscrew, pouring him a glass before turning to the kettle to make tea for herself. When she eventually sits down opposite him, William pushes something across the kitchen table towards her. 'Happy birthday,' he says.

Lila looks at him confused. 'How did you kn—'

'You told me, last time I was here, remember?'

'Did I?' Lila shakes her head. She doesn't remember, but then she's been so preoccupied with thoughts of her possible pregnancy perhaps it's not a surprise. 'Well, thank you,' she says, looking down at the small tissue-paper wrapped gift. You really shouldn't have.'

'It's just a little something.' William shifts in his seat as Lila begins to pull at the wrapping. 'It might not be to your taste,' he says, 'so please don't feel obliged to wear it.'

Inside the paper is a small black box. When she lifts the lid she sees a fine silver chain with a circular pendant nestled on black velvet. She holds it up to the light: an oval about the size of a fifty pence piece made from finely beaten silver with three small raised flecks within. The metal has been worked so expertly it feels as thin and delicate as a sheet of paper between her fingers. Lila stares at the pendant and knows instantly what it is: three seeds inside a papery pod. It's a seed head – an *honesty* seed head – just like the ones growing around the cottage; just like the ones she'd found in the upstairs bedroom when she arrived all those months ago.

'It's beautiful,' she says, fingering the delicate necklace. 'Is it—'

'Yes,' he nods, knowing what she's going to ask before she can finish her sentence. 'It's one of Evelyn's. I think she'd like you to have it.'

'Really?'

William nods.

She holds the chain up to her neck.

'Here, let me.'

He reaches over and brushes the hair from the back of her neck then fastens it in place.

'I want to see it.' She heads into the front room and admires the necklace in the mirror above the fireplace, grinning back at William where he stands just behind, watching. The pendant gleams like a silver coin in the hollow of her throat. She reaches up, smoothing her fingers once more over the delicate metal. 'Thank you. I love it.'

'Good,' says William. In the reflection of the mirror, his eyes seem to shine just a little too brightly. 'It suits you. Mum will be thrilled.'

Evelyn, she thinks, of course; it must be hard watching her deteriorate. 'How *is* she?' she asks as they return to the kitchen table.

'She's fine. She keeps asking after you though. You must come and visit us again, when you get back from London. That is,' he adds quickly, '*if* you come back.'

Lila nods and takes a sip of her tea.

William cocks his head to one side. 'You look different. What is it?'

Lila smiles. She wonders for a moment whether to tell him about the possible pregnancy, but then decides against it. Not yet. Not until she knows for sure and has had a chance to tell Tom. However she feels about him right now, Tom should be first. 'Must be all that swimming I've been doing,' she says.

'I have to say,' he glances curiously about the cottage, 'it looks as though you're almost finished here.'

'Yes,' she admits, following his gaze around the room. 'I was thinking the same thing earlier.' The interior is no longer dingy and draped in cobwebs and dust, but a welcoming space of light and colour. The walls and ceilings gleam a crisp, clean white, setting off the characterful wooden beams slung low across the ceilings. Lila has restored and painted a shabby dresser picked up in a local junk shop, installed it along the wall next to the window seat and lined its shelves with an eclectic array of glass bottles found about the cottage grounds. Colourful curtains cut from an antique patchwork quilt frame each window. There are fresh meadow flowers on the window sill and fruit in an earthenware bowl on the table.

Through the open doorway she can see the sofa standing beneath the window in its new linen slip covers and scattered with colourful cushions, as well as the low coffee table fashioned from the log rescued from the forest. The floorboards have been repaired and polished and gleam a warm honey colour beneath the new jute rug. Above the fireplace hangs a large, speckled mirror, reflecting the light from the windows back into the interior. Upon the mantel

Lila has lined coveted treasure from her walks: a giant pine cone, a polished stone, the long feather from a pheasant's tail, an old milk bottle filled with cowslips.

Upstairs the bedrooms are now cheery and bright. William's antique bed is covered with pillows and a colourful patchwork quilt gifted by Evelyn, while a fresh sheaf of green honesty seed heads has been hung up to dry, homage to the previous occupants. Beside the bed stands an upturned wooden crate with a vintage lamp and a pile of books resting beside it.

Only the spare room remains empty, its floorboards repaired from the water damage and its walls freshly painted but for the rectangle where the strange, faded mural remains. Every time she's thought about painting over it, something has stopped her. She's not sure why, but she isn't quite ready to cover it up. Not yet.

As Lila lets her mind wander through the cottage she can't help smiling; she knows she's done a good job. She's respected the property, honoured its past, and yet transformed it into an inviting space to be. She's made it into a home. Whose home, however, she still has no idea.

It's as if William has read her mind: 'Have you thought about what you're going to do with this place?'

Lila shakes her head. 'I don't know. I wondered about getting a valuation done, seeing what the property market is like up here.' She thinks for a moment. 'But you know, I've worked so hard. I feel as though I've come to know every inch of this place one way or another . . . and there are other improvements I'd like to make too, given time.' She casts her gaze about. 'You know, heating . . . a proper bathroom.' She sighs and slides her hands to her stomach. 'It'll be hard to give this up but I suppose real life beckons down south. I can't hide away for ever.'

She can admit it to herself now; she has been hiding – from her grief, and from Tom and from the message hidden within her dreams. But the time for hiding is over. She wants to confront the future and the truth head on, whatever it brings. She has to understand about the fall once and for all. She shakes herself. 'Anyway, it's

297

not as if I have to make any immediate decisions, is it? Summer's coming. Perhaps it would be fun to come back and hang out here for a bit . . . to enjoy the lake and the cottage. Maybe I'll just hold off from making any big decisions for the time being.'

'Yes,' agrees William, 'there's no need to rush. Enjoy your birthday with your friends and family in London.' He takes a sip of wine. 'Has Tom got anything special lined up?'

Lila shrugs. 'I'm not sure. He's booked a dinner somewhere, I think . . . and I'm having lunch with Mum.' Lila smiles. 'She's coming from France especially.'

William drains the last of the wine and stands. 'Well, I hope you have a lovely time.' Rosie jumps up from her spot by the hearth and winds herself about his legs. 'Come along, Rosie, time for us to leave.'

Lila shows them both to the front door where the first stars are beginning to speckle the darkening sky. 'Thank you for the gift. I love it. Will you thank Evelyn for me too?'

William nods. 'Of course.' He reaches out and touches one of the clematis buds hanging off the vine creeping its way up the front of the cottage. 'This will be in flower soon.'

Lila smiles. 'Something to come back for.'

He nods and as he and Rosie disappear over the crest of the ridge she shuts the door behind him and leans hard against it, her hands instinctively rising up – one to rest on her belly, the other to the necklace hanging about her neck. A gift of honesty; it's more appropriate than William could ever know. Whatever happens next, she knows the time for indecision is over. It's time to face Tom and work out where they go from here.

* * *

The city rises up to greet her like a grey cardboard cut-out propped against the horizon. The urban landscape is a shock after the peace and relative stillness of the countryside. It is all movement and noise. Slowly, she navigates her way through increasingly familiar streets and tries not to jump at the blare of a bus horn, the brash shouts of schoolkids, music pumping from a car window. She feels a little ridiculous; she's always prided herself on her London savvy but after weeks away in the countryside, she is like a muddled tourist or a hermit resurfacing from a period of self-imposed exile. It's a relief when she finally pulls into their street and parks the car.

Opening the front door, her 'hello' echoes down the hallway. She flings her bag onto the floor before spotting Tom's note on the side table. She glances over his brief apology for not being there to welcome her back in person, as well as the directions to the Soho restaurant he has booked for dinner. *7 p.m.: I'll meet you there.*

Lila is relieved. She has an hour or two alone. It's plenty of time. She reaches into her handbag and pulls the pregnancy test from its paper bag, studies the cardboard box carefully then heads upstairs to the bathroom.

She's been thinking of nothing else virtually the whole way home. She's got to be pregnant, surely: the metallic taste in her mouth, the bloated sensation in her belly, her tender, swollen breasts? And yet it still doesn't make any sense. It took them twelve months of trying to conceive Milly. Now, after just one night – Valentine's night – could they have conceived another child? She doesn't know whether to laugh or cry. The last time she took a pregnancy test she was with Tom, the two of them squeezed into the bathroom, waiting impatiently for the minutes to pass. Back then, they had been filled with nothing but hope and longing, but this time it is different. This time *she* feels different.

She is afraid. Afraid because she's not sure she can do it again – afraid for the fragile new life inside her – and afraid for the perilous state of her marriage. She's not so naive as to think another baby can just paper over the cracks and make everything all right again. If she is pregnant, how on earth will she do this? How will she not spend every moment agonising and worrying? She can't think straight for terror.

Taking the white stick from its cellophane wrapper, she follows the printed instructions carefully then balances the stick on the edge of the sink and walks away. She doesn't cheat; she doesn't peek early. Instead she wanders into the bedroom and opens her closet.

Clothes she hasn't worn in months hang forgotten on their hangers, dresses and suits she used to shrug on every day for work. She flicks through them and selects an old favourite – a knee-length dress in a stretchy green fabric – and pulls it on. She smooths the material over her body and turns this way and that in the mirror, assessing her reflection. There is no visible trace of a bump; if anything, the dress is a little too big for her now and she wonders if she's kidding herself. She's been doing all that physical work . . . and swimming every day . . . but wouldn't the dress be tighter? She pushes the thought away and reaches instead for her make-up bag, carefully applying foundation, mascara, blusher and a slick of colour to her lips. She pulls a brush through her hair then stands back and surveys her face. Too much? She grabs a tissue and wipes most of the make-up off again, leaving just the mascara and a smear of lipstick behind. Then, when she can stand it no longer, she returns to the bathroom and reaches for the test.

* * *

The restaurant is an elegant new place tucked down a cobbled lane in Soho. Lila glances around at her surroundings as the solemn-faced maître d' leads her to an intimate corner table where Tom is already seated. There are white tablecloths, flickering candles, chandeliers and clinking glasses all accompanied by the genteel hum of expensively dressed patrons. Lila tugs at her dress and tries to keep pace with the man weaving through the tables. It's clear Tom is pushing the boat out and she knows she should be grateful, but as she moves across the restaurant floor she feels nothing but discomfort. She used to be good at this but tonight she feels awkward in her dress and heels and a million miles away from the rustic pleasures of the cottage. Suddenly she wishes she had done something different with her hair, or that she hadn't wiped all that make-up off. She has forgotten how this works.

Tom looks up as she draws near, lays his BlackBerry on the table and half stands, reaching out to her with a hand. 'There you are,' he says and kisses her on the cheek while the maître d' pulls back her chair and then snaps open the curled fabric of her napkin, laying it with a flourish across her lap. 'Happy birthday. You look lovely.'

'Thank you.' She fusses with her hair, tucking it behind her ears then releasing it again.

'An aperitif perhaps, Madame?' offers the waiter. 'Champagne?'

'No thank you,' she says, 'just a sparkling water.'

Tom glances at her. 'But it's your birthday. We should be celebrating.'

'I know. I'll have a glass of wine later.'

Tom looks stung. 'Or perhaps you're just not in the mood to celebrate?'

She shoots him a look. What does he mean by *that*?

'Very good, madame,' says the maître d' and melts away seamlessly.

Tom and Lila stare at each other and Lila has to take a breath. She has forgotten how handsome he is — his eyes dark and his shaven skin smooth and glowing, the white scar on his cheek illuminated in the candlelight — but he feels like a stranger, someone she is meeting for the very first time and the thought makes her stomach lurch. She wants to reach out for his hand, but she stops herself.

'A work colleague recommended this place,' he says, glancing about the restaurant. 'It's supposed to be good. We were lucky to get a table.'

'It's lovely. Thank you.'

Tom nods. 'So you got back OK?'

'Yes.'

He casts his gaze over her. 'You look different.' He eyes her carefully. 'Less make-up?'

Lila gives a little nod.

'It suits you. I never thought you needed all that gunk.' His eyes narrow as he studies her and Lila fights the urge to turn away. 'And you've caught the sun. Your freckles are back.'

Lila is relieved to see him smile, at last. 'It's all that time I've been spending outdoors. You should see the place, Tom. It's looking really good.'

Tom nods but she sees his smile falter and notices how his eyes drop away from hers. 'Is that an invitation?'

Lila looks at him for a moment. 'You don't need an invitation.'

'Don't I?' He lifts his gaze, this time in a challenge. 'I told you how I felt.'

Lila shakes her head. She'd thought she was the one treading uncertain territory but it seems Tom is equally unsure of himself. A waiter appears before them with a tall glass of sparkling water. He places it on the table before her. 'We'll need a few more minutes before we order,' says Tom.

'Very good, sir.'

Lila reaches for her drink. Beads of condensation are already forming on the outside of the glass, sparkling golden in the candle-light. She takes a sip then returns it carefully to the table and eyes Tom. He is staring down at the menu. 'I'm told the pork belly is very good . . . as is the duck. But really I'm sure it will all be excellent.'

'Tom,' she says, unable to wait any longer, unable to take any more of their stilted conversation, 'there's something I have to tell you.'

He glances up, his eyes dark and unreadable, then shuts the menu with a snap and lays it on the edge of the table. 'I think I know what this is about, but go on.'

'You do?' Lila is confused. How?

'Yes.' He nods. 'It's about William, isn't it?'

'William?'

'Yes. Or rather *you* and William.' There's a look in his eyes she hasn't seen before, a cool detachment.

'Me and William?'

'Yes,' he sighs. 'You know, if you came all this way to tell me that you're leaving me for William then we probably could have spared us both the embarrassment of dinner, but do go on.' She hears the edge in his voice.

'You think I'm here to tell you that I'm leaving you . . . for William?'

'Yes.' He eyes her carefully then gives a bitter laugh. 'Oh come off it, you've been hiding out in your little love nest for months now. Don't you think it's time you told me the truth?'

Lila's hands jump instinctively to the silver pendant hanging around her neck. Honesty. That's what she's come for. 'This isn't about William,' she says, but Tom is staring at the necklace, his eyes narrowing.

'Very nice. Did *he* give it to you?'

'Yes, but—'

'I wish you would just come out and say it. You've kept me dangling for months now, and I've been more than patient, Lila. I've been hoping you'd come back to me . . . that if I just gave you a little time . . . but I can see now that it's not going to happen. You've fallen for him, haven't you?'

'Tom!' Lila's cheeks flush at the thought of her and William, together. 'Would you just li—'

But her blushes only seem to convince him further. He pushes back his chair and rises from the table. 'I'm sorry, would you excuse me. I think I need some air.' He turns on his heel and strides away across the dining room before she can say another word.

Lila stares after him, speechless. What just happened? She looks hopelessly to the floor and sees Tom's napkin there, an incongruous white splash against the charcoal carpet. A waiter walks by and picks it up, folds it carefully then lays it across Tom's empty chair. 'Everything all right, Madame?'

'Yes . . . thank you.' She shakes her head. Did she just imagine all that? Tom thinks she's having an affair? With William? It's preposterous. She has to follow him. She has to explain. 'I just have to . . . I need . . .' She looks at the waiter helplessly. 'We'll be right back. Sorry.'

The waiter nods and Lila reaches for her handbag and races after Tom across the restaurant floor, ignoring the curious glances of the other diners. She slips past the long mahogany bar with its rows of colourful bottles and sparkling cocktail glasses, then out into the foyer where the heavy wooden door onto the street is just slamming shut. She bursts through it and spies Tom walking quickly down the dark Soho lane.

'Tom,' she yells, 'Tom, come back!'

Hearing her voice, he spins to face her, his face cast in shadow, his eyes an angry gleam.

'We need to talk,' she implores.

'We need to talk?' He throws his arms wide. 'That's rich, Lila. I've wanted to talk to you for months now, but you've been so cold, so evasive. Now you're finally here, I can only assume you've come to tell me, finally, that our marriage is over. But really, you needn't have bothered. We're probably beyond that now, don't you think? A text or an email would have sufficed.'

'Tom.' She moves until she is standing before him. 'I honestly don't know what you're talking about.' She reaches out for him but he pulls his arm away, the fabric of his jacket sliding through her fingers. 'Just stop. All this talk about me and William . . . it's ridiculous.'

'Is it?' He eyes the necklace again.

'This? It's a birthday gift, from William and his mother. There's nothing going on.'

He eyes her carefully, but he doesn't back away and she seizes her chance. 'Tom, I'm here. I'm here now, aren't I?'

He shakes his head. 'I know I said I'd stay away but I didn't think . . . I didn't expect . . .' He gives a bitter laugh. 'We've had no contact at all these last few weeks. It's felt as though you've been trying to sever any connection you have with me. It's like we have nothing between us any more . . . nothing real . . . nothing of substance anyway.'

She flinches, the image of their absent daughter floating between them. She swallows and tries to explain. 'But *you* said you didn't want to come . . .' He raises an eyebrow at her and she tries again. 'I've had so much going through my mind. I needed some time.'

'Time to work out how you feel about William?'

'No. God, will you stop going on about William, please. He's just a friend. It's other things. Things I've been remembering.' She hesitates, then realises that she might as well tell him. She's got nothing left to lose except the thin sliver of truth she senses dangling just beyond reach. She takes a deep breath and tries again. 'I've been remembering things. About that day . . . when I fell. I – I don't think I was alone. I remember someone being there – an argument – and then their hands on me.'

Tom is staring, as if she is insane. 'You think someone was there when you fell?'

She holds his gaze and her meaning hits him like a physical punch. He reels backwards. 'You think someone was there? That they *pushed* you down the stairs?' His eyes are wide with horror. 'Lila, this is serious. This is . . . my God. We have to go to the police.'

Lila can't meet his eye. 'Tom, just answer me something first.'

He nods.

'I need to know if you were there . . . in the house . . . when I fell?'

Tom's eyes grow wide. 'What?'

Lila bites her lip. 'Please, I need to know.'

He studies her with growing horror. 'You think it was *me*? You think *I* was there? You think *I* pushed you?' He shakes his head then suddenly crouches low to the ground and puts his head in his hands. 'Oh God, Lila. I don't know what is going on with us but this . . . this is so fucked up.'

The look on his face says it all. She can see amid the disbelief and confusion the devastating impact her accusation has had and she understands at last that she has got it spectacularly wrong. The pain in his eyes is clear to read: it's the pain of an innocent man accused. One look in his eyes and she knows that Tom would never hurt her. She wants to rewind. She wants to take her words back, to be sitting at that table in the restaurant still, but it's too late and she can't take her accusation back – not now.

Tom looks up at her, still struggling to comprehend. 'Honestly, Lila, what are you asking me? You think I'd hurt you . . . you think I'd hurt our baby?'

'Forget it.' She says. 'Just come back inside. Let's talk in the restaurant.'

'No. I can't face it in there.' He rubs his eyes and slumps down further to the ground, all strength leaving his body.

She stands there in the cobbled lane, helpless and uncertain. Out of the darkness, a group of young women totter towards them on high heels, giddy and giggling. 'Come on, Tom. We can't stay here – not like this. Shouldn't we go back in?'

Finally he stands, but instead of heading for the restaurant he turns and heads north towards Oxford Circus. 'Are you coming?' he asks over his shoulder, the exhaustion evident in his voice.

Slowly, she follows him down the street. As they near Oxford Street the orange light of a black cab appears out of the shadows. Tom flags it down and ushers her into the back and Lila sits there in the furthest corner of the back seat, watching as the lights and life of London speed past the window. She sees a rowdy stag party spill from a bar, eight drunken men crowing and posturing around their unfortunate friend who is dressed for humiliation in a huge yellow banana suit. Further along a couple of policemen talk to a homeless person slumped on a makeshift cardboard bed in a doorway. A girl in tiny silver hotpants argues with her boyfriend. A bouncer turns a drunken lad away at the door to a nightclub. The business of another Saturday night revolves all around them but Lila and Tom remain silent, locked within their private black bubble, the half-metre of physical distance between them belying the echoing chasm of confusion and pain.

* * *

As the cab pulls up to the house, Tom pays the driver and hops out, holding the car door open for Lila. She follows him up the path to the front door and watches as he turns his key in the lock, snaps on the hall light, then pushes the door shut behind them.

'Do you want a cup of tea?' she asks.

He shrugs.

'I'll put the kettle on.'

Neither of them move. Lila looks down and sees her holdall still sitting by the front door where she threw it just hours earlier.

She hasn't even unpacked yet. The thought comes to her then that she could reach for it, head out the front door and drive away again . . . back to the lake, back to the cottage. She could run.

But she's sick of running. She's sick of all these half-spoken truths and all the things that remain unsaid between them. And, most importantly, there is still something that she needs to tell him. Gently, she reaches for his hand. He starts at her touch, but allows her to take it. 'Come with me,' she says and she leads him into the front room, indicates for him to take the chair beside the fireplace then sits herself on the sofa opposite. He eyes her warily then turns away. Lila takes a deep breath. 'I'm pregnant,' she says, keeping her gaze focused purely on him.

Tom looks at her then, his eyes darting to her face. 'You're . . . pregnant?'

She nods.

Confusion races across his face. 'Is it . . . is it . . . ?'

'Is it yours?' she asks with a sigh. What a mess: what should be the happiest news of all is filled with pain and suspicion. 'Of course it's yours. I told you, there's *nothing* going on with William. He's just a friend.'

Tom thinks for a moment. 'Valentine's Day?'

Lila nods again.

Tom can't help himself; the fraction of a curve appears at the corners of his mouth. 'Lila. Why didn't you say something? In the restaurant.'

'You didn't give me a chance.'

He shakes his head. 'Pregnant.'

'I've only just found out for sure. I did a test, just before I came to meet you.'

Tom runs his hands through his hair. 'I can't keep up.'

Lila hesitates. More than anything, she realises, she wants him to hold her. 'Tom, I'm scared.'

He swallows and then nods. 'Me too.'

They stare at each other across the room. 'Where did we go so wrong?'

She shakes her head. 'I don't know.' She wants to ask him then, she wants to ask the one question that burns on the tip of her tongue: *Is it too late?*

But before she can say the words he is there, on the sofa beside her. He places his hand on the flat of her stomach. 'There's a baby,' he says, staring into her eyes. She nods and then he opens his arms to her. 'Together,' he says. 'We have to do this together. No more of this distance between us. Agreed?'

She nods and feels the first warm tear slide down her cheek.

'No more running away?'

'No.'

Tom pulls her closer and speaks into her ear. 'I have a suggestion.'

'What's that?' she half sobs.

'Let's start the night over. Let's stay here and talk about this – all of this.'

Lila leans into his body and rests her head against the curve of his shoulder. 'That sounds good.' And it does. Suddenly she wants nothing more than to be nestled in his arms there at home – in *their* home.

'We should phone the restaurant,' she says with a half smile into his shoulder. 'We should explain.'

Tom gives a low chuckle. 'Explain that I thought you were having an affair? That you thought I'd thrown you down the stairs? That we're pregnant and absolutely bricking it?'

Lila's smile widens. 'When you put it like that . . .'

'I'll call them with my credit card details in the morning.'

'You'll never get a table there again.'

'Oh who cares? It was pretty up itself. Confit pig cheek and truffle-infused dauphinoise?' He rolls his eyes at her. 'You know what I really fancy?' he asks.

She shakes her head.

'A curry – from our place down the road. Are you in?'

She nods. 'I'm in.'

* * *

She wakes in the morning still wrapped in Tom's arms, the sound of his mobile phone shrieking at them from the bedside table. He untangles himself and reaches for the phone, mumbling a greeting into the handset. Lila lies in bed half listening, and thinks about how nice it is to be home, back in her husband's arms, back in their bed.

She runs her hands across her stomach, feels her skin, tight and smooth like the skin of a drum. Three months pregnant. Not just her secret any more, but hers and Tom's. A secret shared.

Tom's voice is rising in tone. He curses into the phone and she knows before he's even hung up what he's going to say.

'Trouble at the site?' she asks.

'Yes.'

'So you won't be coming to lunch with Mum?'

He shakes his head. 'Sorry. Do you mind?'

'No, it's OK.'

'Thank you.' He kisses the top of her head. 'Give her my apologies? Tell her it was unavoidable.' Lila nods. 'Are you going to tell her about the baby?'

Lila nods again. 'I think so. A bit of good news . . . it's probably just what she needs after the last few months.'

'Good.' He kisses her on the mouth then slides out of bed, reaching for a T-shirt. Lila watches as he pulls it down over his torso.

'I was thinking . . .' she starts, more than a little hesitantly.

'Uh-huh . . .' Tom is pulling on his jeans, patting down the pockets.

'Maybe you could come up to the cottage this summer. Spend a few weeks there with me – treat it like a holiday.' She eyes him nervously. 'What do you think?'

Tom turns to look at her. 'As soon as I can get away from the Stratford site, sure, why not?'

She smiles and he leans over and kisses her again. 'I like seeing you back in our bed. Don't get up – not yet.'

* * *

The sun darts in and out of fast-moving clouds as she drives out along the A40 to Buckinghamshire. It's a day for blowing away the cobwebs and Lila rolls down her car window to enjoy the sensation of air rushing through her hair and over her skin. Humming along to the car stereo and tapping her fingers on the steering wheel, she is still in a good mood as she arrives in the familiar commuter-belt town and pulls up the drive of her parents' house. The privet hedge has been neatly trimmed and the lawn imprinted with immaculate chequerboard stripes in the fashion her father had always favoured. She sees pale pink peonies and clumps of butter-yellow primroses scattered throughout the flower beds, as well as extravagant bursts of purple alliums beneath the arched stone windows of the old gothic mansion. It's certainly a beautiful house – well-proportioned and ornate – but as Lila turns the car engine off, she wrestles with her feelings. The mantle of her teenage self resettles heavily upon her shoulders. Why does that happen, she wonders? Why does coming home always make her feel like the kid she once was?

She doesn't need to ring the doorbell. Her mother has been watching for her and throws the front door open as she approaches. 'Happy birthday, darling,' she says, greeting her with a hug. 'Did you have a fun night with Tom? He told me he was taking you to that smart new restaurant . . . the one run by that chef off the telly, you know, the rather dishy one?'

Lila realises she hasn't watched TV in months, but she nods anyway. 'Yes.' She has no idea how to explain the events of the previous night so she just goes along with the story, for the sake of ease. 'It was great. Very glam. Amazing menu.' It's not really a lie.

'Oh good.' She takes a step back and gives her a sweeping look. 'You look lovely. That's a very pretty scarf.' She reaches out to touch the colourful silk looped around Lila's neck.

'Thank you. It was my birthday present from Tom.'

'He has good taste, doesn't he? I'll just get my jacket and I'll be right with you. I thought we'd go to the pub up the hill for lunch. My treat.'

'Sounds great.' Lila waits on the doorstep while her mother fusses and flaps in the hallway gathering her belongings, then escorts her to the car.

As they drive through the town Lila sees the familiar markers of her youth: the newsagent where she spent her pocket money on penny sweets, the park where her father helped her wobble along on her first bike, the pub where she bought her first under-age drink. It had been a good childhood, she supposed. Nothing that would make much of a story. No major angst of any kind. Just a lingering sort of loneliness, perhaps, the sort she assumed many only-children suffered from. She could remember asking her parents once or twice if she could have a brother or a sister, but none had been forthcoming and she'd stopped asking the day her mother had told her that she couldn't have any more children. 'I had some difficulties . . . complications after your birth,' she'd said rather mysteriously, but feeling in some way responsible, Lila had dropped the subject and it had never been mentioned again.

They wind their way up a steep country lane, past the old stone church where they'd held her father's funeral, and on past rows of pretty flint-and-brick cottages until they reach the pub nestled on an immaculate village green high up in the Chiltern Hills. Lila parks her car next to a bank of gleaming sports cars and then guides her mother into the restaurant area. They order drinks and her mother hands a credit card to the young man behind the bar. 'I'll start a tab,' she says.

They carry their menus to a table in the window and as they seat themselves on a low velvet bench the sun disappears behind the clouds, casting the dining room in sudden gloom. Through the window Lila can see barrels of geraniums fluttering in the breeze.

'He's famous,' her mother offers in a whisper, nodding her head in the direction of a wrinkled man with a deep mahogany tan and a suspiciously full head of dark hair, holding court at the bar.

Lila squints and recognises him as someone from a long-running TV sitcom. 'Oh yes,' she says, giving her mother a wink, 'it's *that* kind of place, isn't it?'

'Your father did some legal work for him once. Apparently he's a *very* difficult man . . . tight as a tick, too.' She blushes. 'At least, that's what your father always said.'

Lila smirks and turns her attention to the menu. When they have chosen she heads back to the bar to place their order: sardines for her mother, a ploughman's for her. Returning to the table, she sees the gift her mother has placed at her setting.

'For your birthday,' she says.

'Thanks, Mum.' Lila pulls the wrapping off and discovers a gold shoebox and, nestled inside, a pair of red velvet slippers. She looks at her mother, then back to the slippers. They are quirky and a surprise – her mother usually goes in for designer handbags and expensive cashmere sweaters – but Lila likes them. A lot. 'They're lovely, Mum, thank you.' She bends down, slides off one of her ballet flats and tries a slipper on for size. 'A perfect fit.'

Her mother tucks a loose strand of her fair hair behind her ears. 'I saw them on a market stall in France. They reminded me . . . well, they reminded me of you. I hoped you'd like them.' She swallows.

Lila smooths her fingers across the scarlet fabric. 'They're great. Thank you.'

'I thought they were a bit of fun.'

Lila studies her mother for a moment, trying to read her face, trying to understand why she should suddenly look so sad. She wonders if she is back for good this time, or if it's just another flying visit and is about to ask when she is interrupted by a waitress arriving at the table with their food. Lila looks away from her mother's dish. It wafts a pungent garlic smell and the sardines swim in a pool of greasy butter, their cloudy eyes staring up at her, unseeing. The sight and smell makes Lila feel a little nauseous so she tears off a piece of bread from her roll and chews it slowly.

'So, have I told you about my new book club?' her mother asks as she skilfully strips the sardines of their flesh with her knife and fork.

Lila shakes her head.

'I've just joined. There are twelve of us: eleven women and one brave man. We meet once a month and each of us takes a turn to choose the book and host the evening.'

Lila half listens, twisting her lemonade round and round on a bar mat. The last time she visited this pub her father had still been alive. It was just after her university graduation. They'd celebrated with a bottle of champagne and her parents had quizzed her over her plans. 'So,' her father had said over the top of his champagne flute, 'here she is, our little girl, all grown up. What does the future hold for you now, Lila?'

She'd taken a long sip of champagne. 'I was thinking of heading to London. Some friends of mine are getting a place. I want to get a job – maybe in brand consultancy or interior design. I don't mind starting at the bottom . . . working my way up.' She'd been nervous, she remembers, desperate for his approval.

Her father had looked seriously at her. 'Is that what you *really* want to do?'

She'd nodded and held her breath.

'Well, Lila, you have to follow your dreams,' he'd said, looking at her wistfully. 'You have to do the thing you truly love. Sometimes I think your mother and I gave up too easily on our ideals.'

She'd shot her mum a look but she'd just shrugged back at her. He got like that sometimes – regretful, maudlin – and they both knew to change the subject when he did.

The sun makes another appearance from behind a cloud. It glowers at them through the window. Lila can feel it beating onto her back. The bread is sticking in her throat. She swallows it down with another glug of lemonade. She is too hot. She unwraps her scarf and lays it on the seat beside her. She cuts a slice of Cheddar and places it to her lips.

'Are you all right? You've gone quite green.'

Lila nods and tries to clear her throat. She could tell her mother about the pregnancy now, she realises, but she's still struggling and, thankfully, her mum continues with her monologue. She can't decide which book to choose for the following month's meeting. Lila chews her food slowly as the merits of two literary novels are compared, until she realises silence has fallen over the table once more. She looks up with a half smile, unsure whether it is agreement or dissent that is required of her, but it's neither. Her mother seems to have forgotten all about the book club. Instead, her hand has flown to her mouth and she is gazing at Lila in the most peculiar way – startled, as if she has seen a ghost. 'Oh . . . oh my,' she stutters.

Lila glances down at her top. Has she spilt something? Have the buttons of her blouse come undone?

'Your – your necklace.' The blood drains from her mother's face.

Lila raises her hand to her neck. She fingers the silver pendant. 'This one?'

Her mother's eyes are fixed on her neck. 'It's just – it looks – just like hers. Wh-where did you get it?'

Lila gives her a strange look. 'It was a present. From a friend.'

'Which friend? What's her name?'

Lila shakes her head. 'It's a *he* . . . *his* name is William.' Her mother just stares at her, so Lila continues. 'He's someone I met up at the cottage.'

'What cottage?'

'You know, the one I've been staying at, doing up. I *did* tell you about it.'

Her mother's eyes are wide and she seems to be having trouble swallowing. She reaches for her glass of water and takes a sip. When she has recovered she turns back to Lila. 'Darling,' she says, 'where is this cottage exactly?'

Lila swallows. 'Didn't I say? It's up in the Peak District, but it's kind of hard to explain.'

'Try.' It comes out sounding harsh, like an order.

'I don't know,' she begins, 'it's in the far north, near a village called Little Ramsdale, nestled in a small valley beside—' She doesn't get a chance to finish the sentence. Her mother does it for her.

'—beside a lake.'

'Yes,' says Lila, intrigued. 'How did you know that? Mum, are you OK? Is something wrong?'

Lila watches as her mother pushes her plate of greasy fish bones to one side. She puts her fingers to the collar of her shirt and tries to loosen it, as though she is struggling to breathe. Lila watches her carefully, but there is something else nagging at her now. She has missed something. She replays their conversation again and suddenly they are there again: three familiar words echoing in her head.

Just. Like. Hers.

They are almost the exact words from her dream. The words she is sure she heard following behind her as she tumbled down the stairs. And suddenly, with a cold, creeping, realisation, Lila knows who was in the house with her the day she fell. It wasn't Tom. It wasn't him she had argued with and fled down the landing from. It wasn't him who had followed, crying out those words. It wasn't his hands that had lunged for her, pulled at her, sent her off balance. It wasn't his eyes hers had turned to meet as she'd clawed at the air, panic-stricken, knowing there was nothing to stop her going over, nothing to stop her from toppling down the stairs, cartwheeling and ricocheting all the way down.

It wasn't Tom. It was her mother.

Lila stares across at her for a moment. 'What did you mean,' she asks, trying to steady her voice, '"just like *hers*"?'

Her mother glances away. 'Sorry?'

'The necklace . . . you said it was "just like hers". Who did you mean?'

Her pale face visibly reddens but she swallows and shakes her head. 'No, I don't think so.'

Lila tilts her head to one side, eyes her carefully then takes a breath. 'Why did you do it, Mum?'

'Do what?'

'Why did you lie about what happened? That day, in my house, on the stairs?'

Her mother opens her mouth to speak but Lila holds up her hand; she isn't finished. 'You were there, weren't you?'

Her mum remains silent and so Lila continues, piecing things together out loud. 'You didn't see me through the letter box. You didn't let yourself in with the spare key and call the ambulance, did you? I'd already let you inside. You came upstairs with me, to help me find something to wear. I remember now. I let you in. I was in a flap. I was moaning about how I couldn't find anything nice to wear that still fitted over my bump.' Her mother's face is a picture of horror but Lila doesn't stop. 'I remember. You followed me upstairs, came and sat on the bed while I tried on clothes.'

She shakes her head. 'No, that's not—'

'That's when I asked you about Dad, isn't it? I wanted to talk to you about him . . . about his affairs and about how he'd treated you.' She sees her wince. 'He was gone – but I wanted to talk to *you* . . . to try to understand it . . . to try to understand your relationship. But you got so cross. You screamed at me to stop and I said "no". I said I was sick of the lies. Of the pretence. I wanted to understand why you stayed with him, in such a toxic relationship.'

'It wasn't toxic.' She says it under her breath, so that Lila has to lean in to hear her mother's words. 'It was love. True love.'

Lila gives a tiny snort. 'Love? There wasn't much love in that house, not in all the years I was there. You jabbed at each other like fencers, trying to make contact, trying to score points whenever you could. That wasn't love.'

'Stop it.'

'It wasn't. But you got so angry, didn't you? When I dared to criticise Dad and your devotion to him, no matter what he did, no matter how many women he slept with. You were enraged, like you are now, except here we are in a public place and oh, no,' Lila gives a bitter laugh, 'we mustn't make a fuss, must we? God forbid we draw attention to ourselves or actually speak the truth for once.'

Her mother glances about angrily. 'For God's sake just stop, Lila. You don't know what you're talking about.'

'All I wanted to know was *why* you put up with it? All I wanted to understand was why you allowed him to make you so unhappy. But you couldn't bear to hear the truth. I remember it all now.' And she does. In a sudden rush Lila is back there in her bedroom, facing off with her mother across a double bed strewn with clothes.

'Don't talk about your father like that, not when he's not here to defend himself,' her mother had screamed, still raw with grief.

'But if we couldn't talk about it when he was alive and we can't talk about it now he's gone, when, Mum?'

'Why are you doing this? Why are you trying to upset me like this?' she'd cried. 'I've given you everything,' she'd implored.

'I'm not trying to upset you, Mum; I'm just trying to understand things. To understand *him*. Why were we never enough for him?'

Tears had coursed down her mother's cheeks. 'We were enough, Lila.'

'Are you still trying to deny his affairs, his lack of commitment?'

'Stop it, just stop it.'

'He was my father, Mum, but you know sometimes he wasn't a nice man. It doesn't hurt to admit it.'

Her mother had stared at her then, her eyes had swept over her, from head to toe, and Lila had been filled with the strangest sensation, that her mother was seeing her, and yet not seeing her. She'd shaken her head. 'All this time . . . you're just like her.'

Lila had barely heard, fury ringing loudly in her ears. 'I can't stand this,' she'd said and had moved to leave the room, but her mother hadn't wanted to let her go.

'Don't walk out of here. Don't leave the conversation like this. I won't have it.'

Lila remembers it all now, pushing past and racing away down the hallway, her mother calling for her to come back. 'Lila! Stop, Lila!' her voice echoing down the landing, but Lila had lumbered on, the swell of her belly slowing her. She had almost been at the top of the stairs, just reaching for the banister when she felt her mother's hands grabbing at her, trying to pull her back, but somehow tipping her off balance so that she stumbled and teetered before falling headlong down the stairs.

'You tripped me,' she says, her voice barely a whisper. 'You sent me over.'

'No. I was trying to stop you. I didn't want you to leave. I wanted to talk about it.'

'Your hands.' Lila shivers. 'I remember. I can still feel them.'

'I just wanted you to stop. I just wanted you to listen. I wanted you to think about what you were saying and to understand the sacrifices we made for you. You father and I, we loved you – so much. I couldn't hear those awful words coming from your mouth. You were so angry. You looked . . . you looked . . .'

'What?' asks Lila. 'I looked what?'

'Just like her.' She says it in a small voice.

Lila stares at her in fascination. 'Like who?'

But her mother is crying now and she just sits there and shakes her head, reaches into her handbag for a handkerchief, sniffs and wipes at her tears. 'You were running away from me and I didn't want to lose you. I couldn't lose you. Not after everything else. I reached out to stop you. I just wanted to hold you, to talk to you . . . but I must have put you off balance. You stumbled. You fell. The stairs were right there. You fell all the way down, toppled right over and landed at the bottom.' She bites her lip. 'You weren't moving. I was so scared. I thought you were dead. I thought it was my punishment.'

'Your punishment? For what?'

Her mother just shakes her head again. 'I called the ambulance right away, then I waited with you for them to come.' She is weeping openly now. 'I was so scared. I sat beside you in the ambulance and I held your hand. I called Tom and told him what had happened. I wanted to be there for you. I wanted to help.'

Lila stares at her. 'But you couldn't help. No one could. My baby was coming – too early. It was your fault.'

'No. It was a terrible accident.'

'So why lie about it? Why lie about being there with me in the first place?' Lila reaches for her scarf and bag then stands. She can't bear to hear any more. She isn't sure what to believe, but she knows she can't sit there next to her mother and think about this madness another moment. Her mother has lied to her, over and over, and she can't stand to hear one more word leave her mouth.

'Where are you going?'

'Home.'

'Don't go. Let's talk this through. I need you to understand.'

'Oh, I think I understand. All these months I *knew* there was something. I've been blaming myself . . . told myself I was going crazy with strange nightmares and fragments of memories . . . and yet you were there. You were there with me. You were responsible.'

'No. I never wanted any of this to happen. I was going to talk to you about it but when you came round in the hospital and didn't seem to remember' – Lila sees her mother at least has the good grace to look ashamed – 'there didn't seem to be anything to be gained by dredging it up again. I didn't want to upset you any more than you were already. You had so much to deal with.'

'So you lied?' Lila stares down at her through narrowed eyes. She can feel the barman's curious gaze from across the room but she doesn't care. She shakes her head. 'You don't have any idea, do you, what I've been through these last few months?'

Her mother casts about desperately. 'Don't go,' she pleads. 'Let's talk this through.'

But Lila shakes her head again. 'No. All I want right now is for you to leave me alone.'

She turns and stalks through the dining room, ignoring the glances and raised eyebrows of the other customers as she half runs, half walks out of the pub. The whole way to the car she expects to feel her mother's hands at her back, to hear her plaintive cries, but as she draws closer to the car, the only voice she hears calling out to her is a man's. 'Excuse me,' she hears, 'excuse me, miss . . .'

She turns around in a daze, and eyes the young barman racing towards her.

'Is this yours?' he asks, holding out her mother's credit card. 'I think you left it behind the bar.'

Lila looks at him, confused.

He half shrugs then looks down and reads the name printed across the bottom. 'Are you Freya? Mrs Freya Everard?'

Lila stares at him for a long moment then shakes her head. 'No,' she says, 'Freya's my mother. It's *her* card. You'll find her in the restaurant.'

'Oh,' says the man, looking a little sheepish, 'my mistake. Sorry to bother you.'

She hurls her bag into the passenger seat and starts the car with an angry roar. Lies. It's all lies. At that moment she doesn't care if she never sees her mother again. Too angry for tears, she revs the engine again and speeds out of the car park with a spray of gravel. She circles the village green once and then races all the way back to London without so much as a backwards glance.

22

MAY

1981

The May Day celebration is Simon's idea. He broaches it with them over dinner one night. 'It's traditional,' he tells them. 'We've survived winter. It was bloody hard, but we did it and now we should celebrate. We should show appreciation for what the land has provided us with so far . . . and ask for luck with this year's crops. After all, new life is coming.' Kat notices his eyes flick to Freya's swollen belly.

'Our crops?' laughs Ben. 'Steady on, mate. You make it sound as though we've been out in peasant smocks sowing fields of wheat and corn.'

'Oi!' protests Carla, 'they might not be fields but I've been working hard out there. We've got rhubarb, and lettuces coming through, the first pea shoots too. Soon we'll have carrots, marrows, strawberries, beans, maybe even some tomatoes if we're lucky.'

Simon smiles. 'So, what do you all think? We deserve a little celebration, right?'

'How do we even know it's May Day?' asks Kat. 'I lost track of dates a long time ago.'

'Well, it's definitely the right month, that's a start isn't it? What does it matter if it's the first or the twenty-first? Let's just enjoy ourselves. It's been too long since we had a little fun.'

Kat shrugs. 'Let's do it,' she says, trying to conjure some enthusiasm, but when she looks across at Freya with her head bowed and her enormous stomach protruding over the top of the table, Kat feels her bitterness coil and constrict around her guts.

* * *

Ben builds a stone hearth down on the shore of the lake and fetches kindling and logs. He fashions a basic but effective grill. Simon takes the fishing rods out onto the lake and ends their run of bad luck by catching four juicy perch within an hour. Kat helps Carla in the vegetable garden and they return to the cottage triumphant with spring greens and a bowl of tiny pink radishes. Mac does his bit too. He strikes out early with the traps and gun and arrives back that afternoon with a brace of plump wood pigeons and fragrant wild garlic pulled from the forest floor. Kat sees him holding the birds up for Freya's inspection, her sister congratulating him with a smile and the lightest touch on his sleeve. As the kitchen fills with produce, their excitement grows. It's as though they are all trying to banish the memory of the recent weeks of stress and discord.

Watching her friends, Kat is reminded of how it felt all those months ago when they had first arrived at the lake, all of them giddy with the freedom and excitement of discovering a place all to themselves. Somehow it feels as though they are coming full circle. It's there in the return of the yellow cowslips and white puffs of water hemlock growing near the lake, there in the blush of pink honesty flowers blooming near the cottage and in the forget-me-nots meandering across the grassy bank. The valley is alive once more with plants and insects, the splash of ducklings and the shimmering warmth and light she remembers from a year ago.

'See,' says Simon, wrapping an arm companionably around her shoulders, 'this is going to be fun.'

She nods. It *is* a good idea. After a long winter of sickness and hunger Kat can see that they need something to celebrate and for the first time in ages it feels as though they are pulling together again, a group united by a common purpose. She leans into Simon and beams up at him with her brightest smile.

'Where did Freya get to?' he asks, ruining the moment.

'Beats me. You know,' she adds, 'I'm not sure she's contributed anything to the meal tonight.'

Simon sighs. 'I suppose we can let her off, in her condition.'

Kat nods again but inside she simmers. Why should Freya be let off the hard work? They all excuse her now, for being big and slow, for drifting around aimlessly, lost in her own world, but it annoys Kat. She lives there with them all. She should be made to join in.

* * *

She finds her sister on the fallen tree trunk down near the water's edge, gazing intently at something hidden within her cupped hands. She is wearing her usual shapeless dress, her velvet slippers and her hair in a loose tangle around her shoulders. 'Are you going to help us today . . . or what?' Kat has meant to sound encouraging, but instead the words come out stiff and angry.

Freya just shrugs and Kat feels her anger flare. Is she really *still* punishing her for Wilbur? It's been days and she has hardly spoken to her.

'We've got fish as well as Mac's pigeons for dinner tonight.' Kat cranes her neck and sees the dragonfly nestled on the palm of her sister's hand, its body shining iridescent green in the sunlight. 'Is it alive?'

Freya nods and Kat watches as the breeze catches a strand of her sister's fair hair and lifts it away from her face. She stares at her, transfixed. For just a moment it's as though the faintest outline of someone else has been overlaid onto her sister's profile; it fuses in place for a split second before vanishing. Kat blinks. 'You remind me of her, you know,' she says.

Freya can't help her curiosity. 'Who?'

'Mum.'

Finally, Freya turns to Kat and studies her with eyes as clear and blue as the lake before her. 'I don't remember her.' She hesitates. 'What was she like?'

Kat thinks. 'Fair, like you, and fun too . . . when she wasn't drunk . . . or high. She liked to sing . . . she loved that song, "Pretty

Woman", you know the one. She'd sing it over and over. Sometimes she would spin us round the kitchen, grab us under our arms and twirl us round and round until we begged her to stop. Do you remember that?'

Freya shakes her head, but a small smile creeps across her face. She turns away from Kat to hide it. 'I wish I could remember. I'm jealous that you do.'

Kat gapes. '*You're* jealous of *me*?'

Freya nods but she won't look at her.

Kat would laugh out loud if it wasn't so ridiculous. She would gladly swap her memories. They are lodged like shadows deep in her subconscious but the sight of her sister, pregnant and waddling about the place, has unlocked them from somewhere inside. She remembers their mother shuffling about the tiny flat, her belly jutting like a football beneath a thin, cotton dress; then later, a screaming baby in her arms and their father red-faced and shouting, *shut that bloody baby up!* She sees a young Freya toddling around in a dirty nappy, emptying a packet of cigarettes out across the floor; her mother weeping over a plate of burnt sausages as she reaches, unseeing, for the vodka bottle beside the sink. It isn't much, but she *does* remember.

'Would you ever try to find her?' Freya asks.

'No.' Kat shakes her head. 'The last time she left us . . .' Kat swallows. 'If those men hadn't arrived from the electricity company with their warrant . . . they said we could have died.' She shakes her head. 'I have no desire to find her.'

Kat notices her sister's shoulders sink a little lower. Both of them understand how it is: there is no one else. They are all they've got and that's why Freya won't leave now. Even though she is miserable, there is nowhere else for her to go. So she stays, and every day she grows bigger with Simon's child, and every day Kat's jealousy and bitterness grows a little stronger. It creeps up through her like the thick green vines climbing across the exterior of the cottage. She can feel it tangling around her heart, squeezing the life out of it. It's such a messed-up situation and Kat has no idea how to fix it.

All she knows is that things can't carry on as they are because like it or not, the baby is coming.

Freya reaches out a finger and gently touches the body of the dragonfly still resting in her palm. Its wings flitter before falling still, the creature reluctant to leave its sanctuary. Freya lifts her hand to her mouth and gently blows beneath the bug so that finally, on the current of her breath, the dragonfly takes flight and buzzes out over the surface of the lake, vanishing into the powder blue sky.

'Come on,' says Kat, 'we should help the others.'

* * *

As they gather down by the shores of the lake, half of the valley is in shadow, the other half still bathed in sunlight, as if a giant curtain waits to be drawn across the scene. Mac's pigeons have been plucked and skewered and sit cooking on the grill alongside the fish. Ben strums quietly on his guitar. Carla sits behind Freya, brushing her hair while Mac watches on silently. Kat perches next to Simon on the fallen tree, the two of them drinking beer and chatting about the best fishing spots in the lake. The night is easy and informal until Simon stands and urges them all to gather round.

'Uh-oh,' laughs Ben. 'Simon's getting on his soapbox.'

'You can laugh,' says Simon, smiling, 'but we've come through a really tough winter and I think a few words are in order.'

Kat watches him, the relaxed way he stands: his weight resting on one foot, a pale hip bone jutting above the waistband of his low-slung jeans, a bottle of beer cradled at his chest. He cuts a striking figure against the backdrop of the lake and she realises she has no idea what he is about to say.

'We said we were going to give this place a year and we're not far off. I think we should be proud of ourselves. We've proved we can do it. We've made a great start. Frankly, there's nothing stopping us, as far as I can see, from doing another year . . . and another.' Simon looks around at them all hopefully and Kat turns, trying to read the expressions on her friends' faces.

Ben and Carla stare down into their beer bottles. Mac gazes out over the lake. Freya's gaze is downcast. No one looks particularly enthusiastic about another year at the cottage. 'Oh, come on, guys, don't tell me you're not up for it?'

Ben clears his throat. 'First things first, mate, let's finish this year, shall we?'

Carla nods her agreement and no one else says anything.

Simon shrugs, nonplussed. 'OK. So be it.' He swigs the last of his beer then chucks the bottle onto the grass at his feet and rubs his hands together briskly. 'So, I realised that it just wouldn't be a proper May Day celebration without a May Queen, right?' He grins and Kat goes very still, watching as Simon leans across and produces a looping chain from behind the fallen tree, a pretty woven crown made from cowslips, wood anemones and pink honesty flowers gathered from around the cottage. She knows it's ridiculous but as Simon holds the crown up in the faltering evening light, Kat knows she wants it more than anything she's ever wanted in her life. She wants Simon to choose her. She wants him to pick her in front of the rest of them, to prove once and for all that *she* is his choice. 'Not bad eh, for a clumsy fellow like me?' He holds it aloft and looks at each of them in turn.

'Honestly, mate,' says Ben, letting out a loud belch, 'you can forget the speech. Just plonk it here,' he says, pointing to his own head. 'I accept.'

They all laugh but Simon silences them. 'No. There's only one person who fits this crown . . . someone who symbolises the future of our little settlement.' He smiles at Kat and she feels her breath catch at the back of her throat. 'And that's you,' he says, turning to Freya.

Kat's eyes dart to her sister. Of course. Freya. She tries to swallow down her disappointment as Freya glances from Simon to Kat, then back to Simon. Her face is a picture of horror. Simon walks over and places the floral crown on her sister's head but Freya surprises them all by ripping it off and throwing it back at him. 'I don't want it.'

Simon looks confused. 'But it's for you.'

Kat sees Carla and Ben exchange a look. Mac sits up a little taller, leaning into the circle, his gaze fixed on Freya.

'Give it to Kat,' says Freya, and she pushes herself up awkwardly from the ground and makes to leave. 'She's the one who wants it.'

'I don't want it,' Kat lies, her cheeks flushing red.

'But it's yours, Freya,' says Simon. 'I made it for you.'

Mac clears his throat. 'You heard what she said: she doesn't want it.'

'What was that?' Simon turns on Mac, his eyes ablaze. 'Is there something you'd like to say?'

But Mac doesn't get a chance to speak again. It is Freya who rounds on him, a fire burning in her eyes. 'I told you, Simon. I. Don't. Want. It. I don't want *anything* from you.'

Simon studies her for a moment then breaks into a smile. 'Come now, it's just a bit of fun.'

'No,' she says, 'it's not. You know exactly what you're doing, manipulating us all like this.' She stands in front of them, a formidable sight, the swell of her belly jutting before her, her eyes glittering, her hair shining golden in the late evening sunshine. 'I'm sick of this game. I'm sick of pretending that this is some incredible commune built on hard work and self-sufficiency. Can't you all see it's nothing but a pack of lies?' Freya moves as if to leave the group.

'What exactly is a pack of lies?' asks Simon, his eyes gleaming dangerously. 'Tell us, Freya. Tell us what you take umbrage with, this life that has given you so much and asked so little of you in return?'

Freya flings her arms out wide. 'This valley, this cottage we're living in, setting ourselves apart from the rest of the world . . . it's all an illusion. We pat ourselves on the back for being so independent, so different but there's nothing radical about what we're doing here.' She spins to Simon again. 'And you, Simon, you talk about truth and sincerity like it's the very foundation of everything we've built, but the truth is that you wouldn't know *truth* if it came flying out of those bushes there and smacked you in the face.'

'Freya,' warns Kat. 'That's enough.'

327

But Simon just smiles and shakes his head. 'Go on.'

'I really think—' intervenes Kat, a bad feeling growing in the pit of her stomach.

But Freya can't stop now. 'You want to know the truth, Simon? The real truth? About this land we're living on? About this cottage?'

Simon gives a slow nod.

Freya smiles grimly. 'I'm sorry to burst your bubble but we're not squatting here. We're not doing anything even vaguely rebellious or daring. We're not proving a point. We're not changing the world.' She pauses, her eyes ablaze. 'All we're doing is living rent-free in an outbuilding on Mac's mother's farm.'

Everyone gapes at Freya.

'This isn't independence,' she spits, 'this is a load of lazy graduates fresh from college living like trust-fund babies off Mac's inheritance . . . all of you too scared to enter the real world.'

Kat stares at Freya in horror. The woman at the farm is Mac's *mother*? She turns to Mac, waiting for him to deny it, but he is staring down at the ground, his cheeks on fire.

Freya hasn't finished yet. 'You think you're changing the world, Simon, living like this? But you're not. All you're doing is hiding. Hiding from real work and responsibility. What have you truly contributed in the last year, Simon? Nothing. That's what.'

'No,' says Simon calmly, 'you're wrong.'

'Come on then, let's look at the facts.' Freya's eyes flash with anger. 'Where do you think the chickens came from, Simon? The piglet? Why do you think this place was never claimed by anyone? Why do you think no one came to throw us out of the house, off the land? That woman with the dog who came by to check us out and then happily sauntered away and never came back: Mac's mum. Who do you think left us that basket of food on Christmas Day? Mac's mum. Have you never asked yourself these questions, Simon, or did it not fit into your vision, your grand image of yourself as the great provider, master of us all?' Kat sees Freya wince and place one hand upon her belly.

'Freya, that's enough,' says Kat. 'You're upsetting yourself.'

'Mac?' Simon turns to Mac, expecting a denial but Mac says nothing. He doesn't even look up. He just sits there, staring at the ground. Simon turns to Kat, his face turning a strange grey colour. 'Did anyone else know about this? Did you know about Mac's mum? You saw her, after all.'

'I – I – I found the farm but I didn't . . .' She doesn't get a chance to explain further. Simon has silenced her with a hand. 'So everyone knew this, except for me?'

Ben shakes his head. 'You had me fooled, Mac.'

'And me,' agrees Carla.

Freya seems to have recovered. She shakes her head. 'All of this, it's just an elaborate game of *Simon Says* and we're the idiots for playing along.' She turns back to him. 'I see what you're doing. The others might not see it but I do. Divide and conquer; it's pathetic. You should be ashamed of yourself.'

Freya stomps off across the grass, away towards the trees. Kat holds her breath. She wonders for a moment whether she should chase after her but the twist of anger in Simon's face stops her. She gazes up at him. She wants to go to him, to wrap her arms around him and tell him everything will be OK. She wants to tell him that it doesn't matter, that she still believes in him. She wants to pick up the shattered pieces of his dream and help him rebuild them.

But she doesn't get a chance to go to him, because he surprises her by shaking his head, his face breaking into a thin smile. 'Wow. Pregnant women and their hormones. Who knew?' He says it in a light-hearted way but the words fail to raise a smile from anyone else. 'Where does she think she's going, anyway?' he asks. 'It's getting dark.'

'I'll go,' mumbles Mac and he peels away from the group and trots after Freya, trailing her across the grassy bank and down towards the woods.

'Couldn't wait to get away from us,' mutters Ben.

'Why didn't he tell us?' Carla shakes her head then reaches for Ben's hand. Kat sees another look pass between the two of them.

With Mac gone, Simon slumps down onto the tree trunk. Kat knows she should be pleased. Freya's revelations have been far more spectacular than even she could have hoped for. She'd thought she might use the information that Freya had been visiting the farm to drive a wedge between Simon and her sister, but instead Freya has shattered all of their illusions about the cottage and their work there in one fell swoop. There is no way that Simon will be able to forgive Freya. Perhaps now he will help her leave? Hope flutters up from somewhere deep inside. Or perhaps he will want to leave himself? Maybe he will finally give up on the cottage and they will slip away to start again, somewhere else, back in the real world where they can make a proper life together. Just the two of them.

'You know,' says Simon after a little while, 'everything Freya said, it doesn't actually make a difference.'

'What do you mean?' asks Kat.

'Well, think about it, what does it matter who owns this place, who's helped us out? We've still done the majority of it on our own. It's still our hard work that's kept us here. If anything,' he adds, warming to his argument, 'knowing it's Mac's mum's place just gives us added security. We can stay here now without any fear of being chucked off the land, don't you see?'

Kat studies him. Does he really mean that? Is he honestly going to pretend that Freya's revelations don't mean a thing to them?

The four of them sit around the campfire, a heavy silence falling as they contemplate the truth of their situation. The sun slips behind the hillside. The embers of the fire begin to crumble and fade but no one thinks to fetch more wood. Kat is just wondering whether to head back to the cottage when a loud shout echoes out across the water. They turn towards the trees, to where Mac has followed Freya, and watch as he bursts from between the solid grey trunks. None of them move, they just watch him run, getting closer and closer until finally, he draws up before them. 'It's Freya,' he pants, his hands on his knees as he tries to catch his breath.

'What is it?' Kat asks.

He looks up at her, takes another ragged breath. 'I think . . . I think she's going to have the baby.'

Kat shakes her head. 'It's too early. She's not due for another month or so.'

Mac shakes his head. 'I know. Come on. Quickly. I need your help.'

Kat doesn't move.

'Come on!' shouts Mac.

Kat rises and follows Mac back into the woods and it's only as they enter the shadows of the trees that she realises Simon hasn't followed. She turns to see him still slumped on the log, still staring out across the water.

'What are you waiting for?' asks Mac, and she turns and follows him into the dark interior of the forest.

Freya is leaning against a tree trunk, her head on her arms, her legs splayed wide as she sways to some silent, internal rhythm. Every so often she emits a strange, low groan; the sort of lowing sound Kat has only ever heard a cow make.

'Freya?' says Kat, approaching warily. 'Is it the baby? Is it coming?'

'I don't know,' she says, turning to her sister. 'I think my waters broke. I thought I'd wet myself but there's this pain. It comes and goes. I'm scared. I don't want to have the baby here. I don't want to be alone.'

'Don't be scared,' says Kat, 'we're here now. You're not alone.' She looks at Mac helplessly but he just shrugs. He doesn't know what to do either.

Freya leans back against the tree and lets out another groan. 'It hurts.'

'Do you think you can walk?'

'I'm not sure.'

'Let's try. We'll help you. We should get you back to the cottage, don't you think, Mac?'

But Mac seems paralysed with fear. He just stares at them both, wide-eyed and pale in the deepening twilight.

God, she thinks, so much for Simon's pep talk about Mother Nature taking care of things. None of them have a clue. She looks around at the dense woodland and realises for the first time in ages just how far they are from *any* kind of help. She swallows down her fear.

Somehow they half carry, half drag Freya out of the woods and up to the cottage, Mac holding her on one side, Kat on the other. She is heavy and bears down on them as the contractions continue to rip through her body. Kat knows she is supposed to time them so she counts in her head, until she realises that she doesn't actually know what she's counting: is it the length of time that the contraction lasts, or the length of rest time that comes between them? She isn't sure, and even if she were, she wouldn't know what it meant. How quickly are they supposed to come? Why don't they know this? They should have tried to get a book about it, at least.

Freya makes their job even harder by pushing them away. She doesn't want to be alone, but she doesn't seem to want to be touched either. Once or twice she sinks to the ground on her knees. 'Make it stop,' she pleads.

'Hold on to her,' she tells Mac, afraid that if they let her down on the damp ground, they won't get her back up again. Kat knows nothing about childbirth but she's pretty sure it's not supposed to happen this early or this quickly, and she certainly knows enough to realise that you shouldn't have a baby outside on a muddy forest floor.

Finally, they get her through the front door and into the cottage. 'Upstairs?' asks Mac.

'No,' says Freya. 'I can't.'

'Yes you can,' says Kat.

'What can *I* do?' asks Carla, appearing white-faced from the kitchen.

Kat notices her own shaking hands and takes a breath. 'Boil some water. Find us some clean bedding or towels, something to wrap the baby in when it comes. We'll need the oil lamps up there too.'

Carla disappears like a rabbit back into her burrow.

'Where's Simon?' asks Mac.

'I don't know.' Kat looks about and wishes he were there. 'Come on, Freya, we're going to get you up into the bedroom. You can lie on the mattress.'

'No,' says Freya. She clings to the banister as another contraction tears through her. When it is finished Kat guides her to the stairs. 'Come on. We'll take them quickly, before the next one comes. It will be quieter up there . . . more private.'

It's a relief when they finally get Freya upstairs. Kat wants to lay her down on one of the mattresses in their room but Freya refuses. 'I can't. It's agony. Let me stand.' Kat doesn't know what to do. In the movies she's seen women are always lying down when they have a baby, but she doesn't fancy trying to fight Freya, not in the state she's in, so they guide her to the window ledge where she leans over the sill and rides out the next contraction. They are definitely getting stronger, and longer. Kat doesn't need to time them to know that. She looks around at the dingy room in desperation. This is *all* wrong.

Mac takes Kat to one side. 'What can I do?' he asks helplessly.

Kat shakes her head. 'Why does everyone keep asking me that?'

He shrugs. 'I could go for help?'

'Who?'

He doesn't quite meet her eye. 'My mum?'

Kat stiffens. She imagines another person in the house – someone from the outside world – and knows instantly how Simon would feel about it. 'We don't need help. We'll manage on our own.'

Mac throws another worried glance back at Freya. 'How much longer, do you think?'

She sighs. 'I don't know, Mac. I guess we just wait and see.'

'Should I leave?' He is asking Kat but this time it's Freya who replies.

'No,' she groans. 'Stay, please.'

Freya labours for what feels like hours. She paces. She groans. She clings to the window sill. Once or twice she tries lying down, but quickly gets up again when the pain is too intense. It is pitch black outside when Kat finally gets Freya down onto the mattress and gently lifts the hem of her nightdress to examine her. She has no idea what she is looking for. She drops the fabric and stares at her sister's face, her hot cheeks glistening with sweat and tears. Why on earth did they think they could do this at the cottage with no electricity, no hot water, no professional help of any kind? It's sheer madness.

'Do you want some water?' she asks. 'A cool flannel?'

Freya groans and nods.

'Do you feel like pushing?' It's something she remembers hearing a nurse say in a film.

Freya shakes her head. 'I want Evelyn.' She grits her teeth through another contraction.

Evelyn? Kat exchanges a glance with Mac. 'Your mum?'

Mac nods.

Kat feels a flash of jealousy. Freya wants Evelyn, the woman she saw up at the farm. She wants Mac's mum, not her. She takes a breath then swallows her pride. 'How long would it take if you did fetch her?'

'An hour . . . maybe more. I'd have to take the car. It's further by road, but quicker than walking across the moors at night.'

'There's no time,' groans Freya. 'It's coming.'

Simon appears at the bedroom door, a large pan of hot water in his hands. 'Carla told me to bring this up.'

Freya lifts her head off the mattress and bares her teeth. 'Get out,' she screams.

Kat turns to Simon. 'Here, give it to me. It's probably best if you leave us to it.'

Simon runs his hands through his hair. It's the first time Kat has ever seen him look scared. 'Is she going to be OK? Will the baby be OK?'

'I don't know, Simon,' she snaps. Everything feels too primitive and dangerous. She never should have listened to him. Freya should be with doctors and nurses who know what they're doing, in a sterile hospital environment, not lying on a dirty mattress in a dingy old room. This isn't good. This isn't safe. She feels uncontrollable terror rise up and forces herself to take a breath and swallow it down.

'Get him out of here,' cries Freya. 'I don't want him here.'

Kat gives Simon a look and he shuffles out of the doorway, his footsteps creaking back down the staircase.

'I want to move . . . need to . . . turn over.'

Kat helps Freya shift onto her hands and knees on the mattress, her face burrowed into a pillow. She stifles a groan.

'Do you want to push now?'

Freya nods and moans.

'OK.' She lifts her sister's dress and sees her bare thighs slick with sweat and her body opening up like a flower in bloom. It's all so primal, so graphic. Kat can't believe what she is seeing. Freya stretches and groans again. There is the curve of a little skull pushing at her insides. She cries out in agony.

'I think I can see a head,' Kat says. This is good. Head first is good, she's sure of it. She feels Mac move to her side. She had forgotten he was in the room with them but suddenly she is pleased to have him there next to her. She glances up at him and he gives an encouraging nod.

Freya screams, and then, with a slithering trickle of scarlet blood, a head pops miraculously from her body. It is purple and covered in white stuff, the faintest fuzz of fair hair on its scalp. Kat is repulsed. It doesn't look like any baby she's seen before, but she knows she must help. She moves across and, driven by instinct, holds the head gently in place.

'The head's out, Freya. Can you push again?'

'Wait,' says Mac, suddenly. 'You have to check the cord. You have to check that the cord isn't wrapped around the baby's neck.'

Kat gapes at him. 'How?'

'Put your fingers in, feel for it.'

Kat shakes her head. 'I can't.'

'Yes you can. You have to.'

'I don't know what I'm doing.'

'Try.'

But this time it's Kat who is paralysed with fear.

'Move out the way,' says Mac.

Kat steps back and allows Mac at her sister. She watches as he gently feels around where the baby's neck should be. Freya whimpers. 'I'm sorry,' says Mac, 'nearly done.' Then he steps back. 'It's OK, Freya. You can push . . . on the next contraction, OK?'

Freya seems to know what she's doing now, basic instinct driving her on. She waits and pants and then on the next contraction she screams and pushes the body of the baby out in one slippery move. The baby is quick and wet but Kat manages to catch it in a sheet. She stares down at the small purple body and tries to control the shaking in her legs. It's a baby. A *real* baby. 'It's a girl,' she says.

'The afterbirth,' says Mac, 'we have to deliver the afterbirth.'

'What do we do with the baby?' asks Kat. She looks down at it helplessly. A little girl. Still purple. Not moving. Not making any sound. 'Is it OK?'

Mac comes across and takes the baby in his arms. He holds her in the sheet and Kat watches in amazement as he puts his finger gently into her mouth, then massages her delicate chest with the palm of his hand. It is ominously quiet in the room. Kat helps Freya move onto her back and on the next contraction her sister moans and the afterbirth slithers out onto the mattress between her legs. Freya barely notices, her eyes are fixed upon Mac and the baby. 'Is she OK?'

'Hold on,' says Kat. Her eyes dart to Mac's. He continues to massage the baby. 'What are you doing?' she asks.

Mac doesn't speak. The silence is electrifying. Kat holds her breath until the silence is shattered by the piercing wail of the baby. She opens her mouth and her screwed-up eyes and takes a great gulp of air, then wails again.

Mac and Kat smile at each other, the relief evident in their eyes as Freya sobs gently into the mattress, 'She's OK. She's OK.'

Mac takes a pair of scissors, washes them in the hot water Simon brought up and then cuts the umbilical cord. Then he moves across to Freya and hands her the tiny newborn wrapped in the sheet. She is no longer a frightening purple but pink and alert, her little hands flailing at the air, her mouth opening and closing like a fish taking her first breaths on land.

Freya peers down at the tiny bundle in her arms. 'Hello,' she says and the tears fall down her face, a steady stream of joy and pain flowing onto her bloody dress. 'Hello, little girl.'

'How did you know to do that?' asks Kat, still astonished at Mac's miracle. 'How did you know to check the cord . . . and to massage the baby like that?'

He shrugs. 'I saw my dad do it once with a calf.' He can't seem to take his eyes off the baby and Kat remembers what Freya told her all those months ago; how she couldn't be sure about *that* night. It's always been assumed that the baby is Simon's, but she wonders now about Mac. Could the baby be his?

Kat smiles. 'Well, you did a good job. Well done,' and Mac hangs his head, embarrassed by her praise, then slips quietly from the room.

* * *

The baby is tiny, with tufts of fair hair and flailing limbs that grab at the air. Her face is scrunched closed, like the bud of a flower waiting to bloom. Now that the horror and noise and mess of the birth are over, Freya seems calmer. She holds the baby close to her breast and murmurs quietly, soothing words Kat can't quite make out. In the space of a few minutes it seems her sister has been transformed, no longer a girl but a mother now. With high spots of colour on her pale cheeks and her eyes glittering like diamonds Kat thinks she looks beautiful. She wonders if they should try to take Freya and the baby to a hospital, get them checked out, but looking at the two of them together, it's hard to believe mother and child could need anything but each other. The visceral chaos of just moments ago seems like a lifetime away.

There is a loud clearing of a throat. Kat turns to see Simon standing in the doorway. He is gazing at Freya and the baby in awe. 'Mac told me the baby had arrived.'

Kat nods and watches him warily from the edge of the bed as he steps into the room.

'I've brought you something,' he says, not to Kat, but to her sister and he steps closer, his shadow falling over the bed. Kat sees her sister draw the infant closer.

'It's a Moses basket,' Simon continues. 'I found it ages ago. I've cleaned it up . . . for the baby.'

Freya nods but she doesn't say anything.

'So, a baby girl?' Simon smiles. 'What will you call her?'

'Lila.' She throws the name at him like a challenge.

'That's lovely.' He smiles and bends down, reaches out a finger and draws back the purple knitted blanket from around her face. 'She's beautiful.'

Freya softens slightly, her heart already filled with a mother's pride. 'Yes,' she agrees.

Simon peers more closely. 'She has my nose, don't you think?'

And just like that the tension is back; Kat sees Freya's shoulders curve around the baby as she stares daggers at Simon. It is the first time he has vocalised his paternity, his responsibility, and both sisters understand at last what he is doing there: Simon is staking his claim. 'She won't want for anything. You'll see,' he says.

'I . . . we don't—' Freya fumbles for the words.

'Shhhhh,' soothes Simon, rising up from his crouched position, blocking Kat's view, 'you must be tired. Nothing matters now but you and Lila. You must get some rest.' He turns to Kat. 'You must be tired too,' he says. 'I'll stay here a while. Why don't you go? Take a break.'

Kat understands the dismissal – she feels it like a slap to the face. She nods once and stands, moves towards the door then turns back for a final look. Simon shifts and behind him, cast in shadow, she sees Freya's panic-stricken look. 'Wait,' she says to Kat, 'don't you want to hold her?'

Kat hesitates, one hand on the door latch. She has never held anything so small or precious in her life. 'No, it's OK. I'll come back later.'

'No, please,' urges Freya. 'You're her auntie.' She offers the baby up and Kat sees what she is trying to do. She is trying to include her in some way, trying to keep her involved; but Kat shakes her head. Can't she see? She will never be part of this now. *Auntie*. Not mother. Not wife. Not even Simon's lover any more. She looks at the three of them there before her, the image of a perfect, newly made family and she feels her grief well up for everything she has ever lost. She swallows. 'Maybe later,' she says, and she ducks out of the room before the tears can begin to fall.

The sun blooms on the horizon, a peach-coloured dawn illuminating the hills and glimmering upon the still lake. Although Kat is exhausted, her mind is buzzing and she knows she won't sleep. In the space of twenty-four hours everything has changed. There's a baby in the house. Baby Lila: Simon and Freya's daughter.

For some reason Kat had thought that things might be better when the baby came – that it would all be over; but the infant's physical presence, the sound of its crying, its undeniable, needy presence only seems to be evidence now of things really just beginning. For all Simon's idealistic posturing, Kat knows that their life at the cottage is nothing more than a house of cards that has begun to crumble spectacularly all around them.

She hears a wail from upstairs, followed by Freya's gentle shushing. Kat is dizzy with tiredness but she knows she cannot be in the house. She sees Ben curled on the sofa and Carla slumped at his feet on a beanbag, both of them dead to the world. Gently, she extricates a sweater from beneath Ben's feet, then pulls on her boots and slips out the back door.

She starts at the sight of Mac slumped on the back step, his head resting on his knees, something silver dangling between his fingers where it catches the light.

'Hey,' she says, 'are you OK?' When he looks up she sees the fresh red welt beneath his left eye, the skin already beginning to swell and bruise. 'What happened?'

Mac shrugs. 'Simon. Seems he's a little less forgiving than the rest of you.'

Kat nods. The tension has been building between them for weeks; it has always seemed like a matter of time. 'You should put something on it. It looks nasty.'

But Mac just shrugs. 'Is Freya OK?'

'Simon's with her.' She looks again at the object glinting in his hand. 'What's that?' she asks.

He lifts it to the light and Kat sees it is a necklace, a fine chain with a silver pendant in the shape of an oval hanging from the loop. 'It's for Freya,' he says, 'for her baby.'

Kat nods. Poor Mac, even if the baby *is* his he will never stand a chance against Simon, not now he has laid claim to her. Anyone can see that. She peers more closely at the necklace. The pendant is paper-thin with three little marks at its centre. It looks familiar but in her foggy state she can't quite identify it.

'It's honesty,' says Mac, seeing her puzzled look. 'An honesty seed head. Freya likes them so much . . . I thought . . . I thought . . .'

Kat can't help it; her laugh is a harsh bark. Honesty. Mac is giving the gift of honesty, at long last. That's priceless.

'God, Kat, this is all so screwed up,' says Mac. 'How did we end up like this?'

She nods but she has no words of comfort for him. It is — it's all *so* screwed up. She could stay there with him. She could ask him the barrage of questions that buzz in her head: why he lied when he first brought them to the lake all those months ago. Why he never told them his mother owned the cottage, or that she knew they were there. That it was her who had gifted them the chickens, the pig, the Christmas turkey. But then perhaps the signs were there? Perhaps it was just that none of them had cared to look for them, far too comfortable as they were, living out their naive little fantasy. No one thought to delve below the surface of their existence . . . no one except Freya.

'You must have been laughing at us the whole time,' she says, her voice flat. It's ridiculous. She'd always thought that Simon was in control, making decisions, leading the group, but perhaps all along it was Mac. It's too confusing. She can't think straight. She's too tired.

'No,' says Mac, 'I wasn't. I only ever wanted us to be together. To be friends. I only ever wanted to be accepted.'

She leaves him crouched beside the back door and heads down to the edge of the lake where the boggy ground squelches and sucks at her boots. Her fingers trail across the feathery tops of the reeds. Now that she has seen Freya with the baby and the proprietary way Simon hovered over them both she knows that it will never be over. Nothing she can do will sever the connection between them. They will always have the baby, the bond between them that can't be broken. Simon will never let them go.

She knows it's twisted, but she doesn't even care that their connection may have been born from something ugly and violent and – if Freya is telling the truth – from something she never wanted, because she is *still* jealous. Freya has what she wants most deeply of all: Simon's child and a family to call her own. Her sister has been anointed queen, and even in a crumbling house of cards, that makes her the winner. Kat looks out over the choppy surface of the water and sighs. Who would care if she took off right now and never came back? Who would care if she just filled her pockets with rocks and waded into the lake until the water closed over her?

A breeze is picking up. The reeds seem to whisper to her, dark secrets. She reaches for a handful of the sharp green blades and pulls them, like knives, through the clenched palm of her hand. She feels her own warm blood fill her fist. The wind murmurs. It rustles through the treetops and shivers through the tall green stems of the deadly water hemlock at the edge of the lake. Kat studies the plant for a moment, remembering Mac's warning. Carried on the breeze comes another high-pitched wail; shrill and needy, it echoes out across the valley. Kat reaches out and pulls a stem of hemlock clean out of the ground. Pale roots hang like limp fingers at her side as she carries it back up to the house, her face turned to the wind and a thin trail of blood dripping from her clenched fist onto the grass behind her.

23

LILA

June

Lila is paying for groceries in the village shop when her mobile phone rings. 'Is that yours or mine, love?' asks Sally from behind the till.

'Mine, sorry.' Lila looks down at the screen and sees MUM MOBILE flashing on the display.

'I don't mind if you answer it,' says Sally, watching her with obvious curiosity.

Lila shakes her head and returns her phone to the bottom of her handbag. 'No, it's OK.'

'Not a lover's tiff, I hope?' Sally places a packet of butter into the canvas shopping bag.

Lila gives her an enigmatic smile. 'Something like that.' She knows Sally is bursting to know more but she can't get into it, not here.

'You must be entertaining?' she says, packing the fruit cake and a packet of shortbread at the top of the shopping bag where they won't be crushed.

'Yes, I invited William over for afternoon tea, as a thank you. He's been teaching me to swim,' she adds, seeing the woman's eyebrows shoot skyward.

'He was in here just the other day,' she says. 'He was telling me you've done wonders with that cottage of yours.' She grins at her.

'He's very kind,' says Lila. 'I've just tried to make it a little more habitable.'

'Well, it's nice that you've met some of the locals . . . made a *special* friend.'

She senses a lingering question in the woman's words. It's hardly surprising; a blossoming friendship between a pregnant woman and a brooding farmer would definitely make for interesting village gossip and it doesn't take a genius to work out where Sally's mind is going. Lila shrugs it off. Some things are just too hard to explain. She reaches for the shopping bag. 'Come and visit me,' she suggests. 'Join me for a cup of tea sometime. I'll show you round the cottage myself. You'd be very welcome.'

'Oooh,' says Sally, 'I'd love that. Thank you, dear.' She leans across and pats her on the hand. 'You take care of yourself,' she looks meaningfully at Lila's growing bump, 'and that baby of yours, OK?'

Lila smiles. 'I will.'

* * *

Fast-moving clouds shift spotlights of sun over the surrounding hills. Lila takes it slow along the country lanes, enjoying the huge sky and the rolling green pastures on either side. Her mother has been calling every day since their disastrous pub lunch but Lila just can't bring herself to speak to her. She knows now that it was *her* who'd been there at the time of her fall. She knows that she lied about being in the house. But none of it makes any sense. Why would she do that? What was her mother so afraid of? And even if she didn't *push* her, even if it was, as she'd said, a terrible accident, that doesn't explain why she would lie about it. There are three words still ringing in her head: *just like her*. What do they mean? Just like *who*? She knows they form the missing piece of the puzzle, but to get the answers she must see her mother again, and that's something she's not prepared to do. Her biggest and most overwhelming desire is to protect her baby and returning to the cottage had felt like the most natural thing in the world, this time with Tom's blessing.

They had attended the scan together in London just before she'd left. It had been the twenty-third, exactly a year since her fall and

Milly's premature birth. When they'd realised the coincidence they had been nervous; they'd watched in anxious silence as a fuzzy picture of their baby, nestled in the soft curve of her body, had appeared on the screen. In the centre of the image had been a rapid black and white blinking. 'There's the heartbeat,' the technician had told them.

Tom had squeezed her hand and leaned over to kiss the side of her cheek where the tears streamed down her face. 'See?' he'd said. 'Everything's OK.'

She'd nodded but known she would still be nervous, jumpy at every twinge, every kick, every flutter. 'I know. But how do I stop worrying?' she'd half cried, half laughed.

It had been the technician who had answered her. 'You don't,' she'd smiled. 'That's what being a parent is. Alongside all that hope and all that love comes the worry. It's normal.'

'Yes,' Tom had nodded, 'this is just the beginning,' and Lila had smiled at him then and known that whatever came next, they would face it together, their relationship weathered now, but somehow stronger than before.

He has promised to join her as soon as he can for a couple of weeks together at the lake, a much-needed holiday. She will figure out the mess with her mother after that. She doesn't have the energy for anything else right now.

Lila bumps her car along the dirt track, no longer boggy with spring rain but dry and dusty, baked hard after a week of early summer sunshine. She winds down the window and enjoys the breeze in her hair, listens to the low hum of bees buzzing around the dog rose blooms and the sweet song of a blackbird as it warbles in the hedgerow. Whenever she drives up the track now she has the overwhelming sensation of coming home and she knows, deep down, that she doesn't want to part with the place. She's hoping to persuade Tom when he's next up that they should keep it on. She wants it to be their bolthole, a place for them to retreat to when London gets too much. And when they're not using it they could loan it out to friends. It's still rustic and remote, but it has its charms.

As she rounds the bend, the sight of a sleek navy blue car parked beside the old wooden gate makes her slam on the brakes. The force sends her lurching forwards in her seat. She recognises the number plate at once: it's her mother's Volvo. Lila stares at the car in horror. How on earth has she found her? Tom is the only one who could have possibly given her directions. Bloody Tom, she'd told him she didn't want him talking to her mother. She's going to kill him when she next sees him.

The car ahead is empty so she pulls up behind it, grabs her shopping bags and makes her way through the gate and into the high grass of the meadow. By the time she has stomped to the shade of the alder trees she's decided to let her mother say her piece and then send her on her way. No drama, no arguments. As she cuts her way through the tall trees she wills herself to be calm. Think of the baby, she tells herself.

She is almost at the cottage and still there is no sign of her mother. She looks around. She isn't waiting at the front door, or lurking in the garden. For a moment she wonders if she has imagined the Volvo parked on the track, wonders if she has finally lost her mind, but when she squints out across the lake she sees her, a silhouette seated on the collapsed tree down by the lake. She has her back to Lila and sits gazing out over the water, one foot raised up onto the trunk and her hands clasped around her knee, her blond hair catching in the breeze. She looks comfortable, somehow at home, and the thought brings another surge of anger. How dare she come here? This is *her* place.

She dumps the groceries up near the cottage and makes her way down the bank towards the lake, the swish of her feet through the long grass giving her away. Her mother turns and watches her approach, her face blank, her eyes masked behind dark sunglasses. Lila studies the disconcerting black orbs of them but refuses to drop her gaze. This is her terrain – she won't look away. Eventually, when she is just a couple of metres away, she stops with her hands on her hips and regards her. 'How did you find me? Was it Tom?'

Her mother shakes her head. 'A lucky guess.'

Lila is confused. 'A *what*?'

'When I saw your necklace everything fell into place.'

'My necklace?' She reaches up and rubs the thin silver disc between her fingers. 'I don't understand.'

'The honesty, it grows all around here, doesn't it?'

'Yes, but how did you know I was *here*?'

She ignores the question. 'Did Mac give it to you?' she asks, nodding her head at the pendant.

'Mac?' Lila shakes her head.

Her mother removes her glasses. 'I've been having nightmares ever since I saw you last . . . about how you might have come to own that necklace. For one awful moment I thought *she* might have given it to you. But I knew that was impossible. It has to be Mac. It's the only explanation.'

Mac? *Who* is Mac? Lila touches the pendant. It feels warm and solid beneath her fingers.

'I wasn't sure I'd remember my way here, but it came back to me immediately: the hidden turning for the track, the gate into the meadow, even the wet-mulch smell of the woods hasn't changed. I haven't been here in thirty years and yet it feels like it could have been yesterday.'

Without her sunglasses on Lila can see her mother looks different; no longer polished and immaculately groomed, but somehow unravelled, dishevelled. There are dark shadows beneath her eyes and the first hint of her roots growing through the pale blond highlights of her hair. Lila realises she has never seen her mother so sunken in on herself, not even in those early days after her father died.

'I dream about this place, you know.' She says it so softly the words almost don't make it to Lila's ears before they are whipped away on the breeze and carried out across the lake.

'This place?' Lila stares at her mother, still utterly bewildered. She feels as though she's fallen into one of her more disturbing dreams.

'I peered through the windows,' she adds, indicating the cottage behind them with a jerk of her head, 'before you arrived. You've done a wonderful job. Out here it's virtually the same but I wouldn't have recognised the cottage from the interior.'

'Mum, you're not making any sense.' Lila wants to shake her. She wonders if she has finally cracked under the strain of losing her father, if the grief has somehow sent her mad. She is just about to press her to explain when the sound of a barking dog shatters the silence between them.

She spins around and sees the black and white flash of Rosie burst over the crest of the bank. The dog sprints towards Lila and comes to a grinding halt at her feet. She pants and grins and waits for Lila to pat her. Moments later, William appears at the top of the bank. He raises his hand to shield his eyes from the sun and gazes down at them. She can't be certain but when he sees her with her mother, she's sure she sees him take a step backwards, as if he would turn around and disappear the way he has just come, if it wasn't already too late. Oh no, thinks Lila: afternoon tea.

William makes his way slowly towards them, the sound of his boots thumping on the dry ground as he goes. 'You're early,' says Lila, offering him a weak smile. 'I should introduce you to my mother.' She's about to do the proper introductions but her mother gets there first.

'Hello, Mac,' she says, greeting him with a thin smile.

William shuffles uncomfortably by the fallen tree. He looks from her mother, to Lila, then back to her mother. There is something inscrutable in his face. 'Hello,' he says at last.

Lila glances between them, confused. 'You two know each other?'

Her mother doesn't seem to hear. She only has eyes for William. 'So,' she says with a harsh laugh, 'you thought it was time, did you? Thought you'd step in and intervene, after all these years?'

William clears his throat. Lila can see he is nervous. He shifts his weight from foot to foot and gazes out over the lake. 'Simon's gone.' He seems to be having trouble looking at her mother. 'I think it's time we were all honest with each other. Lila deserves to know the truth, don't you think?'

'What do I deserve to know? What are you both talking about? Who the hell is Mac?' Lila stares from her mother to William and back to her mother in bewilderment. 'Will one of you please tell me what's going on here?'

William scuffs one of his boots across the ground.

Lila turns to her mother but she doesn't say a word, she just continues to stare at William through narrowed eyes.

'Don't you think she looks just like her?' he manages, finally. 'The resemblance is striking.'

Her mother nods and Lila is shocked to see a single tear slide down her drawn face. 'She does.'

'If you're not going to tell her, I will,' says William, the faintest hint of a threat in his voice.

'Little Mac,' says her mother, 'all grown up and finally taking charge.'

Lila stamps her foot like a child. 'If one of you doesn't tell me what's going on right this minute I'm going to leave you both here and drive straight back to London.'

'Come and sit down, will you?' Her mother pats the trunk beside her.

'I don't want to sit down. I want you to tell me what's going on.'

'Please.'

Lila stomps across the grass and sits at the far end of the log. She glares at her mother, wills her to speak.

'This old tree nearly killed me, you know?' Her mother reaches out to smooth the puckered grooves of the tree's weeping eye with her fingertips. She rubs the knotted wood then looks to Lila with a faint smile.

Lila shakes her head in irritation. 'What?'

'I was right here when it came down in a storm. It missed me by a metre or two.'

'When were you here? *Why* were you here?'

But her mother doesn't answer. 'You think I was weak staying with your father all those years, don't you? You accused me of being too passive, for putting up with his affairs, his indiscretions, but I

348

wasn't. I wasn't a victim. I was happy to make sacrifices for your father . . . and for you, Lila. We were a family.'

She reaches out to take her hand but Lila pulls away. She doesn't want comfort from her; she wants an explanation. Out of the corner of her eye she sees William settle himself on the ground, Rosie curling companionably at his side. He is a distance away but she can tell from the tension in his shoulders, the way he holds his head, that he is listening to every word her mother says. Somehow, she feels reassured to know that he is there. 'Go on,' she says.

'Your father and I had to make a lot of difficult choices . . . you might never truly know what we gave up, but it's important that you understand that we both loved you, always. All I ever wanted was for us to be a family.'

As if from nowhere, a gust of wind swirls across the lake and scuttles on through the alder leaves. The air fills with the sound of the whispering trees. Shadows dance across the water but Lila barely notices, so intently is she focused on her mother's words.

'I am your mother, Lila. I'm the one who raised you and loved you, fed and clothed you, nursed you when you were sick and dressed your cuts and bruises when you fell. I was the one that was there for you – no matter what.' She swallows hard and Lila can see she is fighting tears. Then finally, she raises her head to look at Lila. 'But my name isn't Freya.'

Lila gapes at her mother.

'My name is Kat – Katherine. Freya was my sister. *She* was your birth mother.'

Lila wants to laugh. The words leaving her mother's mouth are nonsensical. Ridiculous. She sees her mother glance again at the pendant hanging from her neck.

'That necklace you're wearing once belonged to Freya, your real mother. It was hers. Mac gave it to her.' She stops and corrects herself. 'Sorry, *William* gave it to her.'

Lila looks across to William. He lifts his head to meet her gaze and gives her the slightest nod, half affirmation, half apology, before dropping his eyes down to the ground, fixing them on a stray clump of daisies. She can't process what her mother has just told her so she focuses on the incidentals. Mackenzie Farm. William Mackenzie. Mac, to his friends? The cogs turn in her mind and one small piece of the puzzle slots into place.

Lila stares at William, then back to her mother where she sits on the fallen tree, her eyes glistening with tears. Somewhere high above them a kite wheels as a dark silhouette in the sky. Beside the cottage the honesty shivers in the breeze. After all that has happened, after all the murkiness of the past and the strange dreams and fragments of broken memories, Lila understands that she is about to hear the truth — at last.

She turns away from the cottage and the honesty and back to the woman sitting on the tree trunk. 'Tell me,' she says, challenging her with her gaze, 'tell me all of it.' And as the sun shines down on them and the trees rustle and whisper their secrets to the lake, Lila listens intently as her mother reveals the final, hidden chapter of their story.

2 4

JUNE

1981

Ben and Carla are the first to go. They steal away in the dead of night like teenage runaways, taking nothing but their rucksacks, Ben's battered guitar and half the cash left in the money tin. Simon is furious to discover them gone. 'How dare they? What about friendship? What about loyalty? What about the bloody vegetable garden?' He takes the gun outside and vents his anger at the unsuspecting ducks drifting on the lake. Shots ring out angrily across the valley and Kat's shoulders tense at every echoing boom. Upstairs the baby begins to cry.

Kat pretends to share Simon's indignation. To his face she nods and declares Ben and Carla's actions a gross betrayal, but secretly she is relieved. She understands that finally it is happening. The house of cards is crumbling. There are just four of them left at the lake now – five if you count the baby. It seems as though the last few pieces are being moved into place on a chequerboard and Kat feels sure that the game they have played for almost a year is drawing to its conclusion.

There are complications though. Freya won't get out of bed. She lies on the mattress in the corner of the upstairs room, her gaze fixed to the clouds drifting past the window as the baby sleeps beside her, snuffling and gurgling in the Moses basket beneath the knitted purple blanket. When she cries, Freya reaches for her and silences her at her breast. Kat hears her singing lullabies, her soft melody reminding her of something from her childhood; something from a long, long time ago; the sour smell of vodka and the soft-crooning voice of their own mother.

Kat climbs the stairs with fresh nettle tea and toast and finds her sister crying into her quilt. 'Shhhh . . .' she says, 'it's OK.'

'I can't do this.' Freya's voice is flat. 'I can't stay here.'

'You're tired. You need to eat something. Here.' She tries to hand her the plate of toast but Freya ignores it.

'What about Evelyn? Will she come?'

'We'll see. She's a busy woman. You know she has a farm to run.'

'But you've asked her?'

Kat nods but she can't hold her sister's eye. Even though Freya has been asking for Mac's mum, she and Simon have privately agreed not to invite her. They don't want *her* – a virtual stranger – poking around in their business and, for the time being at least, Mac seems to be following their lead.

Freya visibly slumps. 'I suppose you know that Simon wants the baby. He says he wants to help me raise her.' She swallows and then looks up at Kat with panic-stricken eyes. 'He's written to his parents. He's told them about me . . . and Lila. He's asked them for money . . . so we can . . . so we can carry on here.' She buries her face in the pillow.

Kat feels a surge of bitterness. Of course, she thinks, of course he'd ask them for help *now*. She tries to swallow her anger. 'Shhhh . . .' she says to Freya, 'you're overwrought. You have to keep your strength up, for the baby.'

Freya doesn't respond, she just sniffs into the pillow, so Kat leaves the plate of food on the floor beside the bed and moves across the room. It's so quiet she's assumed the baby is asleep, but when she peers over the edge of the basket she sees that Lila is wide awake and staring up at her with her huge navy eyes, lips sucking at her fist. She stares down at the baby, gazes into her knowing blue eyes, studies the tiny curve of her nose and the sprouting fuzz of hair on her head. She looks and looks but she can't see anything of either Simon *or* Mac in the baby's features. She's just a baby – small and wrinkled. She watches her for a moment longer, then turns on her heel and leaves the room.

'God,' she says, jumping at the sight of Mac hovering at the top of the stairs, 'I wish you'd stop doing that. You made me jump.'

'Sorry.' He shuffles on the landing, hands in his pockets. 'How is she?'

Kat shrugs. 'She's tired.'

'The baby's OK?'

Kat nods and the sound of Freya's soft weeping escapes from beneath the door.

'I've heard . . . that sometimes . . .'

Kat shifts impatiently.

'. . . some women can get depressed, you know, after a baby.' He eyes Kat. 'Do you think she's all right? Are you sure we shouldn't send for my mum?'

Kat is tired. She hasn't been sleeping well either, not since the night the baby was born. The cottage is too small and the baby's frequent crying disturbs them all. 'Tell me something,' she sighs, 'why do you all seem to think *I* have the answers?'

'Because you're her sister.'

'Well maybe someone should have told *her* that before she slept with *my* boyfriend.'

A pink flush spreads across Mac's cheeks but he continues anyway. 'I could help. I could take her somewhere – somewhere far away.' He doesn't need to say from whom; it's plainly clear.

Kat gives a low, angry laugh. 'You think he's just going to let you waltz out of here with them both? You've seen the way he looks at that baby. It's his new project – more than me, or Freya, or this damn cottage will ever be.'

'But maybe that's not his decision to make, maybe—'

Kat shakes her head. 'If you love her so much, Mac, you figure it out. Step up. Be the hero.' She stomps down the stairs. Bloody Mac, none of this would have happened in the first place if he hadn't brought them to this stupid lake and let Simon play his silly games.

* * *

Without Carla and Ben around, the atmosphere in the house takes on a sombre, oppressive air, like the hours before a storm when the sky fills with dense black clouds and everything falls quiet and still. With Ben gone, food preparation has become sporadic and it's strange to look out across the vegetable plot and no longer see Carla's form bent over a row of lettuces, or fixing wire strings for the runner beans. Kat misses her cheery face and her light, easy laughter. The only sounds in the house these days are the slamming of doors, the hungry wails of the baby or Freya's incessant weeping. Kat just wants it all to end. She wants it to be over.

* * *

She takes Freya a plate of scrambled eggs and a bowl of fresh strawberries plucked from the garden. Freya's face is tear-stained and blotchy but she doesn't even acknowledge the food tray; she is too busy scribbling on a piece of paper.

'There's going to be a royal wedding,' Kat says – a peace offering – but Freya doesn't look up. 'Charles and Diana. Simon says the papers are full of it . . . that they're calling it a real-life *fairy tale*.' Freya remains silent. 'What are you doing?' Kat asks eventually, noting the silver honesty pendant winking at her sister's throat, realising Mac must have given it to her after all. As she waits for an answer she moves across the room and stares at the sleeping baby in the basket.

'I'm giving you what you want,' says Freya finally, her voice flat and expressionless.

'And what do I want?' Kat asks, not looking up from the baby, watching her tiny chest rise and fall, up and down.

'Simon.'

Kat turns to Freya then and shakes her head. 'It's not that simple.'

Freya holds her gaze for a moment then turns away. She folds the piece of paper carefully in half and then slides it beneath her pillow.

Kat sees the tangle of her sister's hair, her red-rimmed eyes, her dishevelled nightdress and sighs. Maybe Mac is right; maybe she

354

isn't coping. 'You should come downstairs,' she tries, 'get some fresh air. It might make you feel better.' But Freya just sinks down below the covers and closes her eyes. 'Suit yourself.'

* * *

It feels like too long since any of them have eaten a proper meal. Longer since they've slept. The bread is all gone and they are nearly out of milk powder and rice. Kat feels hunger yank at her belly like a dog tugging at the end of a huge, immovable object. She wanders through the garden and finds a cluster of green beans, a handful of berries. She doesn't wait but pushes them into her mouth and chews quickly. They taste of soil and sunshine in her mouth and jostle and grumble in her guts afterwards.

'There are rabbits all over the hillside,' says Simon, coming through the back door, the rifle propped on his shoulder. I've been watching them through the sights.'

Mac nods. 'We should check the traps.'

She must hear them go because Freya appears in the kitchen a few minutes later. Kat is surprised to see her out of bed. Her face is pale but there are high spots of colour on her cheeks and her eyes shine like glass. The baby is clasped close to her breast.

'You're up,' says Kat. 'I've just boiled some water. Would you like tea?'

Freya nods and takes a seat at the table. She pulls the baby close and bends her head, as if to breathe in the warm scent of her. She seems different. Agitated.

'Are you OK?' Kat asks, eyeing her.

Freya nods again but still she doesn't speak.

Kat moves about the kitchen. She finds nettle leaves in the pantry and chops them on a board. Then she splashes hot water over them and pushes the mug towards Freya. Her sister still wears her nightie; it's crumpled from wear and gives off the faint smell of stale milk. She has forgotten to do up the buttons after feeding the baby and Kat can just make out the pale curve of her breast. There is no shine to her any more, no light in her skin. Her hair hangs lank and greasy around her shoulders and an angry red pimple blooms on her chin. Freya doesn't seem to notice her sister's close scrutiny; she just reaches for the mug and drinks deeply.

'You should get some fresh air,' Kat suggests. 'It would do you good. It's a lovely day.'

Freya nods and stares into her mug.

'I'll look after the baby if you like.'

Freya looks down at her lap as if seeing the baby for the first time. She nods. 'I need to wash . . .' she says, her voice cracking. 'A swim in the lake.' She reaches up to touch a clump of her greasy hair and Kat smiles, relieved.

'That's a good idea. It will make you feel so much better.'

'You'll look after Lila?'

Kat smiles. 'I'd love to.'

Freya finishes her mug of tea and stands. She holds the baby close, breathing in the scent of her once more, before handing her to Kat. 'Look after her.'

'Of course I will. I'm not completely inept. We'll be right here, won't we?' She smiles down at the baby, then looks to her sister and is startled to see tears welling again in Freya's eyes. 'Don't cry,' she says, 'it's the baby who's supposed to cry all the time – not you. Everything will be OK, somehow, you'll see. It's just going to take a little time to adjust.'

Freya nods and leaves the kitchen without a backwards glance. Kat watches her through the window as she heads out across the grassy bank and then sways down towards the water. She stumbles once, rights herself, and then wades into the shallows.

Kat turns back to the baby in her arms. 'Silly Freya,' she croons to the infant, 'she's still wearing her nightie.'

The baby is warm and light in her arms. Sunlight filters through the window and lands on her shoulders and neck. Kat closes her eyes, her ears tuning in to the drowsy buzz of a bee caught at the window. She hears the gentle splash of Freya bathing in the lake. There is something soporific about holding a sleeping baby, something calming about her sweet perfumed skin and the gentle

356

rise and fall of her breathing. Lila's snuffling noises mingle with the lazy, faraway splash of Freya moving through the water. The sleepless nights are catching up with her. Kat allows her breath to rise and fall in time with the baby's chest. She'll open her eyes. Any moment now and she'll open them. One more minute with the warm sun on her back and this baby sleeping peacefully in her arms. One more minute.

* * *

It's a cry that wakes her. Kat jumps and glances down at the baby in her arms, surprised to see her still nestled there safely, still sound asleep. She grips her close. How irresponsible; she could have dropped her.

The sun has shifted. She can tell straight away that it's moved on its trajectory for it no longer shines through the window onto her back but slants upon the stone wall opposite. The room has lost its bright yellow glare. From far away she can hear the sound of rapid movement through water. There is more shouting. Simon and Mac must be back.

'No!' she hears. It is Mac's voice. 'No, no, no.' There is a terrible desperation to it that turns her blood cold.

She stands quickly and moves to the window, still clutching the dozing baby close, and looks out towards the lake, where she can just make out Mac and Simon wrestling with something heavy in the water, out at the thin line where the pale green shallows end and the water takes on a deeper, darker hue.

The baby shifts in her arms, opens its mouth and lets out a tiny mewl of protest. 'Shhhh . . .' says Kat, her eyes flicking back to the boys in the water. What on earth are they doing?

Mac is still fully dressed, even down to his boots and they are dragging something up onto the shoreline, something pale, flowing white. She peers more closely and gasps when she understands what it is. Then she is out the back door and running as fast as she can with the baby in her arms to the lake's edge.

'Freya,' she cries. 'Freya.'

Her sister lies at the edge of the lake, her face grey and mottled, her eyes open and staring. Her lips are a shocking blue and wet hair snakes down in dark tendrils over her neck and chest. Mac pulls her close, presses her cold body against his warm one, begs her to stir, but Freya doesn't respond.

He lays her back again and his focus changes. Kat watches as he hooks his fingers inside her mouth, tilts her head then presses his hands together above her heart and begins to pump with his hands. He counts steadily, then leans over and breathes his own warm life into her mouth. Once, twice, then he moves to her chest and begins to press again.

'Come on,' he breathes and Kat watches, her heart in her mouth, as he moves over her sister, willing her to live.

Simon stands a little way behind him, his face white and clammy. She moves across and leans into him, buries her face into the warmth of his shoulder, unable to watch any more.

'Breathe,' urges Mac. 'Just breathe.' Over and over he works on her. He won't give up. Ten minutes. Fifteen minutes. He is intent and sweating but he won't give up, not until Simon steps forwards and places one hand on his shoulder and tells him that it's over.

Mac's hands go still on her chest. He sits back on his heels and stares up at the fading blue sky. It's only then that Kat sees the tears streaming down his face. He rises unsteadily and takes a step towards the lake, lifts his hands then rests them on the back of his head and looks to the heavens. 'No,' he screams, one terrible word echoing out over the lake and bouncing off the surrounding hills.

'Mate,' says Simon, reaching for him, trying to console him but Mac shakes him off, stares at him as if he is a complete stranger.

Kat stands motionless on the bank. She gazes down at her sister, no longer Freya but a stiffer, paler imitation, a fallen marble statue lying on the grass. As the clouds shift overhead, a shard of evening sun falls onto her pale skin and catches the thin silver chain at her neck, its oval pendant shining, for just a moment, as bright as sunshine. Kat stares at Freya, her beautiful, broken sister, and she begins to cry.

At first they don't know what do with her, so they just leave her body lying there at the shoreline beneath the darkening sky. None of them have any words. Kat fetches a blanket for the baby from her room, swaddles her tightly and they sit slumped around the kitchen table, silenced by shock, as twilight slowly draws its curtains across the valley. Eventually the baby stirs and begins to cry. 'She's hungry,' says Kat. 'What do we do?'

Mac stares, unseeing.

'Do we have anything to give her?' asks Simon, his voice cracking with emotion.

Kat feels a sudden desperation grip at her. What do you give a four-week-old baby that has only ever drunk her mother's breast milk? She stands, rummages helplessly in the larder, and returns with the near-empty tin of milk powder. She holds it up to the boys as a question but they don't have an answer so she mixes some with warm water from the pan she boiled earlier and tries to give it to the baby on a teaspoon. The baby gurgles and chokes then spits it out.

'Come on, little one,' she wills and tries again but the baby turns her head and begins to wail. Kat runs her hands through her hair in frustration.

'This is so messed up.' Simon shakes his head. 'I can't think straight.'

'We should call an ambulance,' says Mac, his voice flat. 'The police might need to be involved. I could go to mum's . . . make some calls.'

Kat throws him a frightened glance. 'Will we get into trouble?'

'They'll need to do an inquest. An autopsy. There will be questions. She was a strong swimmer. It doesn't make sense that she drowned.'

Kat presses her knuckles to her lips. 'You mean they'll cut her open? I can't bear it.'

Simon shakes his head. The baby is still crying and he reaches for her, takes her from Kat, tries bouncing her a few times. 'Not yet. We don't tell anyone yet.'

She sees Mac shake his head in obvious frustration, but there is the more urgent matter of the hungry baby to attend to.

'Try the milk again.'

Simon does, and this time the baby seems to manage a drip, then another.

'It can't be good for her. We need to buy a bottle . . . some proper baby formula.' Kat begins to cry quietly as the absence of Freya hits home.

'What we need to do is tell someone,' says Mac through gritted teeth, 'at least notify her family.'

Kat shakes her head. 'But there's no one to tell. *We're* her family.'

'So what do we do?'

The three of them look around at each other, bewildered.

* * *

In the end none of them can bear the thought of her lying out there in the dark beside the lake so they carry Freya's body inside the cottage and lay her on the sofa. The sight of her, cold and lifeless, is horrifying. Kat arranges her nightdress so it covers her once more, fastens the buttons still undone at her chest.

'Get her something to wear, will you?' says Mac. 'I don't want to leave her in this wet nightie. It doesn't seem right.'

Kat nods and climbs the creaking staircase. When she returns she is holding one of Freya's favourite dresses, an aspirin bottle and a ripped sheet of paper in her hand. She can't stop the tears coursing down her cheeks. 'I – I found these – on her bed. The aspirin bottle's . . .' she chokes back a sob, 'it's empty.' She holds the paper out to them both and lets them read the few, sparse words scrawled upon its white surface in Freya's hand, a fat ink blot marking the last letter of her hastily scribbled name where the nib of the pen has caught on the paper.

Forgive me, but I just can't bear to be here any longer.

Freya

Mac reads the words aloud then slumps down beside the sofa, his head in his hands, trying to hide the tears that pour down his face.

* * *

The baby wails and screams for almost three intolerable hours, each of them pacing and rocking and shushing her desperately in turn, but when she has finally exhausted herself and fallen asleep, they sit around the table, the piece of paper lying like an accusation between them.

'It's my fault. I should've . . . I could've . . .' Kat bites down on her hand, tries to stop the sob that falls from her mouth.

'None of us knew . . . none of us understood . . .' Mac swallows. 'What do we do?'

Simon shakes his head. 'I don't know. I don't know anything any more.'

He looks so undone, so broken, a world away from the poised, confident man she remembers from just a few days ago. Watching him, Kat realises that it falls upon her to take charge. 'No police,' she says quietly.

'Why not? There should be an inquest.' Mac is staring at her, challenging her.

She straightens her shoulders and meets his gaze. 'I'm her sister, and I say no police. What good will it do now? Freya chose this. We'll probably never understand why, but at least we know the truth. What good will calling the police do? What else can they tell us? She was depressed. We should have helped her. We all know we've failed her.'

Mac shakes his head. 'Why would she do it?' he asks, his voice barely a whisper. 'I don't understand. I thought we'd agreed . . .'

Simon's eyes narrow. 'Thought you'd agreed *what*?'

Mac clears his throat. 'She was going to come away with me.'

Simon studies him for a moment. 'Bullshit.'

Mac lifts his chin a fraction. 'I was going to help her . . . we were going to find somewhere . . . for her and the baby. She said it was what she wanted. She said she wanted a . . . "a way out".' His voice chokes on the last three words and he closes his eyes to stop the tears. When he has composed himself he continues. 'I didn't think she meant *this*.'

Kat shudders. 'We have to do right by Freya,' she says, 'but we have to do right by her baby now too. Freya is gone, but Lila is here and she needs us. We need to get her milk . . . proper baby milk. We need formula and bottles. That should be the priority.'

At the mention of Freya's baby, Mac's eyes clear. He nods and stands, moves across to the dresser. 'You're right,' he says and he opens the tin. 'We've got twenty quid left.' He holds it out to them like a question and Kat nods. 'I'll be as quick as I can.'

It takes him two hours to find a late-night store selling baby formula and bottles. While he is gone, Kat and Simon sit in the kitchen. Simon barely moves, can hardly speak. Thankfully the baby sleeps on, oblivious to the drama unfolding around her.

'It's the end of everything,' says Simon finally. 'What are we doing to do?' He turns to stare at Kat. 'What am *I* going to do? I can't manage a baby, not on my own.' His voice cracks. Kat sees that his hands are trembling, that reality is sinking in.

She studies him for a moment. She has never seen him so lost, so adrift. She moves around the table and puts a comforting arm around his shoulders, then whispers into his ear. 'You don't have to do this on your own. You've got me. We'll do it together. I'll help you.' Kat shushes him, holds him close while his tears fall. 'Shhh . . . I'm here and I promise I won't leave you.'

She rubs his back and holds him tight and watches as his tears fall onto the rose-coloured fabric of her shirt, turning it a deep and violent red.

* * *

In the end they do it because they think it's what Freya would have wanted, a quiet funeral beside the lake, near the alder trees and the clumps of honesty that she loved so much. No authorities, no fuss. Kat dresses Freya in one of her prettiest dresses, brushes her hair, straightens the silver necklace lying in the hollow of her throat. When she is ready, she leans down and kisses her sister on her cool, pale lips. 'I'm sorry,' she whispers. 'I'm sorry for all of it.'

Mac stands watching by the door, his face ashen. 'Ready?'

Kat nods and Mac moves into the room. He stands beside Freya, gazing down at her perfectly still body. He strokes a strand of her fair hair away from her face then reaches out to remove the silver chain from around her neck. 'For the baby,' he explains and Kat nods and watches as he slides the necklace into his pocket.

They bury her beside the lake. No one says anything as she is lowered into the muddy grave the boys have dug beneath the boughs of a tall alder tree. Kat holds the baby close, and as the first shovel-loads of soil are thrown, her tears begin to flow. She weeps hot, angry tears for her sister and the mother her niece will never know.

Simon and Mac take it in turns to cover her with earth. When they have finished, all that is left is a mound of bare earth rising up out of the ground. Tears course down Mac's dirt-streaked face, but Simon just stands there, shivering even though the day is warm.

'Should we say something?' asks Mac, but none of them can think of anything to say. They wander aimlessly back to the cottage where Kat tries again with the bottle of formula and finally the baby opens her mouth and sucks. She drains it quickly and falls into an easy sleep in her arms.

'Poor little duck,' says Kat, holding her close. She feels heat on her skin and looks up to see Simon watching her.

* * *

They pass another day in a fog, the three adults drifting about the house like ghosts, barely seeing, barely speaking, only the unrelenting demands of the baby girl in their care keeping any semblance of a routine going. Later, when they find themselves down beside the fallen tree at the lakeside, the three of them drawn to the spot by some unseen force, pulling them back to the site of the tragedy, they begin to talk about the future.

'I've been thinking,' says Mac, breaking the silence. 'I could take her.'

'Who?' asks Kat, confused.

'Lila. I'll look after her.'

Kat glances down at the baby sleeping in the crook of her arm and shakes her head. 'That's good of you, Mac, but—'

'I want to. For Freya.'

But Kat shakes her head again. 'No. She's our blood, Mac. Simon's daughter, my niece. She's our responsibility. We should raise her.'

'I can't do it,' says Simon, his head in his hands.

'Yes you can,' says Kat firmly. 'I'll help you. I'll be right there beside you.' She pats him on the shoulder. 'You have to be strong. You're her father.' Mac clears his throat but Kat ignores him. 'She needs her father. She needs a mother. You and I can do it together, Simon.'

'Where would we go? We can't stay here now – not after this.' His questions are like the whines of a plaintive child, all of his decisiveness and grandeur gone.

'To your parents,' says Kat, and she holds up her hand when she sees his initial protest. 'You wrote to them about the baby, didn't you?'

He nods, ashamed.

'Well they can't exactly turn you away, not with a wife and child.'

'Wife?' asks Simon.

'If we're married . . . if they know she's *our* baby . . . what would be so scandalous about that? We'd be returning to them with their

364

first grandchild. It might take some time but they will grow to love her.' She reaches across and squeezes his hand. 'They'll help us.' She can feel Mac's hard stare but she only has eyes for Simon. 'I know they will.'

'I really think—' begins Mac.

'No, Mac,' snaps Kat, 'this isn't your problem. It has nothing to do with you now. Think of Lila. Think about what this little girl needs. Two parents. Security. A family. We can provide that for her. What do you have? What can *you* offer her?'

Mac shakes his head. 'I want to help.' He scuffs his shoes angrily across the ground.

'I know,' says Kat, more softly now, 'but Freya is gone. We must think about the baby.'

As if on cue, Lila begins to stir. Kat rises smoothly and moves across to place her gently in Simon's arms. He sniffs and then holds her close, buries his face in the baby's warm skin. 'When will we leave?' he asks, after he has composed himself.

'As soon as possible. There's no reason to stay, not now.'

Silence surrounds them.

'Take my car,' says Mac.

Kat nods her thanks. 'We'll return it as soon as we can.'

Mac hangs his head. There is nothing left to say.

They don't take much, just a few clothes, the bottles, nappies and formula that Mac bought with the last of their money. As Kat packs their meagre belongings into bags, Mac enters the bedroom and slides the honesty necklace across the window sill towards her. 'For Lila,' he says, when she's old enough.' Kat nods, and smiles at him, but when she's checked around one last time and dragged her bags from the room, the necklace still lies there upon the sill, winking in the summer sunshine beneath the dried white stems of the honesty Freya picked only months before.

They carry the bags out across the meadow under a blazing sky and stow them in the boot of the car. Simon takes the wheel. 'We forgot the Moses basket,' he says suddenly, looking down at the baby in Kat's arms, where she sits beside him in the passenger seat.

'It doesn't matter,' says Kat, waving the loss away. 'We'll get her new things. This is a fresh start, for all of us.'

Simon puts the key into the ignition and starts up Mac's car. The engine revs. Kat sees Mac standing by the gate; he watches them go, raises one hand in sad farewell as they pass by and bounce out onto the track. Kat hugs the baby tightly to her breast.

Halfway down the track Simon slams on the breaks. 'Fuck,' he says.

'What?'

'I told them.' He turns to her, his eyes wide. 'I told them about Freya. In my letter.' He shakes his head, the misery written all over his face. 'This is never going to work.'

Kat studies him for a moment, surprised to see how undone he is. She takes a breath and is equally surprised by her own contrasting sense of calm. 'It's simple,' she says finally, '*I'll* be Freya.'

Simon gapes at her. 'I don't know,' he says, 'it doesn't feel right. It doesn't feel respectful.'

Kat holds the baby close, breathes in the scent of her sweet skin. 'Think about it,' she says quietly. 'We could honour Freya by continuing her name in this way. It would be meaningful, don't you think? For Lila.'

He shakes his head. 'I – I . . .'

She eyes him. 'Do this one thing for me, Simon. Is it too much to ask? Is it too much to pretend that it's Kat that we buried under the alder trees, not Freya? Give me this one thing. Give Lila back her mother. Give her the family she was meant to have.'

Simon shakes his head. She can see he doesn't like it, but she knows he will give her this.

* * *

After they are gone, Mac walks back to the empty cottage and enters through the front door. His footsteps echo loudly on the floorboards and the dust spins as flecks of gold in the shafts of light falling through the windows. He studies the empty beer bottles and the overflowing ashtray on the upturned crate, Simon's paperback still splayed on the arm of a chair, the empty log basket standing beside the fire. In the kitchen the mugs from their last cup of tea remain on the table alongside the empty milk powder tin. Upstairs he traces the faded outline of Carla's funny mural with his finger, six stick figures dancing with joy across the blank canvas of the wall. In the second bedroom, the one Kat shared with Freya, he discovers the silver necklace lying in a pool of sunlight beneath the whispering stems of the honesty seed heads. He reaches for it and slips it deep into his pocket, his fingers tracing the raised surface of the pendant, with its three seeds safely stowed inside their fragile, papery case. Three seeds. He'd asked his mother to make it with three: Mac, Freya and Lila, the family he'd secretly hoped they might be.

Downstairs he finds the Moses basket Kat and Simon have forgotten. The sight of it cold and empty is enough to bring tears to his eyes. He holds the purple blanket close to his face for a moment, thinks about Freya, her slender fingers knitting the wool, holding the warm body of her baby tight, and can't look at it a moment longer. He places the blanket inside the basket and stows them both out of sight, in the dusty cupboard beneath the stairs.

Outside, he unlatches the chicken coop door and coaxes the disgruntled birds, pecking and scratching, into an empty wooden crate. For one lonely moment he hesitates at the doorway to the cottage, looking out across the flat, mirrored surface of the lake. It is still, silent, unchanged by any of the events it has witnessed over the past year. Nothing about the lake, the surrounding landscape gives away the secrets of the year they have spent there. The lake has closed up behind them. The trees continue to sway in the summer breeze. The only evidence of the tragedy is the one, freshly dug mound of earth lying in the shade of the alder trees. Mac stands in the doorway, the sun on his face and his shadow falling in a dark triangle into the emptiness of the cottage, then he pulls the door closed behind him, lifts the crate with the chickens, and begins to make his way back towards the meadow and the long, winding path that will carry him home.

25

LILA

July

'I still can't get my head round it.' Tom reaches for the wine bottle and pours himself another glass. They are sitting in the cottage kitchen, their empty dinner plates and a flickering white candle on the table between them. 'So your mother's real name is *Kat*. But she's not your mother, she's your aunt?'

Lila nods. 'I know it sounds crazy. I'd have thought she'd completely lost it if William hadn't been there with us, listening and corroborating it all.'

Tom shakes his head. 'So they were a group of friends who dropped out and lived up here for a year? They didn't realise that this place – an old shepherds' cottage, did you say . . . ?' Lila nods. '. . . belonged to William's family? He never told them?'

Lila nods again.

'Wily old dog.' He looks around at the cottage. 'It's hard to remember now the state this place was in, but it must have been a tough existence.' Tom takes another sip of his wine. 'So has William explained why he gave the cottage to you – the key and the map – in such strange circumstances? Why do it anonymously like that?' He shakes his head. 'Why wasn't he up front with you?'

Lila reaches out to catch a stream of wax running down the side of the candle onto the scrubbed wooden table. She watches as it cools and turns opaque on the tip of her finger. 'He said he wanted me to have it. He felt that the place belonged to me, in some way, but that he didn't think I'd accept it if he just gave it to me – him a total stranger and all. And he worried if he revealed too much of himself that I would talk to Mum – you know, Kat – and that she would persuade me, somehow, not to come. He wanted me to visit the cottage and see it for myself, to see if I liked it up here. I think he was hoping I would fall in love with the place and want to discover its history for myself. I believe he thought I deserved to know the truth about Freya, but he had no idea who I would be after all these years . . . if I would even want the cottage . . . or want to look below the surface of the life Kat and Simon had created for me.'

'But you did, didn't you?'

Lila nods. It had been strange, that afternoon at the lake with Kat and William, Kat explaining in her cool, calm way about Freya, about the mother Lila had never known. It had been a shock, of course, but as Kat had unravelled the tale and pulled the threads of the past together, Lila had felt a strange relief dawning with the truth. It somehow made sense – all her odd dreams, her strange feelings of déjà vu, her immediate sense of connection to the place.

Poor Freya, a woman of delicate beauty, too young and too fragile to handle the pressures of motherhood. Post-natal depression, that's what Kat and William had put her suicide down to – and it certainly seemed to make sense – but Lila doesn't know how she feels about it all now. It's hard to grieve for something – or someone – you never knew. And yet in some small way she feels connected to Freya, to the memory of her biological mother, perhaps through her grief for Milly. Freya must have been terribly ill to see no other way out and Lila knows she has wrestled with her own dark impulses since her daughter's death.

She'd asked William and Kat to show her where they'd buried Freya and they'd stood solemnly in the shadows of the trees as Lila had tried to conjure words and emotions for a mother she had never known. She wanted words that felt meaningful and real, but nothing Kat had told her felt real yet and standing there in the sun-dappled light, staring at a patch of earth, she'd just felt weary and sad and when she'd finally turned away from the glade, away from Kat and

William, she'd realised there was only one person she wanted to be with at that moment. She'd walked to her car and phoned her husband that afternoon.

* * *

Tom wakes her early the next morning. 'Lila,' he says, shaking her gently, 'Lila, wake up. It's time.'

She shifts and stirs in the antique bed, then opens her eyes and remembers.

'Are you ready?' he asks.

She pushes herself up and looks to the window where a thin grey light breaks through the curtains. 'Yes,' she says, 'I'm ready.'

They paddle out in the rowing boat to the centre of the lake just as the sun begins to crest the tops of the hills. The sky is scattered with slow-moving cloud lit amber from beneath by the breaking dawn. The boat moves easily through the water, gliding between the fiery clouds reflected onto the still surface of the lake. It is painfully beautiful and Lila hugs her knees close to her chest and swallows down the ache at the back of her throat. She knows this is the right thing to do but now that the time has come she is a little overwhelmed.

When they reach the centre of the lake, where the water lies dark and still, Tom slows the boat and pulls the oars in. He leans across and lifts the small white box they have brought with them onto his lap.

'Do you want to do it?' he asks.

'Let's both.'

Tom nods and opens the box. He reaches inside and pulls out a handful of ash, scattering it across the water, both of them watching as it drifts in the light breeze then settles like pollen on the surface of the lake. He hands the box to Lila and she reaches in and does the same. Together, beneath the blazing clouds, they scatter the ashes of their daughter.

When they have finished, Lila looks across and sees the tears sliding down her husband's face. She can't help it; she rises from the opposite end of the boat and tentatively moves across the hull until she is nestled in his arms. 'She'll always be with us,' she says.

Tom nods and moves his hands to Lila's belly. 'The first thing I'm going to tell this baby all about is their brave, big sister Milly and how special she was.'

Lila smiles and they sit entwined together a while longer, just floating and watching the patterns of the clouds shifting upon the mirrored lake.

* * *

It's the perfect afternoon for a barbecue – the air still and warm, the sun beating down on the lake making it shimmer and gleam like a sheet of silver. They have caught fish, picked herbs from the garden and William and Evelyn have arrived with lamb skewers and a salad to add to the feast. Lila wanders down from the cottage with a bowl of wild strawberries, her feet bare and her summer dress billowing out behind her as she goes.

'It's so peaceful here,' says Evelyn, looking out across the water from the deckchair they have positioned for her in the shade of the trees. 'Have I been here before?'

'Yes,' says William gently. 'You have. With Albert . . . and me.'

Evelyn thinks for a moment then smiles. 'I remember. I'd hitch my skirts up and paddle . . . right over there. It was lovely.'

'Well there's nothing stopping you now,' says Lila, 'we don't mind.'

Evelyn's eyes twinkle at the thought. 'If you'll help me with my shoes?'

Lila bends down and helps Evelyn remove her sturdy shoes and wrinkled stockings, then holds her hand and guides her carefully into the shallows. Evelyn gasps with delight as the cool water ripples about her feet, then stands with her eyes closed, listening to the gentle lapping of the water and enjoying the sensation of the sun on her face. Lila stands beside her and lifts the hem of her cotton dress above her knees. There are clouds of midges dancing further out upon the water, they shimmer in the sunlight like dust. Lila closes her eyes and breathes deeply.

'Look at you two,' smiles William from the bank, 'what a picture.'

*　*　*

It's as they're laying out lunch on a picnic blanket down beside the lake that Lila notices her husband's nervous glances up towards the line of trees and the meadow beyond. 'What's wrong?' she asks.

Tom tries to hold her gaze, then sighs and looks away. 'Now,' he says, holding up his hands, 'I don't want you to get cross . . .'

She eyes him. 'What have you done?'

'I *might* have invited your mum to join us. Sorry,' he corrects himself, 'I mean Kat.' He shakes his head. 'God it's confusing.'

'You invited her here . . . to the lake . . . *today*?'

Tom winces. 'Sorry. Was that a *really* bad idea?'

She gives him a look.

'I thought you should see each other . . . at least begin the process of talking . . . you know, clear the air?' He looks at her hopefully.

Lila shakes her head then glances up towards the meadow. She takes a deep breath. 'Well, did she say she would come?'

'She said she'd try but . . . you know . . . I think she felt pretty awkward about it.'

Lila nods. Part of her thinks *good*, she wants her to feel awkward, wants her to stay away . . . but another part of her feels trepidation – and something else too – hope, perhaps, that she might join them? That they might be able to begin to clear the air? The truth is Lila's not sure what she wants. It's been a startling revelation to piece together the tragic circumstances surrounding her fall, to learn about Freya, but it still doesn't change the fact that it is Kat she has grown up with. All this time, it's been Kat who has loved her, raised her as her own. Does that make her any less her mother? She doesn't know.

'Are you angry?' Tom asks.

Lila shrugs. 'No, I'm not angry. Not with you, anyway,' she adds pointedly. She glances back towards the meadow again. She can't help it. Suddenly she is nervous too. She hasn't seen Kat since that afternoon last month, when she'd surprised her at the lake. That day, Lila had sat on the edge of the tree trunk for a long time, listening to her mother's explanation, occasionally glancing across to William, and when Kat had finished, Lila had just sat there in silence.

'Well?' her mother had asked.

Lila had shaken her head. 'Well what? What do you want me to say?'

'Are you angry? Do you hate me for not telling you sooner?'

Lila had taken a deep breath. 'I don't know. I can't get my head around it.'

They'd sat quietly for a little while longer and then, to buy herself some thinking time more than anything else, Lila had offered to show Kat around the renovated cottage. 'Only if you want to. You know, seeing as you used to live there . . .'

Kat had studied her for a moment. 'Yes, I would like that . . . very much.'

William remained tactfully down by the lake while the two of them had wandered up the grassy bank to the front door of the cottage, now painted the same duck egg blue as her kitchen cabinets. Lila held it open for Kat then watched as she moved about the place, exclaiming over the renovations, admiring the changes. She'd commented on the gleaming paintwork, the re-upholstered furniture, the fresh light feel of the place and she'd paused to study familiar objects salvaged from the past as she went – a chipped plate – an old milk bottle – a pile of musty books. Up in the spare bedroom she'd stood for a long time before the faded mural still evident on the wall. She hadn't said a word, just reached out one hand to trace the thin shape of the girl with long plaited hair and Lila had turned away as the tears had begun to slide down Kat's face.

It must have been hard, Lila realised, revisiting the place after all those years; memories of what they had shared there still echoing around them. But as she'd watched her mother move through the cottage, Lila hadn't been able to shake the uneasy feeling that something was still off. Was it really all out there now? Was that really everything? She'd tried hard, ever since, to begin the journey towards acceptance . . . towards forgiveness . . . but there was no denying the distance between them now.

'Well,' says Lila, turning to Tom, 'you've invited her. Let's see if she comes.'

Tom reaches for her hand and gives it a reassuring squeeze.

* * *

They eat lunch sitting on picnic rugs in the shade of the alder trees. Lila glances around occasionally, her eyes drawn to the trees and the meadow. She wonders about Kat, whether she will come, but the afternoon drifts on and she never materialises and soon Lila is too soporific with food and pregnancy and sunshine to maintain her agitated state. She lies back on the picnic rug and plucks at stray dandelions while Rosie sprawls panting at her feet. A little further away Evelyn dozes in the deckchair, a floppy straw hat tipped over her eyes. Tom sits on the crumpled tree trunk beside William, both of them throwing stones out into the lake until after a while, he stands and stretches. 'I thought I'd try a little fishing. Anyone object if I take the boat out?'

Lila knows what he's doing and throws him a grateful glance. She watches as he gathers his fishing gear and pushes the boat out into the water, rowing out towards the centre of the lake. When he is a distance away, Lila moves across to where William still sits on the old tree stump and perches beside him. There is something she has to ask him, but she is afraid and so she waits a moment, summoning her courage. When she does finally speak, she finds it easier not to look at him. 'Kat told me something, after you'd left us the other day. She said, as we were being truthful, that there was one last thing I should know.'

'What's that?' asks William, intrigued.

'Apparently Freya once told her that *you* could have been my father.' Lila blushes and picks at a dry piece of bark beside her. She still can't bring herself to look at him. 'Is it – is it possible?'

William clears his throat. He squints out over the water, to where Tom sits silhouetted against the sun, then pulls his gaze back to Lila. 'I don't honestly know why Freya told your mother that. Perhaps she thought Kat would go easier on her if it had been me that got her pregnant and not Simon.' He shakes his head. 'But I'm afraid it's not true. Freya and I never slept together. Not once.'

Lila feels a tiny flash of disappointment.

'There was one night . . .' continues William, his voice a little hoarse. 'We came close . . . Kat probably told you. We were so young . . . stupid really. It was just one crazy night when things got a little . . .' he clears his throat again, 'out of control. But . . . it didn't seem right. I wanted her, but not like that – not when we were all so messed up.' He swallows and looks out across the lake. 'I loved Freya. I just never knew how to tell her. That necklace, when you were born, it was the only way I could think of to show her.'

Lila reaches for the pendant at her neck. It feels strange but somehow also comforting to know that her birth mother once wore it. Her fingers brush the three raised seeds inside the circular disc. Three: Mac. Freya. Lila. The three of them nestled together inside a world as fragile and thin as paper. Lila sees the glassy sheen of William's eyes and gives him a moment to compose himself. 'That's a shame,' she says with a shy, sideways smile. 'You would have made a good dad.'

They both stare out across the water, watching as Tom baits the fishing line and hooks it out across the water. 'What was she like?' she asks, eventually.

'Freya?' William sighs. 'Lovely. She was very creative; she had your eye for design, a talent for looking at the landscape or a corner of a house and making it more beautiful. She was always making things, or picking flowers, sewing and knitting. But she was young and, I think, a little in awe of Kat. They had an interesting dynamic, sometimes more like mother and daughter than sisters, but it was complicated. Freya was such a bright light, she drew attention like a flame, and yet she didn't court it; sometimes she seemed to prefer to hide in Kat's shadow. It was when she fell pregnant that everything changed. It was hard for Kat . . . and Simon was so domineering, so insistent about the way things should be done and the rules of the cottage that none of us knew what to do to help her. You could see it in Freya's eyes; she was like a caged animal. She was trapped.' He shakes his head. 'I'll always regret that I didn't do more.'

Lila feels William's pain. She reaches out to touch his hand and he turns and smiles sadly.

'You do look incredibly like her, you know; it's rather startling . . . especially now you're pregnant.' He smiles again. 'Mum loved her too. She relished her visits to the farm. She used to say that Freya arriving was like that moment when the sun finally bursts through a bank of cloud.'

Lila swallows and then turns to glances out towards the dark line of trees fringing the lake. She can't help it; that disconcerting feeling is back, the one of being watched. It's her imagination, she knows, probably fired up by all this talk of Freya. She swallows again and tries to shake the feeling away. 'Did you really think she was going to leave with you?'

William nods. 'I really did. We'd talked about it only the day before. I told her we could go anywhere, that I would help her.' He sighs. 'I'll never understand why she did it . . . why I wasn't enough for her and her baby . . . why she made that choice . . . and why she left you. For a while I was so angry with her. I suppose I didn't understand about post-natal depression.'

Lila reaches for his hand and squeezes it gently. 'I'm sorry,' she says.

'Oh I've had a lot of time to think about it over the years. Kat and Simon made the right decision. Simon *was* your father and Kat was your aunt. Perhaps choosing not to tell you about Freya was the kindest choice. It would have been a hard thing to hear at any age.' He turns to her. 'Even now?'

Lila nods and glances out to the boat. 'It's hard, but I'm glad I know.' She watches as a swift plummets towards the surface of the lake to snatch up an unsuspecting insect, before swooping back into the blue. 'But all this time, she's been pretending to be Freya . . . it's a little odd, don't you think?'

'It's strange, I'll admit that . . . but she *had* just lost her sister. Perhaps she thought she could start again with Simon, with you – create a real family. It was the one thing she always wanted, after all: a family.' He shakes his head. 'Grief does funny things to us all.'

Lila nods. She's learned a thing or two about grief and the darkness it can cast this past year. It's hard to believe that she is the same woman who just one year ago sat in a park and considered, even for a fleeting moment, stealing someone else's child.

'Perhaps she did it to remember her sister,' continues William. 'Or perhaps she wanted to do it for you . . . so you could in some small way still have them both in your life.' He turns to look back out over the lake. 'I suppose that's a question for Kat, not me. The truth is I'm not sure I'll ever totally understand what happened here that year.'

A dragonfly zips past and hovers over the shallows, its wings beating so fast she can hear the thrum, low and steady like the distant buzz of a helicopter; it remains there a moment, then darts to the reeds where it settles on a slender stem of green. Further out on the lake Tom splashes the oars though the water. William begins to say something then hesitates. He swallows and then tries again. 'So how are things between you and Tom now?'

Lila smiles. 'We're good. We're moving into a good place. Things feel different, a little beaten-down, more weathered, but I think we're coming out the other side stronger for it. We seem to understand each other now . . . and I'm not going to run away any more,' she adds with another small smile.

'I think I've learned something about grief, this past year. I know that it will always be with me – be a part of me. But I also know that I don't have to hide it. I don't have to be ashamed of it. I love my daughter, Milly, and I will always be her mum. The love and the grief and the joy and the pain and all the emotion – good and bad – all of it that's yet to come . . . well, that's who I am, isn't it?'

She smiles at him. 'I feel like I'm stepping out of a year of shadows, into a brighter place.'

William nods and Lila knows he understands. 'And how are things between you and Kat?' he asks.

Lila swallows. She glances up towards the meadow then looks back to the boat. 'It's going to take time,' she says quietly. 'I'm angry that she and Dad kept the truth about Freya from me for so long. It's hard not to look back on our family and feel like it was all one big lie. But they were young. Kat had just lost her sister and she was left holding a four-week-old baby. It must have been terribly traumatic. I'm sure they were just trying to do their best, amidst the tragedy of it all.' She shakes her head. 'Well, I *know* it wasn't easy. I saw their marriage.' Lila swallows again and turns to William. 'But I understand now too. I understand why she stayed with him. She was doing it for me . . . and for Freya – holding us together, putting up with Dad's philandering, so that we remained a family. There's no denying it; she truly did love Dad and me.'

William nods.

She smiles a little sadly. 'I think that's something I can understand now: that ache to have a family.' Lila reaches out to touch the moss growing on the fallen tree trunk and a piece comes away in her fingers, soft and spongy. 'I'm still struggling with *that* day though. The fall. She told me a little more about it. I pushed and pushed her for an explanation as to why she'd stayed with Dad for so long. She said I looked so like Freya that day – furious, pregnant – that it had upset her deeply. She almost told me then, apparently, but when I ran away . . . well, she raced after me, tried to stop me and what happened next was just a terrible, tragic accident.' She squints out towards the boat and watches as Tom reels in a small, flipping fish. He unhooks it from the line and then throws it back with a splash, its scales flashing silver in the sunlight. 'The lies . . . they're not easily forgiven but Kat's the only mother I'll ever know. If we're going to continue to have a relationship then we're going to have to find a way to live with them.' She sighs. 'You know, I always knew something wasn't quite right. I never felt quite "at home" with them both. And yet coming here, spending time at the cottage . . . I felt at peace. I felt, at times, like I *was* home.'

'It's amazing what our subconscious can tell us. How a place can speak to us. This *is* where you were born,' says William, gesturing out across the valley. 'It was only a short time in your life, but it's where you spent your first weeks with your biological mother. It's where a massive, life-changing event occurred for you. It's no wonder you feel a connection to the place.'

Lila thinks back to the dreams, the whispers in the trees, the shadows on the lake and her strange sense of déjà vu and she can't help a small shiver. She looks around at the cottage, at the water, and at the trees fringing the lake. 'I've made a decision,' she says finally, 'about the cottage. I'm not going to sell it. I want to keep it on, exactly as it is. We'll come up as much as we can. I want our children to know this place. I want to bring them here and create a new story – one of togetherness and joy.'

William nods. He doesn't say anything but she can see that he is pleased.

'I have to thank you, William. If it hadn't been for you giving me this,' she stretches her arms out wide to encompass the valley, 'I never would have found out the truth about Freya. It was you who gave it to me.'

William smiles and looks down at the gnarly bark on the tree trunk beside him. 'I would have been proud to call you my daughter.'

Lila swallows and blinks back her tears. She looks about and sees the future stretching before them, filmy yet definable, like the thin cirrus veil building in the sky above them. She imagines Evelyn seated in the shade of the trees bouncing a gurgling baby on her lap. She imagines a grinning toddler raised high on Tom's shoulders and a skinny-legged kid beside them, a fishing rod in hand and William leaning over to bait the hook, Rosie wheeling at his heels. She sees herself wading through the shallows or picking flowers in the meadow to lie upon Freya's grave. She closes her eyes and sees all the summers that are yet to come and she knows that whatever happens – with Kat, with William and Evelyn, with Tom and the cottage – she knows there will be family.

She sighs. Somewhere deep inside she feels the first stirrings of life, a gentle but insistent fluttering of a tiny, flailing limb. She feels the baby like a real and present truth – like the shining surface of the lake and the waving fronds of the honesty bushes – and she opens her eyes and smiles.

26

KAT

July

It is late afternoon when Kat makes her way through the high grass of the meadow and over the ridge, before coming to a halt by the blackberry bushes above the cottage. She can see Lila and William far below, seemingly deep in conversation on the fallen tree trunk while an elderly grey-haired lady – is that *really* Evelyn? – dozes in a deckchair. Further out on the water the tin boat bobs in the sunshine with Tom slumped at one end, a fishing rod in his hands. She's driven all the way from Buckinghamshire at Tom's invitation, but it's taken every ounce of her courage to leave the sanctuary of her car and walk these last few hundred metres to the lake, and now that she's here, she's not sure she can do it – she's not sure she can join them all at the water's edge.

She hesitates on the ridge and wonders whether to turn on her heel and leave. No one knows that she is there. She could be gone even before they realise that she came; but while she doesn't feel brave enough to join them, she also knows that she isn't quite ready to leave yet either. Something about the light-dappled water and the wind shivering through the grass and rustling the trees holds her captive so instead of heading down to the lake, she crosses the ridge and heads for the alders, seeking shelter amongst their tall white trunks, losing herself in their shadows.

The memories are everywhere; in the gentle lapping of the water, in the shimmering green honesty seed heads, in the tree trunk

381

lying slumped across the grassy bank, even in the slanted shade cast by the cottage in the late afternoon sun. She accepts each small familiarity like a tiny blade to her heart, like the punishment she knows it to be. Hardest of all, however, is the sight of Mac and Lila, seated together on the tree trunk.

Even though Mac has changed considerably in the past three decades, she can still see a faint outline of the gangly young man he once was, hidden in his more substantial form. And Lila – not identical to Freya, no – but there is something in the high curve of her cheekbone, the fullness of her lips and the long, loose tangle of her fair hair, that reaches out to her like an echo coming from very far away. Watching them together, Kat feels her breath stripped from her once again. If she blinked it could almost be Mac and Freya thirty years ago and she feels a familiar ache for her sister welling up inside her.

She could go to them. She could join them. She could begin the difficult task of forgiveness and healing but something holds her back. Even when Lila glances around once or twice, peering over to where she stands hidden in the shade of the trees, even then she doesn't move. She won't go to her. Not yet.

There are new memories of course now, too. They return, fresh from that day only a month ago when she had come back to the lake to tell Lila the truth about her mother. Stepping inside the cottage for the first time in years had been a strange, discombobulating experience – the cottage at the same time both achingly familiar and utterly transformed. She'd moved through the rooms with her heart thudding like a caged bird in her chest, swelling with the complex emotions of grief and love and loss . . . and pride too, for Lila's hard work and achievements. Afterwards, in an attempt to compose herself, she had walked alone to the far end of the jetty and gazed out over the pristine blue-green surface of the lake. She'd looked around and marvelled at how outside nothing had changed – not the shimmering water or the billowing reeds or the shadows of the trees – and yet at the same time she knew *everything* had.

She'd leaned out over the jetty and stared down into the lake. On the surface she'd seen her own mirror image gazing back at her, no longer the unmarked face of her youth but a middle-aged woman with a fretwork of fine lines around her eyes and the first grey hairs beginning to emerge through the hair dye. But the longer she had peered at her reflection, the more clearly she had seen not just her own reflection, but rather her dark and troubled soul. Simon was gone . . . Lila now a grown woman . . . and the truth – or a shadow of it at least – was out there now, shared and made real. She had told a story as clear and transparent as the shallows closer to shore, and yet at its heart, just like the lake and just like her own soul, lay a dark and murky truth that she knew could never be revealed. She'd rewritten the story as best she could.

Kat stands in the shadows of the copse and shivers. She sees Lila reach out for William's hand and squeeze it tight and the sight of their physical connection only serves to remind Kat of her own separation. She swallows down her loneliness and sinks onto the woodland floor, kneeling among the damp leaves and mulch as she watches from the woods.

Last month, after she'd left the jetty, she had joined Mac – or rather William –as if by some unspoken agreement at the foot of Freya's unmarked grave. There they'd stood and for just a moment neither of them had said anything. She'd known they were both remembering, both mourning. 'Lila's a great girl,' he'd said to her eventually, not looking at her. 'Freya would have been so proud.'

'Yes,' Kat had agreed, trying to control the sob threatening to break free.

William had scraped the grass with the toe of his boot and she had allowed herself a small smile then, remembering it as a gesture of his from many years ago. 'Were you happy with him, Kat?' he'd asked her. 'Was it the life you wanted?'

She'd heard the judgement in his voice and shrugged. Was she happy with Simon? What a complicated question. How strange that everyone seemed so preoccupied, suddenly, with the intricacies of her marriage. First Lila, then William. Was it the life she wanted?

Well that was the easier question to answer. Of course it was the life she wanted. Simon and Lila – they were a proper family – the thing she had always wanted most of all. For all their ups and downs, for the sacrifices she'd had to make in her own life, her own stalled career, she had been careful never to repeat the mistakes of her parents. Lila was always safe, always loved, always cared for. Of that she could be proud. 'Yes,' she'd told William, standing there beside Freya's grave, 'it was the life I wanted.'

What she hadn't told him though, what she hadn't felt able to speak of, was the terrible price that family had come at. She'd always known that Simon would never truly be hers. She hadn't been so foolish as to assume one gold wedding band would make the difference. It didn't make him want her any more than he had during that year at the cottage. But he would never leave her, she knew that, because she had given herself to him at the time he needed her most. She had swept in and accepted his daughter and raised her as her own and for that she knew Simon had always been grateful.

No, Simon had never left her, but there had been other crosses to bear. His parents' snooty disapproval when they'd returned to Buckinghamshire as a newly-married couple. Simon's struggle to resolve his ideals with the role offered to him at his father's firm. The drink . . . the women . . . and perhaps most difficult of all, his gradual hardening towards her as his gratitude slowly morphed into something more akin to simmering resentment. The fact they had never been able to have a child of their own had also cut her deeply. She'd always felt that it would bring her and Simon closer, but it seemed a baby born to them both was just never to be and she had endured her infertility like the sentence she knew it to be.

Sometimes she ached with loneliness – those nights without him, when she'd sat alone in their large, empty home feeling the absence of all that was missing in her life like a cold, hard stone sinking into her soul.

And there had been Lila too: the older she'd grown, the more striking her resemblance to Freya. It had cut her to the quick. Just a glimpse of her daughter drifting through the house in a white nightdress, or meandering through the garden in the sunshine, could make that dark part of her heart throb with pain and her eyes fill with tears. Lila had been both a beautiful blessing and a heartbreaking curse. But she would never stop loving her, never stop caring for her because not only was that the promise she had made to Freya, but it was the only way she could think of to make it up to Lila for her own terrible mistakes. Until the day she died Kat knew she would be trying to make it up to Lila.

The sun is just beginning to slouch behind the furthest hills when Tom drags the tin boat onto the shingle and holds up two silver fish for Lila and William to admire. Kat, still hidden among the trees, shivers in the dwindling light and knows that it's time to leave. Perhaps she will come back another day, when she is feeling braver. With one last glance, she rises from the damp earth and turns her back on the gathering by the lake, carefully winding her way up through the trees towards the meadow.

As she walks through the tall grass she brushes her hands across the bowed heads of wild meadow flowers and remembers her last farewell with Lila, how it had been stiff and yet charged with emotion. 'Will you go back to France?' Lila had asked her, standing beside her car on the overgrown track, barely able to look at her.

Kat had shaken her head. 'Not yet, no. I'll stay a while, I think. In case . . . you know . . . in case you have more questions. Or just want to talk?'

Lila had nodded. 'I'm glad, you know . . . I'm glad it's all finally out in the open . . . that we're finally speaking the truth.' She'd felt Lila's careful gaze sweep over her then. 'We are aren't we,' she'd asked carefully, 'talking with real honesty now?'

Kat had nodded. Honesty, that thing she has been so afraid of for most of her life. She'd breathed deeply, inhaling the familiar, sweet scent of the grass. It was such a fine line, wasn't it – that space between what happens and what is told? Could it still be considered a lie if something was just omitted from the retelling, never spoken out loud? She wasn't sure.

'I should leave,' she'd said, shivering slightly and pulling her cotton wrap more tightly around her shoulders. 'I have a long way to go.'

Lila had leaned in to graze her cheek but Kat, unable to bear the formality, had pulled her daughter to her and held her tight, breathing in the smell of her clean hair and the faint trace of lake water. She'd felt Lila relax for just a moment and then stiffen and begin to pull away. She hadn't wanted to let her go, but she'd known she had to.

* * *

Dusk is falling as Kat steers her car back down the bumpy track. A rabbit darts from the hedgerow, wide-eyed in her headlights. She slams on the brakes then slows, taking the rest of the trail more carefully until she is back on the lane and heading south.

She should have left earlier – but even just standing there watching on the very periphery, she had been reluctant to tear herself away from the shimmering lake and the cottage and the sight of them all down there at the water's edge; the family she had always wanted – born at the highest price.

Gradually the dark moors and twisting country lanes fade away and Kat finds herself driving through the lit streets of a market town. She steers the car round a roundabout, then drops down onto the dual carriageway that will carry her back to the motorway. The road is quiet; just a few cars cruising down the inside lane and a ribbon of cats' eyes darting at her from the central reservation. She has a long way to go, locked in the quietness of her car, and she knows there is nothing now that will prevent her mind from turning in on itself. The lake has pulled her darkest secrets up from the depths, where they dance like shadows on the surface of her mind.

EPILOGUE

Simon stands at the cottage window with the lake glinting through the glass behind him and the baby nestled tightly in his arms. 'Come over here,' he says. 'Look at this.' Kat goes to him and watches as the infant grabs on to his finger, opens her mouth and gives a contented gurgle. 'Isn't she sweet?'

Kat nods. 'Does Freya know she's down here with you?'

'Freya's asleep. We thought we'd have a little father–daughter time, didn't we?' He isn't talking to Kat; he's talking to the baby in a warm, lilting voice, his adoring spotlight focused purely on the infant in his arms. She watches him for a moment, sees his swelling paternal pride, senses his unwavering devotion. Next to it, Kat feels invisible. She realises this is how it will always be now. His flesh and blood first. His *daughter* first.

She is about to turn and leave when he surprises her by removing his finger from the baby's grip and wrapping his free arm around her shoulder. Kat stands for a moment, enjoying the sensation of his warm body pressed against hers. The baby yawns. Kat breathes slowly. She steps outside herself and looks at them momentarily as a stranger might: a family. It's what she's always wanted – but it's not hers. She has no right to this.

'Aren't you a lucky girl?' whispers Simon to the baby. 'You've got everything you could ever need right here . . . your mummy . . . your daddy . . . your auntie Kat.'

She sees it then as clearly as the lake gleaming through the window or the clouds skimming across the sky – Simon is never going to choose. He is never going to give up on the cottage or on Freya and the baby, because Simon has everything *he* could ever want: all three of them right there on a plate. For Kat, it's as though a camera lens is twisted and he comes suddenly into sharp and brilliant focus. He isn't strong or powerful; he is weak. And he is never going to choose. He is never going to choose *her*.

* * *

The baby sleeps peacefully in her arms as she carries her back to their room, but Freya is awake, sitting up in bed scribbling on a sheet of paper.

'What are you doing?' Kat asks, settling the baby in the Moses basket before moving across to a pile of crumpled clothes.

'Nothing,' says Freya, but Kat sees her carefully fold the piece of paper in two and slide it beneath her pillow. There is a flash of silver at the hollow of her sister's neck; she peers more closely and recognises the honesty pendant.

'Nice necklace,' she says.

Freya nods. 'Mac gave it to me – for the baby.'

Kat eyes her sister. She looks different: brighter, lighter, more alive. She wonders what it is that Mac has said to her. She folds a sweater and lays it at the end of the bed. 'There are rabbits on the hills,' she says. 'The boys are going out to check the traps.' She reaches for a pair of jeans.

'Is that right?' Freya stretches.

Kat watches her for a moment. 'I'm going to make some tea. Would you like a cup?'

Freya nods and rolls her shoulders. 'Sure, thank you.' She stands and runs her hands through her hair. 'Urgh. I feel horrible. I need to wash.' Kat continues to busy herself with the stray clothes. 'And I need to use the toilet. Would you mind bringing Lila with you when you come downstairs?'

Kat glances over at the sleeping baby. 'Sure,' she says and watches as her sister leaves the room. She waits for a moment, noticing how the sunlight catches on the opaque honesty placed in the window, making the seed heads shine like mother-of-pearl; but as soon as she hears the back door slam, she darts across the room and slides the sheet of paper out from beneath her sister's pillow, her eyes racing over the words.

Dear Kat

I'm sorry for saying goodbye like this but it really does seem as though it's for the best. Mac and I are going away – we're taking Lila somewhere far from here. I know you love Simon but I will never forgive him for what he did to me and I won't let him have her.

Forgive me, but I just can't bear to be here any longer.

Freya

Kat stares at the words scratched in blue ink, reading them over and over until their true meaning has sunk in. Her eye catches on the ink blot at the end of Freya's name, a sign of her urgency, her haste. Freya and Mac are planning to leave. They will take the baby and go.

She knows she should be happy. She knows this should be the answer to her prayers; in one fell swoop Freya and Lila will be removed from Simon's life for ever and she will remain, victorious with her prize.

Kat stands and hovers over the sleeping baby, staring down at her pale face and the long sweep of her eyelashes. Her niece will have what she and Freya never had: a family. And she will be left with Simon, to start again.

She shakes her head. If only it were that simple. She's seen the way Simon gazes at the baby. She's seen the adoration in his eyes and knows that she will never be enough for him. Not now. They will *all* leave her. Freya and Mac. Lila. Simon. They will *all* leave her and she will be left alone and unloved.

Kat puts her hand to her mouth and bites down hard, trying to control the terrifying emptiness opening up inside her. It is a black chasm yawning and stretching in her belly. This is it: her darkest fears coming true at last. She closes her eyes and tries to breathe . . . tries to hold it together, but all she can see are the pale dangling roots of the water hemlock she has hidden in the pantry. This is it, she thinks. Time to end it all, now, before Simon or Freya can hurt her any more.

*   *   *

She enters the kitchen, places the basket with the sleeping baby carefully on the table. Freya is still outside as Kat retrieves one of the stems of water hemlock from where she has stowed it behind some empty crates. Deadly: that's what Mac had told her. There are plenty of nettles left for Freya's tea but she'll prepare something special for herself. She'll drink it there in the kitchen with Freya and Lila. It will be her own quiet farewell to them all and no one will know what she's done until it's too late.

She chops the plant leaves and roots and places them in two mugs: nettles for Freya, hemlock for Kat. She is careful not to contaminate Freya's mixture with her own. Freya returns and as Kat waits for the water to boil she sits with her sister and watches her feed the baby, enjoying the sight of them. Yes, she thinks, a proper family.

'If it's OK with you, I'll go and take my swim,' says Freya. 'I'll be quick.'

'Don't go,' says Kat hastily, 'not yet. Sit with me a moment longer.' Now it's here – the goodbye neither of them will admit to – she doesn't want the moment to end. 'Stay and drink your tea with me . . . then I'll watch the baby while you wash.'

'If you're sure?' asks Freya.

'Yes,' she says, 'I'm sure.' She allows herself to imagine it then, the slow creep of the poison through her veins. The very last thing she sees will be her niece's face, peaceful and still, evidence of a beautiful future.

Kat stands and turns back to the pan on the range, now billowing steam across the kitchen. She pours water into both mugs then carries them across to the kitchen table. The baby stirs at her sister's breast.

'Look,' says Freya, 'I think she's smiling.'

Kat lowers the mugs to the table and bends to look more closely. 'Oh yes,' she says and reaches for the baby's finger, tears springing in her eyes. 'She's beautiful, isn't she?' She bends down closer and nuzzles the baby's soft skin. 'You've got your mummy's eyes,' she murmurs.

When she looks back to the table she is shocked to see only one mug standing on its surface. She glances across at Freya just in time to see her sister raise the other to her lips.

'Thanks for this,' she says and drinks deep.

'No,' says Kat. 'Not – not . . .' but she can't speak. She just looks on helplessly as her sister drinks from the wrong mug.

'What?' asks Freya, a bemused smile on her lips. 'What is it?'

Kat shakes her head but she cannot move. She feels the blood drain from her face, a hot dart of fear shoot up her spine. She could stop this. She could knock the mug from her sister's hand. Before it's too late.

Freya looks down at the baby, now snuggled in the blanket. She hesitates for just a moment, then says, 'I'm sorry, you know, about the way everything's worked out.'

Kat can hardly look at her. Tears sting her eyes. She struggles to blink them back. It's still not too late. She could do it now. It doesn't have to be this way. She swallows. 'I'm sorry too,' is all she says, eventually.

'I think things will be better from now on. You'll see.' Freya sips her tea slowly, until it is all gone, Kat watching on, mute with distress. 'Thank you,' she says, returning the mug to the table.

Kat nods. She can't take her eyes off the mug. Her mind churns: did she *make* this happen? Did she place it there in front of her . . . just a fraction too close? Was *this* the answer she was looking for, all along? She is dizzy at the thought and reaches out for the table with a steadying hand.

'And you don't mind looking after her?' Freya stands and holds the baby out to her. Kat shakes her head and accepts Lila into her own warm embrace. 'I won't be long, little one.' Freya bends to kiss her baby's pale forehead, reaches out to sweep a lock of hair from her brow then turns and leaves the room.

As Freya makes her way outside, Kat holds the baby close and feels the first of her tears begin to fall. They splash down onto the purple knitted blanket and dissolve into the fabric. Freya continues across the grassy bank and then sways down towards the water. Kat sees her stumble once then right herself before splashing into the shallows. She turns back to the baby in her arms. 'Silly Freya,' she whispers in a soft, sad voice, 'she's still wearing her nightie.'

The baby is warm in her arms. Sunlight filters through the window and lands on her shoulders, her neck. As Freya wades into deeper water, Kat sees her sister's nightdress rise up around her legs and bloom like a waterlily upon the surface of the lake. All she can do is watch and wait with the baby nestled safely in her arms.

ACKNOWLEDGEMENTS

I am indebted to Sarah Lutyens, Kate Mills and Vanessa Radnidge for giving me the courage to pursue this story when it was a whisker away from never being written. Their encouragement, advice and editorial insight were, as always, invaluable. Thank you to everyone at Orion, Hachette Australia and Lutyens & Rubinstein for the talent and flair that went into publishing this book. I also gratefully acknowledge the assistance of the Varuna Writers' House and the Sydney Writers' Room for giving me the time and solitude to complete this novel. Finally, I thank my family and friends for their support. I owe you all heartfelt gratitude for putting up with me on those days when I am lost inside my head – especially my generous-hearted sister Jess, my wonderful children, Jude and Gracie, and my husband, Matt: *'the best time of the day'*, always.

the Shadow Year

READING GROUP NOTES

A READER'S INTRODUCTION TO THE BOOK

The Shadow Year *tells two stories, intricately intertwined, each with a tragedy at its heart.*

Five friends – Kat, Simon, Carla, Ben and Mac – are about to graduate from university, but their future seems bleak. It's 1980, and the newspapers are full of doom and gloom. In a last-ditch attempt at escape, they take off on a summer's day to the Peak District where they stumble upon an abandoned cottage on the shores of a shimmering lake, hidden deep in the heart of the countryside. Isolated and run-down, it offers a retreat, somewhere they can escape from the real world. It's a chance to live the dream, doing exactly as they please, with lazy summer days by the lake and cosy winter evenings around the fire. They decide to stay, convinced they can survive on their own and determined to stick it out no matter what the cost. But as the seasons change, tensions begin to rise, and when Kat's sister, beautiful art student Freya, appears at the door, their idyllic life is turned upside down – with devastating consequences.

Lila and Tom are a young London couple, reeling after the sudden loss of their first baby and struggling to hold their marriage together. Lila lost the baby in a fall but can't remember how it happened, and the memories of that day are coming back to her only slowly, piece by painful piece. When she inherits a remote Peak District cottage from a mystery benefactor, she flees there to spend time alone, away from her husband. Renovating the tumbledown house gives her a renewed sense of purpose, but as she sifts through the evidence left behind thirty years ago by the five young drop-outs, she becomes curious. Why did they leave in such a hurry, with their belongings still strewn about the place? Who are the figures in the mural scrawled on an upstairs wall? And why is there a bullet hole in one of the timber beams in the kitchen? Most disturbing of all, why can't she shake the feeling that someone might be watching her?

As the story of the five young friends unfolds it starts to overlap with Lila's own and, in a harrowing climax on the shores of the lake, secrets that have haunted her family for years are finally exposed. But will all the secrets of that one shadowy year come to light, or will one remain hidden beneath the cool, clear water, never to surface?

AUTHOR INTERVIEW

The Shadow Year is your second novel – was writing it a very different experience from writing your first, Secrets of the Tides? Were you more confident the second time around, or did you find yourself facing a whole new series of challenges?

I know it's a cliché but writing this second novel was like being strapped into a rollercoaster. Some days I felt buoyed by the knowledge I had 'done it' before and confident that I could write another novel (receiving kind comments from generous readers and reviewers of *Secrets of the Tides* was especially heartening), but most days I felt cowed by the weight of expectation and the looming publication deadline. I also didn't make things easy for myself. I stumbled upon the story for *The Shadow Year* while bogged down in the first draft of a very different novel. I was 100,000 words in when the lake and the cottage and the character of a broken young woman (who would eventually become Lila) jumped into my head. I tried to push the ideas away so that I could focus on my work-in-progress but they wouldn't leave me alone. I agonised for a few weeks about ditching the other draft to concentrate on what would become *The Shadow Year*, but eventually I knew in my gut that it was the right thing to do. And just like that – I didn't have time for anxiety and self-doubt – I had to write the story and get it done. The clock was ticking.

Your character Lila shares something with you: she grew up in Buckinghamshire in England, and in a similar period. Did this shared background make it easier for you to 'get into her head' and imagine how she would think, feel and react in different circumstances?

No, Lila grew with me as I wrote the novel. She was very much a 'Londoner' in my head, which added to her fish-out-of-water feelings on arrival in the Peak District. It was only as I began to delve into her early childhood and the life her parents had given her that I decided to base her family home in Buckinghamshire, a place I knew well from my own childhood. The fact that we are of the same generation was perhaps the greatest help to me in trying to get inside her head.

As in your first novel, the setting plays a pivotal role in *The Shadow Year*. Is the beautiful lake in England's Peak District based on a real-life place you know well? What came first – the setting or the story?

The very first thing that came to me about this story was the lake and the abandoned cottage, and the idea of a broken young woman taking solace in the remote surroundings. I didn't know who the woman was or where the lake was for a long time but I knew I had to find an actual area of England that could offer such an extreme sense of detachment. I thought about the Lake District for a while, but eventually settled on the Peak District. I was attracted to the area's diversity – the uplands and escarpments, the rolling hills and farmland as well as the barren moors. The more I researched the landscape and the shifting seasons, the potential for foraging and living off the land, as well as the hazards and pitfalls of such remote living, the more the plot began to fall into place. The story, in many ways, grew quite organically from the setting.

Walden is an American classic, describing Henry David Thoreau's two-year experiment in simple living in a cabin in the woods in Concord, Massachusetts, in the 1850s. You've chosen a quote from Thoreau's book as your epigraph, and one of your characters, Simon, reads his work in the course of your story. Was *Walden* an important reference for you as you wrote *The Shadow Year*? Do you believe that in seeking to understand nature we can understand ourselves?

I read American Studies at Nottingham University and was already acquainted with Thoreau's writing before I started on this novel but as I began to play around with the story, *Walden* came back to me, very clearly. It was so obvious, really: the idea of detachment and escape, of separating yourself from the everyday to understand who you truly are or to make sense of your current life. These are themes Thoreau explores in his writing and themes that are, of course, embedded in *The Shadow Year*. When I began to notice the parallels it seemed clear to me that Simon *had* to be reading *Walden* at the cottage, and then, when I revisited the quote about a lake being 'Earth's eye' I also knew it would make a perfect epigraph. The idea of the lake as an 'eye' is something I have borrowed from Thoreau at the very start of the book, and there is also a scene where Kat studies herself in the lake and ruminates on her own dark nature.

Since completing *The Shadow Year*, I've noticed that both this book and *Secrets of the Tides* contain a strong sense of the power of nature embedded within them – both in terms of its capacity to nurture and heal, as well as to wreak havoc and destroy. On a personal level, I find nature immensely inspiring in my writing. When I am stuck, I'll often take myself outside for a walk. I never feel more free or at peace than when I'm tramping across the English countryside in muddy boots . . . or trekking through shadowy gum trees in the Australian bush . . . or walking along a coastal path, listening to the rise and fall of the ocean. It's a curious thing, isn't it, that act of taking yourself *out* into the world to assist with the more introspective process of creativity or self-discovery?

The structure you've chosen for *The Shadow Year* is interesting: you almost give away the answer to the final mystery in your prologue, but then you manage to keep the reader guessing all the way to the very end. Was it difficult gauging which piece of information to give away when? When you're writing and editing your work, how do you keep track of what the reader already knows and what is yet to be revealed?

I really hope I can keep most readers guessing to the end . . . fingers crossed! It's tricky withholding information from the reader, but it's also a great way to build tension. For me it's one of the best bits of writing – I love playing around with the structure of a story. It's like doing a jigsaw puzzle, but the more I write, the harder it is to see all the pieces clearly. My earliest readers – my sister, my husband, my agent and editor – were vital in helping me to ensure the flow of information was happening at the right time. The prologue was the last passage I wrote. For a while the novel didn't have a prologue at all, but my editor and I kept coming back to the idea. We discussed it a couple of times and in the end I wrote something which I hope is a bit of a tease of what's to come and also sets the scene of the lake and the cottage clearly in the reader's mind.

There are twin tragedies at the heart of this story, and a single character is ultimately responsible for both of them – yet you clearly don't regard the question of blame as a simple one. What draws you to this question of blame, and why did you want to explore it?

Guilt and regret are powerful emotions and I seem to be drawn to writing about characters who suffer deeply from both. It's probably because my stories pivot on dramatic moments and you can't have characters doing extreme or questionable things without the inevitable ruminations over right and wrong. As a writer I like to explore the journey that has led a person to take dramatic action. It's that whole idea of walking around in another person's shoes in order to see the true picture of their life, more so than believing in a simplistic black-and-white version of right and wrong or good and bad. The grey areas of a person's character are far more intriguing, don't you think? It's these areas that can bring that tremor of recognition and make us question our own values and beliefs: what would I do in this situation? Am I capable of such extreme behaviour?

SUGGESTED POINTS FOR
DISCUSSION

- What is the significance of the title *The Shadow Year*? Does it have more than one possible interpretation? What are the shadows it refers to?
- Hannah Richell starts her story with a quote from Thoreau: 'A lake is the landscape's most beautiful and expressive feature. It is the Earth's eye; looking into which the beholder measures the depth of his own nature.' Thoreau believed that it is only by understanding nature that we can understand ourselves. Do you agree?
- The cottage and the lake are so important in *The Shadow Year* that they could almost be considered characters in their own right. Can you imagine this story taking place anywhere else (in Australia, New Zealand or Canada, for example), or could it only have been set in this particular landscape?
- Tom comments to Lila about the cottage's eerie atmosphere: 'There are just some places that feel ... that feel as though something has happened there. I think this cottage might be one of them.' Do you agree with Tom? Can places hold the echoes of the events that have taken place there?
- The story is told from two different perspectives and takes place in two different periods in time. Why might the author have

chosen to present the story in this way? How does this create interest, and what challenges might it pose for the writer?

- The answer to this story's final mystery is hidden in the prologue, though the reader doesn't know it until the last chapter. As you read on, did you think back to the young woman in her nightgown stumbling down to the lake, and did you speculate about who she might be?

- We are nearly halfway through the book before we learn who Lila's father was, and we don't learn who her mother was until the end of the book. Did you start to put this together for yourself before it was revealed? Why do you think the author held this information back, and how did this shape your experience of the story and your feelings about the characters?

- When they first move to the cottage and throw themselves into the hard work of daily survival, Kat feels satisfied and happy, and looks back with regret on 'all those wasted hours spent in lecture theatres ... pondering the abstract ideas and philosophies of the world'. Is education ever wasted? How well did Kat's education prepare her for the practical, ethical and moral dilemmas she soon faces?

- After the night of the magic mushrooms, Kat writes in her diary: 'Of course we were all off our heads but still – some would say that's when we become our true selves, let our real instincts take over.' Do you agree with Kat? How responsible were any of them for the events of that night? Was anyone acting on their true instincts or were they all lost in the moment and blameless in light of their drug-taking?

- At a point within the novel, Kat considers her group of friends to be like 'one unconventional, chaotic family'. Do you agree? If so, what familial roles do they each assume?

- As she is growing up, Simon tells Lila that she should 'never trust a man who doesn't read books'. Do you think this is good advice? Why or why not?

- Lila says she has always loved the pace and the buzz of London, but when she returns from the cottage she compares it unfavourably with the tranquillity of the lake, and thinks of the simple life William and Evelyn lead on their farm. She starts to wonder if her life on the lake is 'real', and London's frenzy no more than an illusion. Is it easier to lead a virtuous or moral life in the countryside than in the city? Does a simple life build moral strength? If so, what went wrong with Simon's experiment at the cottage?

- When she first comes home to London, for Christmas, Lila promises Tom that she won't return to the cottage until things are better between them, but then she breaks that promise. Was she right to do so?

- For a time, Lila suspects that Tom may have been with her when she had her accident and lost their baby, and is keeping this fact hidden from her. Did you ever suspect him? Why or why not?

- Do you believe Kat is the only one to blame for the dual tragedies within the story? Is anyone else culpable? Is it possible – or appropriate – to apportion blame?

- Kat and Freya suffered tragic neglect as children. What effect did this have on their adult lives? Can Kat be held responsible for her mistakes, when her past is taken into account?

- Do you think Kat got the life she deserved?

- There are many animals in *The Shadow Year*, in particular a piglet who trots along behind Freya like a puppy and a lamb on William's farm that is fed by Lila. What symbolism do some of the animals hold in the story? What ideas is the author exploring through them?

- At the end of their time at the cottage, Kat, Simon, Carla and Ben learn that they have never been in any danger of eviction. Does this knowledge change the value of their experiment? And if so, how? Was it wrong of Mac to withhold this information? Does this make him in any way responsible for the tragic events that follow?

- By the end of the story, Lila is pregnant again. Could it have ended satisfactorily if she was not?

- There are twin tragedies at the heart of this story, and a single character – Kat – is ultimately responsible for both of them. She asks for forgiveness for one, but her part in the other remains a secret. Does Kat deserve forgiveness when she is not ready to confess all of her sins?
- Themes of grief, blame and forgiveness are central to Hannah Richell's first novel, *Secrets of the Tides*, and are also central to *The Shadow Year*. Do you think it is possible ever to exhaust these themes? Why or why not?
- What do the motifs of shadows and honesty, woven throughout the book, lend to the story?

FURTHER READING

The Poison Tree – Erin Kelly
My Lover's Lover – Maggie O'Farrell
Gone Girl – Gillian Flynn
Walden – Henry David Thoreau
The Secret History – Donna Tartt
Secrets of the Tides – Hannah Richell